# FOES, FRIENDS, AND LOVERS

## A CYNSTER NEXT GENERATION NOVEL

### STEPHANIE LAURENS

# ABOUT FOES, FRIENDS, AND LOVERS

*#1* New York Times *bestselling author Stephanie Laurens returns with a tale of a gentleman seeking the road to fulfillment and a lady with a richly satisfying life but no certain future.*

*A gentleman searching for a purpose in life sets out to claim his legacy, only to discover that instead of the country residence he'd expected, he's inherited an eccentric community whose enterprises are overseen by a decidedly determined young lady who is disinclined to hand over the reins.*

Gregory Cynster arrives at the property willed to him by his great-aunt with the intention of converting Bellamy Hall into a quiet, comfortable, gentleman's country residence, only to discover the Hall overrun by an eclectic collection of residents engaged in a host of business endeavors under the stewardship of a lady far too young to be managing such reins.

With the other residents of the estate, Caitlin Fergusson has been planning just how to deal with the new owner, but coming face to face with Gregory Cynster throws her and everyone else off their stride. They'd anticipated a bored and disinterested gentleman who, once they'd revealed the income generated by the Hall's community, would be content to leave them undisturbed.

Instead, while Gregory appears the epitome of the London rake they'd expected him to be, they quickly learn he's determined to embrace Bellamy Hall and all its works and claim ownership of the estate.

While the other residents adjust their thinking, the burden of dealing daily with Gregory falls primarily on Caitlin's slender shoulders, yet as he doggedly carves out a place for himself, Caitlin's position as chatelaine-cum-steward seems set to grow redundant. But Caitlin has her own reasons for clinging to the refuge her position at Bellamy Hall represents.

What follows is a dance of revelations, both of others and also of themselves, for Gregory, Caitlin, and the residents of Bellamy Hall. Yet even as they work out what their collective future might hold, a shadowy villain threatens to steal away everything they've created.

*A classic historical romance set in an artisanal community on a country estate. A Cynster Next Generation novel. A full-length historical romance of 118,000 words.*

# OTHER TITLES BY STEPHANIE LAURENS

### Cynster Novels

Devil's Bride

A Rake's Vow

Scandal's Bride

A Rogue's Proposal

A Secret Love

All About Love

All About Passion

On A Wild Night

On A Wicked Dawn

The Perfect Lover

The Ideal Bride

The Truth About Love

What Price Love?

The Taste of Innocence

Temptation and Surrender

### Cynster Sisters Trilogy

Viscount Breckenridge to the Rescue

In Pursuit of Eliza Cynster

The Capture of the Earl of Glencrae

### Cynster Sisters Duo

And Then She Fell

The Taming of Ryder Cavanaugh

### Cynster Specials

The Promise in a Kiss

By Winter's Light

### *Cynster Next Generation Novels*

The Tempting of Thomas Carrick

A Match for Marcus Cynster

The Lady By His Side

An Irresistible Alliance

The Greatest Challenge of Them All

A Conquest Impossible to Resist

The Inevitable Fall of Christopher Cynster

The Games Lovers Play

The Secrets of Lord Grayson Child

Foes, Friends, and Lovers

The Time for Love (August, 2022)

### *Lady Osbaldestone's Christmas Chronicles*

Lady Osbaldestone's Christmas Goose

Lady Osbaldestone and the Missing Christmas Carols

Lady Osbaldestone's Plum Puddings

Lady Osbaldestone's Christmas Intrigue

The Meaning of Love

### *The Casebook of Barnaby Adair Novels*

Where the Heart Leads

The Peculiar Case of Lord Finsbury's Diamonds

The Masterful Mr. Montague

The Curious Case of Lady Latimer's Shoes

Loving Rose: The Redemption of Malcolm Sinclair

The Confounding Case of the Carisbrook Emeralds

The Murder at Mandeville Hall

### *Bastion Club Novels*

Captain Jack's Woman (Prequel)

The Lady Chosen

A Gentleman's Honor

A Lady of His Own

A Fine Passion

To Distraction

Beyond Seduction

The Edge of Desire

Mastered by Love

### Black Cobra Quartet

The Untamed Bride

The Elusive Bride

The Brazen Bride

The Reckless Bride

### The Adventurers Quartet

The Lady's Command

A Buccaneer at Heart

The Daredevil Snared

Lord of the Privateers

### The Cavanaughs

The Designs of Lord Randolph Cavanaugh

The Pursuits of Lord Kit Cavanaugh

The Beguilement of Lady Eustacia Cavanaugh

The Obsessions of Lord Godfrey Cavanaugh

### Other Novels

The Lady Risks All

The Legend of Nimway Hall – 1750: Jacqueline

### Medieval (As M.S.Laurens)

Desire's Prize

### Novellas

Melting Ice – from the anthologies *Rough Around the Edges* and *Scandalous Brides*

Rose in Bloom – from the anthology *Scottish Brides*

Scandalous Lord Dere – from the anthology *Secrets of a Perfect Night*

Lost and Found – from the anthology *Hero, Come Back*

The Fall of Rogue Gerrard – from the anthology *It Happened One Night*

The Seduction of Sebastian Trantor – from the anthology *It Happened One Season*

### Short Stories

The Wedding Planner – from the anthology *Royal Weddings*

A Return Engagement – from the anthology *Royal Bridesmaids*

### UK-Style Regency Romances

Tangled Reins

Four in Hand

Impetuous Innocent

Fair Juno

The Reasons for Marriage

A Lady of Expectations An Unwilling Conquest

A Comfortable Wife

# FOES, FRIENDS, AND LOVERS

FOES, FRIENDS, AND LOVERS

Copyright © 2022 by Savdek Management Proprietary Limited

ISBN: 978-1-925559-52-1

Cover design by Savdek Management Pty. Ltd.

Cover couple photography by Period Images © 2022

First print publication: March, 2022

Savdek Management Proprietary Limited, Melbourne, Australia.

www.stephanielaurens.com

Email: admin@stephanielaurens.com

The names Stephanie Laurens and the Cynsters and the SL Logo are registered trademarks of Savdek Management Proprietary Ltd.

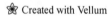 Created with Vellum

# CHAPTER 1

FEBRUARY 16, 1852. ON THE ROAD TO
BELLAMY HALL, NORTHAMPTONSHIRE.

*G*regory Cynster kept his matched bays to a steady pace along the gently winding road heading southwest from Wellingborough. It was barely two o'clock in the afternoon, and despite the chilly temperatures and overcast skies, no rain threatened; he saw no reason to hurry.

Seated beside him, his gentleman's gentleman, Snibbs, who hadn't visited Bellamy Hall before, surveyed the pleasant but unremarkable countryside with eager interest.

Gregory's groom, Melton, occupied the box seat behind Snibbs. Melton had been with Gregory's family all his working life and had visited the Hall several times, including the last time Gregory had been there—for his great-aunt Minnie's funeral in November '43. More than eight years ago, Gregory realized with mild surprise.

*Time passes more swiftly than one thinks.*

Hard on the heels of that thought came another. *And what have I to show for those eight years?*

Much as he didn't want to think it, the answer was: very little.

He'd been drifting. Idly floating through life, utterly purposeless and cast hither and yon by the currents about him. He knew it, but had been unable to fix on a direction—an occupation, a project—that called to him. That excited his interest. So he'd drifted on.

Gregory noticed Snibbs was peering through the trees on their left; glancing that way, he glimpsed several roofs on the other side of long, sloping fields. "That's Earls Barton, the nearest village. Once we take the next turn, the village will come up on our left, and the Hall's lands will lie to our right."

"We've made good time," Melton rumbled.

"Indeed." Gregory spotted the lane that led to the village and also, eventually, to the front gate of Bellamy Hall. He'd spent the last week in Lincolnshire, hunting with friends—a prior engagement he hadn't seen any reason to break—before finally making for the Hall. They'd left the hunting box south of Spalding after breakfast and traveled via Peterborough and Thrapston to High Ferrars, where they'd stopped for lunch before continuing to Wellingborough and out along the road to Northampton.

Gregory slowed his horses and turned onto the lane. Once the pair were trotting steadily, he glanced at where he knew Bellamy Hall to be, although the lie of the land hid the house from view.

He hadn't informed the staff he would be arriving that day, but they had to be expecting him. He'd learned of his unexpected inheritance at the end of January, and the Hall staff would have been informed soon after. The news that he was now the owner of Bellamy Hall had come out of the blue; initially, he hadn't known what to make of it, much less how he felt about it.

Snibbs straightened and pointed through the trees. "Is that it?" Amazement and something like awe tinged his voice.

Gregory looked, then halted the horses. This was the one spot along the lane that afforded a clear view of the house, nearly a mile distant over the fields. He nodded. "That's Bellamy Hall."

Lowering his hands, he drank in the sight. He'd first visited as an infant, and for many years, every summer, he and his family had made the pilgrimage from their home in Kent to spend a few weeks with their mother's aunt, Araminta, Lady Bellamy, better known as Minnie. And forever by Minnie's side had been her devoted companion, Mrs. Timms, known to all as Timms. As he stared across the winter-brown fields at the massive house, he could easily imagine Minnie and Timms eagerly waiting in the parlor to greet and embrace him and ply him with tea, ginger biscuits, and seed cake.

"It's rather…imposing," Snibbs managed.

Gregory's lips twitched. "That's one way of describing it." To the uninitiated, Bellamy Hall was a gothic monstrosity.

The land surrounding the house was relatively flat, allowing the grotesquerie of the hodgepodge of styles—punctuated by random turrets and towers, some round, others square, capped by mismatched roofs—to achieve maximum impact. Built in gray limestone, over the centuries, the original manor hall had sprouted five wings, some of which had floors that didn't align with those of the abutting sections, resulting in a roofline of many and varied heights and uncounted flights of stairs within.

Despite the place's unabashed ugliness, Gregory viewed it with warm affection. He and his siblings had spent many richly satisfying days pretending they were explorers and haunting the twisting corridors, discovering odd alcoves and rooms shut up for years. It was, indeed, a house that stirred imaginations young and old.

Narrowing his eyes, he tried to envision the place as, under his ownership, he hoped it would be—a comfortable, gentleman's country residence. He was there to pick up the reins, assess the situation with the wider estate, and make any decisions necessary to bring the vision in his head into being.

He could imagine himself in the library, comfortably sunk in one of the armchairs, reading the latest news from London. There would be hunting in winter, out of Northampton and nearby Kettering, and in the summer, who knew? He might even host a few of his friends for a house party.

His vision was one of bucolic country peace, soothing and free of social drama. An easygoing, relatively uneventful life that, he felt, would suit him. He could see himself sinking into such an untrammeled existence. Should he feel the need for something more, there was always London, or he could invite his siblings, their spouses, and his associated nieces and nephews to visit, just as he and his siblings had when they'd been children.

He could see it clearly. A quiet, peaceful existence with carefully curated excitements to add spice whenever he wished, with everything under his complete control.

His lips lightly curving, he shook the reins and set the horses trotting again.

They passed the turnoff that led to the village and, shortly after, came to the entrance to the Hall's drive, and he deftly turned the curricle through the perennially open gates.

The first section of the drive was bordered on both sides by closely planted trees. Although the leaves of the beeches and oaks were brown and shriveled, the conifers between were huge and dense and arched over the drive to create a dark tunnel.

The wind was rising. Not quite howling, yet whistling through the trees and rattling the dried leaves in a vaguely menacing way and sending chill fingers sliding over any exposed skin.

Ahead, framed by the end of the tunnel, the sky had darkened, clouds louring, heavy and thick, but as yet showing no overt sign of rain.

The curricle emerged from the tunnel into the open, with neatly clipped lawns rolling away to either side. The drive turned slightly to head directly to the oval forecourt before the house's front door. From the drive, they couldn't see the ruins of Coldchurch Abbey, on the gatehouse of which Bellamy Hall had been built, but Gregory knew the ruins were there, beyond the rear left corner of the roughly rectangular block of the house.

The neatness of the lawns and the shrub-filled beds along the wide front of the house confirmed his assumption that Timms had continued to run the household and estate much as she had in Minnie's day, and he felt certain she would have kept on the staff. The only change he knew of was that the previous butler, Marston, and his wife, who had acted as housekeeper, had retired and moved away, leaving the erstwhile underbutler, Cromwell, to step into the butler's role. Gregory hadn't heard who the current housekeeper was; doubtless, he would soon find out.

He'd last seen Timms in autumn, when she'd visited his parents and uncle and aunt in London. She'd passed, apparently peacefully, in mid-January, when a bout of icy weather had gripped all of England. She'd been buried a week later, but heavy snowfalls blanketing the country had prevented any of the family from attending. They'd been hunkered down in London, Kent, Cambridgeshire, Rutlandshire, and Cornwall and unable to get through.

As the forecourt neared, he slowed his horses and made a mental note to visit Minnie's and Timms's graves.

Under Minnie's will, Timms had been left the house and estate to manage in a caretaker role until Timms's own death. Being a decade or so the elder, Minnie had tasked Timms with selecting which of Minnie's great-nieces or great-nephews should ultimately inherit the Hall, and Timms had chosen Gregory. To his amazement, no one in the family had voiced so much as a quibble or even shown much surprise. The legacy had surprised him, but apparently, others knew or saw something he still didn't; they all thought he was the right person to take up the reins at Bellamy Hall.

Although he'd asked why, no one had explained other than to imply that Timms's reasons were obvious.

He inwardly snorted; he still couldn't see it, but he was there now, about to walk into the house as the new owner of Bellamy Hall.

He didn't draw up in the forecourt but sent the curricle sweeping on, around the north face of the house to the stable yard beyond.

～

Inside Bellamy Hall, seated behind the desk in the study, Caitlin Fergusson examined the figures she'd just jotted down, then tucked her pencil behind her ear and smiled encouragingly at the four people occupying the chairs before the desk. "That should do well enough, at least in this season."

"I'm just glad we've got those porkers to sell." Joshua Bracks, head gardener and principal keeper of the livestock pens, shook his graying head. "I was worried the freeze might have held them back, but they've come along nicely, which is just as well, as the hens don't do well in this weather."

Caitlin smiled reassuringly. "You're keeping the kitchen supplied, which is all we need at this time." She glanced at Julia Witherspoon, sitting beside Joshua. "Your onions should fetch a good price as well."

A large and handsome lady, Julia managed the Hall's kitchen gardens and had a well-developed grasp of what produce would fetch a good price at the local market each month. In her usual regal way, she inclined her head. "I believe so, although I think our shallots and garlic will, in toto, bring in even more."

"That"—Caitlin glanced at her estimation of the likely profits the Hall would make from the market in Wellingborough later that week—"would be very helpful." It was her job to balance the overall budget for the Hall's many enterprises, an undertaking that demanded unrelenting attention to detail.

She looked at the others present—Harry Edgar, who managed the Hall's extensive orchard, and his wife, Jennifer, who ran the cider mill—and arched her brows. "Any thoughts on how your produce will be received this week?"

With a satisfied smile, Harry predicted, "The last of the apples will vanish inside an hour." A quiet gentry-born farmer, he loved his fruit trees and looked on their offerings with justifiable pride. Still smiling, he glanced at his dark-haired wife. "And I expect we'll have a rush over Jen's new plum brandy."

Jennifer smiled, plainly confident in that assessment. "That old recipe you found worked a treat. Like Harry says, people will be lining up for a bottle once the news gets about."

"And of course," Harry added, "we've more of our cider to sell. It's the late-harvest pressing, and that always goes quickly." He met Caitlin's eyes. "I was wondering if we shouldn't add a penny or two to our price."

The others supported the idea, Caitlin included. "As Barnack cider is so prized locally and the last pressing of the season is a limited run, I can't see why those bottles shouldn't go for a premium."

With that decided, all well pleased, they were about to rise when a rap on the door was followed by Nessie, the Hall's cook, sticking her head into the room. She saw them, smiled, and came in. "All the people I wanted to see."

With her apple cheeks, comfortable girth wrapped in a spotless but creased white apron, and gray hair gathered in a knot on top of her head, the older woman was everyone's vision of an experienced cook. She fixed her bright blue eyes on them, and her smile widened. "Now then, I'm seeking a challenge for dinner tonight. So what can you give me to play with?"

Grinning back, they relaxed in their chairs and set their minds to what they could offer Nessie to sate her imaginative cravings. Being well acquainted with the outcome of such endeavors, they were seriously motivated. In the end, Joshua offered a porker already hanging in the cool store, along with two pheasants, and reminded Nessie of the jelly she'd made from the pigs' trotters he'd given her weeks ago. Jennifer promised to send their son with a bottle of the prized plum brandy, and Julia and Nessie put their heads together and came up with a list of vegetables to best complement the viands.

Once everyone was satisfied—and mentally licking their lips in anticipation of the evening meal—the others took their leave of Caitlin and, finally, rose to go.

She was fond of them all and loved her position as chatelaine of Bellamy Hall, but when any of them started talking of their passions, the hours flew. With the previous week's accounts still to be done, she was quietly pleased to see them make for the door.

Then Harry halted and turned to her. "Meant to ask—have you heard anything of our new owner? Are we expecting him anytime soon?"

The others all stopped and looked at her.

She inwardly sighed, but folded her hands and smiled at the group, all of whom were waiting on her answer. "I haven't heard anything at all, but that said, he could turn up any day."

Julia humphed. "Typical of that sort of London gentleman, I fear. No consideration for those his arrival might discombobulate."

Julia wasn't speaking for herself; she was the least likely of the estate's residents to be discombobulated by Mr. Cynster, even should he prove to be the most unconscionable libertine. Others, however, were rather more nervy.

"One has to wonder," Jennifer said, fingers twining, "why he hasn't visited yet." She fixed her gaze on Caitlin's face. "Do you think…that is, what if he's already decided to sell? The Hall and the estate?"

Firmly, Caitlin shook her head. "Even the most disinterested gentleman wouldn't sell an agricultural estate he hasn't stepped foot on for more than eight years. If only to assess what he's inherited, he will come."

Joshua raised his brows. "Perhaps he'll send an agent."

With an authority she didn't truly feel, Caitlin replied, "From all I've gathered of Mr. Cynster's past association with the Hall, especially when his great-aunt was alive, no matter how much of a hedonistic profligate he is, I doubt he would sell the place without at least coming to see what's here." *And run a calculating eye over the Hall's assets.*

From the moment Timms had told her who would inherit—unfortunately only just before Timms had breathed her last—Caitlin had done all she could to learn more about Mr. Gregory Cynster. Cromwell, Jenkins, and a few of the staff who had been at the Hall for decades remembered him, but sadly, their memories were of him as a child or a youth. Along with everyone else on the estate, they had no insights regarding the Hall's new owner as an adult.

Consequently, together with everyone else, not just at the Hall but in the local area, Caitlin had been left to extrapolate from what was expected of, as Julia had put it, "that sort of London gentleman."

As a Cynster, Mr. Gregory Cynster moved in the upper echelons of society. He lived in London—that much, Timms had told her—and was active in the ton. If Caitlin had correctly interpreted the observations

Timms had shared over the past three years, Gregory Cynster enjoyed the archetypal lifestyle of the London-born-and-bred gentleman-rake.

He attended balls and soirées in town. He visited friends and relatives in the country and rode magnificent horses in the hunt. He drove superb cattle hitched to an elegant curricle and squired beautiful ladies—usually young matrons—to ton events and, no doubt, alleviated said ladies' boredom at the drop of their handkerchiefs.

Caitlin's mind wandered into imagining what that would entail...

"I just hope," Harry said, his voice, heavy with dire meaning, snapping her back to the present, "that he doesn't come here wanting to change things."

Caitlin adopted her most confident expression. "Our best guess is that, when he does arrive, Mr. Cynster will look, first and foremost, at what Bellamy Hall can provide in furthering his current lifestyle. Once he sees and appreciates what a well-run and profitable series of businesses Bellamy Hall comprises, I'm confident he'll understand that he has no reason to meddle—indeed, that he would be unwise to attempt it—and, instead, can return to his London pursuits and live comfortably on the income the Hall will provide."

Harry, Nessie, and Julia appeared inclined to accept Caitlin's prophesy, while Jennifer looked like she was considering surreptitiously crossing herself.

But Joshua frowned uncertainly. "Do you think he will?"

Chin firming, Caitlin truthfully replied, "I can't see why not."

Leaving the bays in the stable, in the care of Melton, Jenkins—the head stableman, whom Gregory remembered from long ago—and three suitably reverent stable lads, Gregory walked out of the stable yard and headed for the house, making for the south façade of the house and the side door that the family habitually used.

He'd left Snibbs organizing the luggage they'd brought strapped to the rear of the curricle. The rest of his possessions, and Snibbs's and Melton's, had been consigned to a carter and would be delivered in due course.

On reaching the southwest corner of the house, Gregory paused and looked back. With his hands sunk in the pockets of his greatcoat, he surveyed the buildings around the stable.

Clearly, some things had changed since he'd last been there—or at least since he'd last looked out this way. When he'd come for Minnie's funeral, he hadn't visited the stable so couldn't guess how recent the two barns beyond the stable were. The forge and the carriage barn behind the stable had always been there, but both had been repaired, reroofed, and significantly extended.

Eyes narrowing, he studied the stable; built by Minnie's husband, Sir Humphrey, who'd been a keen rider to hounds, it had always been large. Gregory had assumed that the number of horses would be much reduced by now, yet the stable had seemed busier and more bustling than in his memories. Many of the stalls had been occupied and not solely with carriage horses. While he'd been there, two stable lads had returned from exercising a pair of decent-looking hacks.

What he'd seen had raised several questions, not least being to whom all the horses belonged.

Frowning, he turned and continued along the south façade. He also wanted to know what had occasioned the recent building works; he couldn't imagine what had necessitated the extensions, let alone two more barns.

He reached the side door, opened it, and stepped through, into the usual prevailing gloom; being long and narrow, the majority of the Hall's corridors were perpetually dim. After closing the door and losing what little light the opening had afforded, confident in his memories of the house, he walked on, tacking through two connecting corridors to emerge into the rear of the long front hall.

He wasn't surprised when the sound of his bootheels ringing on the tiles summoned a tall thin man, garbed in severe black and with receding gingery hair and a small yet distinct paunch distending his black waistcoat.

The butler stopped and stared in slack-jawed surprise.

Halting, Gregory smiled. "Cromwell, isn't it?"

The butler started, then his washed-out-blue eyes flared. "Mr. Cynster, sir! We weren't expecting you."

Cromwell stepped forward, then back. He half turned one way, then swung in the opposite direction, then he halted and, wringing his hands, looked at Gregory. "Perhaps I should fetch our chatelaine." Raising both hands, palms outward, in a placating gesture, Cromwell gabbled, "Yes, that's what I should do. If you'll just remain here, sir, I'm sure she won't be a minute. Permit me…"

With that, Cromwell rushed off along one of the corridors.

Gregory stood in the middle of the hall and stared after the butler. "Obviously, I should have sent word."

Caitlin was scanning her latest projections, running her pencil down the column of anticipated profits one last time, when the study door burst open, and Cromwell gasped, "He's here!"

She pondered the total figure. "He who?"

"Mr. Cynster!"

She looked up.

With obvious effort, Cromwell hauled in a huge breath, drew himself up, and announced, "Mr. Gregory Cynster has arrived, miss."

*Damn!* "I see." She glanced at her projections, then laid them aside. She'd prepared herself and the household for this moment, even if she hadn't foreseen said moment arriving today.

*Drat the man. Couldn't he have sent word?*

She hated having situations sprung on her; she much preferred to be in control of events.

She pushed back her chair, hoping by her very calmness to infuse some calm into Cromwell. "Where did you put him?"

Cromwell blinked several times. "Er...I left him in the front hall. He walked in from the rear corridor—from the stables, I suppose—and gave me quite a shock. I didn't expect to see him and didn't know what...where..."

"No matter." Served the blighter right for not having the courtesy to warn the house. She rose and glided around the desk. "Don't worry. I'll see to him."

Cromwell looked much relieved. "He remembered me. I'd better introduce you." He whirled and led the way out of the door he'd left swinging.

Stifling a sigh, Caitlin followed and closed the study door firmly behind her. She stepped out in Cromwell's wake; relieved of responsibility, he was striding on quite eagerly.

She lengthened her stride and used the few moments to rapidly review her plan for dealing with the Hall's new owner. With her strategy clear in her mind, she raised her chin to an angle she hoped would convey supreme assurance and swept into the front hall and came to an abrupt, all-but-teetering halt.

The god in a greatcoat who'd been examining a painting on the wall turned to Cromwell.

His rich hazel gaze rested briefly on the butler, then shifted further to land on Caitlin.

She felt it—the weight of his regard—like a blow. She stopped breathing.

He was tall. Cromwell was tall, but this man was half a head taller. His shoulders were broad, his chest wide, yet the overall impression was one of lean, supple strength. Steel. He reminded her of smooth, tensile steel, like a well-balanced blade that flexed and gave, but never broke.

Her senses registered all that, along with the understated elegance of his clothes, the quality of his boots and heavy greatcoat, but it was his face that transfixed her, that sucked the air from her lungs and left her breathless.

His hazel eyes were a mesmerizing blend of gold and mossy green. Long dark lashes, thick and luxurious, framed them. Beneath the fall of his wind-ruffled dark-brown hair, his forehead was broad, and his dark brows angled in a way that made him look vaguely piratical. Long, lean cheeks, a patrician nose, firm, mobile lips, and a squared chin completed the picture. To her eyes, he was the epitome of a dark angel.

*Or a devil in human guise.*

Trapped in his gaze, she swallowed, desperately scrambling to reassemble her wits.

Gregory drank in the sight of the lovely young woman who had stepped from the shadows of the corridor. He let his eyes feast; she was a sight worthy of such admiration, with her lustrous black hair, sumptuous figure, and strong yet feminine features. Her large almond-shaped eyes were a startling shade of violet blue—pansy blue, his mother would have called it. Her face was a fashionable oval, her complexion flawless, yet while her fine well-arched dark eyebrows, long, nicely curved lashes, and frankly wanton lips were those of a femme fatale, her straight nose and firm chin spoke of a determined disposition and an ironclad will.

His libido stirred. Unmistakably stirred.

*Well, well. What have we here?*

He had to wonder. Perhaps she was one of Minnie's or Timms's charity cases or even a distant relative.

When she continued to stare at him, blinking those wide blue eyes as if trying to make sense of his presence, he ventured, "I'm Gregory Cynster, the new owner. I'm waiting for—"

He stopped. She'd been following Cromwell. He glanced at the butler and saw he was now calm and composed, as if his duty had been discharged and no further weight rested on his shoulders.

Gregory returned his gaze to the woman—lady. His highly attuned senses informed him she was definitely the latter. Yet...hoping against hope, he went on, "Cromwell referred to a chatelaine."

She stiffened slightly and raised her chin a notch higher. "That's me." She frowned slightly and amended, "I'm Caitlin Fergusson, chatelaine of Bellamy Hall."

*No, no, no, no, no!*

If she was his employee, she was entirely out of his reach.

*I can't seduce her.*

While he grappled with that realization, he nevertheless registered the underlying challenge in her declaration and also the faint hint of a burr. She wasn't local. Keeping his frown from his face, he forced himself to view her assessingly.

Had someone informed him that the Hall now had a chatelaine, he still wouldn't have expected her. She was young but, now he looked more closely, perhaps not that young. The youthful bloom on her cheeks might be misleading; it didn't match the awareness in her violet-blue gaze. She had a degree of experience, certainly of people, beyond that commonly found in young ladies of the ton.

She was definitely not reacting to him in the way young ladies normally did. He got an impression of cool starchiness with not a hint of a simper or batted lash to be seen.

She also knew the value of silence, of waiting patiently for the other to make a move...and yes, he and she were definitely on opposing sides of some chessboard.

Lips firming, he conceded, "I see."

The bustle in the stable returned to his mind, along with an awareness of distant sounds of activity at the edge of his perception. A suspicion bloomed that whatever the nature of the household currently at Bellamy Hall, it wasn't what he'd thought he would find.

He'd assumed he would encounter a skeleton staff in a largely silent house. Yet he knew of Minnie's longstanding habit of taking in strays— impecunious relatives, extremely distant connections, and charity cases who had appealed to her kind heart. He should have thought to inquire whether, in that regard, Timms had followed in Minnie's footsteps. As Timms had always been the more practical of the pair, he'd assumed not.

He was increasingly sure his assumptions regarding Bellamy Hall were about to be proved wildly inaccurate.

Regardless, he wanted to know. Now. He nodded to his chatelaine. "Miss Fergusson. Am I right in assuming your role encompasses that of housekeeper?"

She bit her lip, stifling some rash response, and faint color rose in her cheeks, but after a fraught second, she inclined her head haughtily.

He would have wagered she had no idea how haughty—and revealing —the action was. *Who the devil is she?*

Instead of demanding an answer he was perfectly certain he wouldn't get, he said, "While a new owner meeting the staff is often something of a formal affair, in this instance, I would prefer you to escort me around the place and introduce me to whomever we meet, be they staff or…residents currently living at the Hall."

*Damn again!* Caitlin fought to keep her features from reflecting her ire.

Just like that, he'd upended her carefully planned and rehearsed sequence of presentations from the various businesses operating within the Hall. That orchestrated performance had been designed to stun him with their effectiveness, thus encouraging him to leave the Hall rolling along as it was, perfectly successfully under her guidance, while he returned to the bright lights and sins of the capital. Now, instead of that assured presentation, she and whichever residents he and she encountered would have to play their revelations by ear.

Rapidly, she canvassed her options, but could see no way of avoiding acceding to his wishes. Sadly, he *was* the owner of the place, and on behalf of herself and the others on the estate, she was going to have to come to terms with him.

Stiffly, she inclined her head and waved down the corridor leading into the east wing. "I believe we'll find several of our residents this way."

She stepped out, and within a few strides, he was pacing beside her. Glancing back, she found Cromwell ghosting in their wake.

Facing forward, she saw Cynster, too, noticing the butler.

He caught her eye. "I remember Cromwell from earlier visits. He's been here for many years. For how long have you been filling the role of chatelaine?"

At close quarters, his deep voice set something thrumming inside her.

Smothering the disconcerting sensation, she crisply replied, "For just over three years. I arrived in the dead of winter in '49, and when Mrs. Timms offered me the position, I accepted."

"Arrived from where?"

"Farther north." They'd reached the door of the stillroom. Seeking immediate distraction, she knocked and entered. She wouldn't have chosen to introduce him to Alice and Millie first, but beggars couldn't be picky, and she definitely didn't want him asking more questions about where she came from or her years prior to arriving at the Hall.

Alice and Millie were standing on the opposite side of the long table that filled the center of the room. Both women had been stripping leaves from dried herbs and had looked up at their entrance.

Caitlin smiled reassuringly, held her breath, and waved at her companion, who had halted beside her, staring at the evidence of industry spread before them. "Mr. Cynster, allow me to present Miss Alice Penrose, our resident apothecary, and Miss Millie Carter, her apprentice."

He blinked. "Apothecary?"

"Indeed. Alice and her products are highly regarded throughout the district." Caitlin nodded encouragingly to Alice as, having laid aside her herbs, the little apothecary came around the table, a tentative smile on her lips.

Alice was a professional lion and a personal lamb. She was often overcome with shyness until she grew accustomed to a person. Timidly, she offered a hand. "Mr. Cynster. It's a pleasure to make your acquaintance, sir."

Caitlin cast the man beside her a sharp glance and held herself ready to intervene if he was too brash and frightened Alice.

Instead, he smiled gently and charmingly, took Alice's small hand in his much larger one, and exchanged a perfectly polite nod. "Miss Penrose." He released Alice's hand and looked across at Millie. "Miss Carter." Then he looked back at Alice. "I confess I know nothing about being an apothecary. I had no idea Bellamy Hall housed such an...enterprise."

"Oh yes!" Alice's face lit. The apothecary business was her passion; in speaking of that, she stood on firm ground. "I've been here, living at the Hall and using this room"—she gestured to the workshop, once a large parlor—"for over seven years. Mrs. Timms thought it a good idea to have such an enterprise at the Hall. She often told me that she wished I'd come sooner, as she believed having an apothecary to hand would have helped her friend, Lady Bellamy. Sadly, her ladyship had passed before I arrived in the area."

When Alice glanced inquiringly at Caitlin, she nodded encouragingly, and nothing loath when it came to her business, Alice rolled on, "Of course, I focus first on treating all those on the estate. Not just at the Hall itself but on the farms and at the other businesses."

Cromwell had sidled closer. "Best thing for my chest, sir—Miss Alice's poultice. I swear by it."

"I see." Cynster returned his gaze to Alice.

"Beyond that"—Alice surprised Caitlin by gripping Cynster's sleeve and drawing him farther down the room to where Alice's distillation equipment was set up—"we make up the usual tinctures, potions, creams, and powders for all those living around about."

"All the way up to Kettering," Cromwell helpfully added.

"Alice's products also sell well in Northampton," Caitlin put in. "Over the years, her reputation has spread far and wide."

Alice looked suitably modest.

Cynster, meanwhile, appeared faintly confused, although his frown didn't show so much in his features as in his lovely eyes...

He caught her staring and met her gaze.

Immediately, she waved at the door. "Thank you, Alice. I believe some of the others will have come in by now."

"Yes, of course." Alice smiled at Cynster; oddly, it seemed the man didn't trigger any of her usual trepidation. "If you need anything of a medicinal nature, sir, do feel free to consult me."

Gracefully, Cynster inclined his head. "Thank you, Miss Penrose." He nodded equally to Millie, who had remained at the table. "Miss Carter."

Then he turned to Caitlin and, his expression hardening, waved her before him.

He followed her into the corridor and fell to pacing alongside her as she walked briskly around the two short turns that would take them into the rear wing. Before he could ask any of the questions she could all but hear forming in his mind, she stated, "Normally at this time of day, several of our residents are likely to be either consulting with our cook, Nessie, on what supplies are available from our gardens and paddocks or, if they've already spoken with her, delivering the same."

His frown came into being. "Aren't meat and fish procured either from the Home Farm or from local vendors? And surely the kitchen garden produces most vegetables, and the rest comes from local markets?"

That would be the norm at most gentlemen's estates. "Well," she temporized, "yes and no. Matters are handled rather differently here."

"I believe I'm coming to realize that." The muttered words were low and barely audible.

Resisting the urge to prim her lips, she waved down the corridor. "What we call the preparation room is just along here, adjacent to the kitchen." And with any luck, Julia Witherspoon would be there. Caitlin was counting on Julia, a strong woman able to hold her own in any company, to explain how vegetables were procured at the Hall.

They were ten yards from the archway that led into the large preparation room when a high-pitched bleat assaulted their ears and a young goat streaked out of the room and pelted toward them.

Shouts, oaths, and the thunder of boots followed, and Joshua Bracks and his assistant, Hendricks, raced out of the room in pursuit.

Caitlin gasped. Behind her, Cromwell squeaked.

Gregory could barely believe his eyes as the goat barreled down the narrow corridor straight toward him—and his unexpected chatelaine and Cromwell. Without thinking, he gripped her arm and yanked her behind him. He released her just in time to step sideways, the move executed perfectly to startle the goat into deflecting toward the wall, forcing it to halt.

Before the beast could back up, the pursuers fell on it and wrestled it to the ground and, ultimately, into submission.

Once the beast's legs were tied, the larger man hoisted the animal into his arms. He nodded in thanks to Gregory, then turned and carted the animal away, ominously informing the beast, "Off to Nessie with you."

The other man, somewhat slighter and dressed in rather better clothes, got to his feet and brushed himself off.

"Sorry about that. We were just bringing the animal to Nessie for approval." The man eyed Gregory. "We never slaughter any beast unless we're sure it's what Nessie, our cook, wants and needs." He took in Caitlin and Cromwell, and his blue eyes narrowed fractionally. "You must be Cynster." He held out a hand. "Joshua Bracks. For my sins, I'm master of livestock here, as well as the head gardener, but with Julia handling the vegetable garden, Alice taking over the rose garden, and most of the rest parkland, there's precious little for me and my boys to do on the latter front."

"I've just arrived." Gregory grasped the proffered hand and shook it. "Miss Fergusson is showing me around."

"That was quite an accomplished move there." Bracks dipped his head toward the wall. "Used to goats, are you?"

"As a matter of fact, I am. My sister-in-law's uncle—who lives next door to my family home—has bred them for decades. As children, we were often conscripted to help him with his herd."

Bracks nodded. "That would do it. Nothing like learning tricks as a child—they stick with you for life." Brightly, he asked, "What type of goat were they?"

Gregory was happy to answer; he remembered the goats well and could describe them to Bracks's evident satisfaction.

"You must come down to the pens and look over our herd," Bracks said. "I'll be keen to hear what you think."

Before Gregory could agree, his chatelaine intervened. "I can hear Julia in the preparation room, and I should introduce Mr. Cynster to her as well. Perhaps, Joshua, you might first explain what livestock the estate produces."

Bracks was happy to do so. Gregory learned that as well as goats, the Hall produced pigs and chickens, not solely for the estate but also supplying markets and inns at Wellingborough, Kettering, and Northampton.

"Of course," Bracks said, "the lamb and beef come from our farms—from the Hammersleys at Home Farm and the Cruickshanks at Nene Farm. At the pens, we concentrate on the smaller animals."

"I see." Gregory felt he was starting to gain a glimmer of insight, but he remained at a loss as to why the Hall was, apparently, operating as a group of businesses. If he was interpreting what he was hearing correctly.

After confirming with Bracks that, at some point in the near future, he would make his way down to the livestock pens, Gregory allowed his chatelaine to steer him into the large room from which the goat had escaped.

Bracks followed, but after a quick word with the woman who had to be Nessie, the cook, he left via a half-glazed door that opened onto the lawns. In the distance, Gregory saw the other man carrying the goat, presumably to its fate.

With his chatelaine, Gregory approached the cook and the other woman—assuredly another gentlewoman—who were standing beside a table covered with various vegetables.

"Mr. Cynster," Caitlin Fergusson said, "allow me to present Miss Julia Witherspoon, who manages the Hall's kitchen garden."

"A pleasure, Mr. Cynster." A large, bluff woman with a horsey face and a voice that was rather loud, Julia Witherspoon offered him her hand to shake.

He took it and shook it as he would have a man's.

With a nod of approval, Julia retrieved her hand and stated, "My little band of workers and I pride ourselves on the quality of our produce." She waved at the vegetables on the table. "As you can see, our offerings are uniformly superb. It's all about the humus, you see. It's an art, and even if I do say so myself, it's an art we've perfected."

"I see." Gregory's only acquaintance with vegetables was when they were offered to him on a plate. But he was starting to get the hang of what was going on at the Hall. "As well as providing the Hall with your largesse, I take it you sell produce more generally."

That was intended as a question, one Julia Witherspoon was patently prepared to answer at length. It quickly became clear that she was the local authority on vegetable growing and was devoted to nurturing large and healthy crops of every conceivable sort of vegetable, both for the Hall and to sell in the surrounding towns.

Proudly, she informed him, "What with the cabbages, we even manage to turn a tidy profit over the winter months."

Hoping his eyes hadn't glazed, he smiled and nodded, then turned to the other woman. An older, comfortable sort, she was regarding him shrewdly.

"You're the cook, I understand." He smiled winningly. "A decidedly vital person in any large house."

Her lips twitched, then more confidently lifted, and she bobbed. "Indeed, sir. So I'm always telling them."

Miss Fergusson stepped forward. "This is Nessie, and she's one of the true treasures of Bellamy Hall."

"Oh, go on with you, missy." Blushing, Nessie flapped her apron at Miss Fergusson.

"It's true," Cromwell piped up. "Our Nessie's the best hereabouts."

Gregory seized the chance to ask the butler, "How many staff are currently employed in the house?"

Cromwell frowned. "Well, there's the maids—we have six—and the footmen. Only four of those. And of course, there's the kitchen staff."

"Three kitchen maids, two assistants, and three scullery boys," Nessie put in.

"That's the indoor staff," Cromwell said. "Well, excepting the personal maids and menservants, that is. Quite a few of those, of course. When it comes to the outdoor staff, it gets a trifle more complicated, what with several now working alongside Joshua and Jenkins."

Gregory had never inquired as to the staffing at his family's home and had only the vaguest notion of what numbers would be normal for a residence the size of Bellamy Hall. Nevertheless, six maids and four footmen —and the maids weren't even personal maids, and the footmen didn't double as menservants—seemed excessive.

He glanced at his chatelaine. Possibly misreading his look, she waved toward the archway and, to the others, said, "We'd better get on."

With nods and smiles, they parted from Miss Witherspoon and Nessie. As they left the large room, Cromwell mumbled about having to check on the silver and vanished down the corridor in the direction of the kitchen.

Caitlin Fergusson waved Gregory down an intersecting corridor. As he fell in alongside her, she said, "You've now met four of the nine residents—Alice, Millie, Julia, and Joshua all live at the Hall."

*And all are well-born, gentry at the very least.*

That hadn't escaped Gregory's notice. It was strange to encounter so many of that class apparently unrelated yet all living together in one very large house. Several pertinent questions rose in his mind, but before he could voice any, his guide continued, "Two of the others—Mr. Vernon Trowbridge and Mr. Percy Hillside—are the glassblower and head woodworker respectively. They'll both be at their workshops at present, but you'll meet them at dinnertime."

"So that's six of the nine. What of the other three?"

He watched as she drew in a breath, stiffened her spine, and all but visibly girded her loins, then she waved him down another corridor. "At this hour, they'll be in the conservatory."

Caitlin was still battling to tamp down the nerves that had flared when he'd gripped her arm. His fingers had, indeed, felt like steel, but the ease with which he'd dragged her out of danger—the sheer muscular strength he'd so effortlessly deployed—had made her lungs seize.

She didn't know what was wrong with her; she wasn't usually such a vaporous ninny. She didn't know what it was about him, but he set her on edge in a most peculiar way. To develop an irrational sensitivity was the last thing she needed right now; dealing with him was going to be difficult enough without having to cope with that as well.

At least, despite the best efforts of the goat, none of the three business leaders he'd met thus far had muffed their presentations. None had been as polished or as informative as she'd hoped, but none had been a disaster.

That might change with the next three.

To distract herself from that possibility, she volunteered, "The remaining three residents are Melrose Walter, Tristan Fellows, and Hugo Martindale." Mentally crossing her fingers, she added, "All three are painters. They use the conservatory as their studio."

She felt more than saw the incredulous glance her new employer threw her and hurried to explain, "The conservatory has been the painters' domain from well before I arrived. Apparently, the light is critical for their work."

Cromwell had come hurrying after them and had drawn close enough to hear her last words. "Indeed," he added, settling to walk behind them again, "all three of our painter-gentlemen have been with us since shortly after her ladyship died. She knew all three and had encouraged them to stay, and they came for her funeral and remained."

From the corner of her eye, she saw Cynster's jaw tighten, then the muscles eased, and in a frighteningly even tone, he inquired, "Do the painters—like all the others I've met thus far—sell their works?"

She nodded. "They do." She left it at that.

The conservatory lay dead ahead, beyond two half-glazed doors at the end of the corridor.

"It seems that the Hall is a hive of business activity. How many enterprises operate from it?"

"From the Hall itself?"

"From the estate."

"Fifteen." She glanced at him in time to see shock register in his face.

"Fifteen? Good Lord." The words were weak.

She tried to read his expression, but as the shock faded, she was once again unable to guess his thoughts. Nevertheless, while in all physical respects he was precisely as she'd imagined a gentleman-rake would be, he seemed more interested in what was actually going on at the Hall than she—and indeed, the entire company of residents—had expected.

Quite what that augured for their plans, she wasn't at all sure, but his questions, more precisely their tone, were making her uneasy.

They reached the conservatory doors. Peering through the glass, she saw the three painters clustered farther down the long room. Hugo stood to one side of a shoulder-high screen, holding the end of a thin rope that was presumably attached to the animal they'd placed on the table they used for still-life compositions, which was hidden behind the screen. Beyond the screen and table, Melrose and Tristan stood behind their easels as they busily sketched whatever beast they'd posed.

She uttered a silent prayer and, forcing herself not to hold her breath, grasped the handle, opened one door, and led the way inside.

Hugo had been half-asleep. He startled and, eyes flying wide, swung to face them, and abruptly, the leash jerked free of his hand.

"No!" Hugo yelled and dove for the table.

From behind the screen, a chicken erupted, flapping furiously and squawking in panic.

Tristan rushed out from behind his easel as a rabbit squealed, thumped to the ground, and raced toward them, hotly pursued by a young fox.

Caitlin gawped. Cromwell shouted and rushed forward.

The new owner of the Hall swore, dove back, and slammed the door shut just in time to deny the would-be escapees.

Pandemonium ensued.

Caitlin stood perfectly still and watched the three painters, aided by Cromwell, rush around the room, chasing the animals.

It was all too much.

She drew in a deep breath, then in a tone that boded ill for any who did not immediately do exactly as she said, rapped out, "Melrose! Tristan!" When both froze and looked at her, she demanded, "What did you catch them with?"

Tristan blinked. "Oh, ah. Yes—right." He dove beneath the table and extracted a cloth bag. "The stuff's in here—do you think they'll come for it again?"

"Try it," she commanded. "The fox first."

She crossed her arms, tapped her toe, and watched with an expression that told them just how much trouble they were in.

The fox proved the easiest; they'd used a piece of raw chicken to catch it, and the animal was hungry. Tristan tempted it, and when the fox was distracted, Hugo crept close enough to seize the end of the leash again.

The chicken happily settled to peck at a pile of grain, allowing Melrose to scoop it into his arms, while Tristan stretched out on the floor and reached beneath a sofa to lure the rabbit with a lettuce that was certainly stolen from Julia's domain. Eventually, Tristan seized the bunny by the ruff and pulled it out into the light.

The young men—all in their mid-twenties—lined up in front of Caitlin, their expressions the very epitome of shamefaced.

She all but glared at them.

"We're sorry," they chorused.

They'd been forbidden from bringing animals into the house; she'd put down her foot after an episode with three baby goats. But they were going to be even sorrier shortly.

She drew in a tight breath, unfolded her arms, and nodded at the gentleman who, once the danger had passed, had returned to her side. "This is Mr. Gregory Cynster, the Hall's new owner."

Predictably, all three painters' faces fell; the sight would have been comical had the circumstances not been so dire.

"Ah," Melrose said.

She'd warned them how terribly important making a good first impression on the new owner would be—especially for them! She had no idea how to reverse the impact of the past minutes, much less how to explain them away. She drew in a breath and forged on. "Mr. Cynster, allow me to present Mr. Hugo Martindale, Mr. Melrose Walter, and Mr. Tristan Fellows." How was she to cut short the encounter before the three ninnies made things worse?

"Gentlemen." Polite yet repressively distant, Cynster nodded to the three and turned to Caitlin. "Miss Fergusson, I set out early this morning to reach here and would like to rest before dinner."

*Thank God!* Her relief was so profound that she was sure it showed and that Cynster's sharp hazel gaze didn't miss it.

Cromwell stepped up and announced, "Mr. Cynster's room should be ready, but perhaps, sir, if you would remain downstairs until I've assured myself all is well?"

Cynster inclined his head and turned toward the door. "I'll wait in the study."

After bending a last, warning glare on the three penitents, Caitlin quickly caught up and fell in beside Cynster.

As he walked, Gregory drew out his fob watch and consulted it. "What time is dinner?"

"Six o'clock," his chatelaine informed him. "The dressing gong is rung at half past five." She paused, then said, "Unless you would prefer to put dinner back."

He considered that, then shook his head. "No." He slanted her a glance. "This is the country, after all."

Her lips primmed as she held back a no doubt pithy retort.

Facing forward, he allowed Cromwell to lead and the delectable Miss Fergusson to accompany him back to the front hall. What he'd uncovered thus far—a situation only a few steps from a madhouse—was so far removed from what he'd been expecting that he needed to stop and assimilate all he'd seen and heard. He needed to sit quietly so his thoughts could stop spinning.

After the interlude in the conservatory, he also suspected that the denizens of the Hall might benefit from a little time to get themselves organized. He had, admittedly, come upon them unawares. He hadn't sent word, so perhaps he should reserve judgment until they'd had a chance to prepare.

Regardless, he'd never imagined he'd be assessing businesses; he wasn't prepared, either.

They reached the front hall, and his pair of keepers steered him on, into the library. Quite firmly. Almost as if neither had noticed that he'd specified the study.

He didn't argue but instead, once he'd sunk into one of the leather armchairs before the roaring fire and allowed Cromwell to supply him with a well-earned brandy, he dismissed both butler and chatelaine with a nod and an assurance he would be perfectly comfortable until the gong rang.

He watched the pair retreat, sipped the brandy, then frowned and murmured, "What the devil's going on here?"

# CHAPTER 2

"Yes, well. That *wasn't* an ideal way to introduce Mr. Cynster to our household." Caitlin leveled a severe look at the three painters, who all but hung their heads. "However, I hope and believe we'll make a better impression—certainly a more collected one—this evening."

She'd called an emergency meeting of all the business leaders, directing everyone to gather in the conservatory, far distant from the library where Gregory Cynster was presently ensconced. Everyone had come, and all were standing in a loose circle, not far from the door.

Caitlin scanned the faces of the twenty-six people—some couples, others single ladies and gentlemen—responsible for the fifteen active businesses on Bellamy Hall lands, taking in their concern.

Their understandable worry.

All of them—and Caitlin, too—had a great deal invested in the totality that was Bellamy Hall, and not all of that was time and effort. For many, their business was their life's passion and also their principal source of income. Indeed, that was the whole point—the central tenet—of what Lady Bellamy and Timms had created at the Hall.

"First things first," Len Sutton said. "Break it to us gently—what's he like?"

Standing beside her husband, Isabelle Sutton added, "Has he given you any indication of what he intends to do with the Hall?"

Caitlin seized on the second question; she wasn't at all sure how to answer the first. "I got the impression that, at this point, he has an open mind."

As she said the words, she realized they were true. Thinking back, analyzing what she'd gleaned, she continued, "He seemed to have no firm direction in mind—or at least none he allowed me to see. I got the sense he came here to view the place, to see what was here, before making up his mind what he wished to do."

"I only saw him at a distance," Vernon Trowbridge said, "when he was walking from the stables to the house, but he certainly looked the part of your typical London rake. There's no reason why our expectations won't play out—that he won't simply cast an eye over the place, look at the books, see how sound the income is, then happily leave the Hall as it is and merrily head back to the capital to resume his no doubt hedonistic life."

Glancing at Julia, Joshua, and Alice—the three who'd interacted with Cynster—Caitlin saw reflected in their faces the same uncertainty that she felt.

Hugo cleared his throat and tentatively offered, "He seemed a knowing sort. Not a frippery sort of person."

Tristan tugged one earlobe. "He was quick as a flash shutting that door and didn't even fluster when the chicken squawked and ran at him."

That was true. Despite her supreme exasperation at the time, she'd sensed Cynster standing like a rock—immovable and uncompromising—beside her.

She spent a moment dwelling on that, then blinked and said, "Yes, well, I think we can agree that, at this point, we can't be certain of Mr. Cynster's direction regarding the estate. Consequently, I suggest that our most sensible way forward will be to do our level best to impress him with the viability and financial stability of the estate's enterprises and the benefits that will accrue to him if he allows the place to continue as it has been."

They were hoping that, being a London gentleman-rake, Cynster would be a largely absent owner, which would suit everyone there. They'd been rolling along quite happily, first under Lady Bellamy and, for the past eight years, under the gentle hand of Timms, and with Caitlin largely filling those departed ladies' shoes in terms of coordinating the whole, no one saw any need for—much less welcomed the notion of—an intrusive owner.

As a collective, they didn't need anyone to lord it over them.

Recalling what had led to Mr. Cynster's present whereabouts, she added, "That said, we don't want to overwhelm him." She looked around the circle. "Given this is his first evening as owner, perhaps we should limit the presentations to those who would normally be about the dinner table."

The matter was discussed and debated, but relatively quickly, all agreed.

"You may be certain," she assured those who, therefore, would not be making their presentations that evening—Jenkins with the carriage works, Henry Kirk from the forge, Margaret Jenkins and Monica Kirk and their weaving, the Edgars with the orchard and the cider mill, the Suttons from the leatherworks and bindery, Mrs. Poole from the Osiery, and the Cruickshanks, the Hammersleys, the Swithinses, and the Bartons from the four farms—"that I will be urging Mr. Cynster to visit each of your businesses over the coming days."

And she would accompany him to make sure he heard everything relevant to gauging each business's value.

Len Sutton glanced at the fading light outside. "We need to get back. It's nearly time to shut things down."

That was the case for most of those who wouldn't be making presentations that evening. Caitlin thanked everyone for coming so promptly. "Once Mr. Cynster understands how Bellamy Hall operates, I'm sure he'll see the wisdom of leaving things as they are." *And not interfering.* She added, "He didn't strike me as an unreasonable man."

With general farewells, those who didn't live at the Hall departed.

Caitlin turned to those remaining and narrowed her eyes at them. "Now, are you all quite clear on what you need to convey?"

She went over the salient points with them one more time; even the painters proved reasonably competent. "Very well. I'll start the ball rolling by explaining about the Bellamy Hall Fund and how it serves to underwrite the functioning of the entire estate. That will set the overall framework for him and should pave the way for each of you to give a short description of your works, a summary of your markets and your recent profits, and the percentage you pay into the Fund. Please remember to touch on all four points, and if you can stick to the same order, that will doubtless make it easier for him to grasp."

"So, which of us should speak first?" Julia inquired.

"And do those of us who've already met him need to present at all?" Alice asked.

Vernon and Percy hadn't been in the house earlier. Caitlin turned to them. "He insisted on being shown around the house and meeting those who live here, so thus far, he's spoken briefly with Alice and Millie, Julia, Joshua, and our three painters. I would suggest our cause will be best served were you two to take the lead this evening. I'll meet him in the hall, explain about the Fund, and bring him into the drawing room and introduce you two."

Percy nodded. "We'll take it from there and do our spiels."

"Good." Caitlin knew she could count on them. She looked at the others. "It might be best for Julia, Joshua, and Alice and Millie to speak while we're at table, and then you three"—she bent a stern gaze on the painters—"can do your part when we return to the drawing room."

Hugo brightened. "Perhaps he won't want tea and would rather play billiards instead. We could give him a good game, I'm sure."

"No billiards!" Caitlin managed to contain her glare. "This evening is all about informing Mr. Cynster about the businesses at the Hall. We need to make him understand how valuable they, as a collective, are. We can't be certain how long he'll stay. You'll have your chance to make your case properly this evening—don't squander it."

"We won't," a chastened Melrose assured her. "We'll be on our best behavior, truly."

Caitlin gave them a look that translated to: *You'd better be!*

While she'd been speaking with the painters, Julia, Joshua, Alice, and Millie had discussed and agreed on the order in which they would speak. When Caitlin turned to them, they laid out their schedule for her approval, which she gave readily.

The dressing gong sounded, the deep *bong* resonating through the house.

Caitlin shooed everyone to the door. "Don't be late!"

She was the last to leave the conservatory—making sure the painters were on their way upstairs and not ducking back to put one last touch to some work. After closing the door, she hurried not toward the stairs but to the kitchens. There, she found Cromwell and Nessie and checked both had everything they required and all was on track for serving what would be Mr. Cynster's first meal there as owner of the estate.

Cromwell assured her he'd found the right wines in the cellars and the footmen had given the silver an extra polish.

As for the food, "It'll be a meal to remember. Don't you worry,"

Nessie assured her. "We're bound and determined to put our best foot forward, no bones about it."

"All right." Dragging in a calming breath, Caitlin nodded, whirled, and raced for the stairs. She needed to make the right impression herself.

Her eyes on the ground, she hurried along, debating which of her few evening gowns to wear. She pushed through the green-baize-covered door into the rear of the hall and rushed along the side of the massive staircase. She swung around the newel post—and collided with a wall.

One of warm, masculine muscle.

"Oh!" She stumbled back.

A steely arm wrapped about her waist and hauled her upright— against a body of hard, muscled planes. A large hand gripped her upper arm and steadied her, sending a wave of heat rushing through her.

Stunned, wide-eyed, she stared into Gregory Cynster's face. She tried to get her lungs to work and failed.

At close quarters, his moss-and-gold eyes were even more mesmerizing than she'd thought, and his lips...

She blinked. Stared. *What am I doing?*

She lowered her lids and drew in a tight, restricted breath.

His arms fell away, and he stepped back. "My apologies, Miss Fergusson."

Weakly, she waved. "The fault was mine. Sir." She managed another shallow breath. "I wasn't watching where I was going."

From beneath her lashes, she glanced at him—and he was waiting to catch her gaze. One of his eyebrows arched lightly, and his lips were definitely not straight.

She raised her head and tipped up her chin. "If you'll excuse me, I must get on."

Gregory waved her up the stairs and, as she climbed, ascended beside her. The aftereffects of the recent contact were still coursing through him. Pleasant though those were, he recognized burgeoning temptation when it struck him, which, all things considered, suggested he should start viewing his chatelaine as a dangerous distraction.

He couldn't afford to become entangled with her.

*Focus on what you're here to do.*

"I want the study."

"What?" She halted and stared at him.

He halted, too, and narrowed his eyes on her face. "Yes, I went in there, and whoever's been using that desk—"

"You didn't move anything, did you?"

He frowned. "No, I didn't, but whoever's papers those are—given the subject matter, I assume they're the steward's—he'll need to move them. I'm sure there's an estate office somewhere. Now I'm here, he'll need to work from there."

She continued staring at him, but her gaze had grown distant, then she curtly nodded and resumed her upward climb. "I'll take care of it."

Something in her response didn't fit. She glanced back, caught him eyeing her assessingly, and belatedly added, "Sir."

Then she redoubled her pace.

Frowning more definitely—irritated and not quite understanding why—he let her escape and forge ahead, as she patently wished to do.

On reaching the head of the stairs, she rushed off to the left, along the gallery. Cromwell had told Gregory that he'd been given one of the prized turret bedchambers, which lay in the opposite direction.

He stepped into the gallery and turned toward his room and heard a door along the opposite wing close…

He halted.

*That* was what was puzzling him—the part that didn't fit.

Miss Caitlin Fergusson had just gone into one of the bedchambers in what had long been considered the family wing. She was very definitely not the average housekeeper.

"She does call herself a chatelaine." Generally, that meant a glorified housekeeper.

Yet even for a chatelaine, to have a room in that wing seemed strange. Then again, Timms's room had been along there. "Perhaps she and Timms were close."

He considered that as he resumed his trek to his room.

Regardless of all else, one point seemed clear. If he was to make a life for himself at Bellamy Hall, he would need to come to terms with Miss Fergusson.

*One way or another.*

He reached the turret room, went inside, and after closing the door, looked around. It was one of the larger suites in the house, on the first floor looking out over the side lawn toward a stand of old oaks. The furniture was masculine, of heavy dark wood, elegantly carved. The curtains and bedspread were luxurious velvet and satin respectively, in a forest green that complemented the wood of the furniture and the full-height paneling that circled the room.

The window glass was old-fashioned, multipaned diamonds, sparkling clean and entirely in keeping with the rest of the room. A cheery fire burned in the grate of the large fireplace with its carved stone overmantel. Two deeply cushioned armchairs were angled before the hearth, while two tallboys and a heavy armoire stood against the walls.

He halted in the center of the room and glanced around again. All in all, it seemed a fitting haven for the new owner of Bellamy Hall.

~

"He's terribly handsome, isn't he?"

Mary Burton, Caitlin's maid, stood behind Caitlin, who was standing before her open wardrobe, trying to decide which of her favorite gowns to wear.

Brushing out Caitlin's black tresses, Mary continued, "So tall and with such broad shoulders! And his voice!" Despite her forty-plus years of Scottish staidness, Mary shivered deliciously. "Quite goes through one, it does."

Caitlin couldn't disagree; hypocrisy would stretch only so far. Her heart was still beating too fast, and she could all too clearly remember the sensations of that long, lean body hard against hers. Nevertheless... "When it comes to handsome men, I always remember what my grandmother used to say. Handsome is as handsome does, and we've yet to learn what Mr. Cynster intends to do. The blue or the violet?"

Jerked from contemplation of the new owner, Mary looked over Caitlin's shoulder. "The violet tonight. You don't want to dazzle him—not if you're wanting him to concentrate on the businesses, like you said."

Chin firming, Caitlin lifted out the violet-silk gown. "And my amethysts, I think."

Mary ceased plying the brush, took the gown from her hands, and bustled to the bed.

Between them, they got Caitlin gowned, with her hair up in a style more flattering for the evening and the amethysts winking purple about her throat and dangling from her earlobes.

Mary stepped back, surveyed her from head to toe, and sighed. "There, now. You're as prepared as you can be." She grinned. "And you have to admit, having him here is terribly exciting."

Caitlin wasn't sure "exciting" was the word she would have used.

Challenging, confronting—potentially disastrous—seemed much nearer the mark.

They'd assumed Gregory Cynster wouldn't stay long—that he'd look over the estate, comprehend its value, and leave them to it and go. She was starting to believe that the sooner he reached the "go" stage, the better it would be for everyone at the Hall, most definitely including her.

*That's what I need to do. Give him all the information and then, if necessary, actively encourage him to leave.*

With her armor donned, she straightened her spine, raised her head, and with a nod to Mary, swept out to do battle.

Gregory descended the stairs as the house's clocks struck for six o'clock.

While he'd changed his clothes and brushed his hair, by the simple expedient of paying attention to all that reached his ears, he'd confirmed there were several others occupying various chambers in the gargantuan house.

He'd tasked Snibbs with learning all he could via the servants' hall, but suspected that over the next hours, he would be meeting those who resided in the house.

Descending the last flight, he saw a gloriously feminine figure clothed in violet silk hovering just beyond the stairs. Caitlin Fergusson was an undeniably attractive woman…lady.

There was that oddity, again.

Her shoulders rose white and smooth above the gown's modest neckline, and she'd redone her hair. Previously restrained in a severe bun at her nape, the lustrous black tresses had been pulled into a knot on the top of her head, with curls and tendrils artfully hanging about her ears, some long enough to caress her slender throat.

She heard his footsteps and looked up, and inside him, something distinctly primitive stirred.

Ruthlessly reining in his impossible-to-deny interest, he inclined his head and continued down, joining her on the hall tiles.

She gestured to the open doorway behind her. "Before we go into the drawing room, I wanted to mention the Bellamy Hall Fund."

Her gown was of excellent quality, the material expensive and the cut flattering, and if the style was no longer the height of fashion, the gown nevertheless showcased her lush breasts and tiny waist—

"I wondered if you were aware of it."

Her sharply pointed tone struck through the fog of incipient lust. He raised his gaze to her face while his brain replayed her words... He frowned and met her gaze. "No. I haven't heard of any such a thing. What is it?"

She nodded as if she'd expected that. "It's a fund originally set up by the late Lady Bellamy and continued under Timms. The Fund receives regular payments from each of the various enterprises based on the Hall estate. Each business contributes a percentage of their profits, on a sliding scale from fifty to seventy percent, depending on each business's circumstances. As most of the businesses are successful and mature, the majority are paying seventy percent."

She turned toward the drawing room. "In return, the Fund pays for everything connected to the upkeep of the Hall—the staff's wages plus all repairs, not just to the Hall but to every building on the estate. Of course, most food is estate grown, but whatever is bought is paid for out of the Fund."

She glided forward. Mentally reeling, he fell in beside her as she continued, "The Fund also occasionally loans capital to individual businesses to enable larger outlays, such as buying machinery or equipment necessary or desirable to enable the business to prosper or grow."

Halting in the doorway, she arched a brow at him, patently expecting a question or comment.

He was still mentally scrambling. *Why did the Hall's solicitor not mention this?* "That's...astonishing," he managed.

She didn't look impressed. "The Fund has worked well for over a decade, partly because, through it, everyone here is invested in the well-being of the estate as a whole."

He could see how that would work. The fact went some way toward explaining what he'd encountered of people and enterprises thus far.

*But what about the monies left for the estate's upkeep?*

Before his death, Sir Humphrey Bellamy had set aside a significant sum that had been wisely invested and, to this day, produced considerable income. That had been the source of Minnie's wealth; there had never been any shortage of funds at the Hall.

Those monies had passed to Timms and, subsequently, to Gregory. He'd assumed that, over the years, the capital would have eroded, courtesy of the depredations from maintaining the massive house and sizeable estate in good order, but...possibly not. He would have to check with the estate's solicitor.

She started forward again, and side by side, they walked into the drawing room.

He managed not to blink at the size of the gathering. Well-dressed gentlemen and ladies were gathered in small groups, some sipping sherry and everyone amiably chatting; the scene wouldn't have looked out of place in a tonnish London house.

Everyone turned to regard him. He nodded to those he'd met earlier, and with easy smiles, they nodded back. While most returned to their conversations, two older men he hadn't met previously came forward.

Miss Fergusson halted and, as the men joined them, said, "Mr. Cynster, allow me to present Mr. Vernon Trowbridge and Mr. Percy Hillside."

"Cynster." Trowbridge offered his hand, and Gregory gripped it. "Good to see you here."

"Indeed." With a smile, Hillside offered his hand as well, and after he and Gregory had shaken hands, informed him, "We tossed for the honor, and Vernon won. So I'll let him tell you about the glassblowing studio before I bend your ear about fine furniture."

Despite the many questions he had for his chatelaine, Gregory found himself diverted by the two older men and their relaxed, confident, and engaging company. They weren't as old as his parents but somewhere in their forties.

Hillside was slender, with fading brown hair, long hands and bones, and carried the air of a dapper gentleman-about-town.

Trowbridge—Vernon—was older, a salt-and-pepper-haired gentleman of average height and stocky build. "I first met Sir Humphrey when I was a young man. I was in banking, then, and my wife and I occasionally visited here, where Minnie always made us welcome. When my Gwendoline passed...for a while there, I lost my way, but Minnie found me and insisted I return here with her."

Vernon's eyes twinkled. "Second best decision I ever made—the first being to marry Gwen. I came here, and Minnie and Timms worked their wiles, and I ended staying. It was Minnie who encouraged me to follow my passion for glassblowing." Vernon glanced around the gathering. "She insisted she didn't have an artistic bone in her body, but she knew good work when she saw it. She was instrumental in encouraging virtually everyone here."

Gregory nodded. "My uncle—Gerrard Debbington, the painter—credits Minnie's encouragement as pivotal to his career."

"It was much the same for me," Percy said. "I was tootling about town, doing nothing much, bored out of my wits. I'm a distant connection of Sir Humphrey's, and Minnie and Timms had met me at family functions. Timms stumbled across me in town and demanded I give an accounting of myself—you know how she used to do that?"

Gregory grinned. "I do, indeed."

"Well," Percy went on, "what with one thing and another, she hauled me out here, and I ended up setting up the carpentry workshop—working with wood being the one thing I'm good at—and now, my helpers and I make fine furniture."

Miss Fergusson, who had been standing beside Gregory, cleared her throat and looked pointedly at Vernon and Percy.

"That's right," Vernon said. "We're supposed to tell you about our businesses. So, the studio makes fine glassware—I won't bore you with the details; you'll have to stop by and see our range—and we sell through outlets in Northampton as well as directly supplying several of the larger houses around about and others who hear of us through word of mouth. Oh, and in the past six months, we've cleared more than six hundred pounds in profit and paid four hundred of that into the Fund."

Vernon smiled at Caitlin, who nodded approvingly, then both looked at Percy.

Percy grinned. "It's much the same tale for the woodworkers and me. We make damn near anything to order—these days, that accounts for most of our work—and any extra pieces go to shops in Northampton. We've had an excellent past six months, with nearly seven hundred in profits, of which we've contributed four hundred and fifty to the Fund."

Both men were justifiably proud of their achievements; six months' profits of that size were nothing to sneeze at. Gregory could see not just pride but also deep satisfaction shining in their eyes and investing their features. He commended them both, adding, "You've each clearly found your niche."

"That's it exactly," Vernon said. "That's Minnie's legacy, and the true magic of Bellamy Hall."

Miss Fergusson smiled, then something caught her eye.

Following her gaze to the doorway, Gregory saw Cromwell hovering. Having drawn his attention, the butler announced, "Dinner is served, sir, miss."

Gregory turned to his chatelaine, intending to offer his arm—even as he registered the oddity of the impulse—but she waved him toward the door and turned to walk beside him.

Intrigued—distracted—by her again, he quashed the part of him that wanted her closer and obliged her by matching her gliding pace while reflecting that Timms had always eaten with the family. Indeed, she'd been regarded as a family member, meaning of their station, for as long as he could recall. From all he'd observed, Miss Fergusson was of similar ilk.

Glancing back, he saw the rest of the company readily following in a loose, informal configuration. Facing forward, he acknowledged a fact that had been staring him in the face. All those present were gentry-born, perhaps not as well-born as he but of similar social station. Any of them could join ton gatherings without raising eyebrows. But instead of haunting society's spheres, either in London or elsewhere, they'd all opted to run businesses out of Bellamy Hall.

His curiosity was well and truly piqued, especially after speaking with Vernon and Percy.

And then there was Caitlin Fergusson. What was her story?

He slanted a glance her way, but she continued to face forward, her expression mild and entirely uninformative.

Before he could think of a leading question, they reached the dining room, and Cromwell was waiting to seat Gregory in the big carver at the head of the table. As he sat, he noticed the others—still chatting with each other—claim chairs in a manner that suggested those were their customary places.

Miss Fergusson continued to the chair at the table's foot. She sat and was flanked by Vernon and Percy. Meanwhile, footmen held the chairs on either side of Gregory's for Julia and Alice. Beyond Alice sat the three painters, while opposite, beyond Julia, Joshua and Millie claimed their seats.

Gregory wasn't surprised when, as soon as the soup was served, tasted, and exclaimed over, Julia Witherspoon—handsomely turned out in purple-silk taffeta, with her dark hair put up and pearl drops in her ears—launched into a more detailed description than she'd given him earlier of the output of the kitchen garden over the various seasons, followed by a neat summary of the markets and shops through which extra produce was sold. She explained that the kitchen garden supplied the Hall as well as the various other estate families as needed before reporting that, over the six months to December, her "little enterprise" had delivered a profit of two hundred pounds, of which one hundred and thirty had been paid to the Hall fund.

Gregory managed to keep his jaw from dropping. Although less than the profits from the glassblowing and carpentry workshops, to clear two hundred pounds in six months from a kitchen garden while simultaneously supplying the entire estate was no mean feat. Curious, he asked if she had some secret, and with a self-satisfied smile, she explained that she'd realized that certain vegetables were difficult to grow locally and, therefore, in short supply.

"But several of the local ladies and gentlemen have quite a craving." Her smile turned smug. "So I put extra effort into learning to grow those crops, and that's certainly paid off." She nodded across the table. "Alice and Millie helped me work out the best conditions and so on."

The three women shared a smile of pure triumph.

Gregory waited while the empty soup plates were cleared and the main course—a combination of fish, fowl, and meats—was ceremonially laid out. The vegetable dishes were numerous and quite popular, even among the men. Once all were served and had started eating, he found himself waving his fork at the dishes and saying, "This—all of it—is superb." The combination of flavors was hearty and exquisitely sumptuous at the same time. He raised his glass to Cromwell. "My compliments to Nessie. This is, indeed, a welcome feast to remember."

The others around the table echoed the sentiment.

Cromwell beamed. "I'll be sure to convey your appreciation, sir."

"Preferably before dessert," Tristan called, and the others laughed.

As Gregory returned his attention to his plate, Julia explained, "Nessie has been known to substitute bread-and-butter pudding for more flavorsome desserts if she thinks we haven't been properly grateful for her culinary efforts."

Gregory chuckled. "She sounds a character."

Julia nodded. "She is."

Gregory turned to Alice and smiled encouragingly and was unsurprised to discover that she, too, was primed to tell him more about her apothecary business. He listened, recognizing enough to confirm that she truly knew her craft.

When she looked faintly surprised at his questions, he grinned and revealed, "My cousin Lucilla, who lives in Scotland, is active in the same sphere, so I'm passingly acquainted with the use of herbs, tinctures, and such for successfully treating all manner of ailments."

Alice brightened. "That's something of a relief. These days, not everyone is, although I must admit that, around here, most have come to rely on our help when they fall ill."

Prompted by Millie, who had assisted in describing the gamut of their services, Alice proudly reported a substantial profit of over seven hundred and fifty pounds in the past six months, with a full five hundred pounds paid into the collective fund. "It's been a particularly good year for our creams and lotions. The ladies are our best customers these days."

Gregory was beyond impressed. Indeed, he was faintly staggered. If there were fifteen businesses achieving profits of similar levels...

He made a mental note to get onto the estate's solicitor about the monies that plainly weren't being used.

At that moment, dessert appeared. Bowls of trifle, poached pears in syrup, and stuffed oranges were set out on the table as the footmen whisked away their used plates and replaced them with bowls. Everyone eagerly served themselves, and for a few minutes, the room fell silent as they savored.

Then it was Joshua's turn to fill Gregory in on the relative value of certain breeds of pigs and goats, which explained why only certain breeds were raised in the Hall's pens. "If one is going to go to the trouble of breeding and fattening the beasts, there's no sense not aiming to get premium prices."

Given Gregory's knowledge of goats, the conversation got quite technical. He realized how amazing it was to engage in such a discussion over a dinner table, yet a quick glance at the others' faces revealed no hint of boredom. Indeed, it seemed all were truly interested in the details of each other's business.

Caitlin Fergusson's assertion that everyone there was invested in the well-being of the estate as a whole rang true.

As he listened to Joshua's reporting of his profits and payment to the Hall fund—every bit as impressive as those of his peers—Gregory was struck by that broader revelation of collective spirit and the enthusiasm and passion on which it was based. Everyone about the table possessed a strong sense of individual and collective purpose. And he envied them that.

*Isn't that what I've come here hoping to find for myself?*

The realization had him looking about the table with new eyes.

He'd come there intending to take up the reins of the estate and make it into...something. Into some venture that would, he hoped, anchor, absorb, and engage him in the same way Walkhurst Manor anchored Christopher, his older brother, and Alverton and his estates and their family absorbed his sister, Therese.

He was searching for an occupation, one that would give meaning to his life.

Yet Bellamy Hall was a far cry from what he'd expected to find. From what he'd anticipated managing.

Looking around at the faces, he felt as if he'd stepped into a fictional place, not the crazy situation it had initially appeared to be but a gentleman's country estate operating in an entirely unexpected fashion.

He remembered the figures he'd glimpsed on the papers on the study desk. If they were to be believed, the estate was rolling along exceedingly comfortably, and in that day and age, that was no mean feat. That such a success was achieved through the collective efforts of such an eclectic group elevated the accomplishment to a significantly higher level.

For the first time, he felt he was starting to properly see and appreciate what Timms, and Minnie before her, had created at the Hall.

And they'd passed this strange and rather amazing legacy to him.

In accepting the inheritance, he'd assumed responsibility for all that entailed. For everything that existed on the Bellamy Hall estate.

Doubt reared its head. He wasn't at all sure he was the right man for the job.

Then again, none of his cousins to whom Timms might have left the place would have been any better prepared to face this reality and take on the role of owner of Bellamy Hall.

He couldn't walk away. He'd committed to taking the place in hand, to being its defender and protector. And in a curious way, he already felt responsible for this unexpected crew, this odd household. In addition, his family and everyone he knew—everyone whose opinion he valued— would expect him to meet whatever challenges arose and succeed.

Even more importantly, he expected that of himself.

His original vision of his life at Bellamy Hall was already fading, dissipating like morning mist under the sun.

*So...*

Obviously, his immediate way forward necessitated learning all he could about the current state of absolutely everything on the estate.

The others had been chatting among themselves, apparently sensitive to his need to think and assimilate all they'd told him. His gaze roved the table and landed on Caitlin Fergusson, and he added to his mental list the need to learn all he could about the lady who, he was increasingly certain, ran Bellamy Hall.

Caitlin had been watching Gregory Cynster, attempting to gauge his reactions to what he was hearing, but she was too far away to read his eyes, and other than an occasional show of surprise, his features remained uninformative.

Was he impressed? She couldn't tell.

Her gaze had settled on his lips. She forced it up again and discovered he was looking at her. Intently. As if he wanted to read *her* mind.

She swung her gaze to Percy.

*Much less threatening.*

The thought made her inwardly frown. Gregory Cynster was no danger to her…was he?

That an absolute and immediate negative failed to ring in her mind left her even more uncertain.

Cromwell and the footmen proceeded to clear the detritus—all that was left of Nessie's desserts.

Caitlin was unsure what Gregory Cynster would expect. Slowly, she rose and tapped her wine glass, creating a ringing tone that cut through the conversations. When everyone looked her way, she said, "Although it's not our usual practice, if Mr. Cynster would prefer to enjoy a glass of spirits, perhaps, ladies, we might retreat to the drawing room—"

"No need." Cynster smiled at those around the table, his gaze coming to rest on Melrose, Hugo, and Tristan. "I'm happy to continue our discussions in the drawing room."

Plainly, he'd realized theirs was an organized campaign. As none of the other men normally lingered, everyone was happy to rise and stroll back to the drawing room. Leaving Cynster to the care of Julia and Alice, Caitlin paused in the dining room to ask Cromwell to convey her special thanks to Nessie for a job well done. "The entire meal, first to last, was scrumptious."

Cromwell beamed and departed for the kitchens, ferrying the last of the empty platters.

Caitlin smiled. Cromwell was always happy when a meal went off without a hitch.

She lengthened her stride and rejoined the others as they filed into the drawing room. She didn't have to go far to find her charge. Understanding the need to make amends, the three painters had surrounded him just inside the door.

Anxiety flaring, she hurried to join the group. Of all those at the Hall —indeed, on the estate—Melrose, Tristan, and Hugo were the least dependable. Not because they didn't try hard to perform as required but because they were so very easily distracted.

As she neared, she heard Cynster say, "From all I've heard of my uncle Gerrard's career, that at your respective ages, you are selling at all is a significant achievement."

Unsurprisingly, Melrose, Tristan, and Hugo preened.

Their eyes lit on her as she halted beside Gregory, and immediately, Melrose drew breath and concluded his presentation. As soon as he stopped speaking, Tristan launched into his description of his works, what successes he'd had in selling them, and cheerily admitted to the rather small contribution he'd made to the Hall's coffers.

To her relief, Cynster seemed genuinely encouraging. After Hugo had completed his presentation, to her surprise, Cynster asked what compositions they favored. That resulted in an animated discussion during which he held his own.

Relieved, she let the talk run unchecked. It was evident that, through his connection to Sir Gerrard Debbington, who had cut his landscape eyeteeth at Bellamy Hall, Cynster not only understood something of the painterly life but also was not at all inclined to turn up his nose at the notion of an artistic-funded existence.

His continuing questions, most about local opportunities to show their works, demonstrated considerable understanding and also a degree of interest beyond what Caitlin had hoped for in her wildest dreams.

*Surely this is a positive sign that he's able to see and willing to accept that there's value in what's being done at the Hall, even with the painters.*

In truth, a kernel of optimism was taking root as to what Gregory Cynster inheriting the Hall might mean for all those on the estate.

By the time the tea trolley arrived and Gregory held a cup in his hands, he'd accepted beyond question that Bellamy Hall did not and likely never would bear much resemblance to the average country gentleman's estate. With that acceptance, he jettisoned all prospects of ever converting it into that. In all honesty, he was no longer sure he wished to; the residents' passions and enthusiasms had infected him and sunk deep.

Bellamy Hall was something different, a construct that touched some chord inside him and set it thrumming. The concept alone, what he'd understood of it thus far, was intriguing, and the fact that it had existed for so many years, running comfortably along, said a great deal about its long-term financial viability.

Yes, it was different, but was different necessarily a bad thing?

Especially in the current agricultural climate.

He sipped and couldn't help but think that such a progressive collective enterprise would be of considerable interest to his brother-in-law, Devlin, and to Devlin's friend, Lord Grayson Child.

Gregory had joined those gathered around the fireplace. While Alice, Millie, and Julia discussed the progress of Millie's apprenticeship, on the opposite side of the hearth, Vernon, Percy, and Joshua were debating the prospects of taking some of their wares into Kettering one day soon. Possibly on the day of one of the major hunt meets.

In between those groups, Caitlin stood sipping her tea and listening to the three painters, who were making a bid to have her approve some sort of venture, about which she transparently remained unconvinced.

Gregory sipped and glanced around the company again.

One of the most impressive aspects of the household was its collegiality. Everyone seemed content, settled, and at ease with everyone else. He'd detected not the slightest hint of strain or tension, nor the faintest whiff of jealousy. With a group this size, all passionate about their various enterprises, that was nothing short of remarkable.

*Then again, either Minnie or Timms chose these people.*

That said, the group were clearly putting their best face forward for the new owner. He would definitely be checking the accounts and learning more about the Hall fund to assure himself the rosy picture with which he'd been presented was accurate. Despite his worldly cynicism, he suspected he would find it was.

His gaze shifted to Caitlin Fergusson, and he wondered how much his chatelaine had to do with the settled and positive atmosphere. It hadn't escaped his notice that she stood firmly at the center of the household, the lynchpin of its multi-spoked wheel. It was she who managed this miscellany of people—even more difficult, of artisans—and interestingly, despite her being barely older than Millie and the painters, everyone there unquestioningly accepted her rule. Even Percy and Vernon readily bowed to her direction, which, given their backgrounds, was really rather strange.

*Who is she?*

He wanted to know. In that respect, he was eager to meet the estate's steward and hear what he had to say.

He sipped and watched and continued to ponder, especially regarding Caitlin Fergusson, her role at Bellamy Hall, and how he might go about filching the reins of the estate from her.

~

When the gathering in the drawing room broke up, with the ladies leading the way up the stairs and the gentlemen following soon after, Gregory excused himself and retreated to the library, the better to put all he'd learned into some sort of perspective.

Or more accurately, to assemble the disparate pieces of information into a picture he hadn't previously seen.

The lamps had been left alight, but turned low, which suited him. He crossed to the tantalus and examined the decanters, then poured himself a glass and sipped. The brandy was more than acceptable. "Not a bad drop."

Taking the glass, he retired to one of the armchairs by the fire, sat, sipped, and replayed much of the evening's conversations, remembering nuances and noting the questions he hadn't had a chance to ask.

Especially those about his chatelaine.

Eventually, he drained the glass, set it on the table, and left the room. As he climbed the stairs, the house was quieting, but not yet night-silent.

He walked into his turret room to find Snibbs in attendance, hanging up the clothes Gregory had earlier shed.

After closing the door, he walked to one of the armchairs, sat, and asked, "So what have you learned?"

As he'd expected, Snibbs had the entire household committed to memory, and the details of the occupants matched what Gregory had learned. He was more interested in what Snibbs had to say regarding the staff.

"A happier, more contented lot I've yet to meet." Snibbs looked vaguely perturbed. "Never known a place so serene, truth be told. It's almost off-putting."

"Hmm. What does Melton say?"

"Same as me." Snibbs shook out a shirt. "He finds the peace and calm remarkable and said it's the same for the outdoor staff."

Gregory pondered that. "Did he mention whether there's been any noticeable change since last we were here?"

"Well, he said they always were a settled bunch, but they're even more so now. He also said to tell you he's seriously impressed by the stable and the carriage works."

Gregory frowned. "Carriage works?"

"Apparently. And they have their own blacksmith and forge as well. Melton's in alt."

And that, Gregory reflected, truly said something of the Bellamy Hall stable, given that Melton was familiar with several Cynster stables, including the racing stable in Newmarket. "Clearly, I'll need to spend more time in the stable and find out about these carriage works."

"The head stableman, Jenkins, is in charge of the carriage works as well as the stable, and Henry Kirk is the blacksmith."

Gregory tucked away the information. The carriage works and forge must be two of the businesses he'd yet to hear about. Caitlin had mentioned there were fifteen in all; if he counted the painters as one entity, then thus far, he'd heard reports from six. His quest to learn all about everything at the Hall plainly had some way to run.

He glanced at Snibbs. "Anything else?" He didn't want to specifically ask about Miss Fergusson.

"Just that the whole runs remarkably smoothly, and apparently, the chatelaine is well-liked by all. They quite look up to her, all of them, even though she's so young."

"You've met her?"

"No, but I saw her when she came to the kitchen to consult with the cook." Snibbs shot a grin Gregory's way. "Seems they were all wanting to make your first dinner here as the new owner extra special."

"They achieved that and more. Everything was delicious without being overdone." Although Gregory's curiosity over Caitlin Fergusson was driven by an interest far from innocent, a point he intended to keep to himself, he nevertheless asked as airily as he could, "Anything more I should know about the chatelaine?"

He couldn't understand why she so captivated him. Yes, she was attractive, but he'd bedded more beautiful ladies through his years of prowling through the ton, and he'd never felt this degree of attraction to them. There was something about her—something compelling he couldn't put his finger on—that got under his skin and itched. The itch was familiar, one he recognized all too well, but he was at a loss as to why the compulsion was so very intense.

A knowing smirk twisted Snibbs's lips. "I thought you'd want to know about her, but all I've got is that she's been here since January '49 when, with her maid and groom, she got caught in a blizzard, and they were forced to seek shelter here. Apparently, she and Mrs. Timms got on like a house afire, and Mrs. Timms begged her to stay, and she agreed. She's well-born, like Mrs. Timms was, and as I said, the staff adore her." He paused, considering, then went on, "And 'adore' is not too strong a word. I won't be making any unflattering comments about Miss C, as they call her."

Gregory sat back and considered the information. Being possessed of a maid and groom confirmed beyond question that, at the very least, Caitlin Fergusson was upper gentry. But why had she—especially given her age and physical attractiveness—been rambling about the countryside with just a maid and groom?

*And with nowhere to go, given she'd so readily accepted Timms's invitation and no one had come to fetch her away.*

Indeed, he had to wonder what had moved Timms to extend that invitation. He would wager she, at least, had known Caitlin Fergusson's story —all of it. He could readily imagine a strong bond forming between Timms and the younger lady. The pair shared obvious attributes, chief among which was being intensely practical females.

Thinking further, he could imagine that being Timms's protégée explained Caitlin's ready control over the staff and their devotion to her. But the residents?

That was more difficult to understand.

"Anything else?" he asked.

Snibbs made a show of trawling through his memories, but ended shaking his head.

Gregory dismissed him with a wave. "But let me know if you or Melton hear anything that strikes you as odd or unusual."

"Will do." Snibbs executed a perfectly gauged bow and departed.

Gregory sat for a while longer, letting his mind digest what he'd learned, then he rose and got ready for bed.

After turning out the lamp, pleased to discover the bed was soft and comfortable, he slumped beneath the covers, closed his eyes, and considered his overall reaction to all he'd learned about Bellamy Hall.

The truth was he was more engaged, intrigued, and interested than he'd expected to be over the prospects he'd uncovered thus far...and if Bellamy Hall was to be his future, that was no bad thing.

# CHAPTER 3

$\mathcal{G}$regory woke after a sound and refreshing night's sleep, and after summoning Snibbs and plying his razor, he dressed and made his way downstairs.

He went to the breakfast parlor, only to discover that, even though it was barely eight-thirty, most of the household had been and gone before him. Clearly, those who resided at the Hall didn't waste time lolling abed but were out about their business at a commendable hour.

While he ate in solitary splendor, he considered his quest to learn more about the Hall, but decided that his first act had to be to visit Minnie's and Timms's graves. He knew where Minnie was buried and was certain Timms would have been laid to rest close by. Consequently, after quitting the parlor, he made his way out of the south door and, thrusting his hands into his breeches pockets, strolled toward the ruins of Coldchurch Abbey.

The Hall itself was built over part of the original ruins thought to have been the gatehouse, and the lawn to the south of the house hosted several large and weathered standing stones that might once have been a section of a cloister.

Ahead, beyond a low hill, the single remaining arch of the abbey's church rose, wrapped in ghostly streamers of mist that had risen off the nearby river to wreathe the grounds south of the house.

The February morning was chilly and damp, and the skies were sufficiently overcast that it seemed unlikely the sun would break through and dispel the mist anytime soon. At least there was no wind to slice through coats and slide icy fingers past collars.

Under the terms of her will, Minnie had been buried in the old abbey burial ground alongside her late husband, Sir Humphrey Bellamy. Bellamy Hall had been his childhood home, and he'd loved the place with a passion. As had Minnie, and Timms had been equally devoted.

And those Minnie and Timms had gathered into the Hall were continuing that commitment, each in their own way.

Gregory climbed the low hill that lay between the house and the church. As he ambled upward, gravestones—some ancient, others less so—came into view, dotting the downward slope ahead. He reached the crest and saw that someone else was there, crouched beside a grave. He halted, studying the female figure, well-rugged up in a thick pelisse.

Kneeling beside the newest grave, Caitlin Fergusson was arranging flowers in a vase. The next grave along already bore a vase with an arrangement of Christmas roses nestled amid green leaves.

Gregory watched for a moment, then continued his approach.

As he neared, Caitlin lifted the second vase, now bearing early daffodils that had to have come from the conservatory, and placed the tribute at the base of the recent gravestone.

She rose and examined the result, then sensed him nearing and looked his way.

He ignored the faint suspicion he glimpsed in her pansy eyes and, studying the gravestone, confirmed it marked Timms's final resting place.

His gaze still lowered, he murmured, "We all would have come if we'd been able. We were sorry to have missed the service."

He felt Caitlin's gaze on his face. After a moment of indecision, she offered, "We were all here. Every last person on the estate, no matter how hard it was to get here. Some neighbors, too, even though they had to break through drifts to manage it." She paused, then added, "It was a miserable day, but we couldn't let her go alone."

"I'm glad she had people who cared about her there." He accepted without question that Timms had cherished all the odd bods she'd gathered at the Hall.

Caitlin nodded and picked up her basket, clearly intending to depart.

Hurriedly, he looked up. "Do you come here often?" To excuse the intrusive question, he tipped his head toward the three graves—Timms's, Minnie's, and Sir Humphrey's. "I can see the graves are well tended."

She lifted a shoulder. "Every few days, I replace the flowers. Timms loved flowers, and I imagine Minnie did, too. Keeping them fresh is the least I can do."

Gregory glanced at the graves. "I thought Timms would be here, next to Minnie. Over all the years I knew them, they were inseparable—I assumed they would want to be close in death as well." He looked at Caitlin. "I gather you've only been here for three years, yet you're plainly as devoted as any of those who knew Timms for much longer."

Annoyed to feel defensive, Caitlin raised her chin. "She offered me and my maid and groom safe harbor when we needed it."

"When you got caught in the blizzard?"

She nodded. Let him think that was what she'd meant.

"And you stayed."

More question than statement. She turned toward the house. "Timms explained that she needed someone who knew how to manage a household to help her and offered me the position of chatelaine." She shrugged lightly. "That suited me, and I accepted and stayed." She glanced at him. "That's one decision I've never regretted."

A light smile touched his lips. The sight set something fluttering inside her, and she decided she'd dallied there—cocooned in the mists with him—long enough. Tightening her grip on her basket, she started toward the house. "I need to get on."

Of course, he turned to walk beside her. "Where are you going?"

It had been her intention to show him around and introduce him to those business owners he'd yet to meet. Reminding herself of that, she admitted, "This is one of the mornings on which, every week, I visit several of the estate's businesses."

"I see. Which ones are you planning on visiting today?"

"The carriage works, the forge, the glassblowing workshop, the livestock pens, the carpentry workshop, and lastly, the kitchen gardens." She pointed ahead, through the thinning veil of fog, at the large barn behind the stable. "That's the carriage works, and from there, the other businesses I mentioned circle the house, ending with the kitchen gardens, which are located to the north."

He nodded. "I remember the kitchen gardens and the original carriage barn, but several of the other buildings are new to me." He caught her gaze. "If you have no objection, I'll come with you. I need to learn more about the various enterprises located here."

She inclined her head in outwardly easy acceptance and told herself that him learning about the businesses, under her careful guidance no less, was precisely what she'd wanted. Just because her stupid senses had developed some sort of sensitivity to his nearness was no reason to deviate from her carefully calculated path.

To distract herself from her unrelenting physical awareness and the prickling sensation spreading beneath her skin, she inquired, "How long are you planning on remaining at the Hall?" A chatelaine, she felt, could justifiably voice such a question.

She felt him glance at her, his hazel gaze acute, then he faced forward and replied, "I haven't made any plans to leave. At this time, my focus is on learning about the enterprises that contribute to the Bellamy Hall Fund."

Gregory didn't want her pursuing the subject of his ultimate intentions; he wasn't sure he could yet define them to himself. They'd descended the hill and were striding across the relatively flat lawn, with the stable looming ahead. The old carriage barn, apparently now known as the carriage works, lay directly behind the stable. "Tell me about the carriage workshop. It's been rebuilt and extended since last I saw it."

"When was that?"

"When Minnie was still alive. Although I came for her funeral, on that occasion, I didn't go to the stable. While I met Timms several times a year, that occurred either in London or at my family's home in Kent, so I haven't been back to Bellamy Hall for over eight years."

She looked at him. "Your family's home is in the country?"

He nodded. "Walkhurst Manor. It's in the Weald of Kent, roughly midway between Maidstone and Hastings. I grew up there. It's an agricultural estate—crops and orchards, mostly. That was where I learned about goats."

"Ah, yes. The goats. I'd forgotten about that."

Her tone—that of one suddenly seeing a light—had him glancing at her.

He took in her expression and was visited by an insight of his own. "Yes, Miss Fergusson. Although I might have haunted London for the past decade, I'm a country boy, born and bred."

Delicate color rose in her cheeks. "Yes, well, that will make explanations rather easier." A few paces on, she added, "No one here knew that, you see."

Which meant she'd asked. He felt mildly pleased about that.

They approached the carriage works—a large, well-appointed barn in excellent repair.

"The carriage workshop was here when I arrived," Caitlin said. "Indeed, all the Hall's businesses have been in operation for longer than three years—all were established under either Lady Bellamy or Timms." She halted some yards from the open double doors and looked up at the structure. "I believe this was rebuilt about seven years ago. The carriage works came about through Jenkins, the head stableman, and his assistants developing an interest in repairing and, eventually, in constructing carriages. That was after Lady Bellamy died and fewer guests came to the Hall, so Jenkins and his men had little to occupy them." She paused, then added, "I can't recall hearing who suggested the workshop, but I wouldn't be surprised to learn it was Timms."

He nodded. "She was always one to keep herself busy. I suspect she adhered to the philosophy that the devil makes work for idle hands."

She smiled. "Indeed. I'm sure she did."

He tipped his head at the workshop's open doors, through which the thumps and clangs of hammers striking wood and metal could be heard. They advanced and walked into a well-lit space with a high, raftered ceiling and plain wooden walls, every foot of which was covered by racks of tools or shelves of implements and carriage parts.

Jenkins spotted them, set down his hammer, and came forward. He'd been the Hall's head stableman for close to two decades and had met Gregory and his brothers over the years. He knew how much the Cynster family appreciated good horseflesh and also good carriages. He beamed at Gregory and nodded respectfully. "Mr. Cynster, sir. Do you have time for me to show you around?"

Gregory smiled and admitted that was what he was there for, and Jenkins promptly embarked on ushering him around and explaining the basics of the business he and his men had established.

While half of the big barn was given over to housing a handful of carriages—presumably owned by the Hall—plus Gregory's sleek curricle, the rest was divided into a series of five bays, with each bay housing either the skeleton of a new carriage or a carriage awaiting some repair.

Viewing the two undercarriages waiting for springs and bodies to be attached, Gregory admitted, "Spending so much time in London, I always bought my carriages in Long Acre. I never thought about where those in the country would find new carriages."

"There are carriage makers in the major towns, but, for instance, there's only one in Northampton, and his waiting list is longer than your arm. And it's not just a question of new," Jenkins said. "Finding someone to repair a broken joist or spring can be just as difficult. As soon as it became known that on top of keeping all the various carts and carriages on the estate rolling along, we were willing to work on other people's carriages, we've never had a time of not having some project on the go. Right now, we've a waiting list for new carriages that'll see us into next year."

"Is it just the three of you?" Gregory nodded to the other two men, who were working on fixing a new wheel to a gig.

"Nah, it's all of us at different times. Parker—do you remember him?"

Gregory nodded. "He's been here forever."

"Aye, since even before my time. Parker keeps an eye on the horses and makes sure the grooms and stable lads keep up to the mark with them. But once they're done mucking out the stalls and exercising the beasts, most will be in here, lending a hand. Everyone likes to keep busy."

Gregory eyed the bare undercarriages. "What sort of carriages do you make?"

"Anything with wheels," Jenkins proudly proclaimed. "Those two are a cart and a gig, and our current orders range from them to two curricles and even a phaeton." Jenkins grinned. "That'll be a challenge, but we'll meet it."

Gregory smiled back. "I'm impressed."

"Aye, well." Blushing faintly, Jenkins shifted his weight. "I give you fair warning—we'll be studying that curricle of yours for pointers. We haven't seen a carriage of that quality in our barn for a good long while." He arched a brow at Gregory. "Mind if I use it to show the lads what's what? Melton said he didn't think you'd mind."

Gregory nodded. "I don't. By all means, use it as an example."

"Excellent!" Jenkins rubbed his hands, then his gaze landed on Caitlin, waiting with studied patience by the open door. Parker had arrived while Jenkins and Gregory had been talking and had paused to speak with her before heading deeper into the workshop. "Ah, yes." Jenkins returned his gaze to Gregory. "I'm supposed to tell you about our profits. Four hundred this past six months, but that was quieter than usual. We put two hundred and eighty of that into the Hall fund, but we'll be doing better this next six months, for certain."

"Nevertheless, that's an admirable result." *Especially as you're giving so many men employment.* Gregory clapped Jenkins on the shoulder. "Keep up the good work."

With a nod to the other men, he crossed to the door.

Caitlin waved to Jenkins. "Parker gave me your list. I'll add the nails to the order on Thursday."

Jenkins saluted her and turned back to his work.

As Gregory joined Caitlin, she arched a brow. "Impressed?"

"Deeply." He cast a last glance over the workshop. Jenkins had already joined his men, and the three were tightening the wheel nut. Gregory looked at Caitlin. "Where to next?"

"The forge." She pointed at the building that sat to one side of the carriage works, farther from the house.

As they headed that way, she informed him, "Henry Kirk is our blacksmith, and the forge produces not only horseshoes but anything made of iron or steel that people on the estate or around about need. In addition, over recent years, the Kirks have turned their hands to metal sculptures, which, of course, are all the rage. Armillary spheres, sundials, lanterns, posts, and pedestals as well as other pieces."

They reached the wide-open door of the forge. It was a deep building, toward the rear of which sat the forge itself, currently roaring and belching out heat. Gregory stopped on the threshold; the difference in temperatures between the air inside and outside was dramatic.

The blacksmith was standing behind the middle of three anvils set up across the forge. He swung his massive hammer down, and sparks flew, then he raised the tongs he held in his other hand and inspected the horseshoe he was fashioning. He grunted in satisfaction and doused the shoe in a barrel of water standing nearby. Metal hissed and steam rose, dissipating quickly in the heat.

"Henry?" Caitlin called.

The big man looked up, then smiled, put down his tools, and wiping his hands on a rag, strode out to join them.

Gregory saw, in the strange reddish light thrown by the forge, two others, both wearing heavy leather aprons, masks of sorts, and thick leather gauntlets as they manipulated a crucible of molten ore, carefully pouring a golden-red stream of liquid metal into a rather delicate-looking mold.

Gregory drew his gaze from the activity to smile at Henry as the big man halted before them, and Caitlin introduced him.

Henry nodded politely and rumbled words of welcome, then said to

Caitlin, "Glad to see you, Miss C. We need more of that nice leather for grips and more nails for shoeing."

Caitlin nodded. "I'll add both to tomorrow's order."

She glanced at Gregory, and he caught Henry's eye. "Miss Fergusson has told me what you make here."

"Aye—we do the horseshoes, of course, and we also keep all the tools in good nick. Not just the ones used at the Hall itself, but we also work with the farms, keeping their equipment in good condition. Anything metal, we're the people anyone round about talks to." Henry dipped his big head Caitlin's way. "Miss C can tell you we clear a tidy profit every year—the last six months were good. We managed more than seven hundred total and put five of those into the Hall fund."

"I see." Gregory glanced into the shop. "So it's you and two others?"

"Aye." Henry turned to look at the pair, who had finished pouring and had returned the crucible to a stand and were now hauling off their protective layers. "Here, you two. Come and say hello to Mr. Cynster."

Both looked up, and Gregory realized the younger worker was a woman.

The pair grinned—white smiles bright in faintly soot-streaked faces—and came forward.

"This is my daughter, Madge." Henry draped a proud arm around his daughter's shoulders, and she smiled at Gregory and nodded.

Henry went on, "Madge is responsible for all the sculpture we do. Not really blacksmith's work to my way of thinking, but she enjoys it, and it surely brings in the guineas."

Madge smiled fondly at her father, then looked back at Gregory and volunteered, "Many of the local ladies developed a craving for ironwork, and now they've talked of our work to their friends, we find we can sell anything we make through the markets in Northampton and Kettering." She smiled cheekily at her father. "Armillary spheres and the like are far too delicate for ham-fisted men to make, but someone has to do them, so I do."

Henry huffed and beckoned his other worker forward, and a wizened old fellow—with straggly white-gray hair and skin turned to leather long ago—shuffled nearer.

As weak sunlight hit the man's face, Gregory smiled spontaneously. "Blackie, isn't it?" When the man blinked his very blue eyes, Gregory was sure of it. "I remember you from long ago. You used to work in the stable."

Blackie grinned widely, plainly pleased to have been remembered. "Aye, that was me. I remember you as a nipper, always running every-where with that brother of yours. And your sister, too—she was a little miss, no doubt about it." Blackie nodded at Gregory. "I can see you're doing well. Your brother and sister and your baby brother—are they well, too?"

Still smiling, Gregory replied, "Therese is now the Countess of Alver-ton. But you would have seen her when she visited Timms over the past years."

Blackie nodded. "Aye, I did, now you remind me. She and that husband of hers, Lord Alverton."

"They're both well and have three children and a fourth due later in the year. As for Christopher, he married more recently and lives in Kent, while our baby brother is a grown man but not yet of an age to be thinking of marrying."

"Aye, well." Blackie bobbed his head. "It's good to see you back and all."

Gregory sensed a comfortable rapport between the three ranged before him. "So, most of your wares not used on the estate are sold through the regular markets?"

"Aye," Henry replied. "And Blackie and I go to Kettering and Northampton on hunt days. We make good money shoeing the hunters that need it."

"And over the past year," Caitlin put in, showing she'd been listening carefully, "you—Madge, in particular—have received several lucrative commissions."

Madge beamed. "I've been asked to do a set of wall sconces for the church in Wellingborough. That'll be a new string to my bow, so to speak."

Gregory smiled and admitted he was impressed by their industry.

He and Caitlin took their leave, allowing the three to return to their work.

As he and she walked on, he said, "It seems most businesses here have evolved far beyond supplying the estate itself and are drawing customers and, therefore, income from the surrounding communities."

She nodded. "Timms encouraged that, and when I joined the house-hold, I thought it a good move, too." She glanced fleetingly at him. "Aside from the substantial income, the involvement with others beyond the estate's borders creates and fosters goodwill toward the Hall."

She looked back at the carriage workshop. "All those here readily help out our neighbors, but Jenkins and Henry, especially, help some of the poorer farmers for free." She looked ahead and added, "Everyone here remembers what it was like to need a helping hand. We were lucky enough to get one, courtesy of Lady Bellamy and Timms." Her lips quirked upward. "And on top of that, everyone here is proud of their skills. Most will seize any chance to show off."

He chuckled, but as they walked on, he also felt humbled. He could almost hear Minnie, let alone Timms, in Caitlin's words. How much of that resonance was due to the influence of Timms and those at Bellamy Hall, and how much was natural, a sensitivity the three women shared?

Pondering that, he followed her around the corner of the forge, to the wide door of the building that, he realized, abutted the back of the smithy.

Caitlin halted with her charge in the open doorway of Vernon's domain. The glassblowing workshop enclosed the rear of the forge, sharing the massive furnace that glowed in the center of the shop's rear wall. That wall was built to shoulder height, allowing those on the glass-blowing side to easily speak with the blacksmiths.

She spotted Vernon deeper in the shop, discussing something with his apprentice, Terry, and waved to attract the older man's attention.

Vernon noticed and came forward. "Caitlin, my dear—we're in desperate need of more of that fine sand."

She nodded. "I'll send for it later today, but I doubt it'll arrive before the end of next week."

Vernon sighed. "If we have to wait, we'll wait." His gaze shifted to her companion. "Well, Cynster, come to see my works?"

Cynster smiled easily. "I'm here for the tour."

Vernon barked a laugh and waved Gregory in.

Caitlin remained in the doorway and watched as Vernon showed off the delicate vases that were his passion, some in the classical shapes and others more fluid in style. Many were beautifully etched, a technique of which Vernon had become a recognized master.

She felt increasingly confident as she watched Gregory Cynster's reaction to Vernon's exposition. As Vernon had made his presentation yesterday, he focused on imparting a broader understanding of the quality of his creations.

That Cynster was impressed by what he saw was evident. As he and Vernon returned to her, the Hall's new owner appeared sunk in thought. On reaching her, he halted and faced Vernon. "That etching you've been doing—have you thought of incorporating heraldic coats of arms to distinguish individual pieces?"

When Vernon frowned, Cynster elaborated, "I mean on commissioned pieces. For instance, I can think of any number of ton ladies who would be interested in your wares, but even more so if you could incorporate their husbands' coats of arms in the designs. It would make your works not just unique to you but to them as well."

Vernon's face lit. "Yes—I see!"

Cynster tipped his head, clearly envisioning such a creation. "You could even use the animals or symbols in the arms as part of the etched design."

"Indeed! That's an excellent idea." Vernon turned to his apprentice. "Terry—did you hear that? Think we're up to it?"

Terry, a younger man with red hair, grinned widely. "It'd be a challenge, for sure, but we could do it, I'd say."

Vernon turned back to Cynster. "Can you give me some idea of the coats of arms you have in mind? It would give me something to play with, to work up some sketches and try out some ideas."

Apparently equally enthused, Cynster nodded. "I'll check my memory of the arms I have in mind against what I can find in the library—there's bound to be a book on arms there somewhere. I'll hunt it out, check the accuracy of my memory, and make up a few sketches to get you started."

As delighted at the prospect as the three men, Caitlin asked Vernon if he needed anything else ordered in for the project. He asked for several more of the diamond-tipped tools he used, and she promised to put them on the order going out to their supplier that week.

Gregory, meanwhile, was trying to decide which of the many ton ladies he knew should be the recipient of the first of Vernon's new creations. He was tossing up between his grandmother, Horatia, or the dowager matriarch of the entire family, his great-aunt Helena, then he realized both were Cynsters, and he was entirely confident over sketching the Cynster coat of arms. Uncaring that his enthusiasm was blatantly on show, he turned to Vernon. "I know just which coat of arms you should start with. I'll do a sketch for you later today."

"Excellent!" Vernon rubbed his hands together and glanced at Terry. "Well, m'lad, we'd better get on with finishing this commission so we can start on our latest venture."

With smiles and waves to Terry, Gregory and Caitlin walked on.

He noticed she was almost skipping. Then, as if she couldn't suppress her delight for a second longer, she declared, "That was an absolutely inspired idea! I hadn't thought of the implications of you becoming the new owner. You must have myriad connections that Vernon—and several of the others as well—might benefit from."

He considered that and felt moved to point out, "The ladies I know have exacting standards."

Although prim, the grin she shot him was brimful of confidence. "I can assure you the quality of works produced at the Hall is high enough to meet and surpass anyone's standards, no matter how high."

The last words were delivered with something approaching insouciant challenge, and he found himself grinning back. "I, for one, will be eternally grateful should that prove to be so. The notion of never being at a loss for a gift for birthdays and Christmases is beyond appealing."

She laughed—and the sound rippled over his senses, leaving them purring.

Ruthlessly, he shoved his wolfish inclinations as deep as he could and fixed his gaze ahead. After a moment, he managed to refocus his wits. "Where are you taking me now?"

"The livestock pens. Sadly, I doubt any of your ladies would appreciate a gift from Joshua's domain."

He smiled and didn't contradict her, although he could think of several ladies of his acquaintance—his sister and sister-in-law and even some of his cousins—who might be tickled to receive one of Joshua's prize goats.

From the stable, the rear drive rolled away in a northwesterly direction, with the carriage workshop, the forge, and the glassblowing workshop on Gregory and Caitlin's left and the two large barns, staggered one behind the other, on the right. Beyond those, the drive straightened to run northward, along the east boundary of a long line of livestock pens.

Seeing him eyeing the pair of barns, Caitlin asked, "I take it those weren't here the last time you came this way?"

He shook his head. "Which business uses them?"

"They're the carpentry workshops. I understand that originally, it was just the front barn, but the business grew rapidly and soon needed the second barn as well."

Remembering that the carpentry workshop was on her list to visit after the livestock pens, he shifted his gaze to Joshua's domain.

They reached the first pen, which proved to hold six nanny goats with their kids. Joshua and another older man—another of the crew whom

Gregory recognized—were in the pen, examining several kids while the mothers, tied to the rail, looked on suspiciously.

Joshua saw them, smiled, and left what he was doing to join them by the railing fence. "Come to see our beauties, have you?"

Smiling, Gregory admitted, "They appear to be in prime condition." Every animal looked to be in the peak of health.

Joshua waved at the old man, busy releasing the tied nannies, but Gregory preempted the introduction. "Wallace, isn't it?" Gregory smiled as the old man nodded, looking thoroughly pleased to have been remembered. "You used to be called Old Wallace, back then."

"Aye." The old man nodded. "And I'm Old Wallace still, even though Young Wallace—m'son—moved off to Birmingham."

"You and your wife still live in the cottage up that way?" Gregory nodded along the rear drive.

"We do. This is our place. We always knew we'd grow old here, and so we are."

It was a simple statement of loyalty to place that Gregory often heard on his family's estate. He nodded amiably. "It's a good thing, then, that you and the others have the goats and pigs to keep you occupied."

Old Wallace cackled. "Don't forget the chickens. Silly things take more time than the rest."

"That's true enough." Joshua let himself out of the pen and joined Gregory and Caitlin. "Let me show you around."

With a wave to Old Wallace, Gregory fell in beside Joshua, who proceeded to give him a tour of the livestock pens. Along the way, Joshua introduced his younger helper, Hendricks, a countryman in his late thirties who clearly loved raising animals as much as Joshua did.

As they walked on, leaving the pens containing the three different goat breeds Joshua raised, he volunteered, "I've been working with the weavers, Margaret and Monica. Have you met them yet?"

Gregory admitted he hadn't.

"Well, they're exceedingly good at their craft and are experimenting on using the hair from our longhairs"—with a tip of his head, Joshua indicated the last of the goat pens—"which is very fine, to make a softer, finer yarn. Still a bit of an experiment, but it's showing promise."

"So"—Gregory glanced back as they left the goats behind—"you raise one breed for meat, another for milk, and one for their hair?"

Joshua tipped his head from side to side. "More or less, but of course, we get meat and milk from all three. It's just that one lot are better than the other two for milking or meat or hair." They reached the next, much larger pen, which had a very different construction. The lower foot or so was stone, which appeared sunk in the ground. Above that, the fence was woven willow, quite lightweight. Inside the enclosure, a large flock of chickens ran, pecked, and squawked.

"We found that the fence being so shaky"—Joshua demonstrated —"makes the foxes nervous and helps keep them away, and the stone means they can't dig under it." Joshua shrugged. "At night, we still put the lot into the chicken coop, of course. Otherwise, we'd lose too many to owls."

Remembering the eggs he'd enjoyed that morning, Gregory asked, "Does the Hall get all its eggs from this lot?"

Joshua nodded. "We supply all the estate, although the farms have their own chickens. On top of that, we usually have several dozen eggs and a cage or two of birds to sell most market days."

"I see." Gregory doubted the eggs and chickens brought in all that much, but he knew how much prize goats could cost; there was something of a countrywide obsession developing with the animals.

Joshua turned to Caitlin. "My dear, I'd like to start the chickens on that new mix we've been testing. Can you order a ten-pound bag?"

She nodded. "We should get it in by Monday next, with the other grains."

"Wonderful!" Joshua returned his attention to Gregory and, with a proud smile blooming, waved ahead. "And now we come to my favorites —the pigs."

Caitlin stood back and watched as Cynster and Joshua went pen to pen, with Joshua eagerly explaining the value of the various breeds snorting, snuffling, and wallowing in the enclosures.

Old Wallace and Hendricks came up and, leaning on the railing fence, added their observations. She noted that Cynster directed several questions specifically to Old Wallace and Hendricks, drawing them into the discussion.

While Cynster had proved to know quite a bit about goats, with pigs, he was plainly at sea. Caitlin was impressed by his ready acknowledgment of that and his interest in learning about the beasts.

Admittedly, the pigs were the highest-earning animals Joshua and his small crew produced, and Cynster's interest appeared unfeigned and encouraging. He paid particular attention to Joshua's replies regarding the places at which Joshua sold his pigs and the prices he received.

Eyes narrowing, Caitlin studied the Hall's new owner. He was far more genuinely interested in everything he'd been hearing and seeing than she'd expected, and his questions demonstrated a determination to learn far more than he needed to know were he intending to leave the Hall to run as it was and return to London.

*"I haven't made any plans to leave."*

Could he be thinking of taking up permanent residence at the Hall?

She wasn't at all sure what she felt about that prospect.

Neither she nor anyone else there had imagined he would wish to remain and, presumably, play an active role in managing the estate. Everything they'd known about him—admittedly little and primarily based on hearsay—had suggested otherwise.

*Perhaps we were wrong.*

As she watched him talking with Joshua, Old Wallace, and Hendricks, that seemed increasingly possible.

Having him become an active owner might be a very good thing. If he devoted himself to managing the estate, when her years-long exile eventually ended, she would be able to leave with a clear conscience, knowing the estate and its people were in sound hands—indeed, hands that Timms had chosen.

If he was intent on taking up the reins at the Hall, it would be in her best interests to encourage him and ensure that he ran the place at least as well if not better than she did; she could foresee advantages in having him actively involved.

Regarding him assessingly, she suppressed a grimace. Interacting with him, even in a strictly impersonal way, was...unsettling. That was the only accurate description for how he made her feel—as if her nerves were leaping and sparking in a thoroughly disconcerting and definitely distracting way. She assumed the ability had something to do with his status as a recognized rake of the ton—she'd always heard they were a breed apart.

She would have to overcome the ridiculous sensitivity, because if he was to remain and become the active owner of Bellamy Hall, she would need to keep her wits about her.

"I have to ask."

His deep voice jerked her to full awareness—and sent her wits skittering again. Silently, she swore and harried them into order as she watched him and Joshua walk back to her, and Cynster continued, "Have you tried to get your animals to the London markets?" He nodded southward. "With the railway so close and the station at Earls Barton, you could send them on easily enough."

"Hmm." Joshua looked pensive. "I haven't really thought about expanding that far."

Cynster tipped his head toward the pigs. "You would have a ready market there for animals of such quality, and even some of the goats would fetch a good price."

Slowly, Joshua nodded. "It's certainly worth exploring." He paused, then added, "I'll make some inquiries."

"It would be worth a trial at least," Cynster said. "I know nothing about the prices for pigs and goats, yet I feel confident in saying that the prices you'll command down there will be much higher than those locally."

"You're undoubtedly right." Joshua nodded more decisively, including Caitlin in the gesture. "I'll work out how many animals we could offer beyond what we're committed to locally and contact some London livestock agents." Joshua blinked, then grinned. "And if the prices are significantly better, we could think about increasing our herd."

Caitlin laughed, and she and Cynster farewelled Joshua, Old Wallace, and Hendricks. As she and Cynster walked back toward the carpentry barns, she murmured, "By raising the prospect of increasing the herds, you've made them very happy."

A grin split Cynster's face. "I'm delighted to be of service."

Surprisingly, that statement carried the ring of truth. After a moment of pondering that, she ventured, "You've given several business leaders quite a lot to think about."

Sliding his hands into his breeches pockets, he shrugged. "That's part of being a good owner, or so I've always been taught." He glanced back at the pens, then at the glassblowing workshop, the forge, and the carriage works and wryly admitted, "Mind you, I didn't expect to be working with businesses such as these. Thus far, Joshua's domain is the nearest to what I had assumed I would find here. Regardless, it seems senseless not to offer whatever insights I have."

She nodded approvingly. That was exactly the attitude she would most wish the owner of Bellamy Hall to have.

The carpentry barns loomed ahead. As they rounded them, anticipating his questions, she said, "This barn—the first—was built about six years ago, when Percy joined the household. I gather he met Timms in London—how, I've never heard—and she invited him to come and see what he thought of living in the country, and he loved it here, so he stayed."

"Minnie was much the same," Cynster said. "As far back as I can remember, there were always various people here. It was one of those things that gave the place its eccentric character. To my siblings' and my childish eyes, the mix of people at the Hall was just as fantastical as the house itself."

She smiled. "I can see how that might have been. Timms told me she acted as she did—inviting people to come and stay—because she knew that was what Minnie would have wanted her to do."

"I won't argue that. From what I've seen thus far, this is exactly the sort of eclectic yet somehow coherent household Minnie would have delighted in. She was always interested in people and in encouraging them in whatever endeavors most called to them." He paused, then more quietly added, "I suppose, in a way, to achieve their heart's desire."

She looked up as they turned the corner and headed toward the open doors. "That sounds very like Timms as well."

They walked into the carpentry workshop and were immediately assailed by the sharp scent of shaved wood.

Percy glanced up from the chair he was working on, saw them, downed his tools, and came forward. "Cynster! Glad you could make it." Beaming, Percy spread his hands wide, indicating a plethora of pieces of fine furniture in varying stages of completion. "Come—let me show you around."

Gregory went with Percy, while Caitlin remained by the door.

Percy introduced Gregory to the other two craftsmen—Joe and Paul—both of whom were shaping pieces of wood that, ultimately, would fit together as part of a tallboy.

When Gregory asked what specific items they made, Percy replied, "We occasionally make a table or something more practical for someone on the estate—like the bindery worktable we recently made for the Suttons—but as everything that goes out of this workshop is built to last, these days, it's generally pieces of finer furniture for drawing rooms, dining rooms, bedchambers, and the like."

Percy led the way to the piece he'd been working on. "These days, I rarely get time to do anything that's not on order."

That last was said with considerable pride as Percy ran his hand almost lovingly over the curved piece of wood he'd been working on, and when Gregory laid eyes on what was clearly to be the curved back of a dining chair, he could understand the man's absorption. Although as yet unfinished, the carving was exquisite. Gregory could easily see such a piece gracing some duchess's dining room in London... He hesitated, then said, "I made a suggestion to Vernon that I suspect would work just as well for you."

Percy looked up. "Always happy to entertain suggestions."

Gregory explained his notion of ton ladies being drawn to pieces with their husbands' heraldic coat of arms included in the carving. "As that would signal it was an exclusive piece—always a point with ton ladies— and the more I think of it, the more clearly I can see said ladies fighting to place orders. It might well become all the rage, and then you'll be beating them off."

Percy looked intrigued. "Coats of arms, you say?"

"And the animals and symbols that are included in such arms."

Percy's face lit, and Gregory saw him exchange a boyishly eager look with his crew, who had paused in their work to listen.

Gregory grinned. "I told Vernon I'd make a sketch of a coat of arms I think would be useful for him to start with—and perhaps I should add a few others of the husbands of ladies I know." He was thinking of his sister and also of several cousins, all of whom had married titled men.

Percy looked enthused. "If you could give me copies as well, perhaps we could work up a few sample pieces?"

Gregory nodded. "I will. There are two specific coats of arms that, assuming the sample is anything like this"—he nodded at the carved chair back—"I would want to commission pieces with." For Therese and also his uncle Gerrard, both of whom would appreciate such work and could be counted on—if Gregory asked—to spread the word far and wide. "One will be the coat of arms of the Earls of Alverton, and the other will be the Bellamy crest." Gerrard would be tickled with a piece displaying the latter that came from Bellamy Hall. "I'll let you have the sketches as soon as I can and also let you know what sort of pieces I'd like them on."

"Excellent!" Percy clapped his hands and shared an excited look with Joe and Paul. "We'll get on with what we have before us so we'll be ready to take on your challenge as soon as we see the sketches."

With everyone pleased and, indeed, enthused, Gregory farewelled Percy and his men and rejoined Caitlin at the door.

She called to Percy, "Anything you need beyond the usual, Percy?"

"Not this week, m'love, but we will need more of that special glue next week. We're almost out."

"I'll put it on the list," Caitlin assured him. Smiling, she waved Gregory out and turned to walk with him.

As they emerged into the weak warmth as the sun battled to break through the clouds, he asked, "Where to now?"

She pointed at the high stone wall of the large kitchen garden, the front corner of which lay ahead of them on their left, while the rest of the enclosed garden stretched away north, toward the fields. "The entrance, as you probably know, faces the lawn."

They rounded the wall's corner and stepped onto the rectangular section of lawn bound to their left by the front wall of the kitchen garden, ahead by the side wall of the rose garden, and to their right—the south— by the beginning of the rear drive, the side of the stable, and the last section of the drive from the forecourt.

"This is my final stop for the morning." She brandished her now-empty basket. "I've been delegated to bring in the bounty Julia and her helpers will have harvested for Nessie for dinner this evening."

Caitlin led the way through the arched entrance to the garden. As she walked down the central aisle, keeping her eyes peeled for Julia, she was aware that Cynster was looking about him, but with rather less enthusiasm than he'd demonstrated during their visits to the other businesses.

Eventually, she spotted Julia and her helpers, Fred and Moll. The trio were bent over a bed, inspecting cabbages.

Then Julia straightened, pointed at one cabbage, and Fred wielded a wicked-looking knife and lopped the cabbage off its stalk. He expertly trimmed off the outer leaves, leaving a nice tight ball of pale green.

As Caitlin and Cynster drew near, their feet silent on the grassy path, Fred saw them. He handed the cabbage to Julia for a final inspection and ducked his head. "Miss C. Sir."

Juggling the cabbage, Julia turned, as did Moll. The younger girl blushed and bobbed a curtsy to Cynster.

Caitlin smiled reassuringly at Moll and Fred and introduced them to the new owner, then looked at Julia.

"Perfect timing," Julia said. "This cabbage completes Nessie's order."

She stepped out of the bed and carefully placed the cabbage in the basket Caitlin set on the ground.

Once her hands were free, Julia scooped up various vegetables left waiting on the path—carrots, potatoes, two varieties of onions, and several bound sheaves of spinach—and neatly stacked them around the cabbage in the basket.

"There!" Julia dusted off her hands. "That should keep Nessie happy."

Caitlin grinned. "And we all want to keep Nessie happy."

"Indeed." Julia grinned back, then turned to Cynster. "Well, Mr. Cynster. What do you think of our garden?"

He glanced around. "Very comprehensive. I can't say I have many memories to compare with the present, much less that I recognize all you have growing here, even in this season, but I'm certain you've improved on what was here before, and it appears remarkably productive."

Julia took that as an invitation to point out the various beds currently producing, naming the crops in each, and followed with a brief run-down of what plantings would be made over the coming months. "If you do have memories of this space, they'll be of some scraggly old fruit trees. There was not much else here when I arrived, and as we have the main orchard under the Edgars to supply all our fruit, we pulled out the old, half-dead trees and put in more beds." Pausing to survey her domain, Julia heaved a contented, self-satisfied sigh. "It's come along well."

More briskly, she turned to Caitlin. "My dear, could you add pumpkin and squash seeds to our order? And perhaps some of those new beans I mentioned? I'd like to try them and see whether they'll perform for us."

Caitlin nodded. "I'll put those on the list." She bent to pick up the loaded basket.

Before she could, Cynster stooped and grasped the handle. "Allow me."

She drew back. As he raised the basket, easily hoisting the not-incon-siderable weight, she bit her lip. His almost-absentminded tone and the naturalness of the action suggested the intervention was prompted by instinctive good manners—the sort that, for a gentleman like him, stated that no lady should be permitted to lug any heavy weight.

Apparently, she'd already triggered his instincts regarding her true station; she needed to be more careful.

With smiles and an "until later" for Julia, she and Cynster made for the entrance. As they passed through the stone archway, seeking distraction from her awareness of the uncertain ground on which she stood, she focused on him. "I take it you're not particularly keen on vegetables."

He grunted. "I never have been." After a moment, he asked, "What gave me away? Was it my lack of enthusiasm?"

She laughed and admitted it was and let her probably irrational anxiety slip away.

They walked a well-beaten path across the rectangle of lawn, but on reaching the drive, instead of crossing it and following the path onward to the kitchen door—Nessie and her staff would not appreciate the master of the house unexpectedly appearing in their midst while they were in the throes of preparing luncheon—she turned toward the north door of the house, which lay across the drive from the entrance to the rose garden.

Gravel crunched under their feet as they continued along the drive.

She glanced at the rose garden. A smaller walled garden, it was Alice's domain; beneath and around the rosebushes, she grew a huge range of herbs that she and Millie tended and harvested for their various products. But Alice wouldn't be there now—not with the day so advanced —and Alice had already given Caitlin her additions to the orders Caitlin would send out over the coming days.

As if following her thoughts, Cynster asked, "So, the purpose of your visits is to get any additions to orders for items that need to be brought in from outside the estate?"

"And to learn of any difficulty each business might have encountered." She paused, then went on, "I've learned that turning up at the businesses each week gives the business leaders an opportunity to tell me of any issues they have or items they need, and one and all, they remember both better while they're at work. Expecting them to send me a list or remember to tell me over dinner or at some other time simply doesn't work as well."

He nodded, then slanted her a glance. "Your memory must be excellent."

She chuckled and drew out the paper and pencil she carried in one pocket. "My memory is excellent"—she waved the pencil and paper —"but I also make notes as I go."

Amusement danced in his eyes. "Very wise. I hadn't noticed you making your notes." With barely a pause, he continued, "Tell me about the way meals are taken. I gather breakfast is an informal affair."

"Cromwell has the breakfast parlor provisioned from six o'clock— some if not most in the house like to get an early start. I believe Cromwell keeps the dishes warm until nine, then he clears."

"And luncheon?"

"Is always at twelve-thirty, but is also informal in the sense that it's for whoever turns up. The platters are set out on the table in the dining room, and everyone serves themselves."

He nodded. "And dinner?"

She paused, then replied, "Dinner has always been a formal meal, much as it was yesterday, with us meeting in the drawing room, going in to dinner, then retreating to the drawing room again and breaking up after taking tea. Apparently, that was the way Minnie ran things, and Timms kept up the practice." She glanced at him. "Unless you would prefer to dine alone?"

She was relieved when, after the barest moment for thought, he shook his head. "Let's keep things as they are. I usually dine with friends, and obviously, gathering about the dinner table is a valuable way of making all those present feel part of a greater whole."

She was impressed that he'd seen that. She was quick to add, "And before, during, and after dinner creates excellent opportunities to catch up with any issues or broach matters that might affect more than one business." She paused, then went on, "Everyone's relaxed enough to be free with their observations and supportive of each other, and with many of the nearer businesses there, there's no sense of preference being afforded to one and not the other." She glanced at him. "In addition, the other business leaders join us on Wednesday and Sunday evenings, so they're a part of our gatherings, too."

Cynster blinked. "The other business leaders?"

Caitlin grinned. "You've only met about half so far. There's the owners of the Osiery, the orchard and cider mill, the leatherworks and bindery, the weavers, and the four farms as well."

When he frowned, she continued, "The Osiery, the orchard and mill, and the leatherworks and bindery are all down along the riverbank. The weavers are in adjoining cottages on this side of the orchard, and the farms are farther out—Nene and Home Farm are on the other side of the river, while Roxton Farm is on our side of the river but farther east, and Barton Farm fills the northern part of the estate."

"The farms, I knew about," he admitted, "but those other businesses are more recent, I think."

"Most are over five years old, but possibly not as much as eight."

They reached the north door, and he grasped the handle and opened it, then set the door swinging wide and stepped back to allow her to precede him.

Without hesitation, Caitlin walked past him and inside, but she was, once again, very conscious that he was treating her as a lady, not as a chatelaine, an employee. She went along with it; she couldn't afford to make a fuss and, through that, have him focus on what his instincts were plainly telling him.

She halted in the dimness of the corridor. Once he'd entered and shut the door, she held out her hand for the basket. "Nessie and the kitchen staff will be rushing about putting together the platters for luncheon. They won't thank you for throwing them into a fluster."

He frowned, but when she calmly waited, hand commandingly extended, he reluctantly surrendered the heavy basket.

She took it, careful to avoid touching his hand. She hefted the basket onto her hip, but his doubtful expression prodded her into saying, "Don't worry. It's not so heavy I'll collapse while carrying it from here to the kitchen."

He grunted, but then waved her off and turned toward the front hall.

She smiled as she swung the other way. "I'll see you at the luncheon table."

He replied with another grunt.

# CHAPTER 4

*A*fter luncheon, still inwardly marveling at the reality of what Minnie and Timms had created at the Hall, Gregory retreated to the study, determined to learn more.

The study desk had been cleared of all papers. After perusing the ledgers in the bookcases and finding nothing to his purpose, he tugged the bellpull. When Cromwell appeared, Gregory said, "I'm looking for the estate accounts. Where are they?"

Cromwell looked faintly flustered. "Well…er…"

Another point occurred to Gregory. "Regardless, who keeps the accounts?" He'd yet to meet anyone…

His suspicions rose as Cromwell all but flapped and said, "I'll fetch the accounts—and Miss Fergusson."

Gregory watched the door close behind the harried butler, then grunted, returned to the desk, and dropped into the chair behind it to wait.

Five minutes later, Caitlin Fergusson, his exceedingly efficient chatelaine, swept through the door with a pile of ledgers in her arms. She halted before the desk and breezily said, "I didn't know which year you wanted—this year or the one just past."

"The one just past will do."

"You'll want these, then." She set a pair of thick ledgers on the table.

He pointed to the other ledgers she held. "You may as well set those down, too." As she complied, he noticed the door being quietly pulled closed, Cromwell excusing himself from the scene.

Gregory refocused on Caitlin Fergusson's face, taking in her innocent expression. "I'm fairly certain doing estate accounts is not part of a chatelaine's duties."

She'd loosely linked her fingers before her. Now, she lightly shrugged. "Someone had to do it, and there wasn't anyone else."

He frowned. "What happened to the estate's steward?"

"I have no idea. For as long as I've been here, there hasn't been one. As far as I know, there hasn't been a steward since Minnie's time. Timms mentioned that Minnie had an argument with the last one, and after she dismissed him, she refused to appoint a successor. Subsequently, Timms did the accounts."

Slowly, Gregory nodded. "And you took over after Timms."

Caitlin's chin rose a notch. "I've been doing the accounts since I arrived. It was one of the first tasks I took on to help Timms in return for her support. For her letting me and my staff remain here." Her chin elevated a fraction more. "I assure you, I'm more than capable of doing so."

He studied her. There was something wrapped up in all that that she wasn't telling him, but at the moment, that wasn't his primary concern. "All right." He nodded and sat up. "Pull up a chair and, if you would, please take me through the estate accounts."

She rounded the desk and, rather hesitantly, drew up a straight-backed chair.

He scooted the admiral's chair he occupied to his right so she could sit at the desk as well.

She gathered her skirts and sat, her gaze going to the twin ledgers he drew toward them. "From the beginning of last year?"

He nodded, and ruthlessly shoving aside all reaction to her nearness—to the soft warmth of her and the elusive scent of rosemary and orange that rose from her abundant hair to tease his senses—he forced his mind to the task of learning all he could about the expenses of the various businesses.

From the corner of his eye, he saw her bodice swell as she drew in a deeper breath, then she opened the first ledger. "Right, then. The first thing you need to know is how the accounts are laid out."

*How the devil am I supposed to concentrate on that?*

With commendable conciseness, she explained how the ledgers detailed the costs each business accrued through the year. "Obviously, for some, their costs are seasonal, and their profits are, too, while for others

—like the carpentry workshop and carriage works—their costs are more or less steady month to month, but their income tends to arrive in large amounts and at random times. As I understand it, from the first, the Bellamy Hall Fund was essential to balancing the incomings and outgoings, allowing all those involved to have a steady monthly stipend."

"So most here draw a wage of sorts?"

She nodded. "Everyone who works on the entire estate receives some level of monthly payment. Many of the owners, as well as some of the older workers like Parker and Old Wallace, take only a portion of their allocation, preferring to leave the rest as capital in the Fund, accruing interest over the years—a nest egg for when they grow too old to work."

He frowned harder. "Who manages that—the investment of the capital?"

"I gather that was set up in Minnie's day. It's managed by an investment manager—one Mr. Gabriel Cynster." She arched a brow at him. "One of your relatives?"

Gregory snorted. "One of my father's cousins." He nodded in understanding. "And Gabriel's a master investor, so yes, the Fund is in unquestionably good hands."

"That's certainly been my opinion over the years I've been here." She returned her attention to the ledgers and the rows of tiny writing and columns of neat figures. "The other important aspect you need to grasp, one you'll see reflected in the accounts, is that it's the very diversity of the estate businesses that underpins the solid month-to-month returns. The Bellamy Hall estate is not subject to the usual vacillations of income and expense that are common on agricultural estates."

He noticed she spoke with authority, but the concept and what he could see in the accounts as she took him through the entries for January —which was normally a quiet and, relatively speaking, unprofitable month—commanded his full attention.

A tap fell on the door, and it opened to reveal Millie. The young apprentice saw them and balked. "Oh, I thought…that is…" Wide-eyed, she focused on Caitlin, drew breath and blurted, "Alice said we're going to need more alcohol."

"How soon?" Caitlin calmly asked.

Millie grimaced. "As soon as possible. I miscalculated how much we would need last week."

Caitlin waved. "Never mind. I'll send one of the footmen to see what Gordon at the Bells can spare us."

Millie looked relieved. "Thank you." She drew the door closed.

Gregory saw Caitlin was frowning, even as she drew her pencil and paper from her pocket.

"I wonder," she mused, "whether, given the amount of alcohol Alice uses these days, we should speak to the Swithinses or the Bartons—or possibly both—about setting up a still." Looking down, she scribbled a note on her paper.

He remembered he hadn't seen her making notes while they'd been out that morning. "They all think you have a memory like a steel trap, don't they? They never see you taking notes."

A small smile curved her lips. After a moment, she murmured, "A little gloss never hurts one's reputation." She finished her jotting and tucked paper and pencil into her pocket. "Now." She looked back at the accounts. "Where were we?"

She led him steadily through the months, elaborating on how the various expenses shifted between the individual businesses and how the earnings—some random and large, others steady but smaller—allowed a very sound and confident continuation through the year.

"And of course"—she pointed to one large expense in July—"with the accumulation of monies that we set aside, we're able to invest in equipment like this new type of plough."

The door opened, and Cromwell came in. "Miss, Henry Kirk has sent word that Miss Madge's sculpture for Blainey Park is ready to go out. He wants to know if the payment's been received and he can send it off with one of the grooms."

Caitlin nodded. "Tell Henry the payment came in yesterday, so he can arrange for delivery."

"Very good, miss." Cromwell withdrew.

Gregory watched Caitlin as she plainly made some mental note—not a scribbled one, this time—then she looked back at the ledgers, and they continued on.

Over the next hour, they were interrupted three more times by estate people needing information, wanting to add to orders, and seeking permission to take several stones from the old ruins.

With the latter, Caitlin looked at Gregory, but he shook his head. "At this point, you'll know better than I."

She promptly gave permission, but with a range of sensible stipulations he wouldn't have thought to make.

With his own words ringing in his ears, he realized that if he'd learned anything that afternoon, it was that the lynchpin of the entire estate was sitting beside him. And if she wasn't there, he wasn't at all sure the entire enterprise wouldn't fall apart.

And he'd yet to learn of the "other businesses."

He'd been jotting down various questions as they rose in his mind. As they both returned their attention to the ledgers—they'd progressed to September, and the harvest was coming up—the pencil he'd been using caught on his sleeve, and when he shook it free, it rolled toward the edge of the desk between them.

She reached to catch it, and he did, too.

His hand brushed—nearly cupped—the back of hers, and she jerked her hand away as if stung.

"Sorry!" she said.

"My apologies." His words crossed over hers, his tone far too deep.

He fought to unclench his jaw, the effort of not reacting to the sudden, intense flare of awareness momentarily distracting him.

"Now!" She stabbed a finger at one entry. "This refers to…"

He fought to pay attention, but his gaze constantly slid to her face, her profile. She didn't meet his eyes but doggedly continued to take him step by step through the accounts.

She was smarter than he was.

He was going to have to work alongside her—literally beside her, as they now were. He needed her insight; he couldn't go forward to shape any sort of future at Bellamy Hall without her input.

There was no question whatsoever in his mind about getting rid of her; quite aside from the outcry he could all too easily imagine, he wasn't that stupid. The role she filled wasn't one he could simply take over—not in the short term and possibly not in the long term, either. The degree of detail she plainly grasped and deployed on a daily basis…she'd spent three years learning it, and he couldn't hope to emulate her understanding.

While one part of his mind took in the income and expenses in November—noting the expected decline in agricultural returns, which was more than offset by a steep increase in income from the nonagricultural concerns that Caitlin identified as being due to gifts bought in the lead-up to the holiday season—on a deeper level, he took one last look at his earlier vision of a future Bellamy Hall estate under his management, then consigned that vision to the bonfire of discarded dreams.

As she turned the page to the December accounts, he accepted—

specifically and finally and without reservation—that he had to deal with the situation as it was.

Whatever he built out of his inheritance, it had to be based on the Bellamy Hall that was such an amazing going concern.

One part of his mind dwelled on what accepting that actually meant.

When Caitlin came to the end of the year and, finally, closed the second ledger, he stirred and, his gaze on her face, stated, "You were the one who was using the study when I arrived."

He'd recognized her small, precise handwriting on the sheets he'd found when he'd first investigated the room.

Somewhat warily, she met his eyes. "Yes."

When she said nothing more, he inclined his head. "Given that you do the accounts, it's appropriate that you continue to use the study." He saw the surprise she tried to hide. "I'll work from the library."

He pushed back the chair and rose.

She got to her feet more slowly. "Are you sure? I have to confess it would be easier."

He met her gaze. "Not to mention everyone on the estate and no doubt from farther afield expects to find you here."

She struggled to find something to say to that, eventually settling for "As owner, you using the desk in the library does seem more fitting." She smiled at him, plainly pleased to have her domain returned to her. "Thank you, Mr. Cynster."

He grunted and headed for the door. With his hand on the knob, he halted and looked back. "My given name is Gregory. I would prefer you use that."

She blinked, and when he pointedly waited, she rather more quietly replied, "I suppose if you call me Caitlin…"

He smiled and didn't care if his inner wolf showed. "Indeed." With a nod, he opened the door and walked out, leaving her, once more, queen in her domain.

～

That evening, once dinner and the ritual of the tea trolley had been completed and the others had retired to their beds, Gregory walked into the library, now his personal fiefdom. After pouring himself a generous brandy, he settled in one of the armchairs before the fire to digest what he'd learned thus far.

He sipped and let the myriad details and insights he'd gleaned during his first twenty-four hours at Bellamy Hall replay in his mind. After a time, he shifted his focus to what he now accepted he needed to do, namely, to formulate a fresh vision of his future—of his role as owner of Bellamy Hall—a vision that included Caitlin, the business leaders, and ultimately encompassed all productive activities on the estate.

There was still a lot he needed to learn, and expanding his knowledge would have to come first. Until he understood the basis for all he'd seen in the accounts that afternoon, he would have to play matters by ear.

Taking up the reins of Bellamy Hall was proving to be a very different challenge—a much bigger challenge—than he or, indeed, anyone in the family had envisaged.

Of course, Timms and, no doubt, Minnie before her would have known exactly how much adjusting of expectations he would face.

While the family had known of Minnie's habit of taking others under her wing and, subsequently, encouraging them to pursue their dreams, no one had appreciated to what extent that concept, followed over many years, had changed the very nature of the estate.

Glassblowing, fine furniture, iron sculptures, carriages. Those were not the normal output from country estates.

"On the other hand..." He'd seen how the income from those endeavors balanced out and supported the estate's prosperity through what were normally leaner months.

"And if there is a downturn in agricultural prices—like the mess of the corn prices decades ago—this estate will not founder." In fact, given the hugely varied businesses, financially, the estate wouldn't even be stretched.

He needed to adjust his thinking, and a part of that was admitting that such an apparently eclectic, not to say crazy, conglomeration of businesses was by no means a bad thing.

In the long run, it could be a significant advantage.

He also needed to accept that much of the estate's current success rode on Caitlin Fergusson's exceedingly feminine shoulders. She was ridiculously young to fill such a role—to be the anchor and lynchpin for so many businesses run by others far older and more experienced than she —but she had a knack for working with others. He'd already seen ample evidence of that.

Whatever his ultimate goal with respect to the estate turned out to be, he wouldn't achieve it without her.

Without her active help and support.

"Hmm." He took a long swallow of the brandy.

Working alongside Caitlin... He was going to have to figure out how to do that without allowing his attraction to her—or the impact he had on her—to trip him up.

He was far too experienced not to know he affected her, but he had no clue as to how she viewed that. Hopefully, she would gradually get over it —grow accustomed to him—just as he hoped his attraction to her would, over time, fade.

His inner wolf jibbed at that—as if the suggestion he should dismiss that attraction and not pursue it was deeply offensive—but he sternly lectured his wolfish side that that was simply the way things had to be.

He needed to buckle down and get a firm grip on the wholly novel and unexpected challenge Minnie and Timms had—he was perfectly certain deliberately—willed to him.

Feeling distinctly more certain of and settled on his path, he drained his glass, set it down, then rose and headed for bed.

The next morning, Gregory came down to breakfast rather earlier.

The weather was passingly fine, with the sun making a more determined effort than it had the day before to make its presence felt. In the corridor leading to the breakfast parlor, he encountered Julia and Joshua on their way out; they nodded and smiled and continued on their way.

As Gregory had surmised, the inhabitants of the Hall were early birds.

He walked into the breakfast parlor to find Caitlin, Vernon, and Percy still seated about the large round table.

"What-ho, Cynster!" Percy raised his knife in salute. "Come to join us worker types?"

"I have, indeed." With smiles and nods for all three, Gregory headed for the sideboard. "Your collective industry is infectious."

"Don't know about infectious," Vernon replied. "But we do get things done."

"So I've learned." Heaped plate in hand, Gregory rounded the table and drew out the chair opposite Vernon, one place separated from Caitlin. He'd decided to make a concerted effort not to unnecessarily disturb her.

He thanked Cromwell, who arrived to fill his coffee cup, then settled to eat while listening to the discussion between Vernon and Caitlin regarding some sort of special sand Vernon was interested in laying his hands on.

"If I could just find a reliable source," Vernon declared, "one I trusted, and lay my hands on a pound or two, that would at least give me enough to run a few trials and decide if the stuff was worth our while pursuing."

Frowning, Caitlin nodded. "I'll write to the suppliers in Bath and ask if they have any they can send." She narrowed her eyes at Vernon. "A pound? Is that enough?"

He grinned at her. "Two or three or even five would be better."

She huffed and picked up her teacup. "I'll see what I can find. I might have to write to London or Southampton, so don't get your hopes up. Even if I can find any, it won't arrive soon."

"Aye, well." Vernon laid his cutlery across his empty plate. "I'll have to possess my soul in patience."

With a nod to Caitlin, Vernon rose, and Percy followed. In the doorway, they passed Hugo and Melrose as the two painters ambled in.

When the pair joined Gregory and Caitlin at the table, Gregory asked, "Where's Tristan?"

"He's already out." Hugo waved southward. "He wanted to catch the dawn light playing over the ruins."

"It's one of his favorite and most in-demand subjects," Melrose explained. "Lots of ladies like to have a genuine picture of ruins wreathed in mist on their walls, and at this time of year, one can often get especially good mists lit by the rising sun."

Hugo turned to Caitlin. "Miss C, we desperately need those brushes Melrose spoke with you about. The special ones for watercolor works."

Caitlin leveled a look at Melrose. "When was this? I don't recall hearing anything about special brushes."

Melrose's brow furrowed. "I thought I spoke with you last week..." He met Caitlin's eyes and grimaced. "Perhaps not. Can I leave the details on your desk?"

She sighed. "Yes, and I'll order them in, but I can't promise how long they might take."

Hugo shrugged. "I daresay we'll manage if we have to." He glanced at Melrose. "I might try feathers again."

"Down might be better," Melrose offered. "Downy feathers, at least."

Hugo nodded. "You might be right."

Caitlin set down her cup, laid aside her napkin, and pushed back her chair.

Gregory gulped the last of his coffee, nodded to the painters, and followed her from the room. "Caitlin."

She paused in the corridor and, facing him, waited for him to join her. "Yes…Gregory?"

He smiled. "I want you to teach me everything you can about the Bellamy Hall estate."

Caitlin blinked, then turned and slowly continued toward the front hall.

On the one hand, she was delighted that he was openly and apparently genuinely taking a close interest in the Hall's enterprises. On the other, she had to wonder why. Was he merely wanting to get a comprehensive understanding of the businesses that underpinned the estate's financial viability before he returned to his life in London? Or…?

Regardless, the prospect of having him by her side for another half day—at least—left her decidedly uneasy. Indeed, left her prey to conflicting impulses—to happily welcome spending more time with him or run away.

Neither reaction was at all like her.

She couldn't understand why he made her feel so many far-too-powerful urges. Nevertheless, for the good of the Hall and all those who lived there…

She drew in a fortifying breath and evenly replied, "Of course." What else could she say? She summoned an encouraging smile and trained it on his far-too-handsome face. "What precisely do you wish to learn?"

His hazel gaze on her face, he said, "You mentioned visiting other businesses on Wednesday and Thursday. Where would you normally go today?"

"To visit the businesses along the riverbank, returning via the weavers' cottages."

He nodded. "Perfect. I'll accompany you, and you can introduce me to those who run those businesses."

They'd reached the front hall, and he halted and arched a brow at her. "Do we walk or ride?"

"Walk. Riding means the grooms have to catch and saddle horses, and the distance isn't worth it." Briefly, she met his eyes. "Just let me fetch my coat and bonnet, and we can be on our way."

∼

Gregory was waiting in the front hall when Caitlin came down the stairs. She wore the same felted bonnet and full-skirted blue pelisse she'd worn the previous day; both were practical for the season and for strolling a country estate, yet also showed a degree of style that reminded him of all the questions about her to which he'd yet to learn answers.

Indeed, according to Snibbs, no one at the Hall had any idea of where she and her maid and groom hailed from other than it being "to the north."

There was a lot of country north of Northamptonshire.

She stepped from the stairs and gestured down the corridor leading to the south door, and he fell in beside her.

They exited the house and set out on the path across the south lawn. After passing between the standing stones, they toiled up the low hill toward the ruins, but instead of turning right to the burial ground and the ruins of the church, they continued south toward the gleaming ribbon of the river Nene.

At the highest point on the low hill, Caitlin halted and waved at the vista before them. "This spot gives the best view of the estate's lands by the river." She pointed to a roof on the nearer bank, directly south of them and half hidden by trees. "That's the Osiery, so called because they make basket ware from osiers harvested from the abbey's old osier beds. Next on this side"—her arm tracked east to the next group of buildings—"is the cider mill." She shifted to indicate a thick planting of currently leafless trees. "You probably remember the orchard. As you can see, it's quite extensive."

"We—my siblings and I—always wondered if the orchard dated from the time of the abbey."

"I doubt the trees are that old, but the walls around the orchard might well be that ancient."

"Or built of stones from the abbey."

"True. Next, we have the leatherworks." The group of buildings she indicated was some way along from the mill. "The bindery is on the other side of the leatherworks and fronts onto the lane."

"Those are the businesses we're going to visit today?"

"Yes, and the weavers. You can just see the roofs of the two cottages from here. Among those trees."

He squinted and nodded, then looked across the river. "The estate extends on the other side of the Nene, doesn't it?"

"Yes, and Bellamy Hall was lucky. When the railway came through, following the valley, they sited the tracks just beyond the Hall's southern boundary. So Nene Farm"—she pointed to buildings directly south, on the southern bank opposite the Osiery—"and Home Farm"—she gestured farther east—"and Roxton Farm, on the other side of the lane but on this side of the river"—she pointed due east—"were unaffected." She glanced at him. "Not all our neighbors were so fortunate."

He raised his brows. "I can imagine having a railway run through your land, especially when it's on a raised embankment as it is here, creates significant problems."

"Indeed," she said darkly and led the way on.

They descended the gentle slope to the river, to where a wider section, a small lake of sorts, boasted several islands.

"I remember this spot from my childhood. We often came swimming here." The islands and even more the banks lining the pond were thick with coppiced willows.

"You'll remember the willows, then, although they might not have been coppiced at that time."

"They weren't." The path curved to follow the riverbank eastward. A little way ahead, he glimpsed a neat stone cottage with a square stone building beside it. "The Osiery, I assume?"

Caitlin nodded. "The Pooles are Mrs. Poole, her son, William, who's eighteen, and her daughter, Hattie, who's twenty now. Mrs. Poole's a widow and a distant connection of the Bellamys. After the death of Captain Poole, who was in the merchant navy, was confirmed, Timms went to Bristol and invited the Pooles to the Hall to recover from their grief."

That was definitely the sort of thing Timms would have done.

"As it happened, Mrs. Poole was born nearby, and her family had been basket makers for generations, until they died out. She noticed the old willows and took up basket weaving, which she remembered from when she was a child. Nowadays, she and Hattie are regarded as experts in the art, and William manages the osier beds and oversees the preparation of the withies. The larger building is their workshop and storehouse."

"I see." He considered that history, then mildly observed, "If Mrs. Poole's family were basket makers, she would know the ins and outs of the business."

Caitlin nodded. "She definitely does."

That, he reflected, seemed to be a theme at the Hall. Not only did every business owner know their business, but each was passionately devoted to their trade.

They crossed the cobbled yard before the larger building and the cottage. The cottage door stood open. Caitlin tugged the bell chain that hung beside it.

The clanging drew a plain-faced, dark-haired woman to the doorway. She was neatly if austerely dressed, with her hair pulled back in a severe bun, and there was a calmness about her as she nodded and smiled at Caitlin, then bobbed a curtsy to Gregory. "Mr. Cynster?"

He smiled. "Mrs. Poole, I take it. I hope we've called at an opportune time. I fear I know nothing about basket making and would be grateful if you could give me an introduction sufficient to appreciate your craft."

Caitlin wasn't surprised to see Mrs. Poole respond positively to that formal invitation. Lucinda was a very reserved person, and the note Gregory had struck—whether by luck or design—was just the right one to have her unbend.

"By all means, sir." Lucinda waved toward the workshop and stepped out to join them. "Allow me to explain what we do."

Caitlin trailed after the pair as Lucinda guided Gregory through the mysteries of basket making, from the cutting of the young willow canes —"My son, William, does most of the harvesting these days"—to sorting the lengths into a series of stalls to the drying racks.

"We air-dry the canes until they're brown. After that, they can be stored for however long we wish, although for us, that's rarely more than a few months." Lucinda moved on to the long troughs where canes were soaking. "In order to weave, we soak the canes in water again, until the ends can be bent without the bark cracking." She demonstrated. "So these are almost ready, which is good, as Hattie and I plan to start on our next baskets this afternoon."

Lucinda led the way to where Hattie—a fresh-faced young woman with blond curls, her plain gown protected by a thick apron—stood at a table, her fingers flicking as she expertly worked the top of a hamper, creating a strong, whipped rim.

"I see." Gregory watched as if mesmerized. When Hattie finished her edging and tied the last cane off, he raised his gaze to her face, smiled, and reached for the hamper. "May I?"

Hattie blushed and waved, inviting him to take the piece.

Caitlin watched as he lifted it, admiring the even lines, then poked at the weave, testing its strength, before hefting the hamper, noting the weight.

Confident in the quality, Lucinda proudly stated, "That's part of an order from Farringdon Hall." She proceeded to list all the various locals and stately homes the Osiery supplied. "And of course, anything we have left over goes quick as a wink at the Northampton market."

"I'm not surprised." With another smile for Hattie, Gregory set the hamper down. "As I said, I'm no expert, but these are strong yet lightweight and obviously well-made. I've never seen better."

Judging that to be the right note on which to end their visit, Caitlin asked, "Is there anything you need me to add to the orders later this week?"

Mrs. Poole turned to her. "Some of those long-handled iron hooks to manage the bundles would be helpful, and perhaps more hooks for hanging." She waved toward the ceiling. "I was thinking we might try hoisting canes up so we can dry more at a time."

Eyeing the rafters from which such hooks would hang, Caitlin nodded. "I'll see if I can locate something suitable."

She and Gregory took their leave and walked on along the riverbank. After pulling out her list for today, she added Mrs. Poole's request.

Strolling beside her, Gregory waited until Caitlin tucked the list away to say, "That's another small business I would never have thought profitable, yet I take it the Pooles are financially successful."

"Surprisingly so. You'll see it in the accounts, but part of the Poole magic is the connection to her family, the Washburns, who have been in the industry for generations. Mrs. Poole's been quick to see the advantage in keeping the name going—they call one type of basket they make a Washburn basket. Even though the Osiery has only been in operation for six years, the Pooles' work is well-known in the area and is now much sought-after. The Osiery commands the highest prices for basket ware in the county—possibly in the country."

The path followed the curve of the river. Gregory eyed the water rushing past on their right. "I hadn't realized the river rose so high."

"It's often high at this time of year. I've been warned that, along this stretch, the banks can be quite treacherous during winter."

"When we visited, we used to swim along here"—he looked back along the river—"but that was in summer. I don't think I've ever come this way in winter."

He faced forward and smiled as serried ranks of trees—all old, gnarled, and currently leafless—came into view on the slope above the path, which swung away from the riverbank to run beside the orchard wall. Waist-high and built of stones as old as the ruins, the wall enclosed a large plot that contained trees of many different types, each in their own section. "I have vivid memories of the orchard. I especially remember the plums."

They walked on, and another building sited on the riverbank came into view. Gregory studied the more modern stonework and tiled roof. "The cider mill, I take it."

"It was built about twelve years ago," Caitlin informed him. "Prior to that, Jennifer Edgar had been making cider in the Edgars' cottage." She pointed at a stone cottage that stood a short distance beyond the mill.

"Twelve years?" He frowned. "I've definitely visited the Hall over that time, but I suppose I haven't walked this path since I was much younger." He looked more closely at the mill. "So this was one of Minnie's additions—businesses started during her time."

Caitlin nodded. "The Edgars—Harry, Jennifer, and their sons, Johnny and Tom—run the orchard and the mill. The boys attend school at Earls Barton, but spend a lot of time helping out in the orchard and mill. Mrs. Edgar—Jennifer—oversees the cider production. They get extra hands in from the village when they need help for pressing and bottling. Harry, meanwhile, devotes himself to his trees and their harvest."

As they approached the mill, Gregory murmured, "Another successful enterprise?"

Caitlin grinned and waved toward the open door. "Judge for yourself."

They were met at the door by a typical countrywoman—tallish, brown-haired, and neatly garbed in a plain gown—whom Caitlin introduced as Jennifer Edgar. Harry lumbered out of the mill as well, and Gregory shook hands and encouraged the couple to show him around their respective domains.

He spent the next twenty minutes learning about making cider and admiring the press, which, he learned, could run on either water power supplied by a small waterwheel or horse power provided by a large Clydesdale presently grazing in a nearby paddock.

"Necessary, he is," Harry said of the horse, "'cause at harvest times, the river often runs low. Mind you, we press in batches spread over many months, but it's helpful that we don't rely on the river."

Gregory listened attentively as the couple explained the process, from the apples arriving from the orchard all the way through to the bottling and subsequent dispatch to nearby inns, and learned that, as well as their signature cider, the mill also produced a fine perry.

"Smaller run, o'course," Harry said, "but it's become very popular with the ladies round about. It's one of our specialties, now."

With a proud smile, Jennifer added, "Although we sell everything we produce, the perry goes in a flash."

Gregory suspected that making perry from the orchard's pears had been Jennifer's idea. He turned to Harry. "As I mentioned to Miss Fergusson, I remember the orchard of old, but I haven't been this way for at least twelve years. What other fruits does the orchard produce these days?"

Caitlin watched as Harry proudly led Gregory across the path and into the orchard. She trailed the pair, but halted at the orchard wall. Leaning against the stone, she watched as Harry drew Gregory on under the wide old branches, pointing out this and that. She seriously doubted Gregory would know a pear tree from a plum tree, not while they were leafless, but he was definitely paying close attention to all Harry let fall and even asking questions.

Jennifer joined her. Crossing her arms, Jennifer studied the men. After a moment, she said, "He actually seems interested—not like he's just pretending." She hummed, then added, "He might look the part, but he's not what I expected."

Caitlin admitted, "Nor I."

"Has he said when he's leaving?"

"He hasn't made any comment about leaving. Instead, he declared he wants to learn about all the businesses—everything about how the estate runs."

After a moment of silent cogitation, Jennifer offered, "Wanting to know everything about everything doesn't sound as if he's rushing to wash his hands of us."

That was what they'd all assumed he would do.

"No," Caitlin agreed. "It doesn't."

But what Gregory meant to do as the new owner of Bellamy Hall...she honestly couldn't guess.

As the men started back to the orchard gate, she straightened from the wall. "Wanting to know the details of the businesses doesn't mean he intends to stay."

Jennifer lowered her arms and murmured, "We'll just have to wait and see."

Having plainly established a solid rapport, Harry and Gregory stepped onto the path. They shook hands, and Caitlin took her leave of Harry and Jennifer, and she and Gregory walked on. She waved ahead. "The leather-works are next."

Gregory smelled the leatherworks well before he saw the buildings. "They tan the skins here, too?"

She nodded. "That's why they're hard by the river. Luckily, the prevailing winds blow away from the Hall and the village."

He grinned. "That sounds like something Minnie would say. Were the leatherworks established under her aegis?"

"Yes, but the bindery came later. That was Timms. When it was first established, the leatherworks did a good trade in gloves, but as the demand for hand-stitched gloves declined, Timms suggested the family explore bookbinding as an alternative. These days, the bindery contributes a significant percentage of the leatherworks' profit. Although Mrs. Sutton and their daughter, Nell, still make quality gloves, they only work to personal orders."

"Orders from whom?"

"Certain ladies of the ton—introduced to the Suttons' gloves by Minnie and Timms—have become lifelong customers. The prices the Suttons can command for their now-exclusive gloves has enabled the glove making to continue as a viable sideline."

"I see. So gloves, binding books, and what else?"

"Mostly shoes. The Suttons supply finished leather to a host of the Northampton shoemakers. That's the primary market for leather around here, and it's the principal reason the leatherworks is one of the most lucrative businesses on the estate."

In light of that introduction, he was anticipating being impressed, and the Suttons and their enterprise fully lived up to his expectations—indeed, exceeded them. Leonard Sutton and his wife and daughter and their helpers, Morris and Richie, were delighted to welcome him and show him about. He examined the supple leathers they produced and learned that the business had standing orders from the Northampton shoemakers.

"They'll take as much as we can give them," Len Sutton proudly declared.

As for the delicate leather Isabelle Sutton and her daughter, Nell, used to make gloves for their special customers, after handling a pair, Gregory informed the ladies that he fully intended to put in orders for pairs to give as gifts to his female relatives throughout the year. "I never know what to get them, but they'll all love these."

Isabelle and Nell preened.

But shoe leather and gloves weren't where Isabelle Sutton's heart now lay. She waited while Len and Nell spoke with Caitlin about ordering more lye and leatherwork needles, then eagerly escorted Gregory and Caitlin to the building next door, which fronted onto the lane that led to Earls Barton.

The bookbindery was of relatively new construction. "How long has this been a part of your business?" Gregory asked.

"About five years." Isabelle proceeded to show off the equipment they'd brought in, and Gregory found himself quite fascinated by the process.

He liked books, and the quality of the covers Isabelle, Nell, and the others were producing was second to none.

Caitlin couldn't help but smile at the genuine interest that had laid claim to Gregory's often-impassive features.

When he finally dragged himself away from the bindery, and they parted from the Suttons, she set out at a brisk pace up the lane.

He fell in beside her, easily matching her stride. "Are we hurrying?"

"Yes and no. I need to call in at the weavers' cottages, and it's already heading toward noon."

He consulted a fob watch. "Hmm. You're right." A second later, he added, "I was about to say that I could safely promise not to become engrossed in fabrics, but I would have said the same about gloves, so perhaps I'd better wait and see."

She grinned. "You've now seen ample evidence that none of the Hall businesses are lagging when it comes to success."

"Indeed." In a wondering tone, he added, "It's been quite amazing." He scanned ahead, then glanced at her. "Where are these cottages?"

"This way." She turned left, onto the narrow path that led to the twin cottages tucked against a protective rise. "The Jenkinses and the Kirks live here."

"Jenkins of the carriage works and Henry Kirk, the blacksmith?"

She nodded. "And Madge, of course. But Margaret Jenkins and Monica Kirk are talented weavers, and Timms felt their skills shouldn't be overlooked and encouraged them to join forces and set up their weaving business. They take the highest-quality fleece from the Hammersleys at Home Farm and spin that to yarn and weave their pieces here, at their homes."

"Permit me to guess," he said dryly, "their fabrics are much sought-after."

She laughed. "They are indeed. They sell locally through a fabric agent, but most important to their success, they've established a connection with an exclusive shop in Regent Street that sells to the haut ton." She glanced at him. "You might well have seen Margaret and Monica's scarves gracing the throats of a countess or duchess."

He snorted. "If Margaret and Monica's wares live up to the standards of everything else I've seen here, I'll be sending their scarves as gifts to several countesses, a duchess or two, and at least two marchionesses."

She smiled. "Once you see Margaret and Monica's wares and are suitably impressed, you should tell them that. They'll love the idea."

Even before he'd met the two women, Gregory was resigned to doing just that, and sure enough, after he'd inspected the spinning wheels and looms neatly set up in each cottage's front room, the instant he touched the delicate fabric Monica had stretched on her loom, he warned the pair, entirely sincerely, that he would have orders for them to fill.

As Caitlin had predicted, both were chuffed.

After parting from Margaret and Monica with smiles and reiterated promises for future orders, he strode with Caitlin up the lane. As they walked, he reviewed all he'd seen and learned that morning. They turned onto the drive and walked between and beneath the huge old trees.

As they emerged from the tunnel and the Hall rose before them, he said, "I've come to realize that the Bellamy Hall estate is nothing short of remarkable."

He glanced at Caitlin and took in her fond smile.

"That," she said, "is due, first, to Minnie, and to Timms's steady hand after that. Between them, they fostered, nurtured, and grew something that is unique and productive."

He gazed at the Hall's gothic façade. "The estate is a very far cry from the usual disposition of a gentleman's acres. Not being blind, I can see the benefits, especially given the uncertainty that bedevils the profits from agricultural crops and even sheep and cattle."

From the corner of his eye, he saw the sidelong glance she threw him, guessed the thought behind it, and inwardly nodded. "But that's the point, isn't it? Creating such a tapestry of different businesses naturally results in collective security. One type of goods might suddenly be in glut and its price drops, but another business's product will be in high demand, and the prices there will offset the other."

A sense of having finally fully grasped the implications of the composition of the Bellamy Hall estate flooded him.

"Timms told me that Minnie's husband, Sir Humphrey, who was, apparently, a great and very successful investor—"

"He was."

"Well, he taught Minnie that diversifying one's investments into different industries was the cornerstone of success. After Sir Humphrey died and the reins of the estate passed to Minnie, she decided that the same logic should apply to estate management, too, and deliberately sought out different sorts of businesses that could thrive on the estate, and Timms continued in her footsteps."

"To my ultimate benefit, and that of all those on the estate."

"Exactly. Sir Humphrey's farsightedness and Minnie's determination and Timms's devotion to their ideals have paid off."

As they neared the house, he felt as if he'd finally uncovered the truth of the legacy Minnie and Timms had left him. "Now, I understand why there hasn't been a steward in decades." No normal steward would know how to handle this.

For all his life, he, his family, and all those in the ton who knew Minnie had viewed her "hangers-on," as they'd termed them, as a random collection of esoteric folk with odd or unusual interests. Having now met them, he could see that far from being without purpose, Minnie's selection of those whose causes she'd espoused had been deliberate and based on sound judgment and excellent reasoning.

*She's protected the estate from any type of future downturn.*

For no matter what happened in the years to come, at least some of the businesses would be profitable, and most likely, those that remained in the black would do so by a large enough margin to tide the rest over until conditions improved.

And that wasn't taking into account the considerable funds left by Sir Humphrey, Minnie, and subsequently, Timms to ensure the smooth running of the estate. It seemed likely those were simply there, accruing interest year after year—a steadily increasing cushion.

"Good Lord." He shook his head in something akin to disbelief. "This is so much more than I'd envisaged."

Caitlin glanced at his face, took in his rather stunned expression, then looked ahead. "And you haven't yet seen the farms."

# CHAPTER 5

*W*ith Caitlin, Gregory visited the farms the very next day. What he saw added to his understanding of the intertwining of the estate businesses and left him marveling anew at how farsighted Minnie and Timms had been. The two old ladies had grasped what few other landowners had, and the Hall's enterprises meshed together in myriad mutually supporting ways. For instance, the stubbled pastures and any low-quality grain from the cropping farms, Roxton and Barton, were made available to Home Farm and Nene Farm, which ran the estate's large flock of sheep and the local cattle stud respectively, enabling the livestock farms to easily winter their herds. Hides and sheepskins from the livestock farms supplied the leatherworks, and basket ware provided by the Osiery was used on all four farms as well as in most other estate businesses.

Alice and Millie provided remedies for any and all illnesses to the entire estate, human and animal, while the leatherworks provided work boots and heavy gloves to any estate worker who needed them. The forge built and maintained iron and steel equipment, as well as kept every horse properly shod, while the carriage works kept all conveyances in good working order. Every enterprise gave whatever any other enterprise needed free of charge or expectation.

The way the estate community worked together and supported each other was nothing short of remarkable.

On Friday, the day after he'd visited the farms, when, after breakfast,

Gregory settled behind the library desk, he was still struggling to absorb the intricacies of Minnie and Timms's creation. Every time he turned around, he found some new cross-connection that inevitably benefited both businesses involved.

Apparently, Caitlin habitually spent her Fridays ensconced in the study, dealing with orders and the like, which left him with time to further his understanding.

He drew the account ledgers covering the past year to sit squarely before him. It had been only three days since Caitlin had guided him through the entries, but now that he'd seen every business and spoken with the owners—and had gained a far better appreciation of what was going on—he needed to look over the figures again. Illuminated by his new insights, they would tell a much more meaningful story.

As he opened the first ledger, the understanding little smile that had curved Caitlin's lips as she'd handed him the books a few minutes ago rose in his mind. He dwelled on those tempting lips, and his mind, once again, diverted to the fascinating subject of her.

Given she played such a pivotal, central role on the estate, it behooved him to learn more of her. That she was committed to keeping the entire cohort of estate enterprises running optimally, in harness as it were, and strove to achieve that in the easiest, smoothest, least-disruptive fashion was beyond question. She had a sound understanding of the people involved and was committed to their well-being, too. Such unstinting devotion was commendable, especially as, having caught more hints of her soft burr over recent days, he'd adjusted his view of just how far north she hailed from.

He didn't think she'd come from anywhere south of Hadrian's Wall.

In fact, on several occasions, that soft, slight accent had sparked memories of the area around the home of his cousins, Lucilla and Marcus. He was increasingly certain Caitlin Fergusson had lived much of her life somewhere near the Vale of Casphairn.

Yet her origins were but a minor aspect of the conundrum she posed. She was, he estimated, somewhere in her early to mid-twenties. Despite her confidence and assurance, with his well-honed instincts regarding the opposite sex, he simply couldn't see her as any older. And that was the crux of the conundrum. How could a young lady—for she was assuredly that—of only twenty-something summers fill the role of chatelaine in such a commanding fashion?

With such understated aplomb?

And if she was of that age and well-born—as she most definitely seemed to be—shouldn't she be otherwise occupied?

Shouldn't she be off dancing at balls and looking about for a husband? Even in Scotland, that was what young ladies of quality did.

Not that he wished her to leave her post, yet the puzzle she presented nagged at him.

He was missing something, and he had no idea what.

The notion of writing to Lucilla and Marcus, along with their respective spouses, Thomas and Niniver, and asking if any of them knew of a Caitlin Fergusson flitted at the back of his mind, yet he hesitated to do it. Checking in that way seemed unwarrantedly intrusive, almost as if he would be breaking faith, and not just with her but with Timms as well.

No, he wouldn't write.

Hopefully, as she came to know him better, she would tell him anything he needed to know regarding her background and why she'd sought refuge—for far longer than necessary to see out a blizzard—at Bellamy Hall.

*Is she hiding from something?*

He could only hope that as she came to trust him, she would tell him if she was.

He let that conclusion settle in his brain, then sat straighter and refocused on the ledgers before him.

He started at the beginning of the year, reviewing the figures through the prism of his newfound understanding. The accounts now made more sense—and indeed, were a lot more revealing—than they'd been three days ago.

He remained immersed in the figures, gleaning new and deeper insights, until the luncheon gong sounded. He duly repaired to the dining room and enjoyed the company of Julia, Joshua, Percy, Vernon, the three painters, and Caitlin over the shared meal. Apparently, Alice, Millie, and their occasional helper, Gladys, were out on a field trip, which the others explained meant that the three would be tramping through nearby woods and meadows, searching out and gathering ingredients for the various remedies Alice and Millie produced.

After the meal, when he returned to the library, he looked back through the ledgers for the figures for the apothecary business in January, February, and March and noted that while expenses were similar to other months, income was significantly higher over winter, presumably due to sales for the treatment of the usual seasonal ailments.

He sat and considered the likelihood that, for most of the businesses, the highs and lows throughout a year would be reasonably predictable. For instance, some businesses were heavily seasonally dependent, while others were much less so.

"If I worked out the annual pattern for each business, the combination should give an approximation of how the estate as a whole will fare in any month." He thought about that, then muttered, "I wonder if there's any weak month?"

He hunted and found sheets of paper and a sharp pencil and settled to work out projections for each business month to month. "At the very least, I can satisfy myself as to the likely minimum level of monthly income."

He was deep in calculations when a tap fell on the door. Absentmindedly, he called, "Come," and Cromwell walked in.

The butler approached the desk and, when Gregory looked at him inquiringly, said, "Miss Fergusson wonders if she might trouble you for the ledgers for the past year."

Gregory frowned. Those were the only ledgers he had, and she knew he'd intended studying them in detail. "Did she say why she needed them?"

Cromwell's expression suggested that Gregory had asked the right question. "Not precisely, but two grain agents have called, and I gather they wish to reduce the amount of grain they take from the Hall. That or reduce the price they'll pay for it."

Gregory arched his brows. "Is that so?" He shut the ledgers and got to his feet. "I believe I'll return the ledgers to Miss Fergusson myself." He picked them up and made for the door. "I take it she and the agents are in the study?"

Radiating approval, Cromwell hurried to hold the door for him. "Indeed, sir."

Gregory strode for the study. He was glad of the opportunity to see Caitlin in action, not, in this case, as the Hall's chatelaine but in the role of estate steward.

Cromwell hurried alongside him and opened the study door, and Gregory walked in.

Caitlin was seated behind the desk, and the two agents occupied chairs angled before it. Her gaze fixed on him, but not a flicker of an eyelash betrayed whether she was surprised—or possibly relieved—to see him.

He headed for the desk. From her rigid expression, he gathered she was distinctly annoyed, although not with him. From the corner of his eye, he surveyed the agents. Both were of the bluff and hearty type and wore the nondescript attire favored by agricultural agents everywhere; the only notable difference between the pair was that one wore a spotted neckerchief while the other sported a striped one.

Gregory didn't acknowledge the men but walked around the desk and handed the ledgers to Caitlin. "I believe these are the ones you requested."

As she accepted the ledgers, she briefly met his gaze. "Thank you."

Caitlin was hanging on to her temper by a thread. A fraying one. She wasn't sure whether she was happy to see Gregory; there were both pros and cons to his presence. The outcome would depend on how the next minutes played out.

She was a touch surprised when, saying nothing more, he took up a stance, standing to her left, facing the agents. Maintaining an impassive expression, she set down the ledgers, opened the topmost, flicked through several pages, then ran her finger down a column. She found the entry she wanted and tapped the page. "Yes. Here we are. Last year, you paid three shillings a pound for our wheat, two shillings a pound for our barley, and four shillings a pound for our oats." She shut the ledger and looked at the agents. "But this year... What were you offering again?"

Both agents looked at Gregory.

Caitlin didn't shift her gaze from the pair but simply waited, wondering...

To her immense relief, Gregory—*bless him*—said nothing. At all. He, too, merely waited.

Eventually, with uncertainty creeping into their expressions, reluctantly and still somewhat belligerently, the agents returned their gazes to her.

When the pair looked mulish and said nothing, she prompted, "Your offers, gentlemen?"

She wasn't surprised to see their expressions firm and grow truculent.

"Well," the older of the pair said, "like I explained before, we can't stretch to more than a shilling and a half for any grains this year, m'dear." He glanced at Gregory. "We've got a bit of a glut on, as you might have heard."

Caitlin folded her hands on the ledgers and arched her brows in mild surprise. "As it happens, I hadn't heard any whisper of that—at least not for the quality of grain the Hall produces, which, as I'm sure you won't have forgotten, is the highest grade you'll find anywhere. We hit that mark consistently, year after year."

"That may be, dearie, but we aren't obliged to pay the same every year." The older agent shrugged. "We've no reason to, now, have we? Not with all this grain flooding the market."

Caitlin sighed. "Very well, gentlemen. In that case, there seems nothing more to say." Of course, both thought she was about to give in and accept their ludicrous offers. Instead, she tapped the top of the closed ledger with one fingertip and rose, bringing them scrambling to their feet. "Thank you for calling, gentlemen. Sadly, it seems Bellamy Hall is unable to do business with Mercer and Sons Grain Merchants this year. Do pass on my regards to Mr. Mercer, and be sure to assure him that we'll harbor no hard feelings when it comes to selling our grain next year."

Both agents' jaws dropped. Both paled. Utterly dumbfounded, they stared at her.

Serenely, she folded her hands and, her expression entirely unthreatening, waited, exuding the expectation that they would leave.

Gregory struggled to hide a laugh as the elder nearly toppled over as he leaned forward and clutched the edge of the desk.

"Now, now, Miss Fergusson. There's no need to be so hasty."

Caitlin's smile was cool. "Oh?" She arched her brows.

The younger agent tugged at his neckerchief. "I'm sure we can...er, be more accommodating. Bellamy Hall being such a reliable supplier and all."

Caitlin's smile widened, and she waved the men to their seats. "Perhaps we can come to some arrangement."

With his hands clasped behind his back, Gregory stood and watched a master negotiator in action. He could barely conceal his grin when, instead of accepting any reduction in prices, Caitlin succeeded in extracting not just the same prices as last year for their wheat and barley but also held out for a nice increase in the price for the Hall's oats, which apparently were of exceptional quality.

When the agents balked at agreeing to that last stipulation, he decided to lend a hand. He shifted, drawing everyone's gazes, but it was Caitlin's eyes he met. "Don't forget about that fellow who spoke to me in Northampton the other day."

Quick as a flash, she nodded. "I haven't forgotten about him." She turned back to the agents and imperiously inquired, "Well, gentlemen. What say you? Do Mercer and Sons want our oats or not?"

The agents exchanged a startled look, then turned to her and surrendered.

She promptly wrote out a sale note, stating the agreed amount of grain to be supplied and the all-important prices to be paid, and had the older agent sign it.

Once he had, the men rose and took their leave. Gregory had purposely not asked to be introduced and continued to stand back, aloof and distant, and with polite and rather careful nods, the pair departed. They went out of the door, looking distinctly relieved.

Only then did Caitlin grin. She glanced at Gregory. "Thank you. That interjection was just the thing to tip them over the edge."

"You did an excellent job of pushing them to that point." He glanced at the doorway. "Does that happen often? Merchants' agents trying to pressure you to accept lower prices?"

She sank back onto her chair. "Not usually, although he was correct about there being a glut of low-quality grain from last year." Looking up, she met his eyes. "Nevertheless, I suspect that they'd heard of the arrival of the Hall's new owner and thought to try their luck. Most likely, they hoped to be dealing with you, a newcomer to the area and probably not well versed in the prices of grain."

He huffed. "As it happens, they would have caught cold feet there. Selling grain is one of the few farming activities shared between here and Walkhurst."

"Your family's estate?"

He nodded. "In Kent, such crops are a big part of what's grown there. So I do have some idea...." He trailed off, then grimaced. "Although I wouldn't have been as sure as you of the recent prices, and depending on how convincing they were about that glut, I might have believed them and accepted what they offered."

"When they were shown in here and realized they would have to deal with me as usual, I think they hoped to force me into taking the new offer —and them—to you. So it's just as well you came in. They won't try that again, at least not here."

He smiled. "And knowing how men like them talk, the news will get around, and you won't have to do battle with those hoping to prey on my innocence."

She laughed, and he saluted her and headed back to the library, entirely content with the outcome of the unexpected interruption.

The following Tuesday afternoon, Caitlin remembered the assistance Gregory had provided with the grain merchants.

Once more, she was hanging on to her temper by a very thin thread, courtesy of Mr. Coulter, the textile merchant's agent. A short, rotund man who reminded her forcibly of a Pouter pigeon, he sat in the chair before her desk and insisted, yet again, that as the new owner of Bellamy Hall was in residence, it was only right and proper that he, Coulter, deal with that gentleman.

He steadfastly refused to discuss anything at all with her.

He'd stated his decision the instant he'd sat down and, over the past ten minutes, hadn't shifted an inch.

"Proper business practice, Miss Fergusson, dictates that, where practicable, I should negotiate with the ultimate owner rather than a minion."

*Minion?* She bit her lip to smother her immediate retort.

She'd definitely had enough. Meeting Coulter's eyes, her expression utterly uninformative, she arched her brows. "Are you sure?"

Coulter blinked. "Heh?"

Calmly, she elaborated, "Are you sure you want to deal with Mr. Cynster?"

He studied her for an instant, wariness and suspicion blooming in his beady eyes, but then his truculence returned, and he tugged down his straining waistcoat. "I make deals with owners, Miss Fergusson. Not with"—he waved dismissively—"chatelaines."

Lips compressed, she nodded and rose. "Very well. Come with me."

Believing that he was getting his way, Coulter all but bounced to his feet.

She swept from the room, and he resettled his coat and hurried to follow her.

She came upon Cromwell in the front hall. "I take it Mr. Cynster is in the library?"

"Indeed, miss." Cromwell took in Coulter at her heels and, most helpfully, looked concerned.

Caitlin knew Cromwell's anxiety arose because he was bothered by anything out of the ordinary, but Coulter wouldn't know that.

She hid a smirk and swept on, leading the irritating agent to the library.

On reaching the library door, she tapped on the panel. When Gregory called "Come in," she opened the door a fraction, then looked at Coulter, who was eagerly and impatiently crowding behind her. "Just don't say I didn't warn you that Mr. Cynster doesn't like to be disturbed."

"What?" Coulter squeaked.

But she'd already turned and pushed the door wide. Ignoring Coulter, she walked in.

Immediately, she looked at Gregory, seated behind the desk, which, helpfully, faced the door. She'd spoken loudly enough for him to have heard.

Sure enough, he met her eyes, fractionally nodded, then looked past her at Coulter as, not quite so certain now, the agent came rather hesitantly into the room.

Gregory paused with his pen poised above the letter he'd been writing. Understanding that, in dealing with whatever this situation was, he was to play the part of an irascible gentleman who didn't like being interrupted, he leveled a severely disapproving look on the man trailing behind Caitlin and barked, "What's this, then, Miss Fergusson? You know I don't appreciate having my concentration disrupted."

Caitlin halted before the desk, hands clasped before her, the very picture of a dutiful chatelaine. "Indeed, sir. But this gentleman"—she waved at the man who had halted a full pace farther from the desk—"Mr. Coulter, the agent for Kettering Cloth Merchants, who buy and onsell the woolen fabric Mrs. Jenkins and Mrs. Kirk produce, insists that now that you, the owner, are in residence, he will deal only with you."

She reclasped her hands and met Gregory's eyes, plainly consigning Coulter to his mercy.

He glowered at the man. "Well, sir? Is this true?" When Coulter simply stared, Gregory forcefully demanded, "What do you have to say for yourself, sir?"

Coulter gripped his hands tightly and, in a tentative tone, managed, "Well, sir, it's always good policy to ensure I'm dealing with the actual owner. If they're available." He cast a sideways glance at Caitlin. "And, well, especially when dealing with females." He looked at Gregory and essayed a man-to-man expression. "As I'm sure you know, one can never be certain they've quite got their minds around all the nuances of a deal—of contracts and such."

Gregory couldn't help but glance at Caitlin to see what she thought of that. If Coulter had been able to see the glitter in her eyes, much less the set of her lips and chin, he would have run screaming from the room. As it was...

Could they turn the situation to their advantage—assuming Caitlin could control any impulse to throttle the man? Gregory leaned back in his chair and slowly and deliberately set his pen into the pen holder, allowing it to fall into place with a definite *click*.

He stared at Coulter and let the silence stretch until the agent shifted nervously, then quietly asked, "Do you seriously imagine I came into the country so I could spend my time discussing the price of cloth?"

Coulter's eyes flared, and he glanced even more nervously at Caitlin, as if hoping she would rescue him.

Gregory hid a predatory smile and, eyes narrowing, leaned forward, skewering Coulter with his gaze. "Tell me—would you have felt moved to interrupt me had Miss Fergusson been Mr. Fergusson?"

Coulter's eyelids flickered, and he glanced uncertainly at Caitlin. "Yes, well—she's not."

"Of course she's not, man! Yet by my direction, *she* is in charge of arranging all contracts for the sale of Hall products and produce. Surely you don't mean to question my judgment?"

Coulter squirmed. "Of course not, sir."

Gregory nodded. "Just as well. Having recently gone through the past year's accounts, I can testify that Miss Fergusson is more than up to the task. Indeed, she's been highly successful..." He let his words trail away and brought his gaze once more to bear on Coulter, this time with a knowing look. "Or is *that* the real reason you thought to push your way into dealing directly with me rather than negotiating with her—because she knows the worth of our products and will not settle for anything less than an appropriate price?"

Coulter looked faintly green. Agitatedly, he waved his hands. "No, no. It's just..."

Gregory gave him a moment to flounder, then shifted his gaze to Caitlin's studiously straight face. "Miss Fergusson—please take Mr. Coulter back to the study and, if he fails to offer you a price you deem acceptable, have Cromwell show him out."

"Yes, Mr. Cynster."

As Gregory picked up his pen and, already looking down at his letter, arrogantly waved them off, struggling to keep a most unprofessional grin from her face, Caitlin swung around, grasped Coulter's sleeve, and under her breath, hissed, "You'd better come before he loses patience and instructs me not to deal with you at all."

Coulter looked at her with wide eyes, then turned and scurried to the door

~

Half an hour later, Caitlin returned to the library with a wide and richly satisfied, not to say smug, smile wreathing her face.

Gregory looked up as she strolled in, and scanned her features. His lips lifted. "Good price?"

She laughed and averred, "The best we've ever had."

~

Two days later, after a relaxed luncheon, Caitlin and Gregory were on the point of quitting the dining room to return to their respective, now-customary domains when Cromwell appeared, escorting Davy Cruickshank.

Without any of his usual formality, Cromwell said, "Sir, miss, Davy's just come running from Nene Farm." He prodded Davy's shoulder. "Go on, lad. Tell them."

Davy—all of seventeen and lanky with it—glanced nervously at Gregory, then switched his gaze to Caitlin. "It's Mr. Biggs, the cattle agent, miss."

Caitlin groaned. "Let me guess. He's being difficult over the price he'll pay?"

Eyes widening, Davy nodded. "He's saying there's no market for our yearlings, and he's not paying anything like he did last year. Pa says that's not right. He sent me to fetch you."

Caitlin patted Davy's thin shoulder. "Your father's correct, and he did right to send you. If anything, we should be getting more this year than last. I'll come straightaway."

She glanced at Gregory and arched a brow. After their teamwork with the grain agents and the cloth merchant, she had to wonder what they might achieve here—if he was willing.

Meeting her gaze, he smiled in anticipation. "I'll come, too." He looked at Davy. "It'll be faster to take my curricle—you can ride on the back."

Caitlin smothered a laugh as Davy's eyes grew round, and he stuttered a rushed acceptance.

Ten minutes later, Gregory tooled the curricle down the lane that would take them to Nene Farm. The cattle stud lay on the other side of the river, and they had to drive over a humpbacked bridge to cross the swiftly moving water.

When he slowed his horses to take the upward curve, he glanced back at Davy. The lad was sitting on the box seat and hanging onto the rail at the rear of the front seat with both hands. His huge eyes were locked on the horses, and the look on his face stated very clearly that he was having the time of his life.

Gregory hid a grin, then, sobering, glanced at Caitlin before returning his attention to his bays. "This seems to be a pattern."

When she didn't immediately respond, he looked her way and saw she was giving the matter some thought.

He guided the horses down the other side of the bridge, then flicked the reins and set them pacing swiftly again.

"When I took over from Timms," Caitlin said, "some of the agents tried the same thing until they learned that I knew enough to call their bluff and that *I* wasn't bluffing."

*Interesting.* That implied that, even three years ago, she'd known enough about pricing to hold her ground against finagling agents. Most young ladies of her station wouldn't have had a clue.

She went on, "News got around reasonably quickly, and on the whole, they stopped trying to pull the wool over my eyes. But now, I suspect word has gone around that the new owner of Bellamy Hall has taken up residence—and they assume that means you'll have taken over from me —and believing you to be London born and bred with no real idea of the value of things, they're hoping to take advantage."

"I wondered if it was that—that they're hoping to prey on my relative naivete."

"Given this is the third incidence, I think it must be that."

They'd reached the turnoff to the farm. He slowed the horses and made the turn, then set them pacing again.

He glanced at Caitlin. "Given I truly have no idea of the value of cattle—yearling or otherwise—you'll have to take the lead."

The smile that curved her lips boded ill for the poor agent. "I'll be happy to."

As it transpired, neither she nor Gregory had to do very much. The instant the agent, who was facing off with an irate Martin Cruickshank, saw her walking up with Gregory at her back, the man's shoulders slumped, and his aggressive stance wilted.

Caitlin halted before Martin and the agent and, with a wave at Gregory, introduced Biggs.

Gregory acknowledged Biggs with a curt and distant—and thoroughly discouraging—nod, then turned to Caitlin. "You have the field, Miss Fergusson." *Do your damnedest.* Judging by the spark of laughter that lit her eyes, she'd guessed the words he hadn't said. To drive home the point, he looked at Biggs and tipped his head Caitlin's way. "She's the one you have to deal with."

Biggs deflated even further and tried to smother a groan. Almost sheepishly, he met Caitlin's, then Martin's eyes. "Well, it was worth a try. Can't blame a man for trying, can you? Same price as last time?"

"No." Caitlin's response brooked no argument. She met Biggs's eyes. "You're going to have to do better than that, and you know it."

Biggs looked faintly disgusted, but she gave him no time to stew, engaging him in a brisk negotiation. In short order, she wrapped up a deal that significantly exceeded the price Martin had received the previous year, which put a wide smile on Martin's face.

Despite that, Biggs seemed pleased to have got his hands on such fine beasts.

After arranging to return in a few days to take possession of the year-lings, Biggs nodded all around and left.

Martin turned to Caitlin and Gregory and showered them with thanks.

Caitlin smiled at the earnest farmer. "That's what we're here for, Martin. To take care of that side of the business so you can concentrate on what you do best, namely caring for your herd."

Gregory nodded his agreement. "Anything like that, call, and we'll come running."

After they'd exchanged farewells with Martin, he and Caitlin walked to where he'd tied his horses to a rail. Davy had remained there, admiring the beasts.

With no reason to rush back to the Hall, Gregory paused to watch Martin and his cattleman transfer the sold yearlings into a holding pen.

Caitlin halted beside him. After eyeing the young cattle, he said, "They really are fine beasts—even I can see that."

She smiled. "Bit by bit, we'll educate you yet."

He grinned and met her eyes. For a moment, their gazes held, then still smiling widely, he waved her toward the carriage.

When they reached the curricle, he handed her up, then spent a minute talking to Davy while he tried to forget the feel of her slender fingers clasped in his.

Eventually, he took the reins, climbed up, and sat beside her.

And feeling decidedly triumphant, drove back to the Hall at a more leisurely pace.

# CHAPTER 6

On Saturday morning, Gregory sat at the library desk and commenced penning a letter to his sister-in-law Ellen regarding the goats her uncle kept at Bigfield House, the property across the lane from Walkhurst Manor.

All through their childhoods, Gregory and his siblings had played with the goats. Ellen had joined the Bigfield House household only in recent years and, even more recently, had married Gregory's older brother, Christopher, and moved to live at the manor, but she was close to her uncle, and although Sir Humphrey's mind was failing, Gregory knew he would enjoy hearing of the goats at Bellamy Hall, and Ellen could be counted on to pass on any advice or tidbits of information her uncle let fall.

He was nearing the end of the letter when Cromwell tapped on the door; Gregory now recognized the butler's light rap. "Come in, Cromwell." He looked up to see the butler enter, then carefully shut the door behind him.

With a faintly troubled look on his face, Cromwell crossed all the way to the desk before announcing, "There's a…gentleman asking to see you, sir. A Mr. Hagen from Wellingborough, although I believe he's new to the district."

Gregory set down his pen. "I'm fairly certain he's not someone I know." He studied Cromwell's face. "Do you have any idea what he wants?"

"As to that, sir"—Cromwell drew in a breath and pronounced—"I believe the…gentleman is a medical practitioner."

Gregory knew Cromwell's hesitation over labeling the fellow a gentleman was a classic butler's way of indicating disapproval. But why Cromwell would disapprove of a medical man, Gregory didn't know. More, from Cromwell's manner, the man's occupation was supposed to enlighten Gregory in some way, but he couldn't fathom what he was supposed to understand.

"Show him in." On impulse—and because it was the surest way to protect himself from being caught out by things he should know but didn't—he added, "And please ask Miss Fergusson to join us."

Cromwell smiled approvingly. "Very good, sir." He bowed and departed, closing the door behind him.

Gregory laid aside his letter to Ellen and clasped his hands on the blotter as the door opened again, and Cromwell ushered in a man of average height and build, with pale-brown hair and a distinctly round face. He was wearing a neat, dark suit and a tight, thin-lipped expression that suggested he was given to peevishness. Certainly, a growl seemed not far off as he glanced darkly at Cromwell.

In the manner of imperturbable butlers everywhere, Cromwell remained supremely unaffected. "Mr. Hagen, sir. From Wellingborough."

Hagen walked forward and offered his hand. "Mr. Cynster."

Gregory rose and, reaching across the desk, grasped the man's hand and shook it, then waved Hagen to one of the chairs before the desk. Noting Cromwell scurrying out, in languid fashion, Gregory resumed his seat and hoped Caitlin would arrive soon. Something about Hagen set his hackles rising.

He took his time settling behind the desk, then met Hagen's eyes. "Mr. Hagen. I confess I'm wondering what brings you here."

Hagen was sitting bolt upright in the chair. "As to that, Mr. Cynster, I should perhaps inform you that I have recently moved to Wellingborough and set up my medical practice in the town." Hagen noticed the crease in one trouser leg was less than straight and paused to tweak it into perfect alignment. Satisfied, he returned his gaze to Gregory. "It's in my capacity as a medical man that I am here."

"Indeed?" Deliberately, Gregory misunderstood. "I wasn't aware anyone at the Hall was in need of medical assistance."

Hagen frowned. "That's not why I've come."

A light tap fell on the door.

Relieved, Gregory called, "Come," and watched Caitlin slip into the room. She shut the door, then stood beside it with her hands clasped before her, very much the perfect chatelaine.

Gregory nodded to her, but didn't beckon her closer. Hagen missed seeing the nod as he'd glanced around himself.

Having noted who had entered, but plainly dismissing Caitlin as irrelevant to his business, Hagen turned back to Gregory.

Gregory arched his brows, inviting Hagen to continue.

The man's features firmed. "I gather that, until recently, you lived in London, sir, so you'll be aware that medical science is progressing in leaps and bounds. However, I've discovered that, in the countryside, local people, even those of higher station who should know better, cling quite tenaciously to outmoded ways."

Gregory arched a brow. "I daresay that's true, but I continue to be at a loss as to what the opinions of the wider population have to do with me."

Faint but definite color rose in Hagen's cheeks. "The crux of the matter, sir, is this. On making inquiries, I've learned that the majority of those who would benefit from my services prefer, instead, to seek the advice of one Miss Alice Penrose, an apothecary who, I believe, operates under your aegis."

While he might be classed as Alice's landlord, Gregory did not consider himself her overlord in any way, shape, or form. He'd also seen enough orders placed to comprehend how highly regarded the little apothecary was, not just on the estate but throughout the surrounding district.

He therefore had some inkling of what Hagen believed was the justification for his complaint.

Not that he agreed.

Mildly, he stated, "Apothecaries are a highly regarded profession and not solely in country areas."

Hagen sniffed and waved dismissively. "Some—those who approach their art from a suitably scientific perspective—I have no argument with, but sadly, the Apothecary Guild allowed females into their ranks centuries ago and have yet to rectify the error. Consequently, especially in the countryside, apothecaries are often little better than hedge witches, what with their herbal remedies and potions and unguents and utterly unscientific ways."

Hagen's contempt rang clearly.

Still standing by the door in her self-effacing stance, Caitlin had noticeably stiffened. Gregory saw the glare she directed at the back of Hagen's head; he was amazed the man's hair wasn't smoldering. Regardless, that glare clearly conveyed what she thought of Hagen and his attitude.

Calmly, Gregory said, "Be that as it may, as I understand it, no apothecary can force people to consult them. Their customers do so because they wish to, presumably because they have faith in the apothecary's skills."

Hagen leaned forward. "Yes, but don't you see? Those around about with ailments should now come to me! But they won't—not while they blindly cling to the past! To antiquated ways. They insist on seeing the Penrose woman and relying on her herbs and potions!"

Hagen's performance would have been comical had the insult to Alice Penrose not been so blatant. Gregory allowed his features and his tone to harden. "I fear, Hagen, that I remain mystified as to what you believe I should do. From where I sit, I see no reason to interfere in what is plainly long-standing local practice. It is not for me to tell others what to think or do regarding their health."

"Dash it all!" Hagen's hold on his temper was slipping; he thrust a hand through his hair. "Look here—the Penrose female works for you, doesn't she? Even if not technically, she depends on your support. If you were to withdraw it—"

"And why would I do that?" Gregory caught Caitlin's eye and nodded at her to approach; it was clearly time to introduce Hagen to her no doubt more robust opinion. "To be clear, Miss Penrose does not work for me." Gregory looked at Caitlin as she rounded the desk; with her violet eyes flashing fire at the hapless Hagen, she came to stand beside Gregory's chair. "Perhaps, Miss Fergusson, you should explain to Mr. Hagen how matters are managed at Bellamy Hall."

"Indeed, sir." In a crisp, no-nonsense fashion, she rolled on, "Miss Penrose is not in any way a pensioner of the Bellamy Hall estate. She lives here, and her workshop is sited within the Hall, but that is by commercial arrangement. Miss Penrose is an independent businesswoman to whom the Hall acts in the capacity of a landlord. Miss Penrose is widely acknowledged as having a great deal of experience and expertise in treating all manner of maladies, and she and her remedies are highly regarded throughout the county. From the estate's point of view, having Miss Penrose as one of its business members brings both significant revenue and considerable status through being the home of such a respected and worthy member of the community."

When Hagen frowned at Caitlin, Gregory languidly waved and explained, "Miss Fergusson is the Hall's chatelaine and also acts as estate steward. I rely on her knowledge and advice regarding the numerous businesses the estate hosts. That includes Miss Penrose's apothecary business."

Hagen's expression had steadily darkened. Shifting his gaze from Caitlin, he looked at Gregory. "So on the say-so of your chatelaine, you won't do anything about that dratted woman?"

Caitlin glanced at Gregory and saw the last vestige of civility flee his face. His gaze bored into Hagen, and when he spoke, there was a bite in his tone that was positively menacing.

"I suggest, Hagen, that if you wish to expand your practice, the fastest way to do so would be to impress the locals, first, by treating them and their opinions and ways with respect, and second, by actively demonstrating the value of your scientific ways through your treatment of those who do solicit your services. Respect and standing only come through hard work, and both are honors that are bestowed, not rights granted on demand."

Caitlin stared at Gregory with new eyes. This wasn't the man she'd grown accustomed to seeing—that everyone at the Hall had seen. She'd had no idea such steel lay beneath his polished exterior and found the revelation fascinating.

After holding Hagen silent with his gaze for several fraught and weighty seconds, Gregory glanced at her, then looked past her at the bellpull.

With alacrity, she turned, walked to the wall, and tugged the embroidered pull.

She turned back as Gregory, his expression cold and his tone icy, said, "And now, Hagen, I fear Miss Fergusson and I are extremely busy."

The clear implication being that they had better things to do than listen to Hagen's whining.

Slowly, Hagen blinked. He looked like he'd been slapped in the face with a very dead cod.

Caitlin battled to keep her lips straight and her expression blank.

Cromwell must have been waiting for the summons; he opened the door and came in. "You rang, sir?"

"Indeed." Gregory looked at Cromwell. "Mr. Hagen was just leaving. Please show him out."

Hagen opened his mouth, then shut it.

When Gregory looked at him and pointedly raised a brow, Hagen slowly got to his feet. He paused, but then scowled, turned, and marched out. Cromwell followed, shutting the door behind him.

Caitlin looked at Gregory. He stared at the door for a moment, then reached for a partially written letter and set it on the blotter before him. "That will teach me for not acting on Cromwell's recommendation."

"Oh?" She was intrigued. "Did Cromwell say something about Hagen?"

"Not said so much as subtly implied. In best butler fashion, Cromwell kept hesitating over describing Hagen as a gentleman."

"Ah." Grinning, she nodded. "I see."

Gregory sighed. "I should have trusted Cromwell's instincts and acted accordingly. Then I might have spared both our tempers the aggravation of having to deal with such a small-minded fellow." He picked up his pen and brandished it. "I swear I will take this to heart. When it comes to the manner of a man, butlers are always right."

Caitlin laughed and started for the door. "If you have no further need of my advice…"

Without looking up from his letter, he waved her off. "No, no—you're free to go."

As, smiling, she reached for the doorknob, he added, "Incidentally, I'm writing to my sister-in-law, asking her for all she can tell me about her uncle's herd of prize goats. There might be something in her report that Joshua will find useful."

"Very likely." She paused for a second, watching as he bent over the letter, writing rapidly, then she opened the door and left him to his industry.

After shutting the door behind her, she paused. She felt quite chuffed on several counts, including that he'd called for her assistance with Hagen and his unreasonable demands and that, together, they'd seen off the odious doctor. On top of that, she'd been impressed by the strength she'd glimpsed beneath Gregory's sophisticated glamour and felt distinctly heartened by the way he'd risen to Alice's defense.

Indeed, she was starting to believe that he wasn't intending to return to his life in London anytime soon. Possibly not ever. The previous day, his man, Snibbs, had taken possession of a large number of trunks and chests which had been brought from London by carter. Apparently, Snibbs had confirmed that the delivery represented all Gregory's—and Snibbs's and Melton's—worldly goods. That certainly suggested that Gregory had moved in and planned on remaining at the Hall.

That he intended to make the Hall his home.

He'd yet to make any definitive statement regarding his future, yet contrary to their earlier thoughts, she sensed that everyone on the estate, herself included, was now hoping he would stay.

She cast her mind over the recent encounter and realized she was still smiling.

Feeling very much in charity with the world at large, she took one step toward the study, then halted, swung around, and headed for Alice's workshop.

Alice and Millie deserved to know about Hagen and how Gregory had defended them.

On the following Saturday evening, Gregory sat in one corner of the forward-facing seat in the large and ancient Bellamy Hall coach. Although old, the carriage was—courtesy of Jenkins and his men—in excellent repair, and the springs had been replaced, ensuring a remarkably smooth ride.

He was on his way to Loxton Park, the home of the local squire, Lord Loxton. Caitlin had persuaded him that he couldn't decline the Loxtons' invitation, not if he planned to reside at the Hall for any substantial part of the year. The people he would meet tonight were his neighbors, and he would doubtless have reason to interact with them for years if not decades to come.

That was how she'd put it. As he had no plans to leave the Hall other than for short visits to London and to meet with family, he'd been about to reluctantly surrender to her wisdom when she'd capped her arguments by informing him that the local gentry were eaten with curiosity about him. He'd promptly suggested that was a very good reason not to show his face, but she'd countered that if he didn't feed the beast, as it were, their hunger would only escalate.

As he was well aware of the lengths to which matrons with daughters to establish would go in pursuit of an eligible bachelor, he'd capitulated.

They'd taken the old coach because it would comfortably seat all six of the Hall residents attending. As well as Gregory and Caitlin, that included Julia, Joshua, Vernon, and Percy. Alice and Millie had also been invited, but—possibly in response to Hagen's visit—both were in Northampton for a few days, consulting with one of Alice's long-established colleagues there. Doubtless, the obnoxious Hagen's ears had been burning throughout the day.

As the coach rattled on through the encroaching darkness of the winter evening, Gregory fought a losing battle to drag his senses from the lady seated beside him. The rocking of the coach meant that, as she swayed with the movement, her shoulder, sheathed in silk and the velvet of her evening cloak, brushed against his arm.

Such an innocent touch, yet it set his nerves afire and his imagination rioting.

When he'd seen her descending the stairs to join him and the group gathered in the hall, all excitedly chattering, he'd had to blink three times before he'd been sure he had his expression under control.

Before he'd been sure nothing showed of the lust the sight of her had inspired.

Her gown was a stylish confection of pansy-blue silk that left her shoulders bare. Her black hair had been gathered in a knot on the top of her head, with tendrils allowed to hang in corkscrew curls over her nape and provocatively brush the sides of her long, white throat. Her fascinating violet-blue eyes had seemed larger and brighter than ever.

Every subsequent second—as he'd escorted her to the carriage and handed her up, then climbed in and claimed the seat beside her—had been an ordeal. Having her beside him was, on the one hand, absolutely necessary—or so said his instincts—yet having her so close was a serious and continuing source of immense distraction. Not to mention discomfort.

That he was increasingly drawn to her—that this particular itch wasn't going to fade of its own accord or through constant exposure to the source of the irritation—was now evident.

What he should do about it…that was a different matter. Given she was his chatelaine and a vital cog in the machinery of Bellamy Hall, his way forward was anything but clear.

The old coach slowed, then turned through a set of stone gateposts and rolled on along a graveled drive. It was too dark to see much outside, but soon, a pool of warm light enveloped the coach as it drew into a narrow forecourt before a prosperous-looking manor house.

The coachman halted the horses, and the footman dropped to the gravel and came to open the door.

Gregory descended first. He straightened his coat, then turned and offered Caitlin his hand.

She gripped it, and he closed his hand and assisted her down the coach's steep steps. Once on the gravel, she drew her fingers from his clasp, and he forced himself to let her go.

They both stepped aside, and she shook out her skirts while the others joined them. Casting his eye over their number, he had to admit that, dressed for the evening in silks and suits, they might have been guests turning up at a ton ball. Julia looked handsome in her purple-silk gown, while for once, Joshua, Percy, and Vernon looked the part of the gentlemen they actually were.

He glanced around, scanning the forecourt and noting the number of carriages already there and still arriving. Given there were six in their party alone, it seemed this would be a sizeable gathering. Still, it wouldn't be anything like a full-scale ton event; he felt confident he would cope.

As a group, they started up the front steps and were admitted into a well-lit hall. A butler appeared with several footmen to take their coats, then beside Caitlin—too wary to claim her arm—Gregory went forward to meet Lord and Lady Loxton, who were standing in the drawing room doorway, welcoming their guests.

Their party paused to allow those ahead of them to finish exchanging greetings. Gregory seized the moment to study their hosts.

Lady Loxton was a well-endowed matron old enough to have married off her children long ago and, hence, be entirely free to indulge in the enjoyment of entertaining without any ulterior motives. She looked gay and carefree, and there was a sense of settled contentment in her soft, lined face.

Her spouse was a large, heavyset man of about sixty years old. Gray-white curls covered his head, and the features of his heavy-jowled face looked comfortable and well-worn. He was well-dressed, but in a fashion hailing from a decade or so past, yet that, too, contributed to the image of aged yet benign wisdom he projected. A no doubt useful persona, given he was the local magistrate.

The guests in front moved into the drawing room. Caitlin glided forward, and Gregory went with her.

"Cynster." Lord Loxton's heavy expression lightened, and he held out a hand. "Gerald Loxton, sir. Delighted you could join us."

Gregory smiled his easy social smile and shook Loxton's hand. "I'm pleased to have this opportunity to make your and your lady's acquaintance, sir. Thank you both for the invitation." He directed a polite half bow to Lady Loxton and was rewarded with a brilliant smile.

"It is we who are honored to welcome you, sir." Lady Loxton turned her smile on Caitlin. "My dear, I hope I can call on you to deputize for me and introduce Mr. Cynster around. We've several parties yet to join us, so we're stuck here for the nonce."

"Of course." Caitlin had already exchanged warm greetings with her ladyship and had exchanged smiling nods—almost affectionate ones— with his lordship.

Lady Loxton smiled at Gregory with some satisfaction. "While we can't hold a candle to the ton events to which you're accustomed, I hope you'll find our little county gathering a pleasant way to meet those who live round about."

Gregory murmured suitable words of anticipation, then moved on beside Caitlin as she led the way into the room.

Somewhat to his surprise, in what followed, Lady Loxton's expectations were fulfilled. As Caitlin had warned him, the local gentry were indeed curious—about his intentions at the Hall and about what type of man he was—but their interest was mild and relatively unassuming and never pushed into the intrusive.

The local minister, one Reverend Millicombe of All Saints Church in Earls Barton, proved typical of those there, welcoming Gregory warmly and mildly asking if he intended to remain in the area.

He replied with his now-customary answer, namely that, at that time, he had no firm plans to return to London. That he had no intention of making any such plans was a revelation he kept to himself.

After exchanging comments about various walks in the area—Millicombe was a keen rambler—and comparing those with walking trails in the Kentish Weald, the good reverend expressed a hope that he would see Gregory at church one Sunday soon, to which Gregory returned a vague answer, and they parted on that note.

Caitlin continued to act as his guide, smoothly steering him from group to group and making the necessary introductions, for which he was grateful. While he took in the information, matching faces with names and houses and occupations, the exercise also brought to the forefront of his mind an issue that, over recent days, he'd largely forgotten.

His chatelaine was a lady. But more, given the way the local gentry responded to her and she to them, her status was rather higher than anyone else's there. Possibly as high as his.

Possibly higher.

Everyone there was old enough to have developed well-honed antennae for class—something that, in England, had remained a necessary survival skill for millennia—and every person there treated Caitlin Fergusson as if she were…as high-born as he.

Indeed, even he had fallen into the habit of treating her as a social equal. As a lady of his class.

That conscious realization brought the host of questions the observation had previously raised rushing back to his mind.

Why, at her age, was she so content to remain tucked away, more or less socially isolated, at Bellamy Hall?

And the way the other young ladies hung on his every word and watched him so eagerly only underscored Caitlin's lack of interest in pursuing a socially acceptable marriage.

At her age, just like all the other young ladies there, she should be husband hunting.

And the higher her social class, the more that should have been true.

She remained a conundrum, a puzzle he was growing increasingly determined to solve.

Even though she had now introduced him to all those present, he remained by her side as they circulated through the gathering, his awareness and attention focused solely on her.

Caitlin was surprised to find Gregory clinging to her side—almost as if he needed her to protect him from the admittedly overeager and overenthusiastic overtures of the five young ladies among Lady Loxton's guests. But after hearing him deftly—charmingly yet firmly—depressing the pretensions of Miss Holgarth, the most brazen of the five, Caitlin seriously doubted he needed any help.

That said, she could understand why, when two matrons with daughters in tow bore down on them, he murmured by her ear, "Don't you dare leave me."

She fought to quell the shiver that whisper sent slithering down her spine and endeavored to keep her expression unrevealing as, with delighted smiles wreathing their countenances, Mrs. Quinn and Mrs. Moffat engaged.

At first, Caitlin was amused by the various approaches the ladies took in an attempt to winkle invitations to Bellamy Hall. It was not her place to suggest such visits nor to refuse them, but the extent to which the ladies pressed increasingly made her uncomfortable, especially when, from his tone, she sensed Gregory was losing his social patience.

The younger ladies had grown progressively impatient with their mothers' lack of success, and finally, the pair boldly stepped forward and attempted to use their feminine wiles to snare Gregory's attention—only to discover he was perfectly capable of turning into an impervious block. He smiled, he nodded, but he didn't respond as they wished.

Caitlin wondered how long it would be before the witless pair prodded him into saying something cutting and gave thanks when the Loxtons' butler appeared and announced that dinner was served.

Lady Loxton claimed Gregory's arm, while Caitlin smiled on his lordship and accepted the arm he offered her.

Dinner, with the younger people seated together in the center of the table, passed off without incident or, indeed, much social effort on anyone's part. Everyone there, excepting only Gregory, knew each other of old, and the conversations needed no help to flow freely.

But once the company returned en masse to the drawing room, Gregory once again sought out Caitlin. Boldly, without any by-your-leave or even warning, he grasped her hand, twined his arm with hers, and nodded to where the others of their party had gathered in a knot by the fireplace. "Let's join the others, shall we?"

She was ready enough to do so and told herself he was merely seeking safety with her and the others.

As they approached, Julia and Joshua turned, saw them, and smiled.

"Caitlin! Just the person we need," Joshua said.

It transpired that, as often happened at such functions, other guests had seized the opportunity to make inquiries about certain products supplied by the Hall residents present that evening, and several quite valuable orders had been proposed.

Caitlin—with Gregory, plainly interested, by her side—went with Vernon to speak with old Mrs. Hyssop, a wealthy widow, about creating a pair of matching epergnes for her son and daughter-in-law.

"They're in London, you see," Mrs. Hyssop explained, "and I gather such things are all the rage. They've seen your work, Vernon, and asked me to see if you were willing."

Between Vernon and Caitlin, they sorted out the details of the order, leaving Mrs. Hyssop smiling.

As they went to step back, Miss Alcott, Mrs. Hyssop's companion, leaned forward to say, "Miss Fergusson, before you go, can I ask you to mention to Miss Penrose that I would like some more of that cream she makes for my joints? It's quite amazing the relief her preparation gives me." Miss Alcott exchanged a meaningful look with Mrs. Hyssop. "So much better than the exercises that new doctor said were all I could do."

Caitlin smiled and assured Miss Alcott she would mention the matter to Alice, who was sure to send over another pot of her salve.

In turning away from the two older ladies, Caitlin met Gregory's eyes. He arched his brows, and she smiled back. Obviously, Hagen had made no good impression there.

Subsequently, she and Gregory helped Percy settle two orders for straight-backed chairs. In between, Caitlin collected several more orders for Alice, along with two other veiled yet disparaging references to "that new man in Wellingborough."

The most valuable order of the evening came from Sir Henry Ratcliffe, the master of the local hunt. After chatting with Gregory about the sport the hunt had recently seen, Sir Henry turned to Caitlin. "M'dear, I need you to help get me out of the briars. I'd promised to see to getting a new gig for her ladyship, but what with one thing and another, it totally slipped my mind." Sir Henry glanced at Gregory. "Best gigs in the county come from Jenkins and his lads, you know. We at Ratcliffe Hall swear by their workmanship." Sir Henry turned pleading eyes on Caitlin. "If you could put in a good word, m'dear, and ask Jenkins if he can manage to produce one in short order—just the standard gig, nothing fancy—I would be greatly in your and Jenkins's debt."

Caitlin patted Sir Henry's arm. "I'll see what Jenkins can do. If you like, I'll send word once he gives me a date."

"Thank you! Having a date for delivery will placate her ladyship somewhat, at least."

With smiles all around, Caitlin and Gregory moved on.

Eventually, Gregory steered them back to the knot of their compatriots from the Hall.

He found himself regarding the group with an odd mix of affection and satisfaction. All in all, they formed an effective team, and he'd started to feel that he was a part of it. To outside eyes, they might appear a strange, eclectic bunch, but having stepped into the shoes Minnie and Timms had fashioned for him, he'd started to view all Hall residents as his. His people—his to protect and nurture. Strange, but true.

Even stranger was that they'd plainly accepted him in his new role, and even with Caitlin as their champion, with Timms now gone, they needed him there—as the owner of Bellamy Hall, with his background and the unassailable social standing that flowed from that—as their support and, where necessary, shield.

While the group chatted, exchanging tidbits of local news gleaned from the wider company, he glanced around the room. The role he'd played that evening was a real one, an ongoing one—a necessary one to keep what he'd come to view as a vital, active, and distinctly worthwhile collection of enterprises functioning.

Some businesses might be able to go it alone, but all the enterprises on the Hall estate hugely benefited from the established collegiality, not just in terms of encouragement and cross-support but also in terms of financial stability.

Not one of the Hall businesses would ever have to worry about going under because of a bad year.

That deepening understanding—not just of the Hall and its businesses but, even more, the role that had fallen to him to fill—continued to develop as, with the others from Bellamy Hall, he drank tea, and eventually, along with all the other guests, they took their leave of their pleased and satisfied hosts.

They were in the coach and rolling home when he realized he'd applied that word—"home"—to the Hall. He never had before, not even in his dreams.

He dwelled on the revelation and, ultimately, acknowledged that he now viewed Bellamy Hall as his home.

He'd come there hoping to find a real and meaningful role for him to fill, one that would satisfy and fulfill him.

And Minnie, Timms, and the Hall and all its residents had delivered precisely that.

After several moments, he glanced at Caitlin, once again seated beside him. Moonlight filtered through bare branches and gently bathed her face. He studied her features for several seconds, then faced forward again.

He was traveling a road—one he'd started down in coming to Bellamy Hall—but he was yet some way from his ultimate destination.

～

They reached the Hall in the small hours, and after descending from the coach and letting themselves into the house, they made their weary way up the stairs and headed down the corridors to their beds.

Gregory and Caitlin were the last to climb the stairs. Moonlight shone through the windows in the cupola above the front hall and lit their way.

Caitlin wobbled as she stepped off the last stair.

Immediately, Gregory gripped her elbow and steadied her.

Her breath hitched, audible in the silence.

Her gaze flew to his face, and his eyes captured hers.

Shadows and a pervading silence surrounded them and, as seconds passed, seemed to draw closer, tighter, isolating them from the world.

In that moment, there was only him and her—and the attraction that flared, hot and strong, between them.

Impulses crashed through him, pricking, prodding, pushing. His grip fractionally tightened.

Her eyes widened and darkened…

They teetered, both of them, on the brink—a heartbeat from acting.

*You need her. You* need *her.*

*In so many ways.*

He clenched his jaw and, fraction by fraction, forced his fingers to ease.

His hand fell from her arm, and finally, he hauled in a huge breath— and the alluring scent of her wreathed through his brain.

The effort to edge half a step back nearly brought him to his knees.

As he shifted, she hauled in a breath, her breasts rising dramatically. Then she nodded, the small movement graceful yet stiff. "Good night."

The whispered words reached him, and with one last look, she turned away.

"Good night," he murmured and watched her walk away along the corridor to her room until the shadows engulfed her and hid her from his sight.

He waited until he heard her door click shut, then he turned and walked slowly to his room.

Per his instructions, Snibbs hadn't waited up for him. Gregory shrugged out of his coat and set it aside, then walked to the uncurtained window.

He stood and stared out, then looked inward.

On one level, he was happy. Truly happy and eager to engage with whatever the next day might bring.

He'd accepted the challenge. He was committed to succeeding.

Over the past weeks, he'd jettisoned his earlier assumptions and, instead, had wholeheartedly embraced the role the strange creation that was Bellamy Hall needed him to fill.

That was the crux of his contentment. He truly was needed there.

If he was honest, he would admit that he'd been smiling more spontaneously and more frequently over recent days. He'd relaxed and was very definitely finding his feet.

He'd started building his life, but he hadn't yet completed the structure.

The larger part of that challenge lay ahead of him.

And he found that satisfying, too.

He reached for the curtains to draw them across the window, but paused as the lingering heat in his veins reminded him of one obvious and necessary aspect of his future he'd yet to tackle.

But he knew what he needed in that respect, too, didn't he?

He would deal with that—in time.

For now…

He drew the curtains closed, turned to the bed, and firmly shifted his thoughts to the events of the evening and the minor yet satisfying successes he, Caitlin, and the other residents had achieved.

Hopefully, the thud in his blood had faded enough to allow him to sleep.

Caitlin lay in her bed and stared, unseeing, at the ceiling.

Her senses were still whirling, her witless mind utterly engrossed in reliving those moments in the darkened gallery. She had no notion how long it might be before her ability to think rationally returned.

Her lips still throbbed, heated and hungry. She'd been a heartbeat from stretching up and offering them to him.

Thank God she hadn't!

*What if I had?*

And therein lay a source of endless vacillation. One part of her—the eager, youthful, brimful-of-confidence, reckless part she'd reined in for so long—wanted to forge ahead, grasp the tiger's tail, and find out what might be, while the sensible, practical, steadfast, and determined part usually in the ascendant, certainly over the past three years, thought that encouraging herself or him to take another step closer would be a very bad idea.

She was the Hall's chatelaine, and he was the Hall's owner.

Both of them had a responsibility to everyone else on the estate, a responsibility she, for one, considered sacred and would never shirk.

From all she'd seen of and experienced with him over recent days, he wasn't about to set aside his responsibility, either.

Although neither she nor anyone else at the Hall had broached the matter with him, the unvoiced consensus of expectation regarding him had shifted. Increasingly, everyone thought—and even more, hoped—that he would stay.

And that, she admitted to herself, might prove problematic.

On several fronts.

# CHAPTER 7

$\mathcal{T}$he next morning, in light of his previous evening's discussion with Reverend Millicombe, Gregory accompanied Caitlin, Alice, Millie, Vernon, Percy, and Joshua to Sunday service at All Saints Church.

Better he show his face now so that, if necessary, he could miss services later without attracting any special notice, or so his reasoning went. The day was, after all, only the second Sunday he'd been at the Hall; for an unmarried gentleman of his ilk, that was perfectly acceptable observance.

He'd descended for breakfast at his usual time, but Caitlin had already been and gone. The next time he'd laid eyes on her was as the group had gathered in the front hall, ready to depart. She'd glanced at him in surprise, then returned his "Good morning" with a murmured greeting and a dip of her head and, thereafter, had endeavored to behave toward him exactly as she had previously.

At least, outwardly.

He'd wrestled his inner wolf into submission over not provoking her skittering senses, to which, after those fraught moments in the gallery the night before, he was now so much more attuned. With respect to her, he was, he told himself, perfectly willing to play a waiting game.

He walked beside her into the church and discovered that Hall residents traditionally occupied the front pews on the left. Consequently, when Reverend Millicombe stood before the congregation, Gregory was front and center and, unsurprisingly, the recipient of a beaming, welcoming smile.

Millicombe proved to be one of those ministers who had an excellent grasp of the patience of his flock. He kept his sermon concise and his prayers to the point.

A bare forty-five minutes later, the congregation rose, and benediction was said, then everyone followed the reverend up the aisle.

Gregory—as befitted his station—was the first to shake the minister's hand. "An excellent service."

Millicombe beamed. "Now you've found your way here, I hope we'll see you often."

Gregory dipped his head in what might be taken for agreement and moved on. He waited while Caitlin smiled at Millicombe and shared something that made the man laugh, then she joined Gregory on the lawn, and he decided feeling jealous of the minister was utterly ludicrous.

As he'd hoped, the church lawn after Sunday service proved an excellent venue in which to meet the wider circle of local gentry in a neutral setting, with the added benefit that ladies with daughters were less likely to attempt to entrap him under the eye of Millicombe and his wife, who came over to introduce herself, having had to miss the dinner the previous evening due to an illness among the parish flock.

While milling on the lawn, Gregory spotted several of the estate families—those who did not live at the Hall itself—and made a point of exchanging a few words with each group. That seemed to please everyone, including his chatelaine.

He politely asked for introductions to those of the local gentry he hadn't yet met and Caitlin obliged. They also spent a pleasant few minutes chatting with the Loxtons and Mrs. Hyssop and Miss Alcott.

All in all, the outing lived up to his expectations of a pleasant, relaxed country Sunday morning and, he hoped, went some way toward easing his chatelaine's nerves.

After luncheon—a delicious meal that had prompted Gregory and everyone else to send heartfelt compliments to Nessie—he retreated to the library and settled with the ledgers containing the notes of what Caitlin had called the "estate meetings." She'd assured him that he would understand once he read them, and sure enough, after scanning several pages, he appreciated the purpose of the gatherings held at the end of the first week of every month. The notes—detailed yet concise in Caitlin's neat script—recorded the issues discussed, most often some change in circumstances that impacted more than one business.

In the end, he started at the beginning of the previous year and worked his way forward month by month, noting those issues that had been raised and the subsequent reports on how they'd been resolved.

Most had, indeed, been dealt with, yet as of the beginning of the current year, three issues remained outstanding. One was whether the estate needed to investigate shoring up the riverbanks—there were pros and cons—and another was a proposal to extend the chicken coops and enclosures to include a large barn. He was puzzled over why that apparently involved the Bartons of Barton Farm, Julia and the vegetable gardens, and Alice's growing of herbs in the rose garden. There was also a combined project put forward by Jenkins and the Kirks over creating a new yard and storage barn to service both the carriage works and the forge.

Those three proposals had arisen over the past four months, but it was plain from the notes of the most recent meeting, in early February, that Timms's death had stalled all further decisions. Instead, much of that last meeting had been taken up with discussing what those attending expected regarding the new owner.

Wryly, Gregory noted that Caitlin had recorded little of what had been said.

He jotted a list of the three pending proposals, then read back over the notes to glean as much detail as he could.

No doubt because everyone attending would have readily understood what was being suggested, the notes weren't all that much help.

He shut the book containing the notes of the two meetings this year and reached for the other still-open volume that contained the notes from the previous year, intending to shut that as well, when he recalled seeing, at the beginning of that ledger, a list of unresolved issues from the year before. He drew the book to him and found that first page. He ran his finger and his mind down the list. While most of the issues had subsequently been resolved, three, all hailing from '50 at least, were still outstanding.

That seemed strange.

He flicked through the '51 meetings, but while those outstanding issues had been mentioned here and there, they hadn't been further addressed.

He grunted, picked up his pencil, and added those to his list of unresolved issues—the need for a new storage building to be shared by the cider mill and the Osiery, a wood store for general use, and the introduction of a special type of flue to better vent the forge.

All six unresolved proposals altered land use or established structures and thus might well require permission from him as owner. He shut the ledger and set it aside, folded the list, tucked it into his coat pocket, rose, and went in search of his chatelaine-cum-steward.

After several unproductive casts, he ran her to earth in the walled kitchen garden, talking with Julia.

When he joined them, Julia explained that she and her helpers were taking stock of the currently half-empty beds and ruminating on what to grow where in the coming season. "It's important to move things around, you see. Crop rotation, as it were. That makes a sizeable difference to our yields, just as it does with grains and such."

"I see." Before he could say anything else, Julia launched into a description of the tasks needed to be completed in preparation for planting various crops.

He glanced at Caitlin and took in her serene expression—an expression he was coming to understand meant she was thinking of something else. He returned his attention to Julia, still in full dramatic flight, and when she paused for breath, leapt in to say, "It certainly sounds as if you and your helpers"—he nodded encouragingly at Fred and Moll, who had continued digging and weeding respectively—"have a great deal to do before spring comes in."

Thrown off her verbal stride, Julia blinked, then nodded. "Indeed."

"I daresay Caitlin and I should leave you to it." He caught Caitlin's eye. "I have some matters to discuss...unless you and Julia have more details to iron out?"

"No, no." Caitlin smiled brightly—and gratefully—and turned to Julia. "I'll add those extra seeds to the order."

"Thank you." Julia looked around her and frowned. "And yes, I really should get on."

She waved them off, and hiding grins, they started back along the grassy central aisle.

Caitlin sighed. "Julia never knows when to stop—she's so devoted to getting her produce to grow that I think her head is full to bursting with everything to do with that, and once she opens her lips, it all comes pouring out."

"It does seem that way."

She slanted him a glance. "Did you come purely to rescue me, or do you truly have matters to discuss?"

"The latter. Rescuing you was serendipitous. I went through the notes of the estate meetings and found six projects that have yet to be approved." He tugged the list from his pocket and held it out.

She halted under the entrance archway and took it.

He stopped and watched as, with an incipient frown tangling her brows, she scanned the sheet.

"I realize," he said, "that the first three are relatively recent and presumably stalled because of Timms's passing, but the earlier three are also still pending." When she looked up, he caught her eye. "Is there a reason for that? I didn't find any note of the proposals being rejected. They just haven't progressed."

Caitlin glanced around, then pointed to a bench set against the warm stone of the garden wall. "Let's sit."

Once they had, with the wall warm at their backs and the weak afternoon sunshine on their faces, blocking her senses as best she could, she handed him the list and explained, "There are limits to the decisions the business owners—as part owners of the Bellamy Hall Fund—can make regarding physical structures on the estate. All such decisions require the explicit approval of the owner of Bellamy Hall. Essentially, the Fund operates as a cooperative support for the businesses themselves, with the payments for upkeep and maintenance of the Hall viewed as being in lieu of rental."

He frowned. "So maintenance and upkeep…"

"Those, we—meaning Cromwell and I—can arrange without referring to the owner."

He nodded. "But capital works—unsurprisingly—require the owner's specific approval." He glanced at the list. "I had wondered if that was the case."

Determined to ignore the impact of his nearness, she pointed at the first three items. "Those were, as you guessed, stalled because of Timms's death, but with the earlier three, the owners decided that although all three would be required at some point, none were urgent enough to bother Timms. She was meticulous in reviewing the details of such projects, but at that time, she was already ailing, and no one wanted to unnecessarily add to the weight on her shoulders."

She shook her head. "She simply didn't have strength to spare. We wanted to keep her with us for as long as possible, so we put off bringing those projects forward."

"But they're not on the list you made at the start of this year."

"They should have been." She frowned. "I suppose we lost sight of them while working on projects we could advance."

He flicked the list. "So as of now, we have six projects to pursue."

The eagerness in his voice made her smile. "The group meets at the end of this week—on Friday in the study."

He tucked the list back into his pocket. "Can I suggest we move the meetings to the library? Given the size of the gathering, we'll be more comfortable there."

He rose, and she followed suit, smiling as she dipped her head his way. "I'm sure everyone will agree to that."

"Excellent." He glanced at her. "You might spread the word that, on Friday, after the group has dealt with whatever is on their collective plate, I would like to discuss which of these six projects should be commenced first."

They started toward the house, and she grinned. "You'll make everyone very happy."

"Including the chatelaine-cum-steward who looks after the Fund's books?"

She told her leaping heart to desist and raised her chin. "The Fund's accounts are exceedingly healthy, and to be frank, I'll be happier seeing the money put to use—to work, as it were—instead of simply sitting in the bank."

Gregory smiled at the prospect of being actively involved in seeing six projects to completion. "Speaking as the estate's owner, I'm looking forward to making these proposals reality."

That was the unvarnished truth; the thought of having a useful and necessary role to play warmed him. This was what he'd arrived at Bellamy Hall hoping to find, and salvation was there, waiting for him to grasp it.

They crossed the rectangle of lawn, making for the drive.

Caitlin felt deeply pleased by yet more evidence that he intended to be an active owner and also by his transparent readiness to oversee the projects in question, all of which were beyond her ability to manage.

Construction wasn't her forte, but his enthusiasm suggested he felt confident in that arena.

As the sunshine bathed them, she raised her face to the warmth and, lids low, acknowledged how content she was with the way matters were playing out.

The sole of her half-boot skidded on the edging of the drive.

"Oh!" She fought to regain her balance, but started falling backward.

A strong arm banded her back, and Gregory jerked her upright against him.

She smothered a squeal, but then her breasts pressed into his chest, and her eyes met his—and every last smidgen of breath left her lungs.

Even the desire to breathe deserted her.

Time froze while her senses rioted.

The peaks of her breasts crinkled tight. With her gaze locked with his, she fell into the rich moss green of his eyes.

And he stared into hers.

Behind his hazel gaze, she saw…something that made her lungs tighten even more.

That elusive, insubstantial entity prowled, predatory, powerful, yet she sensed that it yearned…

His gaze lowered to her lips, and they throbbed.

And she yearned, too…

She blinked.

She had no idea how long they'd stood there, on the edge of the lawn with her held tight, locked against him.

Her bonnet was askew. Her gaze fixed on his face, slowly, she raised the hand that had come to rest, half gripping, on his shoulder and reached for her headgear.

With his gaze still locked on her lips, he dragged in a breath—as if he was as starved of air as she.

Against her curves, impressed upon them, every muscle in his body felt like tempered steel, even as she registered them tensing further.

Then he moved. Slowly, deliberately—as if she was composed of the most fragile spun glass that might shatter if he moved too quickly—he eased his hold on her. He shifted her fractionally away, setting her on her feet, then stepped back, steadying her.

The instant she stood straight, his arms and hands fell from her.

Immediately, she missed the warmth of his body against hers, missed the sensations…

*Good Lord.*

Her lips ached, as did some urgent impulse inside her.

*I wanted him to kiss me.*

The realization shocked her back to the world.

She tried to speak, then cleared her throat and managed, "Thank you. I…slipped."

"I know." Fleetingly, he met her gaze, then his lashes lowered, hiding his eyes. His voice was deeper and rougher than usual; the resonance reverberated through her breastbone.

She dragged in another breath and forced her gaze across the drive, telling herself she was glad he'd drawn back so she could fill her lungs again.

*What a lie.*

Weakly, she gestured toward the house and started walking.

After an instant's hesitation, he fell in beside her, but as they continued to the house's north door, she was aware that he kept a careful yard between them.

Gone was the relaxed camaraderie of only minutes before. In its place was a heightened awareness that crawled like tiny ants over her skin, setting it prickling and her nerves leaping—in anticipation of a touch that might or might not come.

He reached for the door, pushed it open, waved her inside, then followed.

In the dimness of the corridor, she glanced his way and airily said, "I need to check with Nessie."

His "Of course" sounded strangely distant. His parting nod seemed aloof as well.

She inclined her head in return, then walked down the corridor toward the kitchen—and felt his gaze on her back until she turned the corner and passed out of his sight.

She told herself they would both soon forget the fraught tension of that unexpected moment and revert to how they'd been before, but when afternoon tea was served in the drawing room, as it was on Sunday afternoons, and he walked in to join the company, it was immediately borne in on her, courtesy of her leaping senses, that she'd yet to regain her previous equilibrium.

He smiled and chatted to Julia, who'd undertaken to dispense the tea.

Caitlin remained on the sofa, beside Alice, and kept her gaze fixed on the apothecary's face as she and Millie, on Alice's other side, ran through the herbs they'd managed to acquire during their visit to Alice's friend in Northampton.

"She's found an excellent source of angelica," Alice said, "which is good news for Nessie—she likes to use it in her cakes."

Smiling encouragingly, Caitlin pretended to be interested, but in reality, her attention was locked on the tall figure sipping tea by the fireplace.

Her overactive senses informed her that his gaze had been resting on her for several minutes, but she refused to glance in his direction.

Eventually, he finished his tea, returned his cup to the trolley, and with a general smile and nod, left the room.

She breathed a touch easier.

*I need to keep my head.*

The little voice in her mind was full of sensible directions, but less helpful in explaining how she was to achieve its promptings.

*I need to keep my place here.*

At least for another few years. She couldn't afford to become overly sensitive—missish and mawkish—over him. She couldn't leave. Where would she go?

Of course, there was no viable answer to that, none that would suit her anywhere near as well as being the chatelaine of Bellamy Hall.

Gregory looked down the dining table at his chatelaine-cum-steward and fought back a scowl.

Not solely because she was avoiding him—although as far as his inner wolf was concerned, that was bad enough—but because, despite his most earnest efforts, he couldn't haul his senses from their fixation on her.

He'd never been so afflicted. Ladies were as ladies went; a single, specific lady should have no claim on his awareness, not in the all-consuming way Caitlin Fergusson captured every iota of his attention.

He could pretend otherwise, of course—he was a past master at social pretense—but even while he chatted with Percy and Vernon, who were flanking him at the table that evening, his every sense remained acutely aware of each and every little move Caitlin made.

That afternoon, when she'd landed in his arms—or rather, when he'd hauled her against him and locked her there—the wolf inside him had exulted. In common with his peers, he'd found his sexual desires easy to sate over his years in the ton. More recently, that side of him had grown strangely bored with what was on offer, resulting in a more restless questing, driven by a need for...something more. Something beyond mere sexual gratification.

He couldn't define what that something was, but the instant he'd set eyes on Caitlin Fergusson, his inner self had been convinced that she held the answer to his undefined need.

When he'd had her in his arms, her soft, feminine body and luscious lips had lured him, and he'd wanted nothing more than to seize.

He very nearly had; the impulse had almost overridden his usually ironclad control.

The strength of his reaction had shaken him, but the power in it had further honed his senses, and that underlying impulse—his underlying need—hadn't faded or even dimmed beneath his reasserted control.

Consequently, while outwardly relaxed, as he chatted and smiled with the others, he watched Caitlin and brooded.

His fixation wasn't going to go away; of that, he was now certain. Worse, it had already reached an intensity that made it impossible to ignore.

That meant he was going to have to do something about it.

He couldn't continue in this vein, constantly being so highly aware and so very tense around her; he was going to have to move forward in some way.

*How?*

He'd established beyond all doubt that he needed her help in managing the estate, let alone the household. He couldn't afford to offend her, and the very last thing he wanted to do was to make her uncomfortable to the point she left.

He knew—had known from the first—that he affected her. What he didn't know was in what way. Was she attracted or made uneasy?

That afternoon...for several seconds, he'd thought that she was as deeply, fundamentally ensnared as he, but then she'd apologized and, far too calmly, gone about her business.

Then, during afternoon tea, she'd sent a strong signal by essentially cutting all contact.

Or so it had seemed.

Eyes narrowing fractionally, he studied her down the length of the table. In truth, he wasn't at all sure she wasn't every bit as adept at social pretense as he.

Later, by hook and by crook, he ensured that, as had previously occurred on several evenings, he and Caitlin were the last to go upstairs.

Side by side, they climbed, while behind them, Cromwell took the last lamp left burning in the front hall and vanished through the green-baize-covered door. The door swung shut, and the light behind them died.

Moonlight streamed through the windows in the cupola high above and lit their way. Deeper in the corridors, small wall sconces had been left burning low. One of the footmen would do the rounds at midnight, turning them off and plunging the house into Stygian darkness.

Deliberately, Gregory matched his pace to Caitlin's.

His skin itched with the need to gather her in, with the need to see if...

Beside her, he stepped into the shadowy gallery, the space illuminated solely by diffuse moonlight.

She halted and swung to face him, and he sensed—clearly—that she drew breath and armored herself to meet his gaze.

Instinctively, he responded to the unvoiced challenge and, when he halted, was mere inches away. Close enough that she had to look up to meet his eyes, allowing the moonlight to bathe her face well enough for him to see...

An intense awareness that mirrored his own.

She tried to speak, cleared her throat, and tried again. "Good night." Through huge, luminous eyes, she stared at him as she moistened her lips with the tip of her tongue.

Only the certain knowledge that she was an innocent and the teasing gesture entirely unintentional allowed him to keep his hands at his sides. Regardless, he fisted them against the welling urge to seize her and...

"And about what happened this afternoon, I wanted to thank you—again...for saving me from falling."

*I want you to fall a lot further, all the way into my arms.*

The effort of holding back both words and associated deeds left him leaning—teetering—closer, and he heard her breath catch, saw desire widen her darkened eyes, saw one delicate hand rise as if to seize him as her gaze fastened on his lips.

She was every bit as captive to the desire that flashed between them as he was.

If he took one tiny step closer…what would happen?

He didn't know the answer, and belatedly, experience raised its head and screamed at him—loudly enough for a mind nearly overwhelmed by lust to hear—to stop.

If he touched her now, if he drew her into his arms…he wouldn't be in control.

Not tonight.

Not until he gained some perspective.

She was no lightskirt; he couldn't take advantage of her innocence, and on top of all else, she was living under his roof, literally under his protection.

That was one line he would never cross.

Shackling his instincts and drawing back, easing back from the moonlit brink, was harder than he'd expected, but he clenched his jaw and shoved his unruly impulses deep. Then he drew in enough air to incline his head and, with passable composure, say, "That was, I assure you, entirely my pleasure."

The flash of astonishment in her eyes that he glimpsed as he turned away assured him that she'd heard his true meaning.

"Good night," he called and forced himself to walk toward his room, leaving her where she stood rather than taking her with him.

Sometime during the restless, near-sleepless night Gregory endured after he'd left Caitlin staring at him in stunned surprise in the gallery, he made up his mind to find some way to move forward with her, at least sufficiently to define what might or might not be.

Having decided on that, when he met her at the breakfast table, he took due note of her wary watchfulness and elected to advance slowly.

On Monday afternoon, rather than summoning her to the library—his domain—he tapped on the study door. When she bade him enter, he claimed the chair before her desk and, ignoring her surprise and the suspicion lurking behind it, proceeded to discuss the six pending projects, specifically to determine which she and, from his limited observations, he deemed most urgent.

With the steady expansion of orders for the Pooles' basketry products plus the increased demand for the Edgars' cider, they agreed that the proposed storehouse to be shared by those businesses should be the first project they got underway.

For the rest of the day, they danced around each other, both being careful not to trigger the other's defenses by any inadvertent touch or brush of a shoulder or arm.

Having to watch his every move while, simultaneously, being so excruciatingly aware of her every breath was, he discovered, exhausting.

Consequently, the following day, he left her to complete her usual morning's round of the businesses close to the Hall in the hope that their mutual awareness would ease sufficiently for him to make some progress, however slight, later in the day. Subsequently, by mutual arrangement, after luncheon, they set out—just the pair of them—to walk to the Osiery and the cider mill to discuss the proposed project with the Pooles and the Edgars and scout out the best site for the new storehouse.

Both rugged up against the chilly breeze, they walked briskly past the ruins and on down the path to the river. Looking around, he debated whether to speak now or later.

It was early March, and the first tentative signs of life were showing in the woods that bordered the path, but there was no one else in sight, nothing and no one likely to interrupt a discussion of a personal nature.

And yet...he was conscious of a reluctance to open his lips and speak —to take the risk he had to take and indicate his interest. After all, they had business to deal with; it wouldn't be wise to create awkwardness between them ahead of their meeting with the Pooles and the Edgars. He —and Caitlin—would be better served by him waiting until they were on their way back.

*Best I wait and broach the subject then.*

Somehow.

Yet as the decision echoed in his mind, some small part of him disapproved.

*Isn't this what I always do? Step back from actually taking any step that might significantly alter my future?*

He hid a frown as that small yet determined part nagged, irritated by his inaction. Introspection had never come easily, yet after several moments of consideration, he admitted that he'd developed a habit of waiting to assess how matters might play out rather than make any preemptive proactive move. In retrospect, that habit of waiting for something to happen had contributed in a fairly major way to his lack of any defined purpose in his life.

"Waiting for something to happen" was deliberately passive, and although he didn't like even thinking of himself in such terms, he usually fell into that rut.

He couldn't afford to this time. He wasn't of a mind to risk "something happening" and Caitlin and the nebulous possibility she represented —one he hadn't yet examined all that closely—slipping through his fingers.

She might well have family somewhere. What if one of them fell ill, and she was summoned home? It wouldn't be easy or straightforward for him to leave the Hall to follow and plead his cause somewhere else.

He canvassed the potential problems as a way of screwing up his courage to the sticking point, yet in reality, it wasn't courage he lacked but the will to act.

Today, he swore, he would turn over a new leaf and act rather than wait.

When they were on their way back, the instant an opening appeared, he would seize it and speak.

Just what was he going to say?

Beside Gregory, Caitlin fought a losing battle to keep her mind focused on the new storehouse. She'd given up all hope of dampening her senses to the apparently unavoidable impact of him walking beside her.

They were separated by a perfectly decent space, but that didn't seem to matter. Since that moment she'd spent clutched in his arms, her sensitivity to him had escalated, and her senses' clamoring had grown ever more insistent.

Indeed, the possibility that he was as interested in her as she was in him had eradicated any hope she might have had of reining in her thoughts and potentially foolish imaginings.

It was decidedly unfair that ladies were forced to play a passive role in such matters. If it were left to her, she would face the question of what might or might not lie between them head-on. And if something didn't happen soon to clarify what he thought, she would lose all patience and demand to be told…

Oh, how that prospect tempted her!

In desperation, she wrenched her mind away from the entire subject of her and him and what might be and bluntly asked, "How big do you think the storehouse should be?"

He replied by asking how much space was currently devoted to the completed products of the two businesses.

The query allowed her to distract herself with calculating estimations based on the orders presently waiting to be fulfilled.

They were nearing the riverbank and the osier beds when Gregory pointed to a distant figure, rhythmically wielding a spade close by the bank of the swiftly moving Nene. "What's William doing?"

She looked, then replied, "I suspect he's digging out a dead willow. I gather that, in this season, while he won't be cutting canes, there's still a lot of tending and preparing and cultivating of the willow beds. Apparently digging out or at least breaking up the older rotting stumps allows the surrounding younger willows to spread and, ultimately, yield more shoots."

"I see."

They watched William as they continued along the path, then they and the path swung toward the Osiery, and they left William behind.

Mrs. Poole came out to meet them. After exchanging greetings, they explained their quest, which unsurprisingly gained Mrs. Poole's enthusiastic backing. "I'd almost forgotten about that!" she exclaimed. "One does grow so accustomed to making do."

They discussed the likely construction—stone walls, with a solid timber floor and a good slate roof—then spent some time assessing the space required. In the end, at Gregory's suggestion, they went into the existing building and measured up the space currently given over to storage—crammed storage at that—and tripled it.

Mrs. Poole nodded. "That should give us ample for now as well as room to grow."

They emerged from the building, and Gregory waved toward the cider mill downstream. "As the storehouse is to serve the Osiery and the cider mill, I assume the best place to build it will lie somewhere between."

Mrs. Poole gestured toward the mill. "There's a spot the Edgars and I looked at when we first proposed the storehouse. I can show you if you'd like?"

Caitlin and Gregory readily agreed, and after Mrs. Poole stepped back into the Osiery to let Hattie know she was heading down the path, the three of them set out.

Immediately beyond the Osiery, the path angled to more closely follow the rushing river toward the cider mill and the leatherworks beyond.

They'd just reached the river's edge when a great cry rang out, followed by a distant splash.

They all spun toward the sound, which had come from the other side of the Osiery.

"Oh my God!" Mrs. Poole paled and clapped her hands to her cheeks. "William!"

They all rushed to the edge of the sharply cut bank and peered upstream, toward the osier beds.

"There!" Caitlin pointed to a bobbing dark head and flailing arms.

"He can't swim strongly!" Mrs. Poole wailed. "He's going to drown!"

Gregory cursed and shrugged out of his overcoat, coat, and waistcoat. He thrust the garments at Caitlin, then unwound the muffler from about his neck and gave that to her as well. He didn't have time to take off his boots. He only had a minute to get out in the water if he was to have any hope of intercepting the panicking lad.

He went quickly down the crumbling bank, half sliding as the soft earth gave beneath his weight. Gritting his teeth against the icy coldness, he strode into the rushing water, wary as his boots slipped on the stones lining the riverbed. He locked his gaze on William's head, gauged the power of the water rushing past, then hauled in a breath and plunged into the torrent.

Ignoring the shock of the icy water's embrace, he struck out on a course across the river, angling to intersect William's as the lad was swept downstream.

Although the river was running high, it wasn't outright raging. He was strong enough to battle against the current, pausing now and again to track William.

He realized the lad had caught and was clinging to a broken branch, but both remained trapped in the center of the river, where the current was strongest.

Gregory tacked to where he thought the river would bring William.

*Yes, there!*

He lunged, and his hand hit the end of the branch. He gripped it and surfaced, then shook his hair from his eyes and, along the sodden limb, met William's terrified gaze. "Can you hang on while I drag you to shore?"

"Y-Y-Yes!" William nodded frantically.

"All right." Gregory took stock, then swam around so that he could steer with one arm while dragging the branch behind him. "Just hold on with both hands. Don't try to swim—just use your legs to keep afloat."

Teeth chattering, William nodded.

Gregory started dragging the branch, the lad, and himself toward the shore. Making headway proved more difficult than he'd expected. He was a strong swimmer, but the icy current sapped his energy.

He made inching progress, battling to edge across while simultaneously keeping the current from sweeping them too far and too fast downstream. He started to worry that William, who had to be frozen and who'd ceased even his weak kicking, would lose his grip on the branch. If that happened...

Clenching his jaw to keep his teeth from chattering, Gregory pushed on.

Finally, he got them out of the swiftly running central current, and the drag on his limbs lessened. The cold, however, intensified until the resulting ache seeped into his bones.

He was yards from shore and starting to flag when he heard Caitlin call his name, then a rope slapped into the water just short of his face. He grabbed it and, with a few quick circles of his free arm, wound the rope securely about that forearm, and gripped it tightly.

"Hold on!" Caitlin yelled.

He blinked water from his lashes and looked toward the bank to see Caitlin, Mrs. Poole, and Hattie all grimly anchored one behind the other. They started hauling on the rope.

The rope went taut, then drew him—and the branch and William— slowly but steadily through the water.

Relief flooded him, but did nothing to counteract the cold.

Foot by foot, the women dragged them closer to the bank. Gregory kicked to help them, but it was a weak effort. He looked at William. The lad was done in, but had kept his arms wrapped stubbornly around the branch. "Keep holding on," Gregory encouraged. "We're nearly there."

He looked back to gauge the distance they still had to go and realized he could stand. Relief surged anew, and he put his foot down—only to have the stone he'd thought was on the riverbed roll away.

His boot plunged down into a hole, and suddenly, he was underwater.

He tried to kick upward, only to discover the boot was jammed in a tangle of roots and sodden wood.

Holding his breath, he fought to free his foot, but the boots were too well made; there was no chance of slipping his foot free.

His lungs started to tighten, the urge to breathe building.

He couldn't free the arm trapped in the rope, which the women, not knowing what was happening, were holding taut and lightly tugging, and he couldn't let go of the branch—and William—and use his other hand, either.

For one instant, panic—real fear for his life—gripped him.

*No! I've far too much to live for.*

Eyes closed, lungs burning, chilled to the bone, he pulled back on the rope and, using that tension for leverage, made one last, massive effort to wrench his boot free.

The roots holding it gave. The boot slid free, and he surfaced on a massive gasp.

"Oh, thank God! Thank God!"

The chorus in three voices fell on his ears, then Caitlin, firm and decisive, called, "Just hold on, and we'll pull you in. Just concentrate on holding on!"

It was an order, and in truth, with his strength exhausted, holding on was all he could do.

# CHAPTER 8

*G*rimly determined, working hand over hand, with Mrs. Poole and Hattie, Caitlin strove to pull the men to shore.

The river seemed reluctant to let its captives go, but although their arms burned and their backs ached, neither she nor the other women were about to surrender their precious cargo.

Finally—*finally!*—Gregory staggered onto the lower level of the bank. This wasn't the spot where he'd gone in but farther downstream, where the bank was more stable, and below its lip, a narrow arc of earth formed a cove.

Before he could collapse on the wet ground, Caitlin dropped the rope and leapt down. She managed to duck her shoulder under his and balance his weight while Mrs. Poole and Hattie, who had followed her lead in jumping down, dragged William from the water.

Gregory swayed, and Caitlin wrapped her arms around him and hugged tight. "Are you all right?" A necessary if stupid question.

He looked down at his boots as if surprised to see them at the ends of his legs. "My legs feel like jelly."

She nodded briskly. "You're exhausted." So was she, and she hadn't even gone into the water. Her heart was still racing and pounding. "Here." She steered him to the corner of the small cove where tumbled rocks would serve as steps. "We need to return to the Pooles' and get you warm and dry."

He made an indistinct sound, then weakly sighed, "Warm and dry sounds heavenly."

She glanced back, confirming that William was safely in the hands of his mother, who was ordering Hattie to run back to the house and bring blankets. Hattie promptly leapt up to the bank and ran off.

Caitlin faced forward and put her mind to carefully maneuvering a man who was significantly larger and weighed a great deal more than she did, but whose legs were decidedly wobbly, over the stones and up to the bank.

It was another trial, but together, they conquered it.

At Gregory's suggestion, she left him propped against a nearby tree and went to help Lucinda with William. In the end, Caitlin grasped William's wrists and pulled while Lucinda pushed from behind in order to get William—who was close to collapse—up to the bank.

As soon as Lucinda, who was tallish and strong, had William in hand again, Caitlin collected Gregory's clothes and hurried back to him. After persuading and prodding him into the overcoat, she wrapped his muffler around his neck, draped his coat and waistcoat over her arm, then caught one of his limp arms and drew it over her shoulder. Drawing him away from the support of the tree, she gripped his waist tightly. "Come along— it's not that far."

Of course, the Pooles' cottage was farther than any of them liked. They hadn't gone any great distance before Hattie came pelting back with two thick blankets. Caitlin took one and wrapped it tightly around Gregory, who had started to shiver uncontrollably. His face was white, and every inch of skin she could see seemed the same—close to frozen.

Resuming her place by his side, she urged him on and tried not to think of all the stories of people who survived potentially lethal accidents only to die later of some complication, like a chill or a fever of the lungs.

He was still breathing and more or less walking. She told herself to cling to that and focus on getting him warm again.

The hundred or so yards to the Pooles' cottage seemed like miles, but eventually, hugely relieved that they'd made the distance, she eased a stumbling Gregory through the door. Lucinda had sent Hattie back to the cottage to build up the fire and put water on to boil. As the warmth of the cottage enveloped them, she steered Gregory toward one of the stools set before the hearth. "Hattie, your mother might need help."

Lucinda and William had fallen behind. Hattie nodded and, her eyes wide, raced out of the cottage.

Caitlin eased Gregory down to the stool. Once she was sure he was balanced there, she went to step away, but he caught her hand and, to her surprise, carried it to his lips and brushed an icy kiss to her knuckles.

"Thank you," he croaked.

Her heart was thudding hard and fast. She took refuge in a snort. "I didn't do anything—it was you who jumped into the river."

His lids had drifted closed, but his lips curved in a small smile. "But it was you who thought of fetching the rope, wasn't it?"

Puzzled, she admitted, "Yes."

His tone sank low as he said, "If it hadn't been for that rope..."

She gripped his shoulder hard. "Don't even think it. You're here, and William is, too. That's all that matters."

At that moment, the Pooles arrived and shuffled inside, and Hattie and Lucinda settled William on the second stool. Caitlin rushed to close the door, and Hattie bent and quickly built the already decent fire into a roaring blaze.

Without further ado, the three women set about doing what, in such situations, women always did, namely caring for their menfolk.

They urged William to strip off his wet clothes. Lucinda held up a blanket to protect his modesty, and Hattie brought him dry clothes to don.

"What happened?" Lucinda asked. "You're too experienced to have just fallen in."

From behind the blanket, William mumbled, "It was the root I was hacking to pieces. It was a yard or more back from the bank—safe enough, I thought. Turned out the river had undercut the bank just there, and suddenly, the whole section gave way, and I was in the water."

Lucinda turned her head and, her face a picture of gratitude, looked at Gregory. "Just as well Mr. Cynster was here."

Gregory managed a weak smile and an even weaker dismissive wave. "I only did what any other strong swimmer would have."

"Nevertheless, you have this family's eternal thanks," Lucinda sternly replied, her tone brooking no argument.

Gregory had the sense to smile sweetly and keep his lips shut.

Caitlin had prepared tea and supplied him with a tin mug of the strong, highly sweetened brew and set another mug aside for William.

Once they had William in dry clothes and sitting on the stool, sipping tea, Caitlin and Lucinda studied the lad.

"How do you feel?" Lucinda asked.

William meekly replied, "Chilled to the bone, but the fire and the tea are thawing me out. I swallowed some water, but other than that"—one at a time, he stretched out his long legs, then his arms—"I took no hurt." He glanced at Gregory. "Thanks to Mr. Cynster." He raised his mug to Gregory. "My deepest thanks, sir."

Again, Gregory simply smiled.

Arms crossed, Caitlin regarded William, then glanced at Lucinda. "I'll ask Alice to come down and take a look at him. No need to risk any chest complaints."

Lucinda laid a hand on her arm. "Thank you, my dear. That would greatly ease my mind. Indeed, it was and is a blessing that you are with us as well."

Caitlin also knew to simply smile at comments like that. Briskly, she swung to study Gregory. "Your turn."

His eyes, until then hidden beneath his hooded lids, opened wide. "What?"

Lucinda flicked out the modesty blanket and turned toward him as Caitlin explained, "You need to get out of those sodden clothes."

He stared at the blanket, then at her. "And into what, pray tell?"

That question proved unanswerable.

He was much broader in the shoulders than the slight William, as well as being considerably taller. He grew more and more doggedly resistant to the idea of stripping out of his wet things and, eventually, stood up, shrugged off his overcoat and, spreading his arms and legs, arrayed himself before the fire. As the heat penetrated his clothes, they steamed.

"There," he said challengingly. "I'll be dry enough, soon enough."

Along with Lucinda, Caitlin pressed her lips tight and forbore to point out that his breeches were of tightly woven twill and wouldn't dry quickly, and as for his boots, they still squelched.

Accepting defeat, she thought quickly. The Pooles kept no horse, borrowing those at the Hall or going with neighbors when they needed to venture beyond the estate. She turned to Lucinda and asked if Hattie might go to the Hall and return with the Hall's gig.

Gregory huffed and pointed out that he and she could walk the distance more rapidly than Hattie could return with the gig, and having thought of that, he insisted that walking briskly back to the Hall would, indeed, be the best solution for him. "It'll get my blood flowing, and I'll dry out along the way."

Caitlin glared at him.

He smiled winningly at her. "And once we arrive, I promise to get into a hot bath as soon as you and Snibbs organize one."

She humphed.

Lucinda suggested a compromise, to which he reluctantly agreed. He stripped off his thin and still-damp linen shirt and donned his waistcoat, coat, and overcoat, then allowed Caitlin to rewrap the knitted muffler snugly about his neck.

She didn't meet his eyes, even when she stepped back. She was still struggling to calm her fluster on seeing his naked, exceedingly well-muscled chest. The bunch and play of muscles under his taut skin had been...mesmerizing.

Given she'd seen naked male chests often enough in the past, she was at a loss to account for the distinctly disturbing impact the sight of *his* naked chest had had on her. Her mouth was still watering.

She took refuge in briskness and waved him toward the door. "As you insist on walking back, we should get started."

"Indeed." Lucinda was peering out of the window. "The light's already fading—there might be a storm on the way."

*That's all we need.*

Lucinda turned to Gregory and Caitlin. "Once again, we're deeply in your debt—both of you."

William and Hattie added their fervent thanks as well.

Caitlin left it to Gregory to smile charmingly and demur, then she led the way out of the door Hattie, with a beaming smile of gratitude, held for them.

The chilly breeze that had been blowing earlier had whipped up into an icy wind. Without hesitation or thought, Caitlin took Gregory's arm, twining hers with his, so that if he stumbled or weakened, she could steady him.

He glanced at her—she felt his sharp gaze—but after a second's hesitation, he accepted the contact without protest.

They stepped out smartly along the lane to the Hall, and when, after the first hundred yards, he didn't slow, she allowed herself to breathe a touch easier.

The wind was blowing from the north; there was no way she could shield him from it. She kept firmly holding his arm; that seemed all she could do to help him.

But as they started up the long rise to the top of the low hill beside the ruins, she sensed his strength waning and anxiously grumbled, "We should have taken note of the weather and driven out in the gig."

She felt the distinctly amused glance he threw her as he murmured back, "You couldn't have foreseen me needing to go for a dip."

She suppressed a snort, but the comment sent her thoughts back to those moments when he'd been in the river.

Several paces on, she glanced at his face. "When you were swimming to shore, you went under at one point. Why was that?"

He grimaced. "My boot got trapped in submerged roots. For a while, I couldn't get it out, but luckily, with the rope as leverage, I managed to pull free."

Her blood turned to ice in her veins. At the time, she'd nearly panicked, frantically fearing that he would drown.

She wasn't the least bit reassured by his matter-of-fact recounting. She'd been right. He *had* nearly drowned.

*Nearly died.*

She looked up and, when he glanced at her, trapped his gaze.

She stared at him, then abruptly, stopped walking.

With their arms linked, he halted, too. His expression unreadable, he faced her.

She'd come within minutes, perhaps seconds, of losing him.

*Life's too short to waste even a minute.*

She pulled her arm from his, stepped into him, reached up, set her hands to his lean cheeks, and hauled his lips to hers.

She kissed him and invested the caress with every last iota of her fear and the underlying desire that had birthed it.

Deliberately, she flipped the latch on the box in which she corralled her emotions, all those unruly feelings, and set them free. Free to find expression through her lips, through her touch as she gentled her hold and, wonderingly, stroked his skin.

In blatant desperation, she brazenly pressed against him.

She had to know—now, this minute—if he returned even a fraction of her regard. Today, now, had almost been too late to discover what this was between them—this strange, restless, reckless compulsion.

This *need.*

So lost was she in her focus on kissing him—in impressing on him her wishes and desires—that it was several minutes before she realized that he was kissing her back.

Just as hungrily, just as ardently.

More, he was every bit as lost in the moment as she was.

Joy filled her, and she jettisoned any attempt at rational thought and gave herself up to giddy exploration.

Gregory met her questing tongue with his and matched her hungriness with barely controlled greed. She was the epitome of heat and passion in his arms, her full lips gloriously supple and giving under his.

He supped and savored as her warmth, combined with his response to her blatant demands, sent heat surging beneath his skin, vanquishing the lingering chill.

How long they stood in the lane, locked in each other's arms and communing with lips and tongue, he had no idea, but eventually, a sudden gust of wind blasted and blew, rattling the branches of the trees beside the path, rudely jerking them back to awareness of the here and now.

Albeit reluctantly, they drew apart, their lips separating on a mutual sigh, then they looked around and discovered roiling leaden clouds racing down upon them.

"Good Lord!" She looked at him and met his eyes, and all he saw was wonder, but then she blinked, refocused, and frowned. "We need to get back to the Hall before the storm hits. You've been drenched once already today."

In the grip of eye-opening wonder as well, he stared at her and, somewhat inanely, remarked, "There you are." The one woman he desired above all others. The only woman for him. She was that lady; he knew that as surely as he now recognized he'd spent a good portion of the past decade looking for her and never finding her.

Then reality intruded, but before he could locate his wits let alone his customary sophistication, he heard himself say, "I don't even know who you are or what brought you here."

She blinked at him, then she searched his eyes. Whatever she saw there convinced her to open her lips—he knew beyond question she intended to reveal the mystery of her identity—but along with leaping anticipation, a bone-deep shudder wracked him from head to toe.

Her lips snapped shut, and she regarded him with flaring concern. Then her chin set, and she retook his arm and urged him on. Or tried to. When he didn't move, she met his eyes. "We need to hurry. We have to get you back to the Hall and get you warm again—you must see that."

He teetered. The anxiety in her gaze was entirely real—which was compelling—but so, too, was his need to know who she was—

She gave vent to an agitated, frustrated sound. "I *promise* I'll tell you everything you want to know later. Once you're dry and warm and Alice has given you a clean bill of health." She tugged on his arm. *"Please* come on. We need to get back to the Hall."

He didn't have the necessary strength to stand firm against the plea in her voice and her huge pansy eyes, especially not as he'd started shivering uncontrollably again. "All right. But you will tell me later. After dinner."

Relieved, she nodded. "Later, after dinner. Now, come on."

She tugged mightily, and he consented to get moving.

Whoever she was, he was going to marry her, therefore, he would be wise to keep her sweet.

They reached the Hall literally minutes before the clouds opened and a hard downpour pelted the land. Gregory made straight for his room while Caitlin sought out Snibbs and sent him racing up, followed by a pair of footmen lugging a large copper bathtub.

When, two hours later, once more clothed with his usual sartorial elegance and blessedly warm all the way to his bones, Gregory strolled into the drawing room, it was to discover that everyone had heard of his efforts in rescuing William Poole.

After fielding numerous queries as to his health, he finally reached Caitlin, who was standing with several others by the fireplace and sipping a glass of sherry. He directed a narrow-eyed look her way, only to be told, "It wasn't me."

Julia chipped in, "No, indeed." She bent a mock-severe look on Caitlin. "Our dear Caitlin didn't mention a word about your joint exploits, but she did send Alice down to see William, and Alice brought back the news."

Meanwhile, Alice had been examining Gregory with a keen eye. "You don't appear to have taken any lasting injury from your unexpected immersion."

He inclined his head. "I'm a strong swimmer, so other than a temporary weakness, I've felt no ill effects."

"Well, if you do find a cough coming on, be sure to come and see me," Alice warned. "With an apothecary in the house, it would be the height of silliness to develop an unnecessary fever of the lungs."

Interpreting that—he was sure correctly—as a general admonition based on his sex's predilection for not confessing to weaknesses, he merely nodded and kept his lips shut.

When Cromwell appeared to announce that dinner was served, Gregory turned to Caitlin and offered his arm.

She arched her brow at him—he hadn't offered, and she hadn't taken his arm previously—but when he simply waited, she set aside her empty glass and wound her arm with his, and he led her to the door, with the rest of the company falling in behind them.

He could feel the looks trained on his back as others noted his new courtesy to Caitlin, and those gazes felt smug rather than in any way disapproving.

He walked her to her chair and held it for her, and she sat. As he stepped back to walk up the table to his place, he caught her eye.

*Later, after dinner.*

As if she'd heard the unspoken words, she fractionally inclined her head, and he walked on to claim the carver at the table's other end.

The meal passed off in the usual pleasant fashion he'd come to expect of evenings at the Hall. At home. He definitely thought of the place as that, despite the many with whom he shared the roof.

Smiling benevolently, he lifted his wine glass—one Vernon had made —sipped, sat back, and looked around the table. Savoring the enveloping warmth of companionship as various members of the company contributed to a humorous tale about one of Joshua's goats, Gregory inwardly admitted that, in some strange way, he'd fitted into this group quite neatly.

Quite comfortably.

He sipped again, then set down his glass and returned his attention to his meal. As he delighted in Nessie's offerings, he recalled what had taken him and Caitlin to the river that day. They'd spoken to Mrs. Poole, established her requirements, and raised her hopes, but hadn't got much further. They needed to push on. The Pooles and the Edgars often joined the company for dinner on Wednesdays; he made a mental note that if both families arrived at the Hall tomorrow, they would all make time to pursue the matter of the storehouse.

After dessert had arrived and empty dishes were all that remained on the table, the company rose and returned to the drawing room.

In light of Gregory's ordeal, Cromwell insisted on doing the rounds with the brandy decanter, and along with most of the men, Gregory accepted a glass. Naturally, Cromwell filled Gregory's glass half full while the others received the customary two fingers. When Cromwell retreated, the others teased Gregory, but everyone smiled as they did. They all claimed seats and settled to savor and chat.

Gregory had taken his first appreciative mouthful when someone rang the doorbell, then started hammering on the front door.

Everyone paused and looked toward the open doorway; as the hammering continued, Cromwell, with two burly footmen to back him up, hurried past on their way to the door.

The banging abruptly ceased, and as a chill breeze blew into the otherwise warm room, they heard voices in the hall.

The front door was shut, and the waft of cold air dissipated as a low-voiced argument between Cromwell and some other deep-voiced man continued before petering out.

Three seconds later, Cromwell strode stiffly into the drawing room, a large, shaggy-haired presence at his back.

The man drew every eye in the room. He was taller than even Gregory and was dressed in breeches and riding boots, with a heavy jacket over a distinctive waistcoat of green plaid. His hair was a rioting curly mane that was long enough to brush his shoulders, forming a browny-red corona that framed a face of strong, rugged features.

Cromwell neatly stepped aside—permitting everyone an unimpeded view of the giant—and opened his mouth.

"*Rory?*" Caitlin's shocked voice drew all eyes to her as, with her own eyes huge and her gaze fixed on the newcomer's face, she rose from the sofa. "What's happened?"

The man—Rory—looked around the circle of faces, all once more turned his way, then brought his gaze back to Caitlin and, in the thickest Scots burr Gregory had ever heard, announced, "Och, lass. I've come to take you home."

Every gaze swung back to Caitlin.

Eyes narrowing, Caitlin ignored the intrigued looks and kept her gaze locked on Rory. She didn't dare glance at Gregory, not yet. She'd seen the way Rory was assessing the gathering and suspected she knew why he was there. Reaching for calm, she stated, "If nothing's happened, there's no reason for me to leap into a carriage and head north, is there?"

Rory's attention had wandered, but at that, he looked at her, then frowned.

He opened his mouth, but before he could speak, she tipped up her chin and declared, "Because unless there's some urgent need for my presence there, I would much prefer to remain here." She gestured to those around her. "With my *friends*."

Rory studied her. "Friends, heh?"

She nodded decisively. "Yes, *friends*."

He hesitated, then asked, "So you're happy here?" His accent had largely evaporated.

"Perfectly happy. Thank you for being concerned, but there's really no need."

He heaved a huge sigh, then sheepishly grinned at her. "Well, I suppose that's all right, then."

Finally, she glanced at Gregory and waved at Rory. "Allow me to present my cousin, Rory Fergusson." She didn't bother adding that Rory was a Scot; everyone had heard his performance.

Then she realized why him arriving had been such a shock and whipped her gaze back to him. "How on earth did you find me? It's been three years." She'd been so careful; she'd thought she'd been safe.

He shrugged his massive shoulders. "Easy enough. I tracked Samuel." Samuel was her personal groom, who had come south with her. "What with that mane of white hair and him caring for your piebald mare, ostlers tend to remember the pair long after they've passed. It was like you'd blazed a trail."

And for a hunter like Rory, following such a trail would have been easy. She felt rather deflated.

Gregory had watched the interplay between Caitlin and the Scottish mountain. He set down his glass on a side table, smoothly got to his feet, and approaching the Scotsman, offered his hand. "Cynster. Gregory Cynster. Welcome to Bellamy Hall."

Rory eyed him for an instant, then grasped his hand.

Gregory smiled at the pressure the big man exerted, but he had brothers, too, and he'd been ready for it, which made Rory's lashes flicker, and after releasing Gregory's hand, Rory regarded Gregory with a touch more respect.

"Own this place, do you?" Curiosity was written all over Rory's face, along with lingering suspicion.

Still smiling, Gregory nodded. "I do." And Rory's arrival looked set to markedly add to the evening's entertainment, quite aside from revealing considerably more about his mysterious chatelaine.

Caitlin joined them and laid a hand on Rory's arm. With her other hand, she gestured to the company. "Come and let me introduce you to everyone."

With an amiable nod, Rory went with her.

Gregory remained where he was, watching her guide the huge man around the circle of eager residents. Like him, they were exceedingly curious about what Rory's arrival might mean for Caitlin, whom they all valued highly. That point was evident in the way they, in greeting Rory, reflected their protectiveness of her. Smiling to himself, Gregory returned to pick up his glass and finish his brandy.

When Caitlin had completed introducing Rory to the circle of residents, Gregory joined the pair and smoothly suggested, "I daresay your cousin will have much to tell you. Perhaps he, you, and I should retreat to the library, so he can speak freely."

The look of gratitude Caitlin flashed him confirmed he'd read the situation and her wishes correctly. Reassured, he turned a mildly inquiring look on Rory Fergusson and saw that the mountain had noted Caitlin's glance as well.

Slowly, Rory's gaze returned to Gregory's face, and Rory nodded. "Aye. That might be for the best."

Gregory gestured toward the door. It was plain, at least to him, that Rory still harbored suspicions regarding Gregory's interest in Caitlin. As such suspicions were essentially correct, he remained unperturbed. He glanced at the others, arrayed in small groups about the room. "In that case, I believe we'll bid you all a good night."

The others smiled back and murmured their goodnights, including Rory in their benedictions.

After responding to the company, Caitlin grasped Rory's sleeve and led him from the drawing room. Gregory ambled close behind, ultimately stepping around the pair to open the library door and usher them inside.

He waved them to the armchairs grouped before the crackling fire. As he often took refuge in the library of an evening, Cromwell and the footmen made sure the room was prepared and welcoming.

While Rory and Caitlin sank into the well-padded chairs, Gregory crossed to the tantalus, positioned against the wall nearby. He paused before it and caught Rory's eye. "Something to warm you? I have brandy or whisky, if you would prefer it."

Rory was clearly surprised. "A whisky would be welcome. Thank you."

Gregory turned to the decanters and smiled. Not a trace of accent remained in Rory's speech. And as with Caitlin, his instincts were prompting him to treat Rory as an equal.

He returned to the armchairs, handed Rory a tumbler containing a good two fingers of amber liquid, then cradling his own glass, sat in the armchair next to the one Caitlin had chosen, opposite that of their unexpected guest.

He sipped and watched Rory do the same, then grinned at the shock that overtook the man's until-then-straight face.

Rory held up the glass and squinted at the light reflecting in the golden depths. "This is good Scottish whisky." He looked at Gregory in surprise. "Meaning, really good—the stuff we rarely let past our borders."

Gregory chuckled. "Only to family. That's Glencrae's latest release. Eighteen years old, double malt." Snibbs had brought several bottles from London.

Rory took another sip and closed his eyes as he savored. Reverentially, he breathed, "Ambrosia of the gods." Opening his eyes, he looked questioningly at Gregory. "Family, you say?"

Gregory nodded. "One of my father's cousins married the earl, and through that connection, the family—the males, at least—became devotees of the brew."

Rory huffed. "An excellent taste to be able to develop." He sipped again, and his gaze shifted to Caitlin.

Before either man could speak, Caitlin said, "Before we discuss why Rory has arrived"—she leveled a warning look at her cousin, then shifted her gaze to Gregory—"you need to understand what brought me here. What led to me—and Samuel and Mary—being nearby to be caught out in a blizzard and, thus, to seek shelter here."

Gregory inclined his head. "I'm all ears."

Caitlin held his gaze and, wordlessly, tried to convey that what she was about to say was what she'd been planning to tell him that evening. At much the same time, in much the same place. She drew breath and plunged in. "I was born at Benbeoch Manor, outside the village of Dalmellington, in Ayrshire."

Surprise flared briefly in his eyes, and he inclined his head again. "I know it."

She frowned. "You do?"

He hesitated, then gestured for her to continue. "We can return to that later."

Not wanting to lose her rehearsed thread, she nodded and went on,

"My father was the laird of the Fergussons of Benbeoch. He inherited the title and the estate from his uncle. The estate was prosperous and grew more so under my father's stewardship. My parents were blessed with two children, myself and my younger brother. We had the sort of childhood you might expect, and eventually, I was sent to boarding school in Edinburgh. Sadly, however, my brother, who would have inherited the lairdship and the estate both, died of a fever. Even more sadly, not long after that, when I was eighteen, my parents drowned in a boating accident off the Ayrshire coast."

She refocused on Gregory and saw sympathy and compassion in his gaze. She managed a weak smile. "I inherited the manor and associated estate, while the title of laird of the Fergussons passed to my uncle Patrick —my father's younger brother. There was also the usual stipulation that my inheritance be held by a guardian until I reached the age of twenty-five." She paused, looking back on her life at the time. "I was to have been presented in Edinburgh the following year, but of course, I was in mourning. More to the point, I'd been brought up to believe that my future lay in marriage and leaving Benbeoch, so suddenly finding myself responsible for the estate was...an adjustment. Of course, I'd been trained to run the manor household, as most young ladies would have been, but I knew nothing about the estate as a whole, and I'd never thought of it as mine. But Patrick was named my guardian, and he returned from Glasgow and, with my blessing, took up the reins."

She looked at Rory. "Rory is Patrick's oldest son. He has three brothers—Hamish, Daniel, and Morgan. Uncle Patrick's wife, Megan, had died several years before my parents, and when Patrick returned to Benbeoch Manor—which had been his childhood home—he brought his sons with him."

She smiled fondly at Rory, and he grinned back and nodded his great head, no doubt remembering that time as well. She continued, "We all got on well—my cousins and I. We'd known each other since we were infants, and it was a comfort to have the lads around."

"Family," Gregory murmured.

"Yes. Precisely that. Patrick and his brood—noisy, argumentative, and brooding though they often were—filled the empty spaces. For the first few years, we all rolled along quite happily."

She fell silent, falling prey to her memories, and eventually, Gregory prompted, "But...?"

She refocused on his face and, more seriously, nodded. "Indeed. We grew older—all of us. And Patrick started to get ideas."

Rory shifted his treelike legs, rearranging his huge feet. "Da is a man who gets things done. He's determined and accustomed to making things happen in the way he thinks they should."

"His intentions are always for the best," she hurriedly added, "at least in his eyes."

"And that's the crux of the problem that drove wee Caitlin away." Rory studied her, then shook his shaggy head. "I still don't think you could have done anything other than what you did—run away."

Gregory was frowning. He caught her eye. "What, exactly, was the threat? What caused you to leave your home?"

Well-versed in gentlemen with protective streaks, Caitlin heard the steel that had infused his voice. If she'd had any doubt of where she stood with him—of how he viewed her—that alone would have laid it to rest. The realization distracted her for a moment, then she shook herself and replied, "In a nutshell, Patrick wanted me to marry Rory, thus reuniting the manor and the lairdship and keeping both in the family's hands."

The glance Gregory threw Rory was sharp. "And what did you think of your father's plan?"

For several seconds, Rory's expression remained impassive—and Caitlin feared he was about to be difficult—but then he grimaced and admitted, "Much as I love Caitlin, she's like a sister to me, and on top of that, I know her far too well." He raised his glass to her in a mock toast. "A life being managed to within an inch of my sanity didn't appeal."

Caitlin smiled. "And being married to a hulking great thing like you never featured in my dreams."

Rory grinned. "So you might say we were well-matched in our resistance to Da's plans." He sobered and sipped, then added, "Unfortunately, Da's not the sort you can reason with, not after he's taken an idea into his head and decided that's the way things ought to be."

Caitlin sighed. "Patrick just wouldn't listen. We all tried to point out that trying to force me to marry any of his sons was not going to work. We all argued until we were blue in the face, but it made no difference. Patrick still sees us—all of us—as children to be guided through life. That's been his role and his duty for decades, and he seems unable to grasp that now we're grown, he shouldn't—and indeed, can't—continue to determine our lives for us."

She paused, then went on, "Eventually, he started hinting that he would lock me up until I agreed to marry Rory and Rory agreed."

"Da knew that none of us—me or my brothers—could stomach seeing wee Caitlin held prisoner in her own home for long." Rory grimaced. "Da was pigheadedly certain of his ability to bend me—and the others, too, if it came to that—to his will. The notion that we would stand against him... No matter what we said, he simply refused to believe that we would."

"That," Caitlin said, "was when I started planning to come south. If I can avoid my uncle until my twenty-fifth birthday, when his guardianship ends, then he'll lose all ability to force me to do anything. From that point on, I'll be mistress of Benbeoch Manor and entitled to make my own decisions regarding my future and about everything to do with the estate."

She paused, remembering, then went on, "I wanted to simply disappear, but in such a way that Patrick wouldn't blame Rory and the others. In the end, I concocted a plan to flee from the estate when I was out riding one afternoon. My groom, Samuel, and maid, Mary, were both essential to my plan. They were also devoted and readily agreed to accompany me."

"As guards and for propriety, if nothing else." Rory huffed. "Us lads wouldn't have let her go alone."

She dipped her head. "No, and to be perfectly candid, I wasn't eager to ride off and brave God alone knew what situations by myself." She met Gregory's eyes. "I wasn't fleeing other than out of necessity."

He nodded. "So where did you go? Did you come directly south?"

"It was early January, so we rode south as fast as we were able. We just missed being snowed in in northern England, but we wanted to make things difficult if Patrick sent someone—like Rory—after us, so as soon as we could, we swung to the east, and from York onward, we made sure to keep off the main roads."

"You did well, hiding your trail," Rory said. "It took me forever to follow you down, you'd tacked back and forth so often."

She smiled. "Eventually, we reached Kettering, but south of there, our luck ran out. A freezing blizzard struck out of nowhere, and we were caught on the road—the one that runs along the Hall's northern boundary." She shivered at the memory. "Even used to snow and ice as we were, we thought we were going to die. But Samuel saw a glimmer of light, up high, over the fields, so we slogged and dragged our poor horses in that direction. That beacon we saw was a large lamp Timms—and I understand, Minnie before her—always had lighted and placed in a holder that's suspended just beneath the ceiling of the cupola. The light beams out in all directions through the cupola's windows. That beacon brought us to Bellamy Hall."

Caitlin remembered that night and the massive relief at the warmth, both physical and emotional, with which they'd been greeted. "We were three bedraggled travelers, but Timms and the others here gathered us in." She met Gregory's eyes and smiled. "And as you know, the three of us stayed and found a home."

Rory shifted and scowled at her. "The only reason the lads and I agreed to let you go off like that was…well, we knew you couldn't stay, but you promised you'd write."

"I did write."

"Once! And all you said in that godforsaken letter was that you'd found somewhere safe and comfortable and had decided to stay." Rory snorted. "And the damned letter was posted from London! We had no idea where you'd got to."

He glowered at her, and she frowned back. "You knew I would be back once I turned twenty-five." Puzzled, she continued, "Which brings me to our most pertinent point. Why are you here?"

Rory stared at her belligerently, then sighed and deflated. He drained the last of his whisky, and when Gregory pointed at the empty glass and arched his brows, Rory studied the tumbler, then nodded and held it out. "Aye. A drop more might help with this."

Gregory took the glass, refilled it and his as well, then returned and handed Rory his tumbler. Gregory resumed his seat, sipped, and waited.

Caitlin, too, waited patiently, knowing Rory would have to assemble his thoughts.

Eventually, his lips tightened, and he looked up and met her gaze. "Initially, Da thought—correctly—that you'd run off, but he decided, possibly because of snippets the lads and I let fall and given you'd taken your maid and groom with you, that you'd gone off to sulk with one of your friends in Edinburgh and would be back soon enough."

She nodded. "So he waited." She glanced at Gregory. "We'd hoped he would. He was never one for creating unnecessary fuss among the local gentry, and he especially wouldn't want talk about me running off spreading about."

"Especially given you were the heiress he was supposed to be taking care of." Rory's lips twisted. "We'd picked that right. The lads and I did our best to keep his mind off you, and once the snows set in, which they did soon after you left, he knew there was no way to chase after you. Then, in spring, your letter—which you'd cleverly addressed to Daniel, the quiet one—arrived, and the lads and I relaxed. As the months went on, Da came to believe—helped, I admit, by comments the other three and I dropped here and there—that you were off somewhere, perfectly safe, and would return in your own good time."

Rory paused, sipped, then added, "Mind you, I think he expected you to return within a few months. We did our best to see he was kept occupied with the estate, and months slid past, and you'd been gone a year. About that time, he took up insisting that I track you down. I kept putting him off, deflecting his attention, but he grew wise to that and started talking of hiring a private investigating agent to do the job if I wouldn't. When that didn't make me jump to his tune, he threatened to call in the police. 'Heiress goes missing' and so on. At first, we thought he was just talking, hoping the threat would work, but he grew more and more determined, and eventually, he sat us all down and served up an ultimatum. Either I would come after you, find you, and haul you back—presumably to have him convince you to marry me—or he'd report you as having been kidnapped."

The big man grimaced. "I think he'd figured out that us not being that worried over you meant that we knew something—at least enough to feel reasonably certain you were safe and well. I think he felt—feels—we betrayed him and, most likely, that in a way, we'd all made a fool of him. He worked himself up into such a state, we really thought that, this time, he was in earnest. That if we called his bluff, he would do it. Declaring you kidnapped would ruin you—when you came back, you'd be damaged goods. He knew the threat to your reputation would make me do his bidding. Nevertheless, the others and I used every excuse we could think of to delay, but"—he lifted his huge shoulders in a resigned shrug —"eventually, I had to start off after you."

Gregory watched Caitlin's large cousin send his gaze about the library, taking in the quiet luxury and the understated evidence of wealth.

Bringing his gaze back to Caitlin, Rory studied her shrewdly, then asked, "So you're really comfortable and happy here?"

Gregory looked at Caitlin in time to see her nod decisively. "Yes. I've no wish and no intention of leaving. Not until I need to go north to sort out the estate." She glanced at Gregory. "I'm twenty-three now, and my birthday's in September, so I have nearly eighteen months before I will need to head back."

She wouldn't be going alone. Gregory didn't say so, just dipped his head in understanding.

Indeed, if he and she were to marry, as he was now determined they would, they would need to make peace with the mountain and with the rest of her family as well. In pursuit of that goal, he stirred and, when Caitlin and Rory glanced his way, smiled easily at Rory. "If you're not in any hurry to return to Scotland, why not stay awhile—a week at least—and see for yourself what Caitlin's life here is like? If, as seems likely, on your return, you'll need to argue your and her cases with your father, then the most convincing evidence is what you can claim to have seen with your own eyes."

Rory's expression lightened. "Aye." He nodded. "That's a good thought."

"Caitlin will be able to show you around"—Gregory glanced encouragingly at her—"and you'll see how Bellamy Hall operates. That's something you'll need to appreciate in order to understand Caitlin's position here."

Rory shot a faintly puzzled look at Caitlin, then redirected his gaze to Gregory. "Isn't this the usual sort of estate?"

Gregory felt his lips twitch into a wry smile. "Not quite." He paused, then went on, "Those people you met earlier weren't guests. They're all members of the Hall household, and each of them owns one of the businesses that operates from the estate."

Rory frowned. "I did wonder about that—what they were all doing here and why you could leave them to entertain themselves."

"They all live under the Hall's roof," Caitlin told him. "And there are others who manage other enterprises and live elsewhere on the estate."

Between them, she and Gregory gave Rory a quick introduction to the Bellamy Hall estate and the concept of the Hall fund and how it operated. He was plainly intrigued and asked several questions. In some cases, those questions themselves answered some of Gregory's own queries regarding the Benbeoch estate, while others gave him openings to tease information from Rory and from Caitlin as well without having to own to any personal interest.

Eventually, Rory admitted that he wasn't keen to return to Scotland without Caitlin in tow. "Not for the moment, anyway." He directed a quizzical glance at Caitlin. "Who knows? While looking around this estate of yours, I might find my own place to stop for a while."

Gregory found that suggestion interesting, not least as it underscored the truth of Rory's claim that he harbored no aspirations regarding Benbeoch Manor.

He tried to visualize the manor. "Where, exactly, is Benbeoch Manor? If it's close to the road to Ayr, I must have passed it on several occasions."

Both Rory and Caitlin looked surprised.

It was Rory who answered, "Nay, you can't see the house from the road. It's tucked away beyond the village, on the flank of Benbeoch itself."

"Ah, I see." He nodded. "I remember Dalmellington and the mountain."

Frowning in puzzlement, Caitlin asked, "Why would you have been on that road? It's hardly a major route to Edinburgh or Glasgow."

He smiled. "But it is the most direct route from the Vale of Casphairn to the nearest semblance of civilization."

Caitlin shifted to stare at him. "You know people there? In the Vale?"

He grinned. "My cousins—I suppose, technically, they're second cousins—live there. Lucilla is currently the Lady of the Vale, and her twin, Marcus Cynster—"

"Is the owner of the old Hennessy estate! Aye, and he manages the Carrick estate as well, although it's his wife who's the lady there." Smiling broadly, Rory thumped a fist on his knee. "I *knew* I recognized the name from somewhere."

Caitlin was still staring at Gregory. "You're related to the Lady of the Vale?"

He nodded. "Her father is one of my father's cousins."

"Well!" Rory sat back. He continued to look delighted. "A small world, it certainly is."

Caitlin stared at Rory's now-delighted face and decided she was delighted as well. Although Gregory's connection to the Vale of Casphairn had come as a complete surprise, that meant he was acquainted with the sometimes-different Scottish ways and, therefore, would have a better understanding of her situation.

She was also fairly certain that her big, blustery cousin was, indeed, looking for some way to remain, if not specifically on the estate with her, at least not far away rather than return to his father empty-handed. She could understand that; indeed, she sympathized. And eighteen months wasn't such a long time that, between them, they couldn't find ways to believably excuse a supposedly ongoing search for her.

Feeling decidedly more confident in her ability to manage the situation than she had when Rory had walked in, she glanced at Gregory—currently engaged in an exchange of memories with Rory concerning the hunting around Dalmellington and the Vale—just as the clock on the mantelpiece chimed. She glanced up and saw that the hands were signaling eleven o'clock. Her gaze lowered to the grate. The fire had almost burnt itself out.

She looked at Rory. "I'll have Cromwell prepare a room." She rose and tugged the bellpull that hung beside the mantelpiece.

Both men came to their feet.

Cromwell appeared almost instantly; he had to have been hovering nearby, although how he knew he'd been summoned at that moment, she couldn't imagine. Cromwell half bowed. "Yes, miss?"

"Mr. Fergusson will be staying for at least a week. If you could prepare a suitable room for him?"

"Naturally, miss." Cromwell regarded her almost reproachfully. "Assuming Mr. Fergusson would prefer to be located close to you, I've had the room two doors down from your own prepared. His horse is in the stable, and his bags have been placed in his room."

"Thank you, Cromwell." Caitlin struggled to mute her smile; apparently, the household was ready to embrace any relative of hers. "That's perfect."

"Yes, miss." Cromwell bowed, then held the door as she led Rory and Gregory out.

The three of them strolled toward the front hall.

Rory was looking about, taking in all the side corridors and smaller halls and doors they passed. "This place is a ruddy great monstrosity, isn't it?"

Gregory laughed. "You're not the first to describe it that way."

They reached the front hall and climbed the main stairs.

Gregory halted in the gallery. His gaze briefly touched Caitlin's, then he nodded to Rory. "Good night. In case you're wondering, we don't actually have ghosts—at least not inside the house."

"Good to know." Rory saluted him.

Caitlin waved Rory on, then with a last, questioning glance at Gregory, fell in beside her cousin. They walked down the corridor. She showed him the door to her room as they passed, then continued on to the room Cromwell had assigned to him.

After showing him inside, pointing out the bellpull, and telling him the house had a full complement of staff, she confirmed he had everything he needed for the night, then left him to his rest. She closed the door behind her, then looked back along the corridor to the gallery and the figure waiting there.

A smile curving her lips, she walked past her room and on to where Gregory was leaning on the balustrade and looking down into the now-dark hall.

She joined him, leaning on the polished wood so that their shoulders brushed.

There was nothing of interest in the hall below. She shifted her gaze to his profile and boldly asked, "Has learning that I'm a Scottish heiress changed your view of me?"

His lips lifted, and he glanced her way. "No. Not in the least."

"Are you concerned about Rory coming to retrieve me?"

He shook his head. "In fact, I'm rather glad he arrived." He met her gaze, amusement riding his expression. "Thanks to your cousin, I got the entire story in one sitting." He paused, studying her eyes, then his expression sobered. "I understand why you fled and also why you stayed. This"—he gestured, indicating the Hall around them—"the estate and how it runs, has echoes of what you would be accustomed to on your own lands."

She blinked, then nodded. "I hadn't thought of that, but it's true." After a moment of further thought, she added, "That's likely why I felt so comfortable—why I fitted in so easily."

He nodded. "So this evening's revelations alter nothing between us— rather, if anything, the opposite. Learning of your background only... makes you more desirable in my eyes."

His voice had lowered, deepened, and there was a weight in his gaze that made her inwardly shiver.

In response—in reaction—she smiled and lightly scoffed, "You wouldn't say that if you knew my uncle Patrick."

The epitome of confidence, he grinned and pushed away from the balustrade, and then he was drawing her to him. "We'll see."

The moonlight pouring in from above etched his features and let her see just how focused, how intent on her, he was.

Then he bent his head, and she laid a hand against his lean cheek and stretched up…

Their lips met, and sensation took hold. The hunger she sensed behind the pressure of his mobile lips as they supped—so restrainedly—at hers, lured and enticed. They fascinated and drew her on until she parted her lips, and his tongue surged between, and she would have sagged as her knees went weak, but his arm cinched about her and held her even more tightly against him.

Desire flitted like a rainbow at the edge of her awareness, camouflaged by the escalating yearning, his and hers, that rose to entwine and overwhelm her wits, consigning them to a distant corner of her mind.

This, then, was the prelude to passion—the first step along a road she'd never trod.

Oh, she'd been kissed before, and with desire on the man's part, but never had her desire risen to the call as it did now, surging through her in the moonlit night as he angled his head and drew her deeper into the kiss.

Her hands fell to his lapels, and she clutched tight, anchoring herself in the heady, swirling vortex of sensations. Of feelings and the needs they evoked.

She pressed closer still, kissing him back every bit as hungrily, as greedily and avidly, as he was kissing her.

His hands splayed across her back, and he urged her nearer yet, and her senses waltzed and sang.

She'd never imagined a simple kiss could be this riveting. This enthralling.

This all-consuming.

Gregory had no idea how long they stood communing in the dark. Her lips were the definition of luscious, promisors of paradise beyond imagining.

He ached with a desire more robust, more intense, than any he'd felt in all his years of sexual indulging. What he shared with her seemed so familiar, so similar—the moves, the positions entirely predictable—yet the result was different.

Leagues apart.

And while that was something he couldn't explain, he knew he wanted more.

So much more of her.

Their fires were well alight and burning when, on a strangled gasp, he realized how far they'd come. Sensing control slipping through his fingers—something that had never happened to him before—in sudden desperation, he forced himself to think of her cousin, the shaggy mammoth who was not all that far away.

And who, at any moment, might decide to look out into the corridor.

The image was enough to give him the strength to retreat from the kiss, and eventually, after a surprisingly fraught battle, he released her lips and raised his head.

He was breathing too fast, as was she as he stared—quietly stunned— into her upturned face.

He watched as her lashes fluttered, then rose, revealing passion-darkened eyes that nevertheless gleamed and sparked. Her lips were swollen and slick and slightly parted…

The sight ignited a desire like no other, one that gripped and sank its claws deep.

Blindly, he found her hand and raised her fingers to his lips. His gaze locked with hers, he brushed an ardent kiss to her knuckles, then turned her hand and pressed an even more heated kiss to the center of her palm. "I want—"

She silenced him by placing the fingers of her other hand over his lips. Her eyes had flared. She stared at him for several heavy heartbeats, then her lids fell, and she breathed, "I'm not saying no, but can we see what comes over the next weeks? Until Rory settles or leaves?" She drew a deeper breath, her breasts rising and pressing against his chest, then she looked up and met his eyes. "This is my new life—here, at Bellamy Hall —and I don't want my old life intruding and getting in the way."

He studied her eyes, her face, and realized she hadn't—quite— guessed correctly what he'd intended to ask her.

Until the second in which the words had formed on the tip of his tongue, ready to spill from his lips, he hadn't realized that he'd already reached the point of asking her to marry him.

Rory's arrival or, more likely, his brush with death that afternoon had catapulted him on, over and past all the usual stages of realization and acceptance that men of his ilk were prone to stumble through.

He'd been about to ask her to be his wife, and rather than recoil from the realization, every iota of his wits and his will wanted to embrace it.

His gaze roved her features, drinking in their delicate beauty.

Now he understood how far he'd traveled down that particular road, he wanted to woo her. To use the interval circumstance had created and offer for her hand with all the romance and ceremony she deserved.

If she wanted to wait a few weeks until the question of Rory and what he would do was resolved, then of course he would agree.

Whatever she wanted—that was how matters between them now stood.

He kissed the fingers that had lingered across his lips, then smiled as she lowered her hand. "Very well. We'll wait until Rory decides on his way forward." His smile deepened. "But in the meantime…"

He tightened his arms and drew her close once more.

And when he bent his head and found her lips again, he discovered she was more than willing to follow where he led.

# CHAPTER 9

The following morning, Gregory was lounging in the library, thinking of Caitlin and the pleasures of kissing her, when movement glimpsed from the corner of his eye had him turning his head and looking out of the window.

His chatelaine was walking away from the house, basket on her arm, no doubt embarking on her usual round of the estate's businesses. From the direction in which she was heading, he assumed today's excursion would take in the carriage workshop, the forge, the glassblowing studio, the livestock pens, the carpentry workshop, and the kitchen gardens.

Pacing beside her and looking around eagerly, Rory appeared even larger than he had last night.

Impulse prompted. Gregory got to his feet and set out in pursuit.

He caught up with the pair as they were approaching the carriage works. He nodded to Rory and smiled at Caitlin. "I thought I'd join you."

Amused, she arched a brow, then they passed through the open doorway of the workshop and halted.

Jenkins saw them, downed his tools, and came to greet them.

After introducing Rory, Caitlin and Jenkins embarked on their usual review of orders and progress.

Plainly curious, Rory looked deeper into the workshop, studying the activity in the nearest bay, where several of Jenkins's lads were working on the baseboard of a light carriage.

Gregory explained, "Jenkins was and still is the head stableman here, and there was always a good complement of grooms and stable hands, but over the years, there were fewer and fewer horses and, consequently, less for them to do, so they used their time developing their interest in carriage making. These days, the workshop makes new carriages to order, supplying many of those around about, as well as repairing all types of conveyances."

Rory tipped his head toward where the lads had fixed the baseboard in place. "That's impressive." He glanced at Gregory. "I imagine this lot keep all the estate carts and carriages running smoothly."

Gregory nodded. "They do."

"Were you behind setting this up?"

"The carriage works? No." Gregory added, "I've only recently taken the reins here. All that you'll see was already in place when I came."

Sensing Rory's understandable curiosity, Gregory explained how ownership of the Hall had fallen to him. "I arrived only a few weeks ago, and all the businesses on the estate have been established for several years—indeed, from before Caitlin arrived. I'm still finding my way around and learning as I go."

Rory asked several pertinent and intelligent questions, confirming for Gregory that Caitlin's lumbering cousin wasn't the country bumpkin he might encourage people to think him.

"It sounds a bit like the clan system." Rory tugged at his earlobe, then glanced at his cousin, still engaged with Jenkins. "And Caitlin? What's her role?"

"She more or less runs the place." Gregory felt a degree of pride as he watched her finalize something with Jenkins. "In English terms, she's the chatelaine-cum-steward of Bellamy Hall, but using your Scottish analogy, I suspect she's operating like a clan leader."

His gaze on Caitlin, Rory nodded. "Aye. We do have female lairds. And no matter what she thinks, clan leadership runs in her blood." Glancing sidelong, he met Gregory's eyes. "Seems she might have found her own clan to lead here."

His lips curving, Gregory inclined his head. "I wouldn't disagree."

Caitlin and Jenkins concluded their discussion, and with a nod and a salute to Rory and Gregory, Jenkins went back to his men and their work.

Gregory and Rory returned to Caitlin. She was scribbling on a piece of paper. They halted before her, and she finished her writing, stuffed paper and pencil into her pocket, then waved them on. "The forge is next."

Henry Kirk was pleased to see Caitlin and immediately claimed her attention with a request for some specific sort of iron. Gregory introduced Rory to Blackie and watched in amusement as the two rough-hewn men enthused over the delicacy of one of Madge's creations.

When, eventually, they moved on to the glassblowing studio, it was Gregory whom Vernon wanted a word with; Gregory had given the glass-blower sketches of the Cynster coat of arms, and Vernon wanted more details of the stag. While Gregory and Vernon sketched, Caitlin showed Rory about the workshop.

After that, the three of them headed to the livestock pens. Joshua was delighted to welcome them and, as always, was even more delighted to show off his animals. It transpired that an acquaintance with goats was something all three men possessed, and the minutes inspecting the pens were filled with tales of various instances in which goats had run amok. Gregory took the palm with his description of the lengths to which the wily beasts went to invade his family's hop fields. "Only when the hops are just ripe and perfect for picking, of course. At any other time, they evince no interest whatsoever in those fields."

"Aye, well," Rory said. "Goats are finicky like that. They'll eat just about anything, except what they won't."

The others laughed, and they parted from Joshua and walked back and around to the carpentry workshop.

The instant they walked into the large barn, Rory came alive. Surprised by his flaring interest, Gregory looked around, but could see nothing to account for it. Yet even before Percy reached them, Rory had walked to the nearest bench. While Percy and Caitlin conferred, Gregory watched as the big Scotsman ran a palm almost lovingly over a curved piece of wood that was to be part of a wooden chair. He nodded to Joe, who was shaping a chair seat on the next bench, and ambled across to chat.

The exchange grew quite animated on both sides, then Rory moved on to see what Paul was doing.

Eventually, as Percy and Caitlin reached agreement on several imple-ments to be ordered in, Rory approached the very last bench—the one beyond where Percy had been working on a sideboard. A curiously curved, rather thick piece of smoothed wood stood upright on the bench. Rory gazed at it and, almost reverently, ran a hand over the odd curve.

Percy saw what Rory was doing and left Caitlin to stride down the workshop.

Gregory shared a glance with Caitlin, then they followed the master carpenter.

With his hand resting on the curved wood, Rory smiled at Percy as he joined him. "This is a lovely piece of oak. What's it to be?"

Percy grimaced. "A lute. I've been asked to make one, but I've never made any instrument before, so I'm entirely at sea and just guessing as I go."

With Gregory, Caitlin halted a few feet away. She took in the look on Rory's face. "Oh," she breathed.

Gregory glanced questioningly at her, but her attention remained fixed on her cousin—on his almost beatific expression.

Plainly frustrated, Percy planted his hands on his hips and frowned at the wood. "I hate not knowing what I'm doing, especially with wood."

"Aye. That's never a comfortable feeling." Rory gestured at the curved piece. "If you take a wrong turn, you can't go back."

"Exactly!"

Rory drew in a slow breath. "I could help you with this—if you'd like?"

Startled, Percy looked at Rory. "Man, if you have any suggestions to make, speak!"

"Well, I've made an instrument or two in my time." Handling the wood tenderly, Rory picked it up and turned it in his huge hands. "I've even made something like this lute. See, you'll want to…"

As Rory explained how the lute should be constructed, Caitlin whispered to Gregory, "Rory loves working with wood—carving and shaping and making things. He especially likes to make musical instruments, like harps, guitars, lutes, and such."

They stood and watched, entirely forgotten by Percy and Rory as the pair grew utterly absorbed with the intricacies of constructing the lute.

After several minutes of being unnecessary spectators, Caitlin glanced at Gregory. He met her eyes and tipped his head toward the doorway, and they both took a tentative step back.

Pattering footsteps approaching from outside had them glancing around as Millie, her cheeks lightly flushed from the cold, came hurrying in.

She smiled at Caitlin and Gregory. "Hello." Then she looked past them at Percy. "I just came to see…"

Her words trailed off, and the color in her cheeks deepened.

Caitlin glanced at Rory. Her cousin was standing stock-still, a stunned expression on his face.

"Ah, there you are, my dear. Well timed!" Percy beckoned Millie nearer. "I was just showing this gentleman... I say, have you been introduced?" Percy looked back and forth between the pair, then remembered. "But of course you have! You were there last night when Mr. Fergusson arrived."

His gaze locked on Millie's face, Rory swallowed and croaked, "Just Rory, please."

"Yes, well. Millie, it seems like we're in luck." Percy clapped his hands together. "Rory knows how to make lutes."

"Do you play?" The intensity in Rory's expression was searing.

Millie blushed even more fierily and stammered, "A-A bit." Then she hauled in a breath and more firmly stated, "I haven't really played since I was ten. My aunt taught me."

"Well, then"—Rory picked up the curved limb—"you'll know the pins need to be inset along here."

Millie drifted nearer, and soon all three—Percy, Millie, and Rory—had their heads together.

When Rory asked what design Millie would like to see carved into the finished piece, she replied eagerly, gesturing with both hands.

Percy stepped back, watched the ongoing exchange between Rory and Millie for another moment, then grinned, turned, and walked to Caitlin and Gregory.

Meeting Caitlin's eyes, Percy smiled. "No need for me to act as gooseberry."

"No, indeed." After one last look at the pair, Caitlin glanced at Gregory. "We may as well leave Rory to Millie and her lute. I doubt we'd manage to lure him out, even with food."

Gregory laughed.

They parted from Percy, with Caitlin promising to let him know what she learned about the tools he wanted.

Gregory accompanied Caitlin to her final stop in the kitchen garden. While she consulted with Julia, he considered what they'd just seen. When Caitlin farewelled Julia and turned to leave, he fell in beside her once more. "So, Rory has quite a bit of experience with woodcraft."

She nodded. "His passion is woodcarving—he's made some heart-stoppingly beautiful pieces." She paused, then went on, "He has a very real talent for it, but of course, that's not an occupation my uncle would approve of for his eldest son—indeed, for any of his sons." She met Gregory's gaze. "As you might by now have guessed, my uncle is an exceedingly conservative soul. Men must be men and thus spend their time in manly pursuits."

His lips twitched. "I really can't see anyone thinking Rory less of a man because he likes to carve wood."

She shrugged. "My uncle is prejudiced. And unbelievably stubborn." Eyes narrowing, she added, "And blind."

"Does Rory really know what he's doing with the lute?"

"He does. I've seen several clarsachs he's made. They're Scottish harps, very similar to lutes." Smiling, she met Gregory's eyes. "Rest assured, Millie won't be disappointed."

He smiled back. "I suspect Rory won't be disappointed, either."

She laughed and linked her arm with his, and in thoroughly good spirits, they headed for the house.

After that first day when they'd introduced Rory to the carpentry workshop, other than when he appeared at the dining table, during the day, that was where they would find him, working with absolute focus at the last bench. Under his undeniably skilled hands, Millie's lute was rapidly taking shape.

But two days later, Rory appeared on the rear drive behind the carpentry workshop just as Gregory and Caitlin were setting out in Gregory's curricle. Rory waved them down, and curious, Gregory drew his team—impatient for the outing—to a stamping halt.

Rory grasped the curricle's side rail. "You're on your way to the estate farms, yeah?"

Caitlin nodded. "Yes. Why?"

"Because I think I ought to go along as well." Without waiting for agreement, Rory swung up and squeezed his bulk onto the box seat.

Surprised, Caitlin looked at Gregory.

He shrugged, flicked the reins, and set his pair pacing on.

Their first stop was Barton Farm, where Joe and Fanny Barton watched over the acres responsible for the bulk of the estate's wheat and barley crops. After introducing the Bartons to Rory, Caitlin checked the amounts of seeds Joe had on order, then with all as it should be, they took the main road toward Wellingborough and turned south onto the village lane.

"Nice land around here," Rory called from behind. "It'd be good grazing."

Caitlin tipped her head back and replied, "It's better closer to the river. You'll see."

Gregory sent the bays sweeping on, past the turnoff to the village and around the eastward curve, then swung south onto the lane that led to the bridge across the Nene. Before they reached the river, they turned in to Roxton Farm.

After being introduced, leaving Caitlin and Gregory chatting with Fred and Martha Swithins about their plans for planting, Rory wandered to the edge of the farmyard. Standing before the fence, he looked over the river meadows as if seeing some picture in his mind.

But when Caitlin called him, he came readily and, smiling, took his leave of the Swithinses, then climbed back to the box seat.

Gregory tooled the horses back to the lane. As he turned their heads toward the bridge, Rory rumbled, "There's cattle somewhere near—I can smell them."

Caitlin glanced at him fondly. "The leatherworks I mentioned are just there." She nodded to the buildings bordering the lane. "Are you sure it isn't the tannery you can smell?"

"Nah. Although I can smell that as well—who wouldn't? But live animals smell different."

Gregory wasn't about to argue that. The horses took the bridge in style, drawing an appreciative yelp from Rory. Gregory grinned and, shortly after, slowed the pair and turned onto the drive of Home Farm.

Malcolm Hammersley came out of the barn to greet them.

After being introduced to Rory, Martin asked Caitlin to see if Alice could make up some potion for his sheep.

Rory had noticed the portion of the flock Malcolm had corralled in a nearby pen and wandered across to take a closer look.

Gregory went with him.

Leaning on the railing fence, they studied the sheep. To Gregory, they appeared typical shaggy sheep, but from Rory's expression, he saw something more. Eventually, he offered, "Nice animals. They're heavier-fleeced than what we run at Benbeoch, but I think our lot probably have more meat."

Viewing that as an opening to exploit, Gregory asked about the livestock at Benbeoch and soon had a reasonably good notion of what the estate encompassed.

"Our cropping's light compared to what you have here," Rory said. "You've much richer, deeper pastures, so your productivity will be much higher, but I've always thought, for the best meat, sheep need to forage for their feed, and these fellows here"—he nodded at the flock before them—"have it too easy. Excellent for wool, not so much for meat."

"I'm still learning," Gregory admitted, "but that's what I've gathered. We run for wool rather than meat."

"It's not that we don't have wool at Benbeoch," Rory said, "but it's nothing like the quality you'd get off these." He pushed away from the railing as Caitlin joined them.

She smiled at them both. "Malcolm and I have sorted things out, so we can head to Nene Farm."

They climbed back into the curricle, and Gregory steered the bays out to the lane, then onto the track that ended at Nene Farm.

As he drew the horses to a halt in the farmyard, Rory was already getting out.

"This is more like it." With an eager smile wreathing his face, Rory headed for the nearest paddock.

As it happened, Martin Cruickshank was standing just inside the fence, his hands on his hips as he surveyed the cattle ambling about the lushly grassed field. He heard Rory striding up and turned.

Hurrying after her cousin, Caitlin called out an introduction, but Rory barely waited to ask, "What bloodlines do you run?" He halted at the fence, his gaze locked on the beasts. "Well, I can see they're Angus, mostly, but there's something else there, too."

Martin stared at him. "Aye—and you've a good eye if you can pick that just by looking. We've been working on these for the past decade and more. See…"

Caitlin halted a few paces from the fence and listened as Rory and Martin talked cattle as only two men with cattle breeding in their blood could.

After tying up his horses, Gregory joined her.

They stood and listened, and after several minutes of the often-incomprehensible-to-mere-mortals back-and-forth, he glanced at her. "I feel, once again, that we're decidedly *de trop*."

She lowered her voice. "Rory's in charge of cattle breeding at

Benbeoch. He knows more about the subject than about crafting musical instruments."

Gregory frowned. "Your father—and the estate—will be missing him, then."

"Not really." Briefly, she met his eyes. "My youngest cousin, Morgan, is one of those annoying creatures who is good at anything they turn their hand to, including breeding and managing all types of livestock."

"Ah." Gregory looked at Rory. After a moment, he murmured, "So there's nothing tying Rory to Benbeoch."

She hadn't thought of that, but... "No. There isn't." She followed that train of thought further. "If he wanted to leave, he could, without causing any great problem."

She returned her attention to her cousin and felt as if she was seeing him through new eyes. *Hmm.*

They waited for several more minutes, then Caitlin managed to attract Martin's attention long enough to ask whether he needed anything extra ordered.

"No, thank you, Caitlin. But if you see Millie, could you ask her to make up some of her ointment for treating hooves?" He looked back at the milling cattle. "Just in case."

"You're going to check their hooves?" Rory asked.

Martin nodded. "With the ground down by the river so wet, it pays to be vigilant."

"Aye, it does, that." Rory tipped his head at the cattle. "Their condition's good, considering the season."

Caitlin pointedly said, "I promised to call on Margaret and Monica, so we need to get on."

Rory met Martin's eyes, then glanced at her. "You two go on. I'll stay and help check the hooves."

Martin turned an eager face their way. "That'd be a big help. Not often I have someone whose eye I can trust. Together, we'll be able to get through this lot in half the time."

"Aye, and perhaps you'll show me the rest of the herd afterward?"

Martin beamed. "Of course!"

Hiding smiles, Caitlin and Gregory left the pair and walked back to the curricle.

Gregory offered his hand, and she took it and allowed him to help her to the seat. As she settled her skirts, she realized that her senses no longer leapt at his touch. Instead, they almost purred.

Another happy development.

Gregory sat, flicked the reins, and steered the bays along the drive and onto the lane. After a moment, he voiced the thought their morning's encounters had set humming in his brain. "Do you think Rory came with us today to see if he could find a way to contribute to the Bellamy Hall Fund? Some way other than by making musical instruments?"

"The possibility did cross my mind." Caitlin glanced his way. "This morning, after breakfast, he asked me to explain exactly how the Fund works, so the way the estate operates has definitely been on his mind."

Gregory caught her eye. "How would you feel if he asks to stay and join our, for want of a better term, miscellany?"

She smiled at the description, then sobered. After a moment, she said, "I owe Rory—and Hamish, Daniel, and Morgan—a debt of gratitude. They understood—they always have—and they helped and made it easy for me to leave Benbeoch. I'm not sure I could have managed without their assistance, certainly not in bringing Samuel and Mary with me." She paused, then went on, "I always thought the reason my cousins understood my need to escape Patrick's control over what our lives should be was because they felt the same and wished they could break free, too."

Gregory slowed his horses to take the bridge over the river. "After the initial shock of seeing Rory, I wondered if you were all that surprised."

"That he'd followed me south?" She thought, then replied, "No. I wasn't so surprised that he'd come. As Patrick had been pushing Rory to come after me, him using the opportunity to check that I was safe and well was always on the cards. What I don't think my uncle has correctly foreseen is that, now Rory's left Benbeoch, there's no certainty he'll go back."

Gregory glanced at her. "Having studied Rory over the past days, I can see no reason he wouldn't fit in here, if he was so inclined."

She beamed at him, then squeezed his arm. "Thank you." She looked ahead. "If he wanted to stay, I would be glad of it."

A widening of the verge ahead had Gregory slowing. He eased his horses onto the grassy patch. "I know you want to call at the weavers' cottages, but we've made good time this morning." He looked at her and smiled. "Can I tempt you to take a short stroll by the river, chatelaine-mine?"

She laughed and waved him on. He climbed down, helped her down, then tied the reins to a nearby fence post.

Across the lane, a stile gave onto a narrow path that wound through the meadow to follow the gray ribbon of the river. After helping her over the stile, he continued to hold her hand as they set out, ambling in the late-morning sunshine.

She looked ahead. "It's March—buds are starting to bloom and trees to grow." She pointed ahead. "The hazel catkins are already out, the alder trees aren't far behind, and even the birches are coming along."

He looked, then murmured, "It's the season for new developments." He caught her gaze. "Like us."

She smiled and tipped her head against his shoulder. "A development —is that what our relationship is?"

He looked ahead and, after a moment, replied, "For me, finding you is the next step in…I suppose you might call it 'my evolution.'"

The look she threw him invited explanation.

He smiled and, pacing on, confessed, "I came to Bellamy Hall expecting to find a situation I would shape into the usual country gentleman's estate. While all who were acquainted with Minnie and Timms knew of their habit of taking in an esoteric collection of people, no one had any idea of what they had, in fact, created here, much less knew about the Bellamy Hall Fund. I expected to have to pay for a conventional estate, likely a run-down one needing to be revitalized, from the funds I inherited together with the Hall and, possibly, from my private funds as well. Instead"—he gestured—"I've discovered a thriving, essentially self-funding community." He shook his head. "Indeed, with you filling the roles of chatelaine and steward, the Bellamy Hall estate didn't need me at all."

Abruptly, Caitlin swung across him, forcing him to halt. She looked him in the eye. "You aren't even vaguely considering leaving, are you? Because I'm established here?"

Surprised, he saw the near horror in her eyes and hurried to say, "No. Not at all." He squeezed her hand. "Leaving didn't enter into my plans at any stage." Puzzled, he asked, "Why did you leap to that conclusion?"

She grimaced wryly, shifted aside, and with him keeping pace, started strolling again.

He waited, and eventually, she offered, "Men often don't appreciate a female who knows how to run an estate."

He squeezed her hand more firmly. "That's not me. I don't want to leave"—he glanced sharply at her—"and I definitely don't want you to leave, either."

She nodded, and he looked ahead, recalling his suspicion of two nights before, namely that she hadn't correctly divined what he'd been about to ask her in that revealing moment in the gallery. She hadn't yet realized that, as far as he was concerned, he was committed to marrying her. He swiftly debated, but he'd agreed not to speak until Rory was settled and a little time had passed. He was fairly certain two days didn't qualify.

Reluctantly setting aside the notion of seizing the moment and proposing, instead, he continued, "I'm not particularly good at explaining things—especially not when it comes to what I feel—so bear with me. I was building up to saying that, once I understood the reality of what was here, at the Hall, I realized the role that I'd expected to fill simply didn't exist. However, during these past weeks, going around by your side and learning about the estate as it is, I've seen that there is a role for me as— as I think of it—guardian of the Hall."

Her gaze touched his face, scanning his features.

On hearing his own words, certainty suffused him, and he nodded. "Yes, 'guardian' is the right word. I see myself as a protector, a champion, someone to keep the wolves from outside the Hall's borders at bay."

"Yes!" When he met her eyes, she beamed. "That's precisely what we —all those on the estate—need. A champion who will shield us against threats from beyond the Hall's boundaries."

He smiled, drinking in the joy in her eyes. "You can deal with most of what occurs within our borders, but when it comes to threats from beyond—"

"I can't protect the Hall from those." She nodded. "Until you came, that was my greatest fear—one I'm sure the others felt as well—that something would materialize that we wouldn't be able to handle."

He raised their linked hands and kissed her knuckles. "Clearly, we see matters in the same light." He halted and, when she stopped and faced him, looked into her violet eyes. "And the most unexpected thing I've discovered is how very much better that unforeseen role of protector and defender of the Hall suits me."

Those words rang so very true. Until that moment, his thoughts hadn't crystallized; explaining his thinking had taken him another step on. A further step forward in his evolution, or at least his understanding of that —of how he'd changed.

Holding her gaze, he went on, "My original vision of what my life here would be was an empty one. There was no challenge, no impetus to force me to change and grow. What I've found instead is that necessary challenge—the right one for me. And in learning to meet it, my life is already fuller than I ever imagined it might be."

Raising his hands, he framed her face and searched her eyes. "You and I managing Bellamy Hall together, as a team, is what I want. Please say it's what you want as well."

Her smile was all the answer he needed, and her "Yes" set the seal on the moment.

He bent his head and kissed her, and with blatant eagerness, she kissed him back.

It was a kiss of promise, one filled with wonder and a growing, burgeoning appreciation of what their shared future could be.

Their lips communed, each using the exchange to express their acceptance of the other and of the future they hoped for.

Sadly, as they were standing on the open riverbank and, where she was concerned, he wasn't any longer certain of his control, he kept his hands where they were and, when their passions, entwined, started to rise to compulsive heights, forced himself to pull back and break the hungry exchange.

He tipped his forehead to hers, and they stood and listened to their breathing slow.

Finally, when their passions had cooled and they were breathing evenly, he straightened, smiled into her glorious pansy-blue eyes, and reclaiming her hand, drew her to walk beside him along the path, back toward the lane.

She lifted her face to the sunshine. Her features were relaxed and content, and when her eyes opened, they met his with an assurance, a confidence, that matched his own.

She and Bellamy Hall, and the challenges both brought, were exactly what he needed to become the most complete man he could be.

Looking ahead, he refrained from tightening his grip on her hand, but made a mental vow that he would grasp any opportunity that presented to strengthen his hold on the Hall and on her.

Just in case her uncle turned up with the idea of her returning to Scotland and marrying one of his sons.

That wasn't going to happen.

As much as the estate itself, indeed, arguably even more so, Caitlin Fergusson was an essential, integral element he had to secure to have any hope of achieving his now-desired future.

# CHAPTER 10

*O*n Saturday afternoon, Gregory was relaxing in the Hall library, flicking through the London newspapers, when Cromwell entered.

"Lord Ecton has called, sir."

Gregory frowned. "Ecton?" Unable to place the man, he looked at Cromwell, who was doing an excellent imitation of a rigidly correct butler. "I don't believe I know the man."

"Lord Ecton is a neighbor, sir. His home, Ecton Hall, lies directly to the west and shares a boundary with the Hall estate."

"I see. In that case, please show him in."

"Very good, sir." Cromwell turned and left, leaving Gregory with the distinct impression that he'd behaved correctly.

Curious to meet a neighbor who, apparently, was living in the area yet hadn't rated a mention at either the Loxtons' dinner or on the church lawn, Gregory set aside the newspaper and, when Cromwell returned leading the visitor, uncrossed his legs and got to his feet.

The gentleman who entered on Cromwell's heels was of the type more commonly found gracing the smoking room of a London gentlemen's club. Of average height and build, Ecton was dressed in the height of fashion, his coat a testament to his tailor's art, his trousers perfectly pressed, his silk cravat ostentatiously high, and his waistcoat almost dazzling. The latter garment sported mother-of-pearl buttons huge enough to make Gregory blink.

Ecton's features were passably handsome, and his dark hair was perfectly coiffed. And while his nose was a trifle sharp, his smallish eyes set a little too close together under well-shaped dark brows, and the line of his thin lips appeared rather peevish, none of those imperfections were sufficient to dull the image of a well-heeled, sophisticated London gentleman.

Being one of that breed himself, Gregory knew better than to accept that appearance at face value. Smoothly adopting his London-gentleman-rake persona, he held out his hand. "Lord Ecton."

"Cynster." Ecton gripped Gregory's hand rather limply, then released it and executed a flourishing half bow. "I heard you were in residence, sir, and thought to strike while the iron was hot, so to speak."

Puzzled, Gregory waved Ecton to the armchair opposite his. As his guest gracefully arranged his limbs, Gregory resumed his seat. "I understand our acres run parallel."

"For a short distance, yes." Ecton met Gregory's eyes and smiled self-deprecatingly. "I fear Ecton Hall is much smaller than the Bellamy estate. But of course, London is where we both belong. I believe we have several acquaintances in common. Lord Eccles and Sinclair Kirby. Oh, and Lord Philby, of course. I'm sure you know him."

"I'm aware of those gentlemen," Gregory admitted. All were several years older and ran in a very different set; the named gentlemen were certainly of the ton, but none were exactly highly regarded members of society's elite.

Undeterred by Gregory's guarded tone, Ecton rattled on about recent happenings in the ton. From his airy comments, anyone unaware of the facts might have imagined him a jewel in the haut ton crown.

Gregory knew better.

His distrust of Ecton steadily increased as the man segued into explaining that he'd only just returned to Ecton Hall after spending the earlier months of the year at a succession of hunting and shooting parties in the north. "After that, I returned to London, and it was there that I learned that the old bat who lived here—Mrs. Timms—had finally departed this mortal coil."

Despite his rigidly impassive expression, something must have shown in Gregory's face. Ecton—who Gregory was aware had been watching him like a sly hawk—blinked, then said, "I say, you weren't related to the old dear, were you?"

"No," Gregory replied. "I wasn't." Although, of course, Timms had been an honorary great-aunt and a much-loved one at that. More, Ecton's comment suggested that Timms had had no time for him—which meant that Minnie hadn't had, either—and Gregory knew both ladies had been excellent judges of character. Maintaining his impassive, outwardly relaxed façade, he inquired, "Tell me, Ecton, what brought you here today?"

Ecton spread his arms, indicating everything around them. "I thought to come and have a chat. How are you finding life in this backwater? I daresay you're here purely to put the place in order." Ecton shuddered. "I can't imagine living in such restrictive surroundings—no parties, no dinners, no carousing with one's fellows. Given the company you're accustomed to keeping, you must be missing London already and be desperate to return with all speed." He tipped his head, his gaze sharp as he tried to read Gregory's face. "I know I am. I assure you I'm already counting the days until I can make my escape."

Trying to grasp what the man was about—for he was surely there for some reason—Gregory countered, "So what brought you to the area—to Ecton Hall, which, I assume, is your ancestral home?"

Ecton heaved a dramatic sigh. "Sadly, yes. But as to what brought me here"—Ecton linked his hands around his raised knee and adopted an expression no doubt intended to convey his seriousness—"on learning of Mrs. Timms's demise and asking around, I learned that you had inherited the estate." He met Gregory's eyes. "I have long harbored a desire to buy the Bellamy Hall estate and add its acres to my own, which, as I mentioned, are considerably fewer. Consequently"—leaning back, Ecton released his knee and raised his hands—"here I am, come to make you an offer for this rambling pile."

The smile on Ecton's face didn't reach his eyes, and when Gregory showed no reaction, Ecton hurried on, "I'm aware of the many...shall we politely say 'hangers-on' to which the estate has become home." His lip curled as he sneered, "Country bumpkins, the lot of them, with not an ounce of breeding between them and so caught up in their little hobbies, as if such esoteric endeavors have any value at all in the wider world."

Gregory bit his tongue and fought to ensure that his expression remained inscrutable.

Ecton shook his head and refocused on Gregory. "I'm sure that you'll have seen for yourself what a crazy situation has been allowed to develop here. You must be quite desperate to wash your hands of the entire wretched crew and return to more civilized climes. That said, I assure you I have no intention of taking advantage of your need."

Ecton believed every word of that statement. From all Gregory could see, Ecton possessed not the slightest doubt that Gregory viewed the estate's residents exactly as he did.

"I'm willing to offer a reasonable price, based on the current value of land in the area."

Gregory held up a hand; he'd heard enough. "Thank you for your interest, but I have no wish to sell the estate."

Ecton frowned. "Whyever not?"

Gregory shrugged. "Suffice it to say that I feel no urge to divest myself of the property."

"Not even for ten thousand pounds?"

Gregory smiled tightly. "No. I'm wealthy enough, and the estate was a legacy. I prefer to retain ownership."

Ecton was genuinely puzzled. "I can probably manage a little more…?"

When Ecton looked at him hopefully, Gregory shook his head. "I'm not attempting to drive up your price, Ecton. I truly have no interest in selling."

Having convinced himself otherwise, Ecton didn't believe that. He looked frustrated, but not defeated.

Gregory rose, and reluctantly, Ecton came to his feet.

Gregory waved to the door. "Come. I'll walk you out."

That was a sign of courtesy, one Ecton wouldn't refuse. Transparently wracking his brain as to what else he could say to persuade Gregory to accept his offer, he walked beside Gregory to the front hall, out of the door Cromwell leapt to hold open, and onto the front porch.

There, Gregory paused.

Ecton turned to him. "Thank you for your time, Cynster. Despite your refusal, I believe I'll leave my offer on the table and allow you to think further on it." He paused, then added, "Of course, I can't leave it hanging forever, but no doubt, I'll see you around over coming days."

With that, Ecton nodded somewhat curtly.

Reminding himself that the pompous man was, nevertheless, a neighbor and, thus, it behooved him to maintain good relations, Gregory returned a graceful nod and watched as Ecton descended the steps to where Parker held a pair of showy blacks harnessed to a flashy curricle. Gregory hid a grin; neither horses nor carriage were top of the trees, and

Parker's haughtily dismissive attitude was easy to read, even from a distance.

Ecton remained oblivious. He took the reins, climbed up, gave his horses the office, and drove the beasts far too fast down the drive.

Gregory watched him go. He felt certain that, no matter how unwelcome, Ecton would be back with an increased offer.

*Either that or...?*

The comment from his inner voice, that part of him that listened more to his instincts than his rational brain, left him uneasy.

Or what? Why think that?

What had he seen that he hadn't truly registered?

He didn't know, but he definitely had a bad feeling about Ecton.

Replaying the exchange with Ecton in his mind, he walked slowly back to the library. He sank into the armchair he'd occupied earlier and stared, unseeing, across the room.

Previously, despite his uneasiness, he would have shrugged and left Ecton to do his worst, secure in the knowledge that, whatever Ecton's worst proved to be, he would be able to deflect or block it.

Now, however, he had other people to think of.

People he viewed as his to protect, particularly from the likes of Ecton.

Accepting that and also, given what he'd gleaned of the man, that Ecton would push harder to get Gregory to sell the estate, he weighed up possible defenses, then rose and headed for the study.

When he walked in, Caitlin looked up from the ledger in which she was patiently writing. Several dark curls had escaped to dangle and bounce, caressing the milky satin of her throat, and she'd forgotten a pencil she'd tucked behind one ear.

As he walked forward and dropped into the chair facing her across the desk, she arched her brows.

He smiled faintly and told her of Ecton's visit.

"He wanted to buy the estate?" She frowned. "Why?"

"That was my thought as well. He said he wished to add to his own estate, which is smaller, but why he would want to do that when every second word he lets fall underscores how much he abhors country living, I can't fathom."

"Hmm. From your description—and from all I've heard—he sounds a slippery character."

"You haven't met him?"

She shook her head. "I believe he's rarely at Ecton Hall." She focused on him. "So you refused his offer?"

"Indeed. Yet despite doing so and insisting I was in earnest, I strongly suspect he'll be back. However, I, too, did not form a favorable view of Ecton's character." He met her eyes. "I've decided it would be wise to let the business owners know of his offer and my refusal and, further, to assure them that I have absolutely no intention of selling the estate to Ecton or anyone else. I have no confidence whatsoever that he won't engage in some mischief—I suspect it would be wise to do what we can to spike his guns. I also want to learn what I can about him, and some of the longer-term owners might know more."

She nodded briskly. "All excellent ideas." She laid aside her pen, shut the ledger, and set it aside. "We have a grapevine of sorts that allows anyone at the house to summon all the business owners in the event we need an urgent meeting."

"That's precisely what we need."

She pushed to her feet. "I'll tell Cromwell, and he'll spread the word. We usually meet in the conservatory. We've moved some of the chairs from the music room in there so there's seats for everyone."

The Hall's grapevine, or whatever the mechanism of the summons was, proved surprisingly effective.

An hour later, even those from the farms farther afield had arrived and gathered in the conservatory. Melrose, Tristan, and Hugo had tidied away their easels and helped set out the chairs.

With Caitlin beside him, Gregory stood at one end of the long room and, when everyone was settled, faced the company and told them of Ecton's offer and his refusal.

The looks on all the faces—surprise bleeding into concern and, even after he'd related his dismissal of the offer, lingering uncertainty—prompted him to state, "I want to make it perfectly clear that I will not be selling Bellamy Hall, not to Lord Ecton or anyone else." He paused, then felt compelled to add, "Timms chose me to take on the mantle of owner of the Hall. She knew of and valued what you, together, have built here. Indeed, she was a prime instigator of the remarkable community that currently lives and works on the estate, and I feel honored by the trust she placed in me to act as guardian of her and Lady Bellamy's legacy." He glanced around the circle of faces, meeting each pair of eyes. "I take that responsibility seriously and will do my utmost to ensure the Hall survives and, indeed, thrives."

Shoulders visibly relaxed, and the tension in the room faded.

"Now"—he looked around the company—"what can you tell me about Lord Ecton? I would value any insights you can share."

Caitlin spoke up. "As a relative newcomer, I know little about his lordship, other than that he inherited the estate on the Hall's western boundary from his father some years ago."

Henry Kirk nodded. "Aye, it'd be about six years ago, now. His mother died long ago. I can't recall ever hearing much about her, but his father was a right one—a real gentleman. Can't say the same for the son."

"Not that he's around much," Len Sutton said. "We never see him in the Bells in the village, and apparently, some months after he inherited, he let the staff go. All of them the old lord had kept on. No idea who looks after Ecton Hall these days. Whoever they are, they keep to themselves— much like their master."

The others had little more to offer, although several had observations and memories that confirmed what Henry and Len had said. From the combined comments, Gregory formed a picture of an absentee landlord who had absolutely no interest in his ancestral acres.

That rather begged the question of why Ecton wanted to add the much larger number of actively farmed acres of the Hall estate to his holding.

Gregory frowned. "Is the Ecton land farmed?" He looked at the Hall's farmers.

All shook their heads. Martin Cruickshank explained, "The land that way is rockier—it's the area from which the stones used in the abbey were originally quarried, although that was centuries past, and the old quarry was filled in long ago. But the land's not good for much. A bit of rough grazing, perhaps, but with all the better pastures round about, no one's bothered approaching Ecton to rent his acres. Nor are they likely to, not with the way the man carries on, as if he's so superior to the rest of us."

There were murmurs of agreement all around.

Cromwell, who with Rory—an interested observer—was standing at the rear of the group, loudly cleared his throat.

When Gregory and everyone else looked his way, the butler offered, "I recall that his lordship visited Mrs. Timms on several occasions last year." Cromwell frowned, clearly consulting his memories. "I believe the first time was about a year ago, at the end of winter last year. And he came twice after—later in the summer and again in the autumn."

"Do you know what he spoke with Timms about?" Gregory asked.

"No, sir." Cromwell looked faintly peeved. "Mrs. Timms did not require my attendance, and on all three occasions, Miss Fergusson was out and about the estate."

Gregory frowned. "Did you get the impression that Ecton picked his moments to ensure Timms was alone—that Miss Fergusson wasn't present to hear what he said?"

Cromwell thought, then replied, "To be perfectly candid, sir, I never got the impression his lordship considered anyone but himself."

Gregory huffed a laugh, as did most others. He nodded. "He struck me that way as well."

"That said, sir," Cromwell went on, "from what I overheard and observed when Mrs. Timms summoned me to show his lordship out, I suspect that, on all three occasions, his lordship had offered to buy the estate from the late mistress, but she, as the saying goes, firmly sent him to the right about." The butler smiled. "His lordship didn't take it well."

From Cromwell's expression, those memories were pleasing ones.

Gregory nodded. "Thank you, Cromwell. That confirms that refusing Ecton's offer is what Timms would want."

He'd been sure enough on his own account, but to know that Timms had stood firm against Ecton's blandishments underscored that whatever Ecton was about, it wasn't anything Gregory should waste his time considering.

He looked around the company. "One last thing. For the moment, at least, I think it would be prudent to keep the news of Ecton's offer for the Hall under our collective hats. There's no need for anyone else to know."

Everyone nodded in agreement, and he thanked them for so promptly responding to his request to meet. All assured him that they were pleased to have been consulted. He noted that, to a man and woman, they were relaxed and settled as they filed out of the room to return to their various houses, barns, and workshops.

Caitlin dallied to have a word with the painters. They'd been away for a week on a sketching expedition and had returned only that day.

Gregory followed the others to the door.

As the last of the owners stepped into the corridor, Rory pushed away from the wall against which he'd been leaning and joined Gregory.

Curious, Gregory glanced at the big man and slowed.

Rory waved him through the doorway, then followed and fell into step as Gregory walked toward the front hall.

He saw Rory glance back at Caitlin, noting that she was still engaged.

"So"—facing forward, Rory paced slowly along—"what I got from all of that was that this lordling, Ecton, has land of his own—possibly not good land but land nevertheless. Regardless, he's never around and clearly cares naught for his acres or, indeed, his old home." Rory slanted a look at Gregory. "So why does a man like that want to buy Bellamy Hall?"

Gregory nodded. "Indeed. That's the question to which I want an answer."

In pursuit of that answer, Gregory took himself to church the following morning, accompanying Caitlin and the other Hall residents so inclined. Rory came as well.

After settling in the front pews with Caitlin, Rory, and the others, Gregory surveyed the congregation and wasn't surprised to discover Ecton nowhere in sight.

At the end of the service, he scanned the heads again, but saw no sign of the man.

*Excellent.*

Ecton's absence meant Gregory was free to discuss the man with those of the neighboring gentry who were present that morning.

On reaching the church door, he smiled and shook hands with Reverend Millicombe, who was plainly heartened to see Gregory for the second week in a row.

Retrieving his hand, Gregory glanced around. "I wondered if I would encounter Lord Ecton here this morning."

The good reverend blinked. "Ecton? Is he back?"

His tone suggested that such a happening wasn't a prospect he viewed with any pleasure.

"So I assume," Gregory replied. "He called on me yesterday, but I have no idea how long he plans to remain in the area."

Millicombe's normally benign expression grew severe. "One can but hope," he muttered, but refrained from specifying for what he hoped.

Noting that, Gregory inclined his head and stepped off the narrow porch, allowing Millicombe to smile and greet Caitlin, who introduced Rory, much to Millicombe's delight.

Gregory waited for Caitlin and Rory to step from the porch, then strolled with them onto the lawn where, over the next minutes, most of the congregation gathered. Leaving Caitlin to introduce Rory—who, unsurprisingly, was attracting a good deal of attention—Gregory presumed on the acquaintance garnered the previous week and at the Loxtons' dinner to assess the reactions of the local gentry to the news that Ecton was about.

Universally, that information was met with a resounding lack of enthusiasm.

Although the comments were politely restrained, he was left in no doubt that Ecton was not well liked. Much of the animosity derived from Ecton's cavalier dismissal of all things country.

"He quite turns up his nose at us," Mrs. Hyssop confided. "He actually had the gall to describe us—all of us who used to be his parents' dearest friends—as *provincials*!" Her jowls shook with remembered ire.

Miss Alcott soothingly patted her friend's arm, then looked at Gregory. "Ecton is a sad excuse for a gentleman. If his parents were alive today to see him and how he behaves, they would be so very disappointed."

Mrs. Hyssop nodded. "That they would be, without a doubt."

From Sir Henry Ratcliffe, Gregory learned that the general expectation was that Ecton would soon sell up. "All he's interested in," Sir Henry said, "is cutting a dash in London. It's our fondest hope that he finds a buyer soon. I can tell you he definitely won't be missed."

Finally, Gregory fetched up beside Lord Loxton and was unsurprised to learn that, as local squire and magistrate, his lordship held a very dim, not to say jaundiced, view of Ecton. "A bad egg, sad to say. His father was a particular friend, y'know, but the son?" Leaning heavily on his cane, Lord Loxton made a dismissive, rather rude sound. "Between you and me, Cynster, I would believe almost anything of that boy. His parents were nice, steady, sound people, but sadly, they spoiled the lad first to last. If you want to gauge the result, all you need do is take a look at Ecton Hall. The place is falling apart! Boy's a ne'er-do-well the area can do without. The sooner he ups stakes and leaves, the better we'll be pleased."

As a damning indictment, that would be hard to beat.

After thanking his lordship for his candor, Gregory made his way back to Caitlin's side. As his gaze passed over numerous familiar faces in the crowd, he was glad he'd warned all those from the Hall not to mention Ecton's offer.

The fewer people who knew of that, the better. Given how negatively Ecton was viewed, despite Gregory having no intention of selling the Hall, that Ecton was wanting to buy the larger and more prosperous estate would set tongues furiously wagging and all sorts of hares racing in far too many minds.

But as to why Ecton wanted to buy the Hall, Gregory still had no idea. Indeed, all he'd heard only made Ecton's offer more incomprehensible, not less.

He rejoined Caitlin, Rory, and the others, and they headed to their carriage.

As alongside Caitlin, Gregory ambled, ruminating on all he'd heard, it occurred to him that Ecton was one of those people who valued things— like his estate—purely in terms of what they could give him.

So what was it Ecton thought Bellamy Hall would give him that he didn't already have?

Brows rising, Gregory realized he could phrase that question another way. What was it about the Bellamy Hall estate that Ecton knew, but Gregory didn't?

# CHAPTER 11

*T*he following morning, immediately after breakfast, Gregory closeted himself in the library and diligently wrote to everyone he knew who might have information or insight into what was behind Ecton's sudden interest in acquiring the Bellamy Hall estate.

"Ecton or anyone else," he grumbled. "If I'm to be inundated with offers to buy the place, I want to know why."

He wrote to his father's cousin, Gabriel Cynster, who was a canny investor who could be counted on to have his finger on the pulse of all things financial in England, and also to Montague, who had long been the Cynster family's man-of-business. His firm efficiently oversaw the diverse holdings and investments owned by the many branches of the family; if there was any whisper about Ecton in the City, Montague would have heard of it.

With those letters sealed and set aside, Gregory wrote to his father and mother and to both his brothers. All four knew at least as much as he had about the estate prior to becoming its owner; if there was something in the past that might account for Ecton's interest, his father, his mother, or Christopher might know. In addition, his father would pass Gregory's query on to anyone else in the wider family who might be able to shed light on the matter. And if, by some strange chance, Ecton's reasons were prompted by considerations of estate management, then as the previous and present masters of Walkhurst Manor, his father or Christopher might have insights to offer.

As for Martin, Gregory's little brother was presently dipping his unexpectedly wealthy toe into what Martin termed "industries of the future." If Ecton's wish to purchase Bellamy Hall had anything to do with new industries, Martin might well know.

After finishing the letter to Martin, Gregory bethought himself of his sister, Therese—or more specifically, his brother-in-law, Alverton. He drew out a fresh sheet, checked his nib, then dipped it into the inkpot and started to write. Quite aside from Therese being miffed if Gregory asked everyone else in the family but not them, her husband, Devlin, the Earl of Alverton, was deeply immersed at the highest levels of both political and investment circles. While Gregory seriously doubted Alverton would ever have rubbed shoulders with Ecton—the notion of Ecton swanning about the circles Devlin inhabited was impossible to imagine—if there was some government or industrial proposal afoot that might account for Ecton's desire to acquire Bellamy Hall, Devlin would know.

With that letter added to the pile, Gregory sat back. *Who else?*

Devlin's childhood friend, Lord Grayson Child, had recently married Lady Isadora Descartes, who, it had transpired, owned and operated *The London Crier*, a newspaper that had shot to prominence over recent months with its exclusive reporting of a plot to destroy the telegraph system in England. If Ecton's interest in Bellamy Hall was a part of some wider conspiracy in pursuit of who knew what, then it was possible that Child or, even more likely, Isadora and her people at *The Crier* might have heard some whisper.

By the time he'd signed that letter, he'd realized that Drake Varisey, who had married Gregory's cousin Louisa a few years before, was an obvious person from whom to seek advice. Drake occupied a curious position connected to Whitehall; if any threat to the realm materialized, it was Drake who dealt with it, and he often conscripted Cynsters to the cause. Gregory had assisted in several actions over the years. If Ecton was part of a wider plot, Drake would know of it.

Having finished the letter to Drake—and Louisa—Gregory drew out one last sheet. These days, Toby Cynster was the unofficial lieutenant Drake called on first and most often. While Toby and Gregory's brother, Martin, were close friends, one could never be sure where Toby would be —whether he would be off who knew where doing something secretive for Drake or at home in Newmarket, overseeing the breeding stable at Demon Cynster's stud.

Regardless, Toby was one of those people who heard whispers of all sorts of things. It was possible he and he alone might have heard something that would explain Ecton's offer.

Knowing Nicholas, Toby's older brother, could be relied on to make sure Gregory's letter reached Toby, Gregory addressed his missive to the Cynster Stud at Newmarket. He dropped the letter on the pile on the salver, then counted the stacked missives. Nine. He couldn't think of anyone else to ask. He tapped the pile. "Let's see what comes from these."

He rose and rang for Cromwell and, when the butler arrived, consigned the letters into his care for immediate dispatch.

After Cromwell had left, Gregory ambled to the window and stood looking out. The day was pleasant enough; as the month progressed, the weather was steadily improving. If he wished to visit any of the farther-flung businesses, the afternoon looked set to be fine.

He weighed the pros and cons of telling Caitlin and the others about the letters. The pros were largely indulging his own impulse to share and the reassurance he would gain from having people with whom to discuss any uncertainties, neither of which would do anyone other than him any good. The cons, however, would impact everyone on the estate, feeding unnecessary and certainly unproductive speculation regarding his interest in Ecton's offer.

No. He wouldn't mention his recently dispatched queries. If anything came of them, that would be the time to explain.

With that point decided, he turned his mind to what else he might do to shore up the estate against any possible threat. Against any possible predator. His instincts definitely cast Ecton in that light, and his inner self had zero doubt over what, therefore, his role demanded.

Apropos of that, he'd heard back from the estate's solicitor regarding the funds he'd inherited along with the Hall—those funds Sir Humphrey had set aside for the upkeep of the estate and which Gregory had assumed would have been depleted to keep the place functioning over the years. The solicitor had confirmed that, over the past decade, those funds had not been touched but, instead, had accumulated interest and grown to the point where the current total was significantly greater than Sir Humphrey's initial sum.

Gregory had decided to leave that money where it was, as a sizeable buffer against any unforeseen difficulty or future calamity that might impact the estate. However, while all well and good, those funds were a part of his personal wealth and, of themselves, did not increase the value of the estate itself.

He narrowed his eyes. "Yet increasing the estate's value and hence any putative price will be the surest defense against Ecton or anyone else trying to buy Bellamy Hall."

After several minutes of cogitation, he returned to the desk and hunted through various papers stacked in meaningful piles around the blotter. He located the sheet on which he'd been doodling on and off over the past days, extracted it, laid it on the blotter, and reclaimed his chair.

He picked up a pencil and ran the tip down the entries, alongside many of which were question marks. Prompted by the need to get a clear idea of the value of his holdings prior to making an offer for Caitlin's hand, he'd listed all the businesses operating on the estate. While he held no direct interest in any of them, having now fully comprehended how the Bellamy Hall Fund operated, then given that the Fund paid the salaries of all staff, including those in the house, and also all costs associated with the upkeep of the entire estate, including the Hall itself, thus ensuring that his personal wealth was not called on for such purposes, the financial viability of the Hall's businesses was of significant financial consequence to him.

In a nutshell, the more profitable, stable, and established the Hall's businesses became, the longer they would prosper and the better off he— and his personal wealth—would be.

And over time, the Bellamy Hall estate would escalate in value to him, thus increasing the price for anyone wishing to purchase it.

That was the crucial point.

Quite aside from him not wishing to sell, even if something happened to him and someone else became the estate's guardian, he could ensure that the entity Minnie and Timms had created was so very valuable that no one would ever contemplate dismantling it or selling the estate that hosted it to anyone.

He stared at the list. "There comes a point where even a conglomerate becomes so financially secure that, in essence, it becomes invulnerable."

He was paraphrasing Montague, but that, he decided, would be his new aim. To steer the Bellamy Hall businesses to the point the conglomerate became financially invincible.

Smiling at the thought—at the challenge—he refocused on the list. The question marks indicated businesses he needed to better understand. While he'd been idly doodling, ideas of how to expand those businesses had popped into his brain, but he needed to learn more about their current situations and also what long-term aims the owners might already be harboring.

He gazed at the list. There was potential for improvement in several areas.

His eyes narrowed. "And with Ecton lurking, this might be an excellent time to forge ahead and shore up those businesses."

More, given his intentions regarding Caitlin, strengthening the businesses fell into the category of killing two birds with one stone.

Chin firming, he pushed back the chair, rose, picked up the list, and made for the door.

Later that afternoon, Caitlin was working through the orders, noting those items the businesses required on a regular basis that needed to be reordered as well as those less-regular items where extra might be required, when a tap on the door was followed by Gregory walking in. He wore a faint smile and was carrying a list of his own.

He met her eyes, and his smile deepened. "I hoped I would find you here." He closed the door and came forward to elegantly subside in the chair before her desk. "I have several questions. Not of the businesses as they are but about their potential—how they might expand."

She set down her pencil, folded her hands on her lists, and regarded him with interest. "I'm not sure what you mean."

"I mean"—he waved at the lists and ledgers decorating her desk —"that as chatelaine-cum-steward, you steer the businesses through the here and now, and I've no ambition to dabble in that. You do a far better job of managing the minutia than I ever would. However, given that I have a better grasp than anyone else here of the world outside the Hall's boundaries, I believe I should focus on improving the prospects of the various businesses."

She studied him for several seconds, then asked, "Is this in relation to Ecton's offer?"

He blinked, then, smiling in wry resignation, inclined his head. "I wasn't going to mention the connection, and I suggest we don't when speaking with the others, but it occurred to me that the more prosperous the estate as a whole—all the businesses combined—the more valuable it will obviously be and the more difficult it will become for anyone to even imagine I would sell."

She thought, then arched her brows. "So further expansion and ongoing success would be our shield?"

"Precisely. And if managed correctly, a well-nigh impenetrable one." He consulted his list. "For instance, I've been studying the current costs in each business, and if we look at the forge, I have to ask how competitive is the price that Henry pays for his pig iron?"

She blinked, then admitted, "As far as I know, he has me order from the same supplier in Northampton that he's always used."

"Yet often, simply letting it be known that the Hall order will go to the supplier offering the best deal will be enough to secure a lower price." Gregory scribbled on his list. "And with a lower price for Henry's raw materials, the profits—especially from Madge's sculptures—escalate dramatically."

"Hmm."

"And then there's the way Julia, the Edgars, and the others with fresh produce sell their excess goods. At the moment, they simply take them to the local markets where, given their quality, they vanish within minutes." Gregory met Caitlin's eyes. "I believe they could do much better, even if, in the interests of fostering goodwill among the locals, they still provide some goods to the markets round about."

She listened as he took her through the ideas that had occurred to him. While she privately thought some—like the three painters getting a showing at the Royal Academy—were possibly beyond reach, others were entirely achievable, and she fully understood his reasoning in suggesting those avenues as ways of improving profits.

He came to the end of his list and looked at her. "What do you think? None of these proposals is predicated on doing more work, but on cutting costs where possible and increasing demand, thereby raising prices."

Delighted—not only by the suggestions themselves but also by the evidence of his commitment to the Hall—she smiled unrestrainedly. "I think those ideas are impressive, and I would strongly urge you to present them to the relevant business owners and see what they think."

He smiled back. "Good. I'll accompany you on your rounds tomorrow and put some of these"—he waved his list—"to the test."

~

When, the next day, Caitlin and Gregory visited the businesses closest to the Hall, and he put his ideas to the various owners, she wasn't the least surprised his suggestions were listened to initially with polite curiosity, then with growing interest, and eventually, once he explained the likely impact of the proposed improvements on each business, embraced with eagerness and wholehearted enthusiasm.

In the case of the forge, the carpentry workshop, and the carriage works, Gregory's focus was on lowering the cost of supplies. That said, he made it clear that revising those costs was only the first and easiest step for those three businesses to undertake, but once that was done, he had further ideas of how they might expand.

"Once you have your costs as low as practicable, we'll be able to project what profits might be possible, but to safely extend your business, you need to be certain of your costs."

He left all three owners thinking about their businesses in a way they hadn't previously done.

As for Vernon, he was, at first, taken aback by Gregory's suggestion. "I'm not saying it would be a bad thing to gain membership of the London Glassblowing Society, but well"—Vernon shrugged—"I've never seen the need."

"Not the need," Gregory said, "so much as the benefits. Am I right in assuming they hold exhibitions of members' works?"

"Aye." Vernon nodded. "They do."

"Then look at it this way—just as my earlier suggestion of incorporating coats of arms into your designs will create new customers who will clamor for your works, thus increasing the prices you will be able to command, so, too, exposure via the Glassblowing Society to a wider critical audience will gain your work a higher cachet and a different and potentially more avid group of customers."

Vernon's expression was that of a man viewing an imaginary scene. After several moments, he slowly nodded. "All right. I'll try it. Can't see that it'll hurt."

Gregory grinned and clapped the older man on the shoulder. "Good man. Aside from all else, you and others need to open Londoners' eyes to the artistry that lurks in the countryside."

Vernon laughed and saluted. Eyes twinkling, he said, "We can but try."

Their discussion with Joshua regarding future expansion revolved about the goat herd. As Joshua confirmed, "At present, there are plenty of suppliers of pigs to the local towns, but goats are another matter, and yes, you're right, there's unmet demand there. However, at present, after meeting the needs of the estate, we rarely have any to spare."

Gregory nodded. "Let's make increasing the herd a priority, then."

In the carpentry workshop, they talked to Percy, explaining their new tack of seeking to lower the costs for their raw materials—in Percy's case, high-grade timber—and Gregory floated the idea that a large combined order from the carriage works and carpentry workshop might lower the cost to each business without affecting quality.

Percy saw the sense and seemed intrigued by the idea. "Leave it with me. I'll liaise with Jenkins and see what we can come up with as a joint order."

"If you can give me firm figures, I'll be happy to take it to our suppliers and see what they say." Caitlin glanced at Gregory. "Once we have their reaction, we can decide if it's worthwhile contacting their competitors."

With that decided, they strode off to visit Julia in the kitchen garden.

Somewhat to Caitlin's surprise—she'd always seen Julia as a confident woman—Julia was rather hesitant over Gregory's idea of approaching the main inn in Northampton and negotiating a standing agreement to replace the irregular orders the kitchen gardens, the Edgars, and the Hammersleys occasionally filled. "I'm not sure I could commit to regularly supplying the inn."

Gregory tipped his head. "Why not?" His tone made it clear that, rather than being aggressive, he was interested in her answer.

Julia colored. "Well, obviously, we can't provide the same vegetables all year around."

Gregory smiled encouragingly. "I was thinking more along the lines of agreeing to deliver a crate or two of seasonal produce every week. I noticed that's how they've been ordering from you in the past."

Somewhat reluctantly, Julia admitted that.

When she said nothing more, Caitlin prompted, "So what do you think of the idea?"

Julia met her eyes, then, her color rising, blurted, "To be perfectly candid, I'm hopeless at negotiating. I'm sure to mess things up and make the manager swear never to order from us again."

Gregory blinked. "Actually, that's an excellent point."

Julia looked startled. "It is?"

"I think—in fact, I'm sure," he went on, "that the most effective way of gaining standing orders for you, the Edgars, and the Hammersleys is by combining the orders for all three businesses into one Bellamy Hall order, and for that, it would be inappropriate for any of the owners to be the negotiator." He met Caitlin's eyes. "And while Caitlin could do it, I have a suggestion I think will work better."

He smiled as if seeing some happy prospect. "Don't ask me why, but Snibbs, my gentleman's gentleman, who hasn't had a lot to do since I've been here, is amazingly good at persuading people like the managers of inns to agree to all sorts of deals. I always send him to secure the rooms and meals whenever he travels with me. I went to Ireland not long ago, and having him along made my life immensely easier. And a lot more comfortable."

He looked at Julia. "If you're agreeable, we could meet—you, the Edgars, the Hammersleys, and Snibbs, as well as Caitlin and myself—and thrash out the details of an offer your three groups feel able to agree to, then we'll send Snibbs to speak with the manager and see what he can extract from the man."

For the first time, Julia looked interested. "So all I would have to do is work out how many crates per week?"

"And," Gregory said, "what the minimum price you can accept for them would be. We"—he met Caitlin's eyes again—"can take care of the rest in terms of framing an offer, and Snibbs will then take it to the manager."

Julia thought for a moment more, then raised her head and nodded decisively. "If we can get a reasonable price for those crates—perhaps three a week—that would even things out over the year and, possibly, allow us to put on another worker." Her eyes slowly lit. "I know the Bartons' youngest, Missy, is keen to learn how to grow the things we do."

Caitlin smiled warmly. "There you are, then—that will be another step forward."

They agreed to meet on Friday afternoon and work out the details for a combined approach.

Leaving Julia smiling at nothing as if envisioning a pleasant future only she could see, as Caitlin and Gregory walked back to the house, he murmured, "And if the manager of the main inn isn't interested, we can count on Snibbs to go straight across the road and make the same offer to the next largest inn."

Caitlin linked her arm with his and grinned delightedly as they crossed the gravel to the north door.

The following day, Gregory again accompanied Caitlin on her rounds. At the Osiery, he had little to add to Caitlin's usual checking of orders and requests; given the raw material for the Osiery's products was grown, harvested, and prepared by the Pooles themselves, there was little prospect of cutting costs, and the Pooles were already commanding high prices for their wares.

At the orchard, after Caitlin had completed her checking, he explained to the Edgars his idea of pushing for a standing order from the main Northampton inn, explaining how he and Snibbs, whom he'd consulted on the notion, felt the approach should be framed. Both Edgars were keen, especially Jennifer. "If we had a regular order for our cider, we could expand production."

They left both Edgars happily imagining and walked on to the leatherworks. After Caitlin had taken the revised orders for various treating powders from Len, Gregory explained to the three Suttons—Len, Isabelle, and their daughter, Nell—his ideas for expanding their markets. "I know that, at present, the Northampton shoemakers take most of your leather, but I've discovered that making shoes is not the most lucrative use of the weight of leather you produce. Making saddles is, and I have a contact that—if you're agreeable—I can approach regarding supplying leather for the top-quality, top-of-the-trees saddles used by racing stables at Newmarket."

He added, "Once the shoemakers realize you have an alternative market—and a higher-paying one at that—I suspect they'll be willing to increase the price for whatever leather you can give them."

Len's gaze had grown distant. Slowly, he nodded. "We don't run the tannery at full capacity—we never have. But if there was greater demand..." He refocused on Gregory, and his expression brightened. "We could take more skins from Nene and also from Home Farm. Good sheepskin can be used for a lot of things that will free up more calf leather for the saddles."

Gregory nodded encouragingly. "We're working on another project that will hopefully result in the Home Farm selling more lamb and mutton, so that might work out well."

"Excellent!" Len looked enthused. "Do you need anything from us to send to your contact regarding the saddles?"

They discussed what samples Gregory should send, then with that settled, he turned his attention to Isabelle and Nell. "Mrs. Sutton. Nell. I wondered if you had given any thought to contacting the librarians at Oxford's colleges and also the university library, the Bodleian, regarding rebinding and re-covering those books that require refurbishing?"

Both ladies stared at him, then Isabelle shook her head. "We've never really thought about reaching beyond the local area."

"But," Nell said, "we've done a few libraries for some titled people—Lord Somerton and Sir Sidney Parrish." She glanced at her mother. "Why not try for the college libraries? At least let them know we're here and can do the job as well as anyone."

"At least as well as the London firms the colleges almost certainly pay a pretty penny to." Gregory smiled at the ladies. "Bookbinding in leather isn't as common as binding and covering in cloth. That, I do know. I also know your leather is of exceptionally high quality. Put both those facts together, and I would say you have a good chance of gaining the right sort of attention and, ultimately, lucrative orders from Oxford." He paused, then asked, "Would you like me to test the waters and see if there's any interest?"

Isabelle and Nell exchanged a glance, then both smiled at him and nodded. "Please do," Isabelle said. She glanced at her husband. "If the bindery can expand as well, we'll use virtually every bit of each hide, and the profit per hide will increase."

"And that," Gregory said, smiling, "will be to everyone's benefit."

He and Caitlin took their leave of the Suttons, with both Len and Isabelle promising to send samples of the leather and their tooling for bound books to Gregory for him to use in seeking fresh markets for their goods.

As he and Caitlin started walking toward the weavers' cottages, she studied his face, taking in his serious, calculating expression. "You've really thought...well, widely about the businesses, haven't you?"

He glanced at her, then lightly shrugged. "Once I grasped what each business does and understood what they made, I could, to some extent, put myself in the owners' shoes and look at their enterprises in terms of new possibilities."

He paused as they turned onto the lane, then went on, "I realized that, even if the owners have only been living on the estate for the past five or so years, few of them are Londoners. Most wouldn't know the Oxford colleges while, as an ex-student, I do. I know London, Oxford, Newmarket, and several other towns quite well. That gives me an advantage—a wider view, if you will—that no one else here has."

Briefly, he met her eyes. "I realized that was what I could use to make my contribution to the Bellamy Hall estate." He shrugged again. "Once I thought of it in those terms, it seemed rather obvious."

She was impressed by how he'd drawn on his experience and applied his knowledge to improving the future for those at the Hall. Smiling softly, she linked her arm with his, and together, they walked on.

On Saturday afternoon, with Caitlin, Gregory went searching for Julia. They found her in the kitchen garden with Nessie, selecting vegetables for dinner.

With her basket virtually full, Nessie waved Julia off, and Julia turned to Gregory and Caitlin with an eagerness far removed from her initial hesitation. "Have you worked it out?" she asked Gregory.

"I think so." As arranged, he'd met with Julia, the Hammersleys, and the Edgars yesterday and worked out what each business felt they could contribute to what Snibbs had informed him should be presented as a combined lot put to tender.

By the end of the meeting, Gregory had each business's commitment defined. He'd seen the owners off, then had sat down to work out possible prices. That hadn't been quite so easy; he'd needed to postulate every combination and work out the profits for each.

Checking and rechecking had taken him to lunchtime today. After luncheon, he'd buttonholed Caitlin and run through the possible tenders —the combinations of vegetables, fruits, bottles of cider, lamb and mutton—and the prices he'd calculated that, for each, would result in a sufficiently good profit.

She'd frowned and pored over every little detail. He'd sat back and watched her, rather anxiously, truth be told, but in the end, she'd raised a smiling face and informed him that he was brilliant.

He'd beamed back; no one had ever called him brilliant before, and for her to do so quite literally made his day.

Now, he outlined for Julia the proposals he'd prepared and gave her an idea of the likely returns.

Her eyes grew round, and she breathed, "That, week on week, would mean…" She blinked, then concluded, "Quite a lot." She refocused on him. "Thank you!"

He grinned. "Don't thank me yet. We've got to get the manager of the Northampton Arms to agree."

Julia beamed. "I have every confidence in Snibbs. He's really rather good at appearing arrogantly officious."

Gregory laughed. "He is."

He and Caitlin took their leave of Julia, who wandered off to check on her carrots.

As he walked beside Caitlin toward the archway leading to the side lawn and, ultimately, the house, he was conscious of the pleasure of achievement, a warmth that had spread and taken up residence inside him.

He couldn't remember feeling the like before.

*Is this what satisfaction feels like?*

Caitlin had linked her arm in his. He felt her gaze on his face, then she murmured, "When you first arrived, we didn't know what to expect of you—what sort of owner you would be." When he glanced at her, she smiled and looked ahead. "As it turns out, you've stepped into Timms's shoes, but you've also taken the role of owner and made it into something different. Something more." She glanced at him and, this time, met his gaze and allowed him to see the appreciation warming her violet-blue eyes. "You've become the sort of owner all of us need you to be, and that's becoming more obvious with every passing day."

She looked forward and tipped her head to his shoulder. "Don't think we don't see it, that we, collectively, don't value what you're doing and appreciate the changes you're making."

His heart swelled. "Thank you for telling me that. It…means a lot to me."

And it did. Far more than he would have thought possible a mere month before.

As they crossed the lawn toward the house, he looked up at the turrets and uneven roofline and no longer saw a gothic monstrosity. Now…this was home.

Smiling, he ushered Caitlin through the door and followed.

Everything was going excellently well. Even Ecton's unwanted interest had only led to better days for Gregory and all at Bellamy Hall.

# CHAPTER 12

*T*hree days later, Gregory was enjoying a leisurely breakfast with Caitlin, Rory, and the three painters. The others had already broken their fast and departed.

Seated around the other side of the round table, Melrose, Tristan, and Hugo were earnestly whispering about their works, discussing which particular pieces to show should Gregory's letter to his uncle, Gerrard Debbington, regarding him viewing their work bear fruit. Perhaps understandably, the three were a trifle twitchy over the prospect of displaying their efforts to one who was widely regarded as England's pre-eminent landscape painter.

Beside Gregory, Caitlin was chatting to Rory, seated on her other side.

While attacking a mound of kedgeree, Gregory reflected that over the two weeks since Rory had arrived, Caitlin's cousin had settled into life at the Hall remarkably smoothly—indeed, without a single ripple. Rory had taken to spending his mornings at Nene Farm, helping Martin Cruickshank with the cattle stud, taking luncheon at the Hall in company with whoever was there, then joining Percy in the carpentry workshop, much to Percy's delight and relief. Rory had taken over the crafting of Millie's lute, relieving Percy of that responsibility; Percy had confided that Rory's ability to work with wood was nothing short of amazing, and his carving was exquisite. Consequently, Percy had set Rory to carving the Cynster coat of arms into the back of what would be the love seat that Gregory had commissioned for his great-aunt, along with a second version for his grandmother.

Gregory set down his fork and reached for his coffee cup. Bit by bit, Rory was quietly and methodically carving out a place for himself at the Hall. It was, Gregory thought with a small smile, instructive to watch.

At his and Caitlin's monthly meeting with the business owners the week before, Martin had hung back specifically to complain not of Rory's invaluable insights into managing Martin's breeding stock nor Rory's help about the cattle stud but rather about his—to Martin, frustrating— refusal to accept any form of payment. "Having him work for nothing doesn't sit well with me," Martin had stated, "but he adamantly refuses to accept any coin. He says him getting room and board here is enough."

Caitlin had exchanged a glance with Gregory, which he'd interpreted as saying that, in truth, Rory didn't need the money, but she'd made soothing noises to Martin, then—plainly struck—made the inspired suggestion that, as she knew Rory would, eventually, want to expand his woodcarving into a business of his own, perhaps Home Farm through the Bellamy Hall Fund could underwrite the high-grade wood and tools necessary for that.

Martin had been ready to seize any straw that held out the promise of easing his conscience. He and Caitlin, with Gregory assisting, had worked out the basics of a barter-like exchange. Subsequently, after dinner that evening, when, as they often did, he, Caitlin, and Rory had taken refuge in the library after the others went upstairs, Gregory and Caitlin had put the proposal to Rory and watched the big man's eyes and expression slowly light with quiet joy. Rory had gladly accepted the arrangement.

Gregory glanced sideways at Rory. Sitting beyond Caitlin and enthu- siastically gesticulating, he was explaining what sort of wood—some sort of burl—he was hunting for. "It has to be really gnarly so I can use that as a frame for the face. Like hair, it'll be."

Rory had found his place. Smiling, Gregory returned his attention to his plate. He'd found his place, too, and was remarkably content.

The thought had barely formed when the peace of the morning was shattered by a sound disturbingly close to a roar.

Seconds later, Cromwell came rushing into the breakfast parlor. "Sir! Miss. Mr. Rory! There's another Scotsman here."

Hard on Cromwell's heels, a man strode swiftly into the room.

As along with everyone else, Gregory came to his feet, his first thought was that at least the newcomer wasn't as large as Rory.

"Hamish!" Rory exclaimed, confirming the connection. He waved his hands in a placating gesture. "Calm down."

Frowning direfully, Hamish halted. His blue eyes were lighter than Rory's, and instead of Rory's red-brown hair, Hamish's was more blond than brown and not as curly, but in all other respects, the likeness was compelling.

As Cromwell sidled across to stand behind Gregory's chair, Gregory had no doubt he was facing another Fergusson. Wide-eyed, the three painters edged sideways, out of the direct line of fire.

"Really, Hamish!" Caitlin scowled back far more ferociously. "Is that any way to enter a gentleman's house? You know better."

Hamish had been scanning the room. He returned his gaze to Caitlin. "You're all right." The statement was uttered in a tone of wonder.

"Of course I'm all right," she snapped, then a heartbeat later, inquired, "Have you eaten?"

"Aye. At the inn in the village." Hamish shifted his gaze to Rory. "And what happened to you? Why are you still here?"

Holding Hamish's gaze, Rory calmly stated, "I'm still here because this is a good place, and it's given me the chance to set up as a wood-carver, just as I've always wanted, while keeping my hand in at the cattle stud as well." He studied Hamish. "So why are you here?"

"Because Da sent me after you, just like we thought he would. After you left, he got angstier and angstier and, eventually, dispatched me to find you, and if not you, then Caitlin at least, and I'm supposed to haul whoever I find back home." Hamish glanced around. He spotted the painters and politely nodded, then turned back to Rory and Caitlin and—eyeing Gregory rather curiously—said, "I didn't expect to find you both in the same place."

Caitlin waved at Gregory. "This is Mr. Cynster, the owner of Bellamy Hall."

Gregory promptly held out a hand. "Just Gregory, please."

Hamish gripped his hand, shook, and dipped his head. "Hamish Fergusson, sir. Brother to the hillock over there and cousin to Caitlin."

"Welcome to Bellamy Hall, Hamish." Gregory glanced at Caitlin.

She waved at the chairs. "Why don't we all sit down?"

She, Rory, and Gregory reclaimed their seats, and the three painters crept back to theirs. They returned to their half-eaten breakfasts, plainly intrigued and determined to quietly listen and observe, while Hamish drew out a chair midway between Tristan and Gregory.

Once all were settled, Gregory asked, "Coffee?"

Hamish nodded. "Thank you. A cup would be welcome."

Gregory signaled to Cromwell, who obligingly filled a cup and placed it before their new guest.

Rory was frowning in puzzlement. "I'm the tracker in the family, not you. How did you find us?"

Hamish snorted. "You daft pillock—I just asked after you. The moving mountain. Trust me when I say none of those who had seen you go past had forgotten you."

Rory grunted.

"So now you've found us both," Caitlin said, "what are your plans?"

Hamish sipped the coffee appreciatively, then lowered the cup. "Well, for a start, no more than Rory and you do I plan to go back, no matter what Da fondly believes. I, too, have had enough, so..." He paused, sipped, then continued, "But he made me promise that I would make sure both of you were all right—that you were happy and well—and that I would write back and tell him so as soon as possible, even before I started on persuading you to come back." He met Caitlin's eyes. "I think he's beginning to accept that you might not need rescuing. He truly did use the word 'persuade.'"

Hamish sighed and set down the coffee cup. "I'd like to keep that promise as far as I'm able." He looked at Rory. "You saw how he'd got before you finally gave in and came down to look for Caitlin. It's as if it's finally dawned on him that three years have passed, and we've all grown older, and he no longer knows what's going on—what Caitlin's been doing and, now, what the devil you're doing as well." He flicked a glance at Caitlin. "We—Rory, me, Daniel, and Morgan—did remarkably well in distracting him from you going off, but now, reality's biting with a vengeance, and there's just no putting him off any longer."

Caitlin nodded. "If you write, we'll need to send the letter via London, but I know how to do that."

"Aye, well." Hamish drained his cup, then lowered it and said, "If you can think of some neat way to convince me that you've truly fallen on your feet and are in no danger of any sort, I'll be on my way."

"Why the rush?" Gregory met Hamish's sharp glance with an easy smile and gestured to the house around them. "We have plenty of room and can easily put you up until you decide what you want to do next. Like Rory, you're welcome to stay as long as you wish."

Hamish looked at Caitlin and Rory, taking in their encouraging looks.

"There's no reason to rush off, is there?" Rory pointed out. "Stay awhile and catch your breath and, if you're serious about not going back, figure out what you really want to do." He shrugged. "That was what I did."

Gregory wondered if Hamish would refuse simply to be different from his older brother, but after a moment, Hamish said, "I'm definitely not going back. I've had my fill of farming under Da. There has to be more to life than that."

Rory and Caitlin both nodded in affirmation.

"In that case," Caitlin said, "Cromwell will arrange a room for you near Rory's. But meanwhile, why don't you come with me on my usual Tuesday morning rounds and see some of what's going on at Bellamy Hall?"

"Rounds?" Hamish looked intrigued.

Caitlin rose, bringing everyone else to their feet. They'd all finished their breakfasts, and the three painters, with smiles all around, seized the moment to sidle past Hamish and out of the door.

Gregory would wager the three—who were among the biggest gossips at the Hall—would make straight for Nessie, queen of the gossip circle, to inform her she had another large Scotsman to feed.

Meanwhile, Caitlin explained, "There are various businesses that operate on the estate, and I visit a handful on Tuesday, Wednesday, and Thursday mornings to check if they have anything specific they would like me to add to the Hall's weekly orders, most of which go out on Fridays."

With a wave, she collected Hamish and made for the door.

Gregory and Rory followed.

"Just come and see, then you'll understand." As they headed for the front hall, Caitlin glanced back. "Rory?"

He waved southward. "I'm off to Nene Farm." To Hamish, he said, "It's the cattle stud—one of the Hall's businesses." He studied his brother, then added, "For what it's worth, my advice is to take a good long look around before you decide on your next move."

With that and a general salute, Rory parted from them in the front hall, striding down the corridor to the south door, clearly intending to walk to Nene Farm.

After they'd donned their coats, with Hamish and Gregory, Caitlin left the Hall by the north door. As they walked to her first regular stop at the carriage works, she pointed out the walled gardens and the other buildings scattered along the rear drive. "The livestock pens are at the end, farthest from the house."

Hamish was studying the carpentry barns. "Solid-looking buildings. They look recent."

Caitlin explained how the conglomerate of businesses had evolved, first under the late Lady Bellamy and, subsequently, her lifelong companion, Timms.

Hamish glanced at Gregory, sauntering beside them. "And now, you own the estate."

Smiling slightly, Gregory inclined his head. "I inherited it...in reality, I suppose, from Minnie, the late Lady Bellamy, via Timms. Minnie was my great-aunt."

"So it's a family property?" Hamish asked.

His hands in his pockets, Gregory shrugged. "In a way. It's certainly the place I intend to make my long-term home." He glanced sidelong at Caitlin, a small smile curving his lips. "I look forward to establishing my own family here."

Caitlin was thankful that Hamish was looking ahead and so missed Gregory's smile and the blush that warmed her cheeks in response.

They reached the carriage works, and she introduced Hamish to Jenkins, who came striding up to greet them.

After exchanging cautious nods, Hamish stepped back, outwardly reserved, but Caitlin noted that he was looking all around, taking in everything—and listening as well—as Jenkins described a special type of screw he needed. While Jenkins needed to speak with her regarding his tools and supplies, he also wished to consult Gregory about a new idea he and his lads had for an innovative axle. So Jenkins could demonstrate what he meant, Gregory went with him into one of the bays, leaving Hamish and Caitlin free to talk—for Caitlin to further assure Hamish that all was well with her.

"Tell me," Hamish rumbled, "is he any bother?"

As his gaze was resting on Gregory, Caitlin didn't pretend not to understand. "No bother at all. Gregory and I get on well, and no, you don't get to judge or interfere in my life, Hamish Fergusson—no more than your Da."

Hamish glanced sideways at her, but she rolled straight on, "In fact, I'll make a pact with you—I won't interfere in your love life, and you will keep your nose out of mine."

Hamish's brows rose. "Love life? Is that the way the wind blows, then?"

She put her nose in the air. "Perhaps." Then she reconsidered and said, "Actually, it is, but we're in the early stages of sorting ourselves out, and I don't need any heavy-handed cousins getting in my way."

Given her tone, she wasn't surprised when Hamish—after examining her determined expression—nodded and backed down. "All right."

She wasn't deceived. She knew him, and Rory, too…

Thinking of Rory gave her pause.

When Gregory returned and, looking a trifle distracted by Jenkins's innovation, absentmindedly waved them on, she brightly declared, "I want to go to the carpentry workshops next." Rather than the forge, which she wanted to leave until last.

Gregory glanced at her, but after a second's hesitation, nodded. "Lead on."

She did, checking in with Percy at the main workshop door while Gregory showed Hamish around the various projects underway, including Rory's carving and the lute he was making for Millie, then she rejoined the pair, and the three of them wandered down to the livestock pens.

Hamish was fascinated by the goats, enough to make Caitlin wonder what it was about goats that drew men to them. Gregory, Joshua, and Hamish all stood around and discussed the finer points of the herd and Joshua's plans for expanding it, and through that, Hamish heard about Gregory's efforts to procure standing orders with the inn at Northampton to stabilize the income to some of the businesses.

She knew Hamish was every bit as intelligent as Rory and, if anything, had a better head for business. He was definitely impressed by Gregory's efforts, just as much as he admired Joshua's goats.

When, after duly examining the chickens and pigs, they left the livestock pens, she was crossing her fingers that she, Gregory, and the rest of those Hamish had thus far met had laid at least a foundation for him to understand and, ultimately, accept her and Rory's decisions to remain at Bellamy Hall.

They entered the glassblowing studio, and after speaking briefly to Vernon and introducing Hamish, with her fingers crossed, Caitlin watched the artist in Hamish rise to the lure of Vernon's creations. She listened carefully, but although Hamish talked avidly to Vernon, Hamish didn't reveal any of his personal and very private ambitions.

Standing beside her and watching as well, Gregory bent his head and whispered, "Is Hamish a secret artist?"

Caitlin nodded. "He sculpts, and you can imagine how encouraging his father was over that."

"Even worse than with Rory's musical instruments?"

"To Uncle Patrick, musical instruments had some use, and we Scots do like our music. But purely decorative sculptures? They were totally unacceptable." She met Gregory's eyes. "Hamish learned to keep his inner artist locked away. I'm hoping our last stop will break that lock and have him actively considering what he truly wants in life."

He read her eyes, then nodded.

Hamish was walking back to them, a thoughtful expression on his face.

When he looked up, Caitlin smiled brightly and waved him out of the studio. "On to our last stop—the forge."

They walked into the forge to find Henry bludgeoning a horseshoe. He saw them and grinned and plunged the shoe into a cooling bath. "That's done, and I'm glad you're here, Caitlin. We've run out of tacks for the Clydesdales. We need the longer ones."

Caitlin introduced Hamish, and the two big men—much the same size —eyed each other for a moment, then both smiled and shook hands. Henry offered, "Always pleased to meet one of Caitlin's family."

Gregory exchanged a nod with Henry, then, leaving him and Caitlin discussing tacks, led Hamish deeper into the forge.

Blackie was shaping a new plowshare. He greeted Hamish with a cheery grin, showed him his work, then went back to it.

With Gregory, Hamish approached the third worker in the smithy, a fully aproned, gloved, and visored figure standing at an anvil set to one side of the forge, hammering a much finer piece of metal into an intricate shape.

The figure paused, grasped the complicated spiral with small tongs, and pushed back the visor—displaying a mane of copper-red hair.

Hamish jerked to a halt as he realized the figure was female. Then his gaze went to the piece that Madge, unaware of them, was holding up to the light, squinting as she examined her work for flaws, and as if the piece drew him and he couldn't hold himself back, Hamish walked on.

Madge sensed someone approaching, glanced at Hamish, and smiled. "Hello. Who are you?"

Hamish nodded in greeting. "Hamish Fergusson." He waved toward where Caitlin was still talking to Henry. "Caitlin's cousin."

Madge blinked and, still smiling, glanced briefly at Gregory, then switched her gaze back to Hamish. "She has more than one? Are you Rory's brother?"

"Aye, there's four of us, and she has other cousins, too." Hamish studied Madge's face, then switched his gaze to the metal she held. "What are you making?"

Madge sighed. "It's part of an armillary sphere. A very large one."

"Do you get much call for that sort of thing around here?"

"You'd be surprised. There are a good many country houses around about, and once a lady sees one of my spheres, well, she simply must have one for her garden as well." Madge laid the piece on the anvil. "Unfortunately, each one wants something special, and that often translates to bigger."

"May I?" Hamish gestured to the twisted metal limb.

"I think it's cool enough, but do be careful."

Madge watched as Hamish lifted the piece to eye level, then rotated it to view it from various angles.

From a pace away, Gregory watched, too, and Caitlin, having finished with Henry, joined him.

Hamish lowered the piece and pointed to a section. "That's out by a few degrees. Will that make a difference to how it fits together?"

Madge reclaimed the piece, studied it minutely, then huffed. "Yes, it will. Thank you." She looked up at Hamish. "You have a really excellent eye. Do you draw or sculpt, too?"

Hamish looked bashful. "A bit." He hurriedly added, "But not with metal."

"Oh?" Madge studied him. "With what, then?"

"Stone," he mumbled.

Gregory glanced at Caitlin and saw her eyes light. He lowered his head and murmured in her ear, "Is this why the forge was last on our list?"

Her gaze locked on the pair by the anvil, she nodded.

Madge set down her tongs. "You're a stone sculptor? Then you'll want to take a look at the local stone—Blisworth stone, it's called. It's a gray-tinged limestone, well-formed—I've heard it takes edges well. It's used a lot around here for building."

"Is it?" Hamish looked interested. "Are there many statues made of it?"

"A few." Madge rattled off descriptions of several pieces to be found in local country-house gardens. "And, of course, you should take a look at the various carvings in the ruins."

"Ruins?"

Caitlin and Gregory both grinned at the expression that dawned on Hamish's face as Madge described the ruins as only another artist could.

Caitlin ducked her head and whispered, "I'd forgotten about the abbey church. There's all sorts of carving in there."

Gregory nodded, amused at how visibly Hamish's inner artist was shining through as he asked questions and Madge replied.

Eventually, now radiating enthusiasm, Hamish asked, "Is it easy to get blocks of this stone to work on?"

"Well, the main quarry's at Blisworth, just southeast of Northampton, so only a few miles away. And they often have blocks they'll let you have for a shilling or two—the pieces they carve off to make the larger blocks they need for buildings. The offcuts are often of a decent size and, being limestone, easy enough to cart around." Madge beamed at Hamish. "Mind you, if you do go to the quarry for stone, make sure you take Pa"—she tipped her head at Henry—"or me along. We know the overseer, and he'll do right by you if one of us is with you."

Hamish seemed lost in Madge's smiling eyes. Then he drew in a deep breath, his chest rising dramatically, and nodded decisively. "Thank you." He glanced at Caitlin and Gregory. "I might take you up on that."

"Any time." Madge turned back to her anvil and her stubborn piece. "Now, to get this right."

"I'll leave you to it," Hamish said, "and thank you again."

"My pleasure." Madge spared Hamish one last big smile before refocusing her attention on her work.

Growing thoughtful, Hamish joined Gregory and Caitlin, and after calling a general farewell to Henry, Blackie, and Madge, Gregory, Caitlin, and Hamish strolled out into the weak, nearly midday sunshine.

They were halfway to the house when Hamish planted his boots and halted.

Caitlin and Gregory stopped and looked at him.

He met their gazes and almost defiantly declared, "I want to stay."

Caitlin beamed, and Gregory smiled. "As I said earlier, as with Rory, you're welcome to stay for however long you wish." He glanced at

Caitlin and added, "And if, in time, you decide to start your own business, as Rory is, we'll be able to accommodate that, too." He met Hamish's eyes and confidently stated, "Bellamy Hall is large enough to absorb quite a few more businesses, and at present, we don't have that many on the artistic side of things. You'd be a welcome addition if you stayed."

Hamish clearly wished to seize the offer, but hesitated. He studied Gregory, then looked at Caitlin. "From what I gathered, Rory more or less pays his way by working his magic with the cattle. I'd need to do something similar—I can't be a burden on others while I work on my pieces. That wouldn't be fair."

From her eager expression, Gregory assumed Caitlin had already thought of that and seen the obvious solution.

Sure enough... "The Hammersleys," she said, "run sheep at Home Farm. Not specifically for breeding. More for wool with meat production on the side. Perhaps you might be able to help them?"

Gregory caught Caitlin's eyes. "Why don't you and I take Hamish to Home Farm this afternoon and introduce him to Malcolm?" He looked at Hamish. "I've only been here for about a month, but from what I've gathered, Malcolm could use a pair of knowing hands with the flock, especially as his son, Gordon, is wanting to go off to study engineering."

"That," Caitlin said, decision in her tone, "would take care of virtually three birds with one stone." She looked at Hamish. "If you're willing to consider working with Malcolm?"

Hamish thought, then nodded decisively. "Aye. I enjoy working with sheep, and if that gives me a way to sculpt with good stone, I'm more than happy to help the man out."

"Excellent!" Gregory said and meant it.

The bell summoning them for luncheon tolled from one of the turrets, the sound rolling out over the surrounding buildings and gardens.

"Let's go in for luncheon." Smiling, Caitlin waved Hamish and Gregory on and fell in to walk between them. "Then this afternoon, we'll head to Home Farm and introduce Hamish to some Sassenach sheep."

Four short days later, it was obvious to all that Hamish had rediscovered and, this time, fully embraced his calling. It transpired that, as well as being a gifted stone sculptor, the big man was also an experienced stonemason.

As he'd explained after offering to fix a cracked section of the kitchen garden wall, "It was the only thing about working with stone of which Da approved."

It didn't take long for Gregory and Caitlin to explore the work available for a stonemason in a locality littered with brick- and stone-built houses and cottages, let alone garden walls and terraces. Once they had, they'd explained to Hamish that, his work with Malcolm aside, he quite literally held in his hands the ability to establish a very lucrative business of his own.

"Stonemasonry plus sculpting." Hamish's tone suggested he'd glimpsed Nirvana. "It never occurred to me... Well, up north, we don't have so many houses built of stone blockwork, not like down here, and anyone can throw together a rough stone wall."

They'd had that conversation this morning. Now, with the afternoon sun finally strong enough to strike through his coat and register as warm, Gregory followed Caitlin's trail. According to Julia, whom he'd found admiring her repaired wall, Caitlin had headed into the rose garden.

He found her checking the new growth bursting from the heavily pruned branches.

She heard his footsteps, looked up, saw him, and smiled, and warmth of a different kind blossomed in his chest.

He smiled back, confident and assured. "There you are." He caught her hand, raised her fingers to his lips, and kissed them. Then he settled her hand on his sleeve and turned her toward the bench at the end of the central garden walk.

She looked at him inquiringly. "You were looking for me?"

He nodded. "Given Rory and Hamish's arrivals, and what I've gathered from what they've let fall, I wanted to ask about your family. Your uncle and your other cousins, and any others who might be relevant to"—he caught her gaze—"us."

He was delighted with the way Rory and Hamish had settled into life at the Hall, but felt it would be wise to prepare for the predictable future.

She smiled and, when they reached the stone bench, drew her hand from his arm and sat. She waited until he'd sat beside her, then said, "Well, of the immediate family still at Benbeoch Manor, there's Uncle Patrick and Daniel and Morgan, his younger sons. Daniel is twenty-eight years old, and Morgan is twenty-three, the same age as me."

"I gathered that your uncle was pushing hard to promote a marriage between you and Rory." When she nodded, he went on, "Is there any chance that with, as far as your uncle knows, Rory vanished and out of the running, that he'll press you to marry one of the others? Obviously not Hamish, either, but what about Daniel or Morgan?"

"No." She shook her head. "Daniel is quiet, but he would never be a party to that, and Morgan is like my annoying little brother."

"But does Morgan think of you as an older sister?"

She tipped her head, then grinned. "Now you mention it, he does." She met his eyes. "'Siblings' would be an accurate description of our relationship."

He nodded. "All right. Is there anyone else with aspirations to your hand that I should know about?"

She laughed. "No. And even Rory, as you now know, wasn't any real contender. First to last, that was my uncle's idea." She studied him. "Why are you asking?"

"I'm trying to get some inkling of what hurdles might stand in my path when I apply to your uncle for permission to offer for your hand."

She blinked.

Less certain than he had been, he pointed out, "I should, you realize. Even if, legally speaking, you might not need his permission to marry, he is your guardian, and I'm sure there are clauses in that guardianship we'd rather not have to fight. Yet you won't turn twenty-five for eighteen more months..." He blew out a breath. "Well, I really don't want to wait that long." He couldn't read her expression and felt compelled to ask, "Do you?"

"No." Lips firming, she shook her head. "And you're right. That's a difficulty we'll have to overcome—gaining Uncle Patrick's permission." She gestured vaguely in the direction of the house. "And now Rory and Hamish have deserted his cause and allied with me. I hadn't really thought of that, of how Patrick might react." Eyes a trifle wide, she looked at Gregory. "What if he refuses?"

"We'll negotiate our way around that impasse once it occurs. Let's not invite trouble."

Caitlin sighed and faced forward.

Gregory studied her face, then murmured, "Are you happy here—as chatelaine of Bellamy Hall?"

She looked at the fresh, bronzy-colored shoots sprouting on the bare rose canes. After a moment, she replied, "When I first came to Bellamy Hall, even though it was the height of winter, and we arrived in the middle of a raging blizzard, it felt as if I'd landed in a place that was warm and encouraging, with the perfect conditions for me as a person to bloom and grow. Here, I was instantly appreciated. My skills and talents, such as they are, were recognized, and I was encouraged to use them. That started virtually the day after we arrived. Then, weeks later, as the thaws set in, Timms offered me the position of chatelaine, and it seemed to fit so perfectly that I accepted without hesitation."

She paused, thinking back. "From my first evening here, I've been happy—happier than I've ever been. I've found fulfillment and satisfaction. That's why I've never even thought of leaving." She glanced at him and faintly smiled. "I could have, you know. I had and still have significant funds at my disposal. Rory and the others insisted that I had enough to see me safe for quite some time."

Throughout her revelations, Gregory's gaze had remained steady on her face. Now, voice low, he asked, "So you'll be happy staying? And even remaining as chatelaine-cum-steward, not just for a year or two but for very much longer?"

Her gaze on his eyes, she tipped her head. "Are you asking if, as your wife, I would want to stop being the estate's chatelaine-cum-steward and instead…what? Embroider in the morning room all day?"

His lips twitched, but he stilled them and, with an admirably serious expression, said, "Given the situation, I'm sure you can see that it's a point on which I need reassurance. If in marrying you, I have to find a new chatelaine-cum-steward—"

"Don't even think it." Reaching across, she grasped his lapel and drew him to face her. Obligingly, he swiveled, and she drew his lips to hers, but paused with their lips a whisker apart to state, "If you are here, I'll be perfectly happy to remain at Bellamy Hall for the rest of my days. And if I am here, then there's no possibility you'll ever need anyone else to act as chatelaine-cum-steward. No power on earth will prevent me from filling the role I've spent the past three years making mine."

His lips had curved long before she finished speaking, and as the last syllable fell from her lips, he replied, "I hoped you'd say that."

Then he closed the last fraction of an inch and kissed her.

She kissed him back, glorying in the exchange. To her, this simple pleasure was both novel and exciting, yet also comforting and reassuring; it was patently something that was meant to be.

She'd never before realized that one could communicate through a kiss, yet as she parted her lips and he supped and sipped, then dove deeper, wanting more, a landscape of burgeoning desire bloomed in her mind. His desire and hers, twining and strengthening, one feeding the other and rolling forward, painting an alluring image of what would soon be theirs.

A future she wanted. One she would seize.

She shifted closer, and he did as well, and his arms slid about her and tightened, and she buried her hands in his hair and urged him on.

Warmth—that curious blend of passion and desire—spread beneath her skin.

Hunger and need escalated as his lips played over hers, and their tongues tangled in a sensual duel that heated her blood even further.

Emboldened, she nipped his lower lip, then kissed the imagined hurt away.

He made a sound low in his throat, then his hold on her shifted, and she felt his hand cup her nape, his fingers tangling in her hair as he angled her head and deepened the kiss.

Pleasure bloomed and beckoned. They were rarely truly alone at the Hall, yet at that moment, secreted in the rose garden, there was no one else likely to intrude…

The moments spun out, richly colored with rising passion, warm and heady with intoxicating desire—until the distant but distinctive *clack* of horses' hooves and the crunching of wheels on the gravel of the drive dragged them back to the world.

Reluctantly, they drew back from the kiss.

Gregory looked into her eyes, a frown in his. "What now? Are we expecting anyone?"

As he eased his hold, she inwardly sighed and, accepting that the unwelcome visitor had put an end to the promising interlude, shifted apart and shook her head. "Not that I'm aware of."

He drew away, then rose and tugged his coat straight, muttering, "This better not be another cousin."

Mirroring his reluctant resignation, she stood and straightened her gown. "I seriously doubt it. Hamish arrived less than a week ago. Unless Daniel has lost patience and run away of his own accord, this won't be him." She frowned. "And anyway, whoever this is has driven up in a carriage. Perhaps it's one of our neighbors come to call?"

Gregory had a sudden, very unwelcome premonition of who the visitor might be. Lips firming, he grasped Caitlin's hand. "Come on. We'd better go and see."

She nodded and strode quickly beside him up the central path. "If they ask for either of us, Cromwell doesn't know where we are. He'll panic."

"Hmm." Gregory walked out of the rose garden, onto the drive, around the front corner of the Hall, and on toward the forecourt, then halted.

A flashy curricle with a pair of nervous horses stood before the front steps, and Ecton was standing beside the carriage, holding the reins.

A groom came pelting past, rushing to take charge of the horses.

Gregory released Caitlin's hand and ran his fingers through his hair, smoothing the strands. "I knew he'd be back."

He glanced sidelong at Caitlin; her chatelaine's mask was firmly in place. As he watched, she tucked a strand of dark hair he'd dislodged back into her sensible chignon. He muttered, "I'll have to speak with him."

Briefly, she met his eyes and nodded infinitesimally.

Refocusing on Ecton, Gregory adopted his customary façade of easy-going bonhomie and strode forward. Initially, Caitlin hung back, then followed, correctly trailing a few paces behind him.

For Ecton, they were owner and chatelaine, nothing more.

As he approached, he saw Ecton's attention fix on Caitlin, but then Ecton switched his gaze to Gregory and smiled. "Cynster! Well met!"

Gregory kept his feelings from his face as he halted and shook the hand Ecton offered. "Ecton. I'm surprised you're still in the area. What brings you here this fine afternoon?"

Pointedly, Ecton switched his gaze to Caitlin, who had halted a few paces behind Gregory.

Gregory glanced at her and suppressed a smile at the picture of a dutiful chatelaine she was projecting. He nodded at her. "Thank you, Miss Fergusson. That will be all."

Her eyes sparked before her lids fell, and she inclined her head and walked toward the steps. Her stiff posture screamed that she didn't trust their visitor any more than Gregory did.

He returned his attention to Ecton, who was watching Caitlin climb the steps. As she crossed the porch to the front door, Ecton looked at Gregory, and his smile brightened. "As you say, the day's a fine one. Come—let's walk while we talk."

Gregory suspected that Ecton's unlikely appreciation of bucolic delights had more to do with ensuring there was no possibility of others overhearing them, but consented with a tilt of his head and walked beside Ecton onto the front lawn.

With his gaze on the lawn ahead of them, in genial vein, Ecton commenced, "Now you've spent more time in this ramshackle place, in the dubious company of its many and varied inmates, you must be itching to bolt back to the capital and...shall we say, more sophisticated entertainments."

Gregory was tempted to correct him, but in the interests of getting Ecton to his point in the shortest possible time, let the assumption stand unchallenged.

Ecton glanced up, briefly studied Gregory's face, then smiled and, with growing confidence, stated, "I'm sure you won't have forgotten my offer to buy the place—lock, stock, and barrel, as they say. And given you might feel a certain connection to the place, I'm willing to sweeten my offer. Quite considerably, as a matter of fact. I've taken a look at the situation, and I believe I can take the plunge to the tune of twenty thousand pounds."

From what Gregory had gathered of Ecton's finances, there was little likelihood the man could afford such a sum. He halted. "Ecton—"

"Of course, I would need to stagger the payments, but I'm sure you and I could come to some arrangement—"

"No." Gregory waited until Ecton halted and his gaze reached Gregory's face before evenly and very definitely stating, "I have not changed and will not change my mind. The Hall was entrusted to me, and I will remain its owner. I have no intention of selling the estate, either in whole or in part, now or at any time in the foreseeable future."

Ecton looked mulish, still unwilling to believe, so Gregory rolled on, "It might not suit you, but I like it here. Indeed, I've decided to spend the rest of my life here." He gestured at the gothic monstrosity behind them. "In this ramshackle place with its many and varied and, frankly, interesting and engaging inmates. They are worthy people, and I value their friendship. They don't just grow on one..." His voice trailed away as he realized the truth, and it found its way to his tongue. "I've become one with them. One of them. My place is here, with them."

What he'd intended as a revelation to Ecton had become, in truth, a revelation to himself as well. Not in substance—he'd gradually been shifting to that position over the past weeks—but in the certainty with which the statement now resonated within him.

All the way to his soul.

His place was there. He'd come to Bellamy Hall hoping to discover the right sort of life for him to live, and he'd found it, living there with Minnie and Timms's esoteric collection of people. People those two old ladies had reached out to and helped, and who now honored their memories in helping each other and, indeed, all those about.

This was his new life, and he wanted it and intended to hold on to it.

Ecton blinked. Quite aside from Gregory's words, he'd heard the conviction, the ironclad decision in his tone.

Gregory watched as, slowly, Ecton accepted Gregory's rejection of his offer and the resolution behind it, and a pronounced degree of grim peevishness overtook Ecton's until-then-determinedly-pleasant expression.

Ecton's eyes narrowed to dark shards.

Despite the tension, Gregory had to fight a smile; the man looked every inch the spoilt child Loxton had labeled him. Evenly, Gregory said, "No hard feelings, I hope."

Ecton drew in a long breath, and his features settled into a frankly grim mask. "I had plans, but if they're not to be...?" He slanted a glance at Gregory as if imagining that, after all, he might change his mind.

Gregory felt his features harden. "Sorry, old man. I'm happy here."

That was the simple truth.

Almost curiously, Ecton frowningly studied Gregory's face, then his gaze flitted to the house. His eyes narrowed again, then he curtly nodded and turned toward his curricle. "In that case, I'll say no more about it."

Gregory walked with him to the forecourt and waited at the bottom of the steps as Ecton took the reins from the groom, climbed up to the box, and with the barest of nods to Gregory, flicked the reins and drove his horses—again, too fast—down the drive.

The groom snorted. "An ill-matched pair, that. Nothing like yours, sir."

"No, indeed." Gregory watched Ecton tool down the avenue. The same could be said for Ecton's life. "Nothing like mine at all."

When Ecton had vanished from sight, Gregory dismissed the groom with an absentminded nod and climbed the front steps.

His inner self didn't like Ecton at all; there was something about the man that abraded his instincts and left him uneasy in a way he couldn't immediately explain.

What unsettled him most of all was that he still had no idea why Ecton wanted to buy the Hall.

There had to be a reason, a big and compelling reason, and until he knew what it was, he wouldn't—couldn't—rest easy.

Lips firming, he reached for the front door latch. At this point, all he could do was hope that his usually reliable correspondents-cum-informants would write back soon.

# CHAPTER 13

*I*t was, in fact, a full nine days after Hamish had arrived—days in which all remained calm, well-ordered, and peaceful, and matters moved in their usual slow but positive fashion while spring laid a soft hand over the Hall lands—before Daniel walked into the Hall's breakfast parlor. Unlike his older brothers, he didn't announce his arrival with a roar but with a tentative smile as he meekly followed a now-resigned Cromwell, who halted and formally stated, "Mr. Daniel Fergusson, sir, miss."

Caitlin beamed. "Daniel!" She leapt to her feet and rounded the table, holding out her hands. "We wondered when you'd get here."

Much leaner and slighter than Rory and Hamish, with dark hair and sky-blue eyes, Daniel smiled and grasped her hands.

She gripped his fingers and drew him closer to plant a kiss on his cheek. Stepping back, she studied him. "Did Uncle Patrick send you?"

He nodded. His gaze found his brothers, busily eating hearty breakfasts but also looking inquiringly at him. "Da waited six days after Hamish left. I think he's fairly certain you two haven't come to any harm but have used the chance to scarper off somewhere. As we predicted, he's fretting and fashing over that."

Daniel brought his gaze back to Caitlin and smiled. "That said, I'm fairly certain Da would be surprised to find the two large lumps here with you. I think he imagines that, once they were south of the border, they each went off on their own."

Rory shook his head. "He never did understand that we"—he pointed his fork at Caitlin and Daniel, then circled the tines to include Hamish and himself—"were all of like mind, much less that we might stick together and look out for each other."

"That's just as well," Daniel said, "because otherwise, he'd never have let me come after you."

"Indeed." Caitlin drew Daniel to the table, to the empty chair beside the one Hamish occupied. "Have you breakfasted?"

Daniel nodded. "Aye. Not knowing what I might find here, I ate at the inn in the village."

"Coffee?" Farther around the table, Gregory, his expression mild, interested, and welcoming, raised the coffeepot.

Eagerly, Daniel nodded. "Please. They didn't have anything but weak tea at the inn."

Caitlin poked Daniel's arm and nodded toward Gregory. "That's Mr. Gregory Cynster, the owner of the estate."

Daniel looked conscious and bobbed his head. "Pleased to make your acquaintance, Mr. Cynster."

Smiling, Gregory waved Daniel to the chair. "Just Gregory, and I'm delighted to meet you as well."

With Daniel slipping into the chair and Hamish passing Daniel's cup to Gregory to be filled, Caitlin returned to her place on Gregory's other side. As she reclaimed her seat, she smiled at the others farther down the table, who were still breaking their fasts. As was most often the case, Melrose, Tristan, and Hugo had been the last of the Hall's residents down to the breakfast parlor. In response to the open curiosity in the trio's faces, she replied, "Yes, Daniel is another cousin."

Taking that introduction in his stride, Daniel accepted the filled coffee cup from Hamish, then turned a smile on the three painters. "And yes, despite all appearances, I am, indeed, a full brother to the two already here."

The comment made everyone laugh, and Caitlin reflected that was one of Daniel's gifts, one that certainly came in handy in his usual role of peacemaker among his unruly siblings.

"So," Hamish said, once Daniel had taken a sip of his coffee, "how were things going at Benbeoch with me and Rory both gone?"

Appreciatively, Daniel cradled the coffee cup. "Much as we expected —Morgan is happily managing the entire estate, and no one has really noticed any difference."

Rory grunted. "We've always known he could do it."

"We knew," Hamish said, "but Da never saw it."

Daniel murmured, "He refused to see it."

Rory and Hamish nodded, and Hamish looked at Gregory. "Da truly doesn't need us"—he glanced at his brothers—"any of us, at Benbeoch. Morgan is more than up to the task of managing the whole damn enterprise, and more to the point, he enjoys doing it. He'll be in his element, now."

Daniel and Rory murmured agreement.

Cromwell came in, carrying a rectangular parcel wrapped in brown paper and string. He paused by Daniel's chair. "What did you want done with this, Mr. Fergusson?"

"Oh." Daniel set down his cup, rose, and took the parcel from Cromwell. Then he looked at Caitlin and smiled shyly. "This is for you." He walked around the table and handed it to her. "I hope you like it."

Gregory watched as Caitlin's eyes lit up.

"Thank you." She set the package—about eighteen inches wide and twelve high, but only a few inches deep—on the table, undid the strings, then quickly stripped away the wrapping. "Oh!" She lifted a framed painting free of the paper. She held it up and, with her eyes, devoured the scene depicted in delicate pen strokes and softly colored with watercolor paint. "It's Benbeoch—the manor with the mountain behind."

Bashfully retreating to his chair, Daniel said, "I thought you might like it—in case you got homesick."

"It's *wonderful*. Thank you, Daniel!" Her face glowing with happiness, she angled the painting toward Gregory and pointed at the house. "He's captured the place perfectly, including the way the mountain looms over it." She threw a smiling glance at Daniel. "You've got the atmosphere exactly right."

Studying the painting, what Gregory saw was a lot of gloomy, rather dour shadows. The house appeared...well, the word that sprang to his mind was *severe*. Then again, he'd seen houses in that area of Scotland, and they did tend to share that anchored-in-the-rock, shuttered-against-the-harsh-winters-and-wild-storms look.

The scrape of chair legs on the floor signaled Melrose, Tristan, and Hugo coming to their feet, but instead of slipping out of the door and heading to the conservatory, all three quickly circled the table to stand in a line behind Caitlin's chair and study the painting she was still marveling over.

Gregory watched and waited, curious as to what the painters' verdicts would be.

For a full minute, in complete silence, all three stared at the painting, completely absorbed as they drank it in.

Then something changed. Hugo drew in a long, deep breath and raised his gaze to look at Daniel. "How long have you been drawing and painting?"

Lightly, Daniel shrugged. "Ever since I was a child." He glanced across the table at Rory. "Our mother was an artist. She taught me."

"Well, she taught you damned well," Tristan breathed. "This is *fabulous.*"

Melrose shook himself as if freeing himself of the painting's spell. "I say—you'll have to join us." Face alight, he looked at Daniel. "We paint and draw, too. We must show you the ruins—you'll love them."

Tristan, Hugo, and Melrose left their position to congregate around Daniel.

Within seconds, the group were deep in a discussion of matters painterly.

Rory and Hamish ignored the exclamations and explanations and stoically polished off their breakfasts.

Gregory returned to sipping his coffee and watching Caitlin's face.

Eventually, she raised her gaze to the gaggle of painters and, after listening to their paean of mutual admiration for several moments, smiled fondly. Then she looked at Gregory.

He had no idea what she read in his expression, but she leaned closer and murmured, just for him, "Yes, I do miss it, but that doesn't mean I'm pining to go back." She looked at the painting. "I have a lot of good memories of the place and of my parents there, but this"—she raised the framed painting—"is my past." She met his eyes. "My future lies here. Of that, I'm sure."

He smiled, relieved, reassured, and frankly amazed that she'd seen his sudden panic, much less understood what had been behind it. Watching her gazing so raptly at the picture of her home had sent vulnerability spiking through him, occasioned by a road-to-Damascus epiphany of just how much she meant to him and to everyone else at the Hall. Yes, they were an eclectic bunch, and she was the one who held them all together; she was the Hall's lynchpin without whom they would find it impossible to function.

Daniel had risen and joined the other three, who were imploring him to go with them to the conservatory. He cast an uncertain glance at Caitlin and Gregory.

Caitlin waved him off. "Go, go! Cromwell will have a room prepared for you, and Melrose, Hugo, and Tristan will bring you to the dining room in time for luncheon."

Daniel grinned his thanks and turned to the other three, and in short order, the four departed for more artistic surrounds.

"Well," huffed Rory, once the foursome was out of earshot, "no need to show Daniel around the estate's businesses. He's already found the one he can contribute to."

Caitlin and Hamish nodded, and Hamish added, "He'll do well, too. We always knew he had it in him. He just needs the right sort of encouragement, and the chances are, he'll find it here."

"Indeed." Caitlin set down the painting and pushed back her chair. "And with that settled, I'd better get on with my day."

Gregory put his hand on her wrist, and she stopped before getting to her feet. "A moment, if you would." He looked at Hamish and Rory as the pair set down their knives and forks and mopped their lips with their napkins. "You two as well."

Hamish's and Rory's expressions suggested they were all ears.

Gregory chose his words with some care. "None of you were all that surprised by Daniel's arrival."

Rory snorted. "It was odds on that Da would send him, and we all hoped he would so Daniel could get away as well. Our father's a stubborn bugger—we've all told you that. He'll cling to the hope that something's just delayed me and Hamish, and if he just holds out for a little while longer and does one more thing—like sending Daniel after us—everything will fall out as he wants."

"I see." Gregory met Rory's and Hamish's gazes. "I would like to hear your thoughts on the likelihood of us finding ourselves facing your father sometime soon."

Hamish grimaced. "That's harder to say."

"Aye," Rory agreed. "When Daniel doesn't come back, likely the scales will finally fall from Da's eyes, and he'll be ropable. But will he come after us?" The big man shrugged. "Who can say?"

Gregory tapped a finger on the tablecloth, then asked, "Will he be able to track you?"

"Oh, aye—he's not daft." Hamish nodded across the table at Rory. "He'll know to follow Rory and me, and that'll be easy enough."

"So he is likely to turn up here, breathing fire, at some point?" Gregory looked from one brother to the other.

"I don't know about breathing fire," Rory said, "but if he appears down here, he won't be in any good mood."

Caitlin was frowning. "Will he leave Morgan to manage alone, though?" She looked at her cousins. "He never would have when I was still there."

"Things have changed, lass. Our Morgan's grown and learned, and he's not one anyone messes with. He might take after Daniel in looks and size, but the brains on that lad." Rory shook his head. "He's quick, clever, and knows just how to manage people, Da included." Rory paused, then added, "Truth to tell, if Da does make his way down here, it'll be because Morgan prodded him into it just to be quit of him for a while."

"That, and Da never being able to let well alone." Hamish drained his cup, then set it down. "He'll have had my letter by now, telling him the three of us are well and happily going our own road, but it's likely that will only make him even more determined to bring us to heel and have us following his road, not ours."

Rory snorted. "Not only that. Morgan will have seen that letter, too, and if Da thinks to give our little brother any grief, Morgan will have Da heading south—with Da thinking it's all his idea—faster than you can blink."

Hamish nodded fatalistically. "Aye. That."

Gregory looked from one brother to the other and inwardly sighed. "All right. At least I know where we stand."

Caitlin smiled encouragingly at him and got to her feet.

Gregory and her cousins rose as well.

Caitlin reclaimed her painting and, clearly debating where to hang it, bustled out ahead of the men.

Gregory saw her take the corridor to the study. He parted from Rory and Hamish in the front hall and continued to the library.

He dropped into the chair behind his desk and stared into space while his mind retrod all he'd learned that morning.

Eventually, he refocused on his attempts at improving the financial stability of the Hall's businesses, outlined in the papers spread over the desk's surface. "Obviously," he murmured to himself, "there's more than one reason that I should get my financial affairs, including those of the Hall, in order."

That was, indeed, the issue demanding his most immediate attention, but there was another that, increasingly, hovered in his mind.

He hadn't yet formally asked Caitlin to marry him.

He would have, that night in the gallery, but she'd asked him to wait until the situation with her family clarified and settled, and—as per his habit of allowing anything requiring the slightest emotional effort to roll on in its own time—he'd acquiesced.

Yet over the past weeks, he'd changed. He was no longer so ready to shy from emotional issues as he had been—no longer willing to allow obstacles to deflect or delay him from reaching his goals.

He wanted to ask her—simply and straightforwardly—for her hand, but realistically, how far could they go without her guardian's permission?

"Not all that far" was the answer.

On top of that, while her formally committing herself to him would reassure him on one front, having her acknowledged in any way as his fiancée might be a very bad idea on the Ecton front. There was something about the man that set Gregory's teeth on edge. Put mildly, he sensed the man was almost certainly an outright cad. If Caitlin became known as Gregory's fiancée, he wouldn't put it past Ecton to try to use that in some way to pressure Gregory into selling the Hall.

The last thing he wanted was for Caitlin and their relationship to become some sort of pawn in whatever game Ecton was playing.

"Speaking of which." Gregory glanced at the corner of his desk, but it appeared the mail hadn't yet arrived. He frowned. "Someone better write soon." His need to learn what was behind Ecton's interest in the Hall was escalating by the day.

◇

To Gregory's great relief, replies to his queries about Ecton started rolling in the following day.

Unfortunately, those replies, although loaded with advice, brought little by way of factual information.

The first letter Gregory—ensconced behind his desk in the library—opened came from his father's cousin, Gabriel Cynster, who wrote that he knew nothing of Ecton nor of any issue that, in his view, would materially increase the value of the Bellamy Hall land. However, he warned that an approach of the sort Ecton had made was definitely grounds for caution regarding what the man had in mind.

Montague replied saying much the same thing and that he would continue to pursue information on Ecton's financial standing. While he had no firm evidence as yet in hand, what he'd gleaned from his contacts in the City was not favorable. "In short," Montague wrote, "his lordship might very well be sailing overly close to the wind."

Gregory read the careful phrasing a second time and snorted. "If the quality of the man's horses is any guide, he doesn't have the funds he wants people to believe he has."

Setting those letters—the only two replies he'd received thus far— aside, he hoped the rest of his family and those connections he'd tapped would come up with more solid information about why Ecton wanted to buy the Hall.

Grimacing, Gregory forced his attention back to the details of the improvements he was determined to see made to the Hall's businesses. He wasn't going to wait to learn what Ecton was up to before shoring up the value of the estate.

∼

The next day was Saturday, on which morning most of the business owner-residents were more relaxed about commencing work at the crack of dawn. Consequently, all the residents, including Rory, Hamish, and Daniel, were seated around the breakfast table when Cromwell came in, bearing the salver with the day's mail.

"Early delivery, today." Cromwell paused beside Vernon's chair and laid a thick envelope by Vernon's elbow. "For you, Mr. Trowbridge."

Vernon grunted in surprise, glanced at the envelope, and froze.

While Cromwell circled the table, handing out missives to others, most eyes returned to Vernon, and the conversations faded. It was unusual for the older man to receive letters, let alone one in paper of such weight.

He shook himself, picked up the letter, grasped his knife, and used it to break the large and fancy seal on the letter's back.

Everyone—including Cromwell, who had paused behind Gregory's chair—watched while Vernon spread out the single heavy sheet.

He read, and slowly, his expression lightened. Then he beamed, looked up the table at Gregory and Caitlin, and waved the sheet. "I've been accepted into the London Society of Glassblowers, as a master glassblower with full honors and rights. Consequently"—he glanced again at the letter—"I've been invited to show a selection of my works at the upcoming exhibition later this spring!"

Delighted exclamations erupted around the table, and congratulations rained down on Vernon's head.

Gregory raised his coffee cup. "I give you Vernon Trowbridge, Master Glassblower of the London Society of Glassblowers."

Everyone cheered and drank to Vernon's health and his continuing artistic and financial success.

Later, after the excitement had died down and everyone had finished their breakfast and was streaming from the parlor, Vernon hung back to intercept Gregory, who was ambling at the rear with Caitlin.

Vernon caught Gregory's eye, dipped his head, and fell in to walk on Gregory's other side. His gaze on the carpet, with his hands clasped behind his back, the older man gruffly said, "I wanted to thank you for your suggestion and your encouragement." Briefly, he met Gregory's eyes. "I wouldn't have done it otherwise, but"—raising his head and squaring his shoulders, Vernon nodded decisively—"having the membership really will help."

With gratitude shining in his eyes, Vernon met Gregory's gaze, and Gregory felt Caitlin lightly squeeze his arm.

Vernon nodded again. "So I'd best get to it, but I wouldn't mind your opinion regarding what pieces I choose for the exhibition."

Smiling, Gregory inclined his head. "I'll be honored to help."

Vernon's smile widened. With a salute, he walked on.

Gregory and Caitlin diverted to the front hall, and Gregory stole a quick kiss before they parted and headed down different corridors.

He took his unopened letters to the library, settled behind his desk, and broke the seal on the first of three missives, a reply from his elder brother, Christopher.

Gregory spread the sheet and read:

*Ecton sounds a rum customer. I can't recall ever running into him in London, but as you say you believe he's a few years older than us, I'll check with Sebastian, in case he's run across him...although even as I write that, from what you say of the man, I suspect the chance is slight. As for the estate, I have no clue why Ecton might suddenly develop a desire to purchase it. I haven't heard anything pertinent. Will write if I do.*

*Oh, and Ellen says she's still gathering information on goats from Sir Humphrey, but extracting facts from his memory, which, these days, often*

*goes wandering, is not a simple matter. She'll write shortly with what
she's managed to learn.*

Gregory grunted, laid the letter aside, and reached for the next, in
which his father had written in a neat, businesslike script:

*Dear Son,*

*Neither your mother nor I have met the current Lord Ecton, but your
mother says his parents were lovely people, quiet and countrified but
quality to the core. More on the man from your mother in a moment, but
with regard to a reason why Ecton suddenly wants to buy the Hall,
neither your mother nor I know of any particular feature of the Hall or its
lands that would make it particularly attractive or valuable beyond the
usual uses of a gentleman's acres. So other than Ecton having a deep-
seated desire to extend his holding for some normal farming reason, we
sadly have no insight to offer on that score. I can tell you that Ecton's
own holdings are very much smaller than the Bellamy Hall estate. By
smaller, I mean perhaps a twentieth or less of the area, and from memory,
it's not good land but rocky and unproductive. So if Ecton was of a
farming bent and had come into significant wealth, one might understand
his wish to purchase the Bellamy Hall estate. But as the picture you've
painted is very far from that, I would strongly suspect there's something
rather less straightforward behind his offer.*

*On a more positive note, we were pleased to hear that you've settled
in well at the Hall and have taken up the reins of the estate. We look
forward to further updates.*

*Your father, Vane Cynster*

That last sentence, Gregory knew, was a pointed and, from his father,
who was subtlety personified, strongly worded prod to write more often,
which, if asked, his father would say was for his mother's sake.

Gregory smiled and lowered his gaze to the subsequent paragraphs,
added in his mother's flowing copperplate.

*Dearest Gregory,*

*As your father stated, I have not had the pleasure or otherwise of
meeting the current Lord Ecton. However, I have heard that, to put it
bluntly, his lordship is held in very bad odor among the ladies of the ton. I
have not come across any with a single good or even equable word to say
of him, although most encounters seem to date back several years, to the
time when he first came on the town. Nevertheless, regardless of any
improvement in his demeanor and behavior, as the general consensus is
that his pockets are to let, the prevailing wisdom is that all ladies of good*

*character would do well to avoid him. His friends—although the feeling is they would be more accurately classed as not-that-close acquaintances —are more of a mixed bag. Some are wealthy and of higher rank, but as of this moment, all remain in that category of gentlemen who would not be found in any major hostess's drawing room.*

*Regarding what reason Ecton might have to purchase the Hall estate —and how he might do that without access to significant funds, I do not know—but on that point, you might write to your uncle Gerrard in case he knows something I don't that might explain it. As we are currently fixed at Somersham Place, I am unlikely to see him or Jacqueline in the next weeks.*

*Incidentally, Therese mentioned that she believed you had a chatelaine. Is that correct? If so, what's she like?*

*Your loving mama, Patience Cynster*

He loved his family, but they—especially the females—were inveterate busybodies.

The last of the letters was from Lord Grayson Child and his wife, Isadora—she who was the part owner and editor of *The London Crier*.

Child had written:

*Dear Gregory,*

*What interesting questions you pose. Although neither Izzy nor I have any immediate information to share, both of us have been sufficiently intrigued to attempt a few discreet inquiries. Hennessy is also interested and will see what information his so-called 'snouts' might have. Thus far, all we've gathered is that Ecton is known in certain male social circles, meaning not the sort with which any lady with the barest modicum of sense would seek to associate, and while the other members of those circles are generally men of some wealth, or the sons of same, we've yet to find anyone who can vouch for Ecton's financial standing.*

*More anon.*

*Oh, and Izzy and Hennessy say that if there's any sensational story behind this, please don't forget they exist.*

*Yours, etc. Child*

Setting that letter aside as well, Gregory frowned. It was frustrating that no one had any firm facts, although the consistent reports that suggested Ecton was far from wealthy—or at least, nowhere near having sufficient wealth at his disposal to finance an offer for the Hall—made Gregory wonder if, perhaps, he'd made the offer on behalf of someone else.

Perhaps one of those not-that-close acquaintances who did have that sort of money to spare.

He pondered that, then grunted. Regardless of who was the ultimate buyer, the question of why anyone would wish to buy the Hall—for twenty thousand pounds, no less—remained the critical point of the mystery.

He glanced at the pile of letters. He was still awaiting replies from his younger brother, Martin, his sister and brother-in-law, plus Drake and Louisa, and last but very possibly not least, his cousin Toby. It was entirely possible that one of them might know why Ecton wanted to buy the Hall.

Telling himself that he would simply have to possess his soul in patience, he drew forth his list of the improvements he had in hand and, with a smile, struck out the entry for Vernon and the glassblowing studio.

Then he knuckled down to further his ideas for the other businesses.

Two days later, Gregory stood with Caitlin behind a row of five chairs lined up behind the study desk and endeavored to conceal his smug satisfaction as he watched Julia, the Edgars, and the Hammersleys sign copies of an agreement to supply the principal hotel in Northampton with a regular weekly order of their produce.

The hotel's manager, a fussy individual, was seated on the other side of the desk, with Snibbs standing beside him. In deploying his talent for persuading the commercial classes, Snibbs had come up trumps; he'd convinced the manager that replacing his irregular orders with a standing order was the only way he could hope to secure reliable supply from the Hall businesses. Snibbs had hinted at increased interest from a new hotel in nearby Rushden and even an inquiry from Bedford. In the end, it was the manager who had approached the Hall, not the other way around.

"There!" The manager straightened after signing the last of the copies. He set down the pen and looked across the table. "That will set us up for the coming year, but I do hope you will all give due regard to fulfilling any additional orders we might place."

All three business owners smiled and assured him that his orders would, naturally, take precedence when it came to allocating their harvests between their various customers.

Everyone rose and, across the table, shook hands, then Snibbs rang for Cromwell, who smiled, bowed, and escorted the hotel manager out.

"Well!" Eyes bright, Julia looked at her fellow business owners. "What a coup!"

Jennifer Edgar nodded. "I would never have believed he'd come around to the idea." She smiled at Snibbs. "You worked wonders, Mr. Snibbs."

Snibbs colored; it was the first time in their years-long acquaintance that Gregory had seen Snibbs look remotely bashful.

"Aye," Harry said. "And at those prices, too." He looked at the Hammersleys. "How does the deal stack up for you, Malcolm?"

"It's good," Malcolm said, then he beamed. "Extremely good, truth be told." He looked at Gregory. "But I'm thinking we all owe our thanks to Mr. Cynster here." He dipped his head to Gregory. "Left to ourselves, we would have just continued to grumble about the Northampton Arms' irregular orders and done nothing about it—none of us would have thought of seeking agreements like this." He waved his copy of the agreement.

"Hear, hear!" came from numerous throats, and it was Gregory's turn to feel bashful.

Smiling, Jennifer announced, "I've brought bottles of our latest run of perry to celebrate, if anyone would like to try it?"

Everyone was eager. In the end, the Edgars and Hammersleys joined the Hall's residents for luncheon, and a rowdy celebration, fueled equally by delight over the excellent agreements and Jennifer's rather strong perry, ensued.

At one point, Caitlin leaned her head briefly against Gregory's shoulder, and when he looked at her, she raised her glass, and her smiling eyes met his. "Well done!" She toasted him, then lowering her glass, murmured, "Quite aside from the financial success, this has knitted not just those three businesses but all of us closer together. It's a shared victory. I've never seen us so…united."

Glancing around the table, taking in the high spirits and the strong and, yes, strengthening sense of camaraderie, he murmured back, "I hadn't thought of that, but you're right." He met her gaze and smiled. "That's an additional, unlooked-for benefit."

There was no denying that a group united in common cause was much less vulnerable to attack.

Once luncheon was over and everyone scattered, returning to their regular tasks, Gregory made for the library and the latest batch of letters that had arrived that day. Cromwell had left the letters on the salver on the corner of the library desk. Gregory sat, drew the salver his way, and sorted through the pile, hoping against hope that someone would have written with the solution to the mystifying secret of why Ecton wanted to buy the Hall—so that Gregory would know exactly what threat he and the Hall faced—but...

He grimaced. "Damn." None of the day's letters were from those to whom he'd written.

He sighed, leafed once more through the envelopes, then settled to read a purely social missive from a longtime friend.

Over breakfast the next day, a letter arrived, addressed to Messrs. Walter, Fellows, and Martindale. The three painters, seated next to each other at the table, with Daniel beside them, stared at the letter as if it were a snake.

After several seconds of complete stillness, Rory snorted. "For God's sake, just open it. It can't bite."

The looks on Melrose's, Tristan's, and Hugo's faces stated they weren't entirely convinced of that, but eventually, with every eye now upon them, Melrose, seated between the other two, gingerly picked up the letter, broke the seal, and carefully unfolded the sheet.

Three pairs of eyes locked on the writing, scanning the lines.

"Good Lord!" Tristan's eyes lit. "It's from the owner of an art gallery in London."

"And look here." Holding the letter, Melrose pointed at a paragraph and all but bounced in his chair. "He wants to see our works with a view to including them in an exhibition. He asks particularly for scenes of the ruins and the countryside."

Hugo was equally excited. "He—Mr. Crawford of Crawford Galleries in the Burlington Arcade—writes that we were mentioned in passing by Sir Gerrard Debbington and also by a Mr. Cynster, another artist who shows at the gallery." All four pairs of eyes, Daniel's included, rose to look down the table at Gregory.

"But you don't draw," Melrose said.

Gregory grinned. "Another cousin, Carter Cynster. One of my uncle's protégés."

"Ah." Melrose glanced at the letter, then looked back at Gregory and smiled like a beatific cherub. "But it's you we have to thank for mentioning us to your uncle and his protégé."

He pushed to his feet, and his friends rose with him. As if rehearsed, the three painters laid their hands over their hearts and bowed. "From the bottom of our hearts, we thank you," Melrose said.

"Hear, hear," came from the other two.

The trio straightened, and still smiling beatifically, Melrose said, "You truly can have no idea how much this means to us."

Smiling, too, Gregory replied, "I didn't have to do much, and in reality, what comes of this will be up to you." His gaze on the three, he added, "You can repay me and everyone at the Hall by doing your best to impress Mr. Crawford."

"Lord, yes!" Tristan turned to Hugo and Melrose. "When are we going to go down?"

Melrose picked up the letter and sat again. "It says here…"

The three tossed around possible dates and how long it would take for them to put together the most impressive portfolios.

Eventually, they fell silent, then, again virtually as one, they turned to Daniel, who had been sitting quietly eating beside Hugo. "I say!" Melrose exclaimed. "Did you bring any more paintings with you?"

"Besides that glorious one you gave Caitlin," Tristan clarified.

Daniel waggled his head. "A few."

Hugo beamed and clapped him on the shoulder. "You should come with us and speak with Crawford, too."

Daniel looked uncertain.

The other three deployed their not-inconsiderable persuasive charms.

When it became apparent that Daniel was torn between wanting to seize the chance and his reluctance to appear to be horning in on his new friends' luck, from the other end of the table, Rory rumbled, "Lad?" When Daniel looked up, Rory caught his brother's eye. "When opportunity knocks, a wise man answers the door."

Daniel blinked, and the other three pounced.

The end result was that Tristan, who apparently had the best handwriting, was delegated to write by return mail and inform Crawford that their group had increased by one and that the four of them would bring their current portfolios to him for evaluation on Thursday of the following week.

"That," Melrose declared, "will give us time to polish our offerings and for you"—he looked at Daniel—"to hie to the ruins and put together a few more pieces."

Tristan was poring over the letter. "He—Crawford—definitely wants the ruins. Who knew the old abbey would prove such a godsend?"

Gregory offered, "Anything with a hint of the gothic is very much in vogue in London these days."

"Really?" Tristan's surprise was mirrored by the other three.

Melrose clapped his hands together. "Well, that's perfect for us." He glanced at the other three. "Come on, lads. Let's get to it."

Chairs scraped and, on his feet, Hugo quipped, "Painting our way into our future, just like we've always dreamed."

About to dash off with the others, Tristan paused in the doorway, looked back at Gregory, and smiled. "When we first met you, on that day in the conservatory, we didn't imagine you would prove to be a supporter of our art. How wrong we were, and thank Heaven for it!" He waved the letter. "This is thrilling—just thrilling!"

Along with the others still about the table, Gregory laughed and waved the eager foursome off.

They went, and the conversations about the table returned to more mundane subjects.

A moment later, as she rose to depart on her usual rounds, in passing Gregory's chair, Caitlin laid a hand on his shoulder and lightly gripped.

When he looked up, she caught his eyes and smiled.

Reading pride and an abiding sense of satisfaction in her violet eyes, he smiled back, raised a hand, set his palm over her fingers, and lightly squeezed.

Her smile deepened, and he released her. She left, but that sense of real achievement remained, a pleasurable warmth inside him.

Later that afternoon, Gregory was studying the planting plans and projections for the upcoming season's wheat, barley, and oat crops from Roxton and Barton Farms and wondering about investigating the potential markets for millet and rye when Cromwell—beaming—opened the library door to admit a breathless Isabelle Sutton, closely followed by a smiling Nell.

Setting down his pencil, Gregory looked from one joyous face to the other. "What's happened?"

Isabelle sank onto one of the chairs facing the desk, while Nell perched on the seat of the second chair. Even though plainly breathless, Isabelle smiled radiantly. "We've come to report"—she paused to draw in a deeper breath—"that today, we received letters of interest from three Oxford colleges!"

"Three!" Nell exclaimed.

Isabelle went on, "They want us to come and look at their old books, and they've asked us to bring examples of old books we've re-bound."

"Excellent!" Gregory smiled. "That's very good news."

"What is?" Caitlin came in. She smiled at the other women. "Cromwell warned me there was some excitement."

"Indeed!" Isabelle and Nell turned to Caitlin and poured out their tale.

Meanwhile, Gregory swiveled his admiral's chair and examined the books on the nearby shelves. When the excitement died enough for him to get a word in, he glanced at Isabelle. "Did the bindery re-cover any of the books here?"

It was Nell who answered, "Yes, we did. Quite a few, actually."

The four of them spent the next half hour combing through the tomes, selecting those that Isabelle and Nell felt would best show off their skills.

"That will do," Isabelle declared as she set the eighth book on the pile. "We'll only be able to carry so many with us on the train."

They sat and discussed the conditions they would stipulate.

"I would strongly advise that you insist they bring their books to you at the bindery and fetch them once they're re-bound." Across the desk, Caitlin met Gregory's eyes. "We can't accept responsibility for carting books of such value across the country, even if it's not that far."

Everyone agreed, and they worked out a pricing structure based on the samples they would take.

"That should cover it." Gregory eyed the stack of selected books. "From memory, most of the books in a college library would be similar in size and style to one of these."

"We'll take a big enough range of leather samples to cover anything they're likely to have in their collections." Isabelle's confidence had grown wings. She smiled at her daughter. "We'll manage."

With all decided and a trip to Oxford planned for the following week, Gregory and Caitlin walked mother and daughter down the front steps and waved them on their way.

Once again basking in the pleasurable glow of having steered one of the Hall's businesses to the next level of success, Gregory turned toward the steps.

Having halted one step up, Caitlin met his eyes, then leaned close and kissed him.

A soft, simple, yet alluring kiss. When she drew back, his lips still curved, he arched his brows. "What was that for?"

She laughed, turned, and linked her arm in his. "That," she said, as they climbed the steps, "was a thank-you for being you."

~

The following day brought several replies to his appeals for information about Ecton.

Immediately after luncheon, Gregory closeted himself in the library and delved into the small pile.

The first letter proved to be from Martin—a scrawled note informing Gregory that his younger brother was pursuing the matter of why Ecton wanted to purchase the Hall and would write when he had any insight to share.

Gregory grunted. Reading between Martin's scrappy lines, it sounded as if he thought he might find the answer. Eventually.

Gregory grimaced. "I can but hope."

He laid that missive aside and opened the next, which proved to be from Devlin and Therese. His brother-in-law wrote that he hadn't been able to unearth any hint of Ecton being involved in any legitimate investment scheme or fund. Nor had he found anyone who could tell him anything about the Ecton Hall property as it currently was, which led Devlin to conclude that the land encompassed by Ecton's estate had never featured on anyone's list as holding any significant value. As to why Ecton might want to buy the Hall estate, Devlin was as mystified as Gregory.

Given that, with Therese, Devlin had visited the Hall on several occasions when Timms was alive, Gregory trusted Devlin's assessment, which essentially mirrored his own. The value in the Hall's lands lay in the businesses those lands supported, and Ecton had no interest in such enterprises.

"Curiouser and curiouser," Gregory murmured. If Devlin knew of no investment interest in either the Ecton Hall or Bellamy Hall estates...

Gregory shook his head and read on.

Therese had, of course, added a postscript—a lengthy one—in which she informed Gregory in no uncertain terms that Ecton was *persona non grata* in ton circles. To her knowledge, his lordship had been banned from most of the houses of her acquaintance after a deeply regrettable incident that had occurred in the gardens of Devonshire House, in which instance Ecton had been found to be inebriated beyond recall and subsequently had behaved with such outlandish licentiousness that he'd been jettisoned from the house and effectively banished. And not just from the upper echelons of society.

His sister wrote that the general consensus was that Ecton's pockets were to let and his estate was far too small and encumbered to counteract such a failing. Despite his rank, he was, therefore, not considered worth a glance from even the most desperate of matchmakers. Indeed, Therese wrote, on all fronts, Ecton was considered to be a complete waste of time.

Gregory smiled at his sister's forthright phrasing, but given her position as Devlin's countess and her deep connections throughout all levels of society, Gregory knew he could rely on the veracity of every word she wrote. She might not be giving him chapter and verse, but if she said Ecton was next to penniless, he was.

"So how the devil does he think he'll put together twenty thousand pounds to buy the Hall?" The more Gregory mulled that question, the more he suspected the answer lay along the lines of Ecton never quite coming up with the money.

Frowning, he shook his head. "He must think me a dolt." Certainly one easy to dupe.

The third letter came from Drake and Louisa, although Drake had penned the entire missive, for which small mercy Gregory was grateful. If Louisa had written, there would have been as many pointed questions as pieces of information imparted. And Louisa never forgot unanswered questions.

Deeming himself to have escaped lightly, he swiftly scanned the letter, but for once, Drake had no light to shed on Ecton or on what was driving his interest in the Hall. Beyond confirming that Ecton did not inhabit the better London clubs but was said to run with a very rum set of the disaffected and profligate, Drake had nothing to add regarding Ecton personally. As to Ecton's reason for wanting to buy the Hall, Drake had underlined that he would be very interested in learning what that was.

Gregory snorted. "You and me both."

Drake concluded with a firm request to be informed of the outcome of the situation at the Hall and, especially, of what lay behind Ecton's interest.

"Assuming I ever learn what that is." Gregory set Drake's letter aside, picked up the second-last envelope, and smiled. "Toby."

He broke the seal and unfolded the single sheet. Although younger by some years, Toby was one of those of whom it was said that they had an old head on young shoulders. He was steady and reliable and very, *very* clever. More to the point, Toby often acted as eyes and ears for Drake in many different venues. It was possible he'd run across Ecton somewhere, which was why Gregory had written to him.

Sure enough, Toby had a few insights about the man to share.

*Ecton is a shady character who even his so-called close acquaintances aren't all that fond of. Interestingly, those close acquaintances—hedonistic, profligate, and untrustworthy although they undoubtedly are—nevertheless hail from titled ranks, as does Ecton himself. So he's not slumming. From what I've gathered, the group formed at Eton and have hung together in mutual support of their dissolute and disreputable ways.*

*I suspect they egg one another on in finding outrageous ways to alleviate their boredom. You know the sort. But while I can easily see where the others—there are at least four regulars of the group besides Ecton—get their funds, namely from their long-suffering parents, when it comes to Ecton, who has already come into his patrimony, I haven't been able to find any source of income other than his estate, and you will know the circumstances there better than I.*

Gregory frowned. He reviewed his conversations with Lord Loxton and the other locals. What had they told him about Ecton's estate? Nothing specific, but the implication had been that the estate—and certainly the house—was run-down. More, the Hall's people had been sure that Ecton's acres weren't used for any agricultural production, so there was no money coming in from that.

Toby's information aligned with Therese's assertion that Ecton didn't have a penny to scratch himself with. After a moment of futile speculation over how the man intended to finance the purchase of Bellamy Hall, Gregory shook his head and laid Toby's letter with the rest.

That left him looking at the last letter in the pile.

He stared at it, knowing the writing was familiar… "Aha! Nicholas!" Eagerly, Gregory picked up the letter, opened it, and spread the single sheet. As he read, a smile bloomed and grew, eventually wreathing his face.

On reaching the end of the missive, he sat back, delighted. "It's certainly a good week for the Suttons. With this news, they're financially in the pink. Or more accurately, deep in the black."

He'd sent Nicholas samples of the leathers the Suttons produced, asking if Nicholas felt there would be any interest from the saddlemakers located around Newmarket. As the head of the Cynster racing stables and, these days, with Prudence married and in Ireland, also in overall charge of the Cynster stud, Nicholas wielded significant influence over everything to do with horses in Newmarket, the home of England's Jockey Club.

Gregory had expected Nicholas to show the leather to his saddle-maker and, if the firm showed interest, to put them in touch with Gregory. Instead, Nicholas wrote that the Cynster stables were interested in securing sufficient quantities of the Suttons' leather for their favored saddlemaker to produce new saddles for all their riders, both the racing saddles and the various types of training saddles. Nicholas floated the notion that he would be willing to pay a premium to ensure that the Cynster order was filled as a priority, before any other saddler gained access to the Suttons' product.

Nicholas hadn't explained the avidity of his interest, leaving Gregory to surmise that there was some specific benefit to having saddles made with leather of exceptional quality.

Regardless, he was beyond delighted. On impulse, he rose, folded the letter, tucked it into his coat pocket, and headed for his room.

After changing into breeches and boots, he strode to the stables and had Melton saddle his gray gelding. Melton had retrieved the horse from the Alverton Priory stables soon after Gregory had taken up residence at the Hall; earlier in the year, he'd left the horse—a hunter—with his brother-in-law, assuming that he would travel to Lincolnshire to hunt at some point, but he hadn't had the time.

He smiled at the thought of all he had been doing—had been accomplishing—and with a nod of thanks, took the reins from Melton, swung up to the saddle, and set off along the drive, circling the house to the forecourt, then heading for the leatherworks.

～

An hour later, richly satisfied with the latest outcome of his endeavors to strengthen the Hall's businesses, Gregory rode back into the stable. After surrendering his horse to Melton, he walked out into the late-afternoon sunshine.

He paused in the stable yard and looked up at the looming bulk that was Bellamy Hall. Massive and over-ornate it might be, yet it looked like home.

Felt like home.

Smiling to himself, he started along the drive, making for the house's north door. As he walked, he looked inward, examining the feelings coursing through him—satisfaction, a certain type of pleasure, triumph of a sort, vindication, and quite a few others more nebulous.

*This is the happiest I've felt in years.*

That was the simple truth.

He wondered where Caitlin was. He glanced up, then diverted to the kitchen garden. Pausing under the archway, he looked around.

Julia spotted him and waved. "If you're looking for Caitlin"—she pointed to her left—"she headed for the rose garden."

Smiling, Gregory saluted, turned, and made for the nearby rose garden.

Bathed in spring sunshine, the walled sanctuary was pleasantly warm. He spotted Caitlin among the roses and strode down the central aisle toward her.

She heard him coming, looked up, and smiled in a welcome that warmed him in a way the sun never would.

Smiling in return, he joined her on one of the narrower side paths. He grasped the hand she offered and would have drawn her to him and stolen a kiss, but she glanced warningly to her left.

Looking in that direction, he saw Alice and Millie, heads down, busily snipping at some bushes growing beneath the roses.

Alice glanced up and smiled. "Good afternoon, Gregory. Have you come to steal Caitlin away?"

He grinned. "If I may."

Her eyes twinkling, Alice looked at Caitlin and, with one gloved hand, waved her off. "We can finish here. You'd better go and learn what news our dear owner has to share."

Caitlin turned wide eyes on him. "Do you have news to share?"

"As it happens, I do." He grinned at the apothecary. "Thank you, Alice—you and Millie will assuredly hear all this evening."

Already back at her snipping, Alice raised a hand in acknowledgment. "I'll look forward to it. Hearing of success is always encouraging."

Caitlin allowed him to twine his arm with hers and lead her back to the central path. "By your smugly delighted expression, it's plainly good news."

"Definitely." He told her of Nicholas's request-cum-order. "The thing is the Cynster stables currently rank as the premier Thoroughbred stable for both training and breeding in all of England. Once news of their purchase of Sutton leather for their new saddles gets out, the demand will skyrocket."

"What do the Suttons think of that?"

He half grimaced. "Coming on top of the Oxford inquiries for the bindery, at first, they almost panicked."

"Too much success all at once?"

"Indeed. But I talked them through it, and we agreed it would be best for them to consult with Martin and Malcolm regarding increasing the supply of hides and, depending on what Nene and Home Farm can manage, looking into other sources in the local area. I suggested they keep the business as local as possible so Len can be sure of the quality. It's the quality of Sutton leather and the fine working on the bindings that are the principal advantages of their products, so they won't want to compromise on either in any way."

"Sound advice." She looked at him with open admiration, the sight of which quite went to his head.

He smiled almost inanely. "I left them discussing hiring more workers once the deals are finalized."

"You've plainly taken your role of owner to heart." Approvingly, she met his eyes. "Timms would be cheering you on."

He read her certainty of that in her expression and felt something inside him rejoice.

He wanted to seize the moment. The impulse to go down on bended knee and beg her to marry him waxed strong, but…the specter of Ecton and his doings and the rather more definite obstacle of her uncle loomed in his path.

*Just a little longer.*

Facing forward, he looked up at the house. If Ecton ran true to form and fulfilled local expectations, he would lose patience and leave for London soon. Once he had, the nebulous, ill-defined threat he currently posed would evaporate.

As for her uncle, he would have to be faced and overcome regardless.

*Once Ecton departs, I'll ask her.*

That, he told himself, was a vow.

They reached the door, and he opened it and ushered her inside.

He fell in beside her as they started along the dimly lit corridor.

There was a small alcove farther along, out of sight of the doorway and the front hall. As they drew level, he looped his arm about her waist and stepped smartly sideways, into the alcove's shadows.

She looked up at him, her eyes going wide. "What—?"

He answered by sealing her lips with his, and as she responded and softened, he drew her closer and plunged them both into the kiss, intent on reaching the point at which they'd been forced to break apart the last time they'd been in the rose garden.

And then, interruptions permitting, this time, go further.

# CHAPTER 14

*T*he next day, as was Gregory's wont, after luncheon, he retreated to the library to deal with his correspondence and then work on his plans for the Hall's businesses.

As he walked toward the room that had become his sanctuary, he found he was smiling. All in all, matters at the Hall and on the estate were progressing well—smoothly and in a positive direction. Not only were his first attempts at improvements bearing fruit, but his way forward with Caitlin had clarified.

Her cousins were settling into the fabric of life at the Hall. Rory divided his time between Nene Farm and the carpentry workshop, while Hamish was predictably in demand—at Home Farm for his assistance with the flock and more generally about the estate wherever stonework needed attention. And now there were the new storehouse for the Osiery and cider mill and also an extension for the leatherworks to be built, and in what spare time Hamish had, he was sculpting in the last bay in the carriage works, which Jenkins and his lads had happily surrendered for the stonemason's use. As for Daniel, he'd immediately fallen feetfirst into the company of the painters, so that group had grown from three to four.

Gregory knew Caitlin was pleased and not only because of the ready assimilation of her cousins into Hall life. She was quietly yet openly delighted with Gregory's continuing development of his role as owner of Bellamy Hall.

She was unwaveringly encouraging, and if the kisses and caresses they shared each night before reluctantly parting for their respective beds were any guide, she was as committed as he to the future he was endeavoring to create.

Admittedly, their private hunger had steadily escalated until need was a definite itch beneath their skins, yet he felt increasingly confident that the end to their waiting would soon be in sight.

Ecton would lose patience and depart the area, and her uncle would lose patience and make his move.

Quite what that move would be, Gregory had no idea, but he felt certain he—and Caitlin and her cousins—would meet whatever challenge eventuated.

He reached the library, went in, and shut the door, enclosing himself in a well of peace.

The mail had been somewhat late today, but had, at last, arrived; several letters were piled on the corner of his desk. He picked them up, rounded the desk, sank into his chair, leaned back, and flicked through the envelopes.

One was from Martin.

He tossed the others on the blotter and reached for the letter knife. After breaking the seal, he spread out the sheets—that there were three was an encouraging sign—and eagerly scanned his brother's scrawl.

Martin, it seemed, had managed to uncover what everyone else had so signally failed to find.

"Well, well, well. Thank you, little brother."

Avidly—indeed, admiringly—Gregory read of how Martin and a few of his friends, including Toby and another cousin, Jason Cynster, had taken on learning what Ecton—who, apparently, anyone with half a brain could discern was a bad 'un—was intending to achieve via his offer for the Hall as a private challenge against which to pit their wits and wiles. They'd gone hunting in the dens Ecton and his group were known to favor and, via the judicious use of spirits to loosen tongues, had learned that Ecton had been overheard talking earnestly to a mining company agent about a possible mine on his land.

Subsequently, Martin had checked with Montague, and based on the firm's research, everyone had agreed that the land encompassed by the Ecton Hall estate was far too small to be viable as a mine.

That suggested the reason Ecton wanted the Bellamy Hall estate was so that he could package the land for sale to a mining company.

There was, however, a wrinkle in that hypothesis. Martin being

Martin and, therefore, invariably curious had naturally wondered what element a mine on the Ecton Hall-Bellamy Hall lands might produce. As he pointed out, the answer would significantly impact the value of any such mine and, therefore, the potential value of the Bellamy Hall estate.

Through Montague's, Alverton's, and his own growing list of contacts, Martin had investigated further and had concluded that, in that area, the most likely product of a profitable mine would be ironstone. He added the caveat that Ecton might be targeting some other mineral of worth, but if so, there were no whispers of other minerals of value being found in the vicinity.

A building-stone quarry was always a possibility, but Martin couldn't see how that would be profitable enough to act as a spur for the purchase of Bellamy Hall.

Gregory snorted. Having recently become acquainted with the price of local building stone through Hamish's purchasing of offcuts for sculpting, he concurred. "There's barely a living to be made in such a quarry." Nothing of the level of profit that would push Ecton into action.

Martin had concluded, therefore, that ironstone was the most likely ore Ecton was proposing for his mine, and there were sound reasons to support that hypothesis. Recently, iron had been successfully extracted and smelted from sands dredged from the depths after removal of limestone building blocks at a site north of Wellingborough, not far from the Hall. Consequently, ironstone sands were currently all the rage with mining companies. Martin had also heard reliable reports that several companies were looking to build iron and steel works in Northampton to process the iron extracted from such sands.

Overall, Martin wrote, selling land for an ironstone mine could be a viable and, indeed, highly profitable proposition at that time, and at first glance, the lands of Ecton Hall and Bellamy Hall, lying between Wellingborough and Northampton, were in an excellent position.

However—and Martin had underlined the word three times—from what he recalled of the Bellamy Hall estate, the entire estate lay only fractionally above the level of the Nene, the abbey ruins being the highest point, and even that outcrop barely qualified as a low hill. Consequently, either there would not be ironstone sands beneath the Hall's lands or, if there were, they would be too deep below river level—and therefore, the water table—to make accessing them at all feasible.

Martin's ultimate conclusion was that, unless Ecton was proposing to mine something valuable no one else as yet knew anything about, any proposal of a mine on the Ecton Hall-Bellamy Hall lands should be treated with extreme skepticism, and suspicion would not be uncalled-for.

Gregory stared at Martin's final words, then, frowning, slowly lowered the letter and set it on the blotter.

Every instinct he possessed was stating adamantly that Ecton was up to no good.

He was that sort of man, and his approach over purchasing the Hall had that sort of smell to it.

Eyes narrowing, Gregory stared across the room. "If that's what he's planning, how does he imagine he's going to pull the wool over some mining company's eyes?"

A sudden, startling clamor erupted, coming from the direction of the front hall.

The noise continued. Not quite a roar—more like a bellow.

Suspecting he knew who this would be—a glance at his calendar confirmed that seven days had passed since Daniel had arrived—Gregory pushed back his chair.

He rose as, with the barest of taps, Cromwell opened the door and, looking a trifle wild-eyed, announced, "There's *another* Scotsman here, sir." He gestured toward the front hall. "An older one, and he's demanding to have his sons and his ward delivered to him immediately. Sir?"

Gregory waved Cromwell back and strode for the door. "I'll come and speak with him. Meanwhile, you and the footmen fetch Rory, Hamish, and Daniel. As fast as you can."

Gregory walked down the long corridor toward the front hall, with Cromwell trotting at his heels. Gregory spoke over his shoulder. "You should find Rory in the carpentry workshop, Hamish in the carriage works barn—the last bay—and Daniel, we can but pray, won't have gone out but will be in the conservatory."

Frowning slightly, he continued, "Get those three to the drawing room as fast as you can. Caitlin's gone down to the Osiery." He pulled out his watch and glanced at the face, then tucked the timepiece back into his pocket. "I doubt she'll be back for another hour, but when she returns, tell her her uncle's arrived and direct her to wherever we are at that point."

"Yes, sir."

Gregory stepped out of the corridor and into the front hall.

An older gentleman—in build, more like Daniel than Rory or Hamish

—was standing with his hands fisted by his sides in the middle of the hall and glowering blackly from beneath beetling gray brows.

The gentleman's color was high, and his spine was rigid. The impression Gregory received was of a furious bantam ready to fly into the attack at the slightest provocation.

Smiling charmingly, he strolled forward. "Mr. Fergusson, I presume?" He held out his hand. "I'm Gregory Cynster, and I own this pile. Welcome to Bellamy Hall, sir. We're delighted to see you."

Fergusson blinked and automatically grasped Gregory's hand in a firm, no-nonsense grip. But as their hands parted, Fergusson Senior's aggressive attitude returned. His eyes—a quite-startling blue—locked on Gregory's face in high dudgeon and uncertain suspicion. "I'm here to see my sons, sir, and my ward, and I won't be denied."

"Naturally." Calmly, Gregory waved to the drawing room. "I've sent for your sons—they should be along shortly. Miss Fergusson is presently visiting elsewhere on the estate, but she should be back within the hour." He turned toward the drawing room. "Might I suggest we sit in comfort while we wait?"

As Gregory had hoped, Fergusson was knocked off his stride by the calm, unflustered welcome. Although plainly reluctant, he allowed Gregory to usher him into the drawing room and consented to sink into one of the armchairs before the fireplace, in which a neat fire merrily crackled, throwing out just enough heat to take the lingering chill from the air.

As Gregory claimed the armchair on the other side of the hearth, Fergusson threw him a suspicious look. "I warn you, sir, that I will not be staying." He jutted his chin. "I fully intend to haul all four of my family back to Benbeoch Manor."

Mildly, Gregory responded, "I see." He seriously doubted Patrick Fergusson would find matters so simple. Not even with his younger son. And he certainly wouldn't succeed in winkling Caitlin away from the Hall; it would not be just she and Gregory who would oppose him on that.

"How was your journey?" Gregory asked.

Fergusson, who was staring, beetle-browed, at the open doorway, slanted him a sidelong glance. "I came from north of the border."

Gregory inclined his head. "I know of Dalmellington and the area around it."

"You do?" Fergusson studied him in surprise.

"I have relatives who live near the village of Carsphairn."

Fergusson's brows lowered again, this time in furious thought. Then he had it. He looked at Gregory. "Cynster. You're related to Marcus Cynster?"

"Marcus—and Lucilla, now Lady of the Vale—are cousins. Well, second cousins, to be precise, but we're all quite close." Gregory smiled. "I visit every now and then."

"Do you? Well, in that case, you'll know about our winter snow. It's more or less thawed now, but it wasn't a pleasant slog down to the border."

Gregory sensed the older man relaxing a trifle. He might have induced him to mute his aggressive bullheadedness by a few more degrees—to improve the chances that he would listen properly to his sons —but heavy footsteps approaching across the hall put an end to any further advance on that front.

Rory led the way in, his face set like stone, his bushy hair drawn back in a queue that left the hewn planes of his face exposed. With his hamlike hands loosely fisted at his sides, he appeared the very epitome of a fierce highland warrior; all he lacked was the kilt and a weighted club.

Immediately behind him came Hamish, also grimly determined, followed by Daniel, who, despite his relative youth, likewise appeared ready to fight for his freedom.

Never having had to do that himself, Gregory could nevertheless empathize. From everything he'd gathered and now seen of Patrick Fergusson, he was a man who had grown unshakably accustomed to all members of his family running in his harness.

Rory halted several yards away and nodded at his sire. "Da."

"I'm thoroughly disappointed in you, boy!" Fergusson gripped the arms of the chair as if restraining himself from leaping up and physically confronting his significantly larger son. "I entrusted you with the simple task of finding your cousin and bringing her back to Benbeoch where she belongs. Instead, I find you taking your ease here! Aye—and corrupting your brothers into doing the same. What do you have to say for yourself, heh?"

His gaze steady, Rory shrugged. "Does it matter? You won't listen, anyway, and you'll never understand. But you need to accept that I won't be returning to Benbeoch."

"Won't you, now?" Patrick leaned forward, his eyes narrowing to shards. "If you don't return with me"—he cast an almost-contemptuous glance at his younger sons—"and bring these two to heel as well, I'll cut you off without a penny. How do you imagine you'll manage then?"

Unperturbed, Rory shrugged again. "Exactly as I have been for the past month, or haven't you noticed I haven't been drawing from the estate account?"

Blinking, Patrick eased back; it was apparent to all that, indeed, he hadn't noticed that.

Rory nodded. "Aye, old man. I'm no longer dependent on you or Benbeoch. I've found a place here, and I've started my own business, and it's going well, too."

Patrick looked flummoxed. "Doing what?"

Rory smiled—a genuinely happy smile. "Making musical instruments —wooden ones. I've orders rolling in, more than I can easily fill. They— those hereabouts—are saying I should perhaps take on an apprentice to teach, and I think maybe they're right. I also consult with the local cattle stud—and for that, I admit, I owe a debt to Benbeoch. Not to you, but to old Smithy and the others who taught me all about breeding the beasts."

Patrick was frowning.

Gregory suspected it was Rory's smile—the real emotion behind it— that had given his father greatest pause.

After a tense moment, Patrick switched his gaze to Hamish, standing at Rory's left. "And what about you, heh?" Patrick barked. "You found your calling, too?"

Hamish had relaxed somewhat while Rory had been speaking and stood at ease with his hands clasped behind his back. In response to his father's goading questions, Hamish's smile was almost as content as Rory's. "As it happens, I have. I'm working with stone—both as a stone-mason and also a sculptor—and I've more work than I can handle on both counts already, and I've only been here a few weeks." He tipped his head Rory's way. "I can already see, with orders building as they are, that like Rory, I'll be thinking of taking on an apprentice soon. I also help the Home Farm here with their sheep."

Patrick blinked and blinked, then shifted his gaze to Daniel. Considerably less aggressively—less confidently—he inquired, "And you?"

Again came a radiant smile, one of joy in a life that was fulfilling Daniel's dreams. "There are other painters here, Da, and they've invited me to join their business, and I've agreed. We're heading to London next week to show our pieces to a gallery owner there. He invited us at the recommendation of Sir Gerrard Debbington!"

Patrick made a scoffing sound, although it lacked his earlier certainty. "And he'll pay you what? A few shillings for your daubs? How can you make a living from that?" Sensing weakness, Patrick was working up a head of steam. "And who's this Sir Gerrard Debbington when he's at home, heh?"

Evenly, Gregory said, "I believe my uncle is generally held to be the pre-eminent landscape painter of his generation. Consequently, in the art world, his recommendations tend to open doors to serious opportunities." Smoothly, he went on, "Regarding the painters' business, which runs out of the Hall and thus operates under the estate's aegis, since inheriting the estate earlier this year, I have, of course, run my eye over the profitability of the businesses it supports. I can, therefore, testify that the business based on the painters' joint efforts is very firmly in the black, with the income more than adequate to cover all associated costs as well as providing a nice personal income to the four gentlemen involved. Their pending expansion onto the London—and by that, I mean the ton's—stage will only further elevate the return on their investments of time, effort, and creativity."

Patrick was growing increasingly bewildered. No longer glowering, he stared at Gregory for several long moments, then said. "Are you telling me that"—he glanced at his sons, then flung out a hand at them and looked back at Gregory—"that being a maker of musical instruments and a carver of stone and a painter, for the Lord's sake, are...are..."

"Worthwhile and profitable professions?" Gregory smiled. "Indeed." He looked at the three brothers; they'd grown on him. "I believe I speak for all those living on the estate when I say that your sons have proved to be welcome additions to our ranks." He caught Patrick Fergusson's eye. "They've earned their places among us, and each is respected for the talents and skills they're contributing to our broader enterprise."

Now, Patrick looked concerned, albeit in a fatherly way. But after a moment, his resistance hardened, and he gruffly growled, "If you remain here, I warn you, I'll disinherit the lot of you."

Regardless of the words, anyone who heard them would know he didn't mean them.

Rory sighed. "Da, you've known for years that we take after Mama. We're artists of one stripe or another"—he tipped his head toward his brothers—"all of us. We're never going to be happy or settled at Benbeoch. It never was our home." He paused and slanted a glance at Hamish, who caught it and held it for an instant, then nodded. Rory looked back at Patrick and said, "And speaking of home, it's not just Caitlin being here that makes us feel we've found our place. Both Hamish and I have met ladies"—Rory hauled in a tight breath and let it out with —"who we hope to ask to be our wives. If they accept us, then given Morgan's not going to be ready to front any altar for years, your best chance at being a grandfather will be here."

Patrick looked shocked, but in a taken-aback way. He clearly hadn't thought of that.

Hamish stirred. "So, Da, no matter what you threaten, it won't make us come to heel and follow you back. We've found our places here—"

"Doing what we love," Daniel put in.

Hamish and Rory nodded, and Hamish went on, "So we'll be staying here, alongside Caitlin." Hamish's, Rory's, and Daniel's gazes all switched to Gregory. "And," Hamish continued, "we'll be looking out for her, so you won't need to worry about that."

Patrick swiveled to look at Gregory. After a moment, he asked, almost as if he was afraid to hear the answer, "Caitlin—what's her place here?"

Gregory smiled as reassuringly as he could. "Your niece is the Hall's chatelaine, but she also fills the role of steward. She accepted the post three years ago, when she first came to Bellamy Hall and the position was offered to her by the previous owner."

"A relative of yours?" Patrick asked, clearly still harboring all sorts of suspicions.

Gregory inclined his head. "Mrs. Timms was my great-aunt Lady Bellamy's companion for many years. All the Cynsters consider Timms a member of our family, although technically, she's a close connection."

Patrick was puzzled. "So what does Caitlin do?"

Rory grinned. "What you'd expect her to do, Da. She manages everyone on the entire estate."

Gregory's lips twitched. He straightened them, but inclined his head in agreement. "In a nutshell, that is, indeed, what she does." To Patrick, he said, "There are fifteen active businesses—all profitable and expanding—that operate from the Hall estate. That's not counting Rory's new enterprise or Hamish's stonemasonry business. As Daniel has joined an existing business, we now have seventeen businesses, and Caitlin organizes everything required to keep them running smoothly."

He glanced at the clock on the mantelpiece and saw with some surprise that it was nearly three o'clock. He frowned. "I could give you chapter and verse, which would underscore how vital to everyone—literally everyone on the estate—Caitlin and her abilities are, but..." He looked at Rory, Hamish, and Daniel. "I'm rather concerned that she's not yet here."

Daniel offered, "She told me she was off to the Osiery to speak with Mrs. Poole about an order."

Gregory nodded. "But I would have thought she would have returned by now."

The drawing room doors—which Cromwell had silently shut behind the brothers—were abruptly thrust open, and the normally correct butler, white-faced and close to panicking, pushed through, guiding a gasping William Poole, who was doubled over, trying to catch his breath.

Gregory leapt to his feet as Caitlin's cousins swung around.

Patrick Fergusson pushed out of the chair and peered past his sons.

Gregory strode forward. "William! What's happened?"

"Ran...as fast as...I could," William gasped. He leaned heavily on Cromwell and tried to straighten as his wide eyes found Gregory's face. "It's Miss C, sir. Some blackguard came past and kidnapped her—right off the lane."

"What?" Commandingly, Gregory held up a hand to silence all the other exclamations. "Start at the beginning, William. We know Caitlin went down to see your mother. Did she reach the Osiery?"

William nodded. "Aye. She spoke to Mama and set off again, walking up the lane back toward the Hall." He drew in a deeper breath and rushed on, "Hattie was in the osier beds with me. She was pruning closer to the lane and saw Miss C walk past. Then a carriage came along—one of those gentleman's carriages with two horses between the shafts. Hattie heard the horses and the carriage stop, and she thought that was odd, so she went a little way toward the lane to see what was going on."

William sagged, and Rory stepped in to help him stand. "Easy, lad."

Gregory bit his lip, but couldn't help prompting, "And?"

William hauled in a breath and raised his head. "The carriage had pulled up beside Miss C, and Hattie saw the gentleman in the carriage talking to her. Hattie said she—Miss C—looked shocked, and then the gentleman gave her his hand, and she climbed up to the seat. But she'd no sooner sat than the gentleman grabbed a black sack and pulled it down over Miss C's head. She cried out, but the material cut off the sound, and the man tied a scarf about her head—a gag holding the sack in place— then he grabbed Miss C's hands and bound her wrists with a rope."

William met Gregory's eyes. "Hattie ran to help Miss C, but by the time Hattie reached the lane, the man had whipped up his horses, and the carriage was bowling off. Hattie ran back and got me from the river. She told me what she'd seen, and I came running."

"My thanks to you and to Hattie." Gregory gripped the lad's shoulders and locked his eyes with his. "Did Hattie recognize the man?"

William shook his head. "But she said he was definitely a gentleman. He had dark hair and was tallish, but not as tall as you. Oh, and he was wearing a coat with big buttons—she saw them, even from a distance."

"Ecton," Gregory snarled. He released William and patted the lad on the shoulder. "You did well to come running." He looked at Cromwell. "See he eats and drinks something and rests."

"Aye, sir. Come on, lad. Let's take you to Nessie."

The instant Cromwell turned away with William in his care, Rory rounded on Gregory. "Ecton's that ponce next door, right? The one who offered to buy the estate?"

Gregory narrowed his eyes. "Yes. Twice. I refused both times."

"So now he's kidnapped Caitlin?" Hamish looked stunned.

Gregory knew how he felt. "So it seems. Presumably, he intends to use her as a pawn to force me to sell to him." If so, he wouldn't harm her. Not yet.

Patrick blinked. "Would you agree to sell this place to get Caitlin back?"

"Of course," Gregory replied, "but it won't come to that." His expression hardened as he envisaged what had happened. "Ecton was in his curricle. If he intends to use Caitlin to bargain with me, he won't harm her, but he can't risk going far with an obviously trussed-up lady beside him. He was on the track driving toward Bellamy Hall. Just past the Osiery, there's a turnoff, an arm of the track that continues west along the riverbank south of the ruins to eventually join the lane near the entrance to the Ecton Hall drive."

Gregory met Rory's eyes. "He'll have taken her to Ecton Hall." He swung around and stalked out, into the front hall.

Rory, Hamish, and Daniel were right behind him, with their father on their heels.

Patrick was expostulating, "I can't believe it! You numbskulls let Caitlin wander about alone and unprotected? Of course she got kidnapped!" When Gregory glanced at him, Patrick demanded, "Don't you know how much she's worth?"

It was Gregory's turn to blink. "No, I don't. I hadn't thought of that angle." He wondered if Ecton knew Caitlin was a wealthy heiress.

*That doesn't matter. Finding and freeing her immediately does.*

Grimly determined, he faced forward and strode on—straight out of the house and around to the stable.

Caitlin's cousins kept pace, as did their father.

By the time Gregory had ordered horses for them all—Patrick had demanded a horse as well—the entire stable knew of Ecton's perfidy. Several of the footmen went running from the house, intent on spreading the word.

Tight-lipped, Jenkins, summoned from the carriage works, nodded to Gregory as he settled in his saddle. "The ground between here and the Hall's too uncertain—too many rocks and holes—to ride horses over it. The fastest way for you lot will be around by the track along the river and into Ecton Lane. The rest of us"—with a tip of his head, he indicated the men who were arming themselves with all sorts of implements—"will go direct across the fields. By the time you reach Ecton Hall, we won't be far behind."

Grimly, Gregory nodded. He didn't waste his breath trying to dissuade them from forming a mob; he had no idea what the situation at Ecton Hall would be. He glanced at the Fergussons. His gaze fell on Patrick. His jaw set like iron, the elder Fergusson was swinging up to the saddle.

He saw Gregory looking at him and growled, "I'm coming whether you like it or not."

Gregory nodded. "By all means. You are her legal guardian. Your presence might help."

Patrick's expression softened, and for a second, a desperately worried uncle showed through. Then his features hardened again, and he nodded to Gregory. "Lead on, then—let's go!"

Gregory didn't wait for further encouragement. He led the way out of the stable yard and swung directly south. Behind him, men were gathering—some of the women as well. Caitlin wouldn't lack for rescuers and defenders.

Patrick had seen the same thing. He called across to Gregory. "It seems our Caitlin's well-regarded. Lots of your people are turning out to help her."

From Gregory's other side, Rory yelled back, "'Well-regarded' is a massive understatement! Everyone here loves her."

And that, Gregory thought, was the unvarnished truth.

*And she's no longer your Caitlin—she's ours.*

He shifted into a fast canter, leading the way over the green sward and onto the track that skirted the ruins.

He remembered his first morning at the Hall as its owner, when he'd come upon Caitlin arranging flowers on Minnie's and Timms's graves. He held that image in his mind as he thundered toward Ecton Hall.

~

Caitlin battled to overcome the panic that clawed at her mind.

Unfortunately, breathing deeply wasn't an option.

*Breathe shallowly! Short, light breaths. Slowly. Don't try to fill your lungs!*

She was lying on her side, trussed up—her wrists firmly bound and her ankles as well—but it was the hood of tightly woven black material encasing her head that was the principal source of her panic. That black-guard, Ecton, had cinched a scarf or something similar tightly beneath her nose, pushing the material between her lips; if she tried to breathe too deeply, the material threatened to smother her.

But, she told herself, she hadn't suffocated yet. The weave of the material was fine and only allowed so much air to seep through. Just enough for her to remain conscious as long as she stayed calm and breathed slowly, shallowly, and evenly.

Of course, the hood also meant that she couldn't make any sound louder than a murmur or see anything of her surroundings, which only compounded her fear.

As the minutes dragged by and nothing more happened—no sound, no movement around her—and no hint of anyone or anything being near came to her hyperactive senses, those leaping senses gradually subsided, and the ability to think returned.

*Where am I?*

With something like her customary determination seeping into her mind, she directed her senses outward and tried to analyze what they were telling her.

Was she lying on stone? Surely she was. Cool, unyielding stone, covered in a thick layer of dust. Dry dust, it seemed.

Courtesy of the hood and her long-skirted pelisse, gloves, and boots, not much of her skin was exposed—just slivers on her forearms where the binding about her gloved wrists had rucked up the sleeves of her coat—

but if she concentrated on what those slivers could feel, the air seemed cool but not damp, and from what little she could smell, she didn't think there was anything wet or moldy near.

She wasn't sure how far she could trust her sense of smell, but she didn't think she was outside—not in the open air or even in a shed.

A cellar?

But what had been that horrible noise that had followed after Ecton had shut the door?

Increasingly disgusted over finding herself in the blackguard's clutches and in this predicament, she inwardly shook her head. She hadn't trusted Ecton, not one inch. And she certainly wouldn't have so blindly rushed to clamber into his curricle if he hadn't told her that he'd come racing from the Hall because there'd been a terrible accident, and Gregory had been badly injured and was asking for her.

Of course, she'd all but leapt into Ecton's carriage!

Her mind had been so fixated on Gregory, with imagining him lying injured and wanting her there, she'd immediately focused ahead and hadn't noticed when Ecton had reached behind him. He'd whipped out the hood and yanked it over her head before she'd realized he was a threat. And before she'd been able to scream, he'd gagged her.

She'd tried to fight him off, but given she'd been blind, half-smothered, and fighting to breathe, her efforts had been laughable, and he'd easily bound her wrists as well, then he'd driven somewhere at speed. She'd known better than to throw herself from a racing carriage, yet even now, thinking carefully over the moments, she'd been so shocked and disoriented that she had no idea how far he'd driven before he'd halted his horses.

He'd bent and lashed her boots together before getting down, rounding the carriage, and hoisting her over his shoulder like a sack of potatoes.

She'd tried to struggle, but she'd been dizzy and breathless; it was hardly surprising he'd paid no heed. Instead, he'd carried her up an incline; she'd heard his soles slap on rock.

Had those been stone steps? She wasn't sure.

At that point, she'd stopped fighting and, instead, had tried to think of what to do. All she'd come up with was easing her handkerchief from inside her sleeve—something she could just manage with her bound hands—then letting it flutter and fall free. A clue to her whereabouts that might prove helpful if—*when!*—people came searching for her.

Ecton had come to the end of his climb and walked a few paces on and around, then paused and juggled her while he'd opened a door. Then —and she was sure of this—he'd carried her down seven stone steps. Then he'd walked farther—perhaps ten paces—before halting and lowering her, reasonably gently, to the ground.

The hard ground on which she still lay.

Immediately he'd set her down, he'd swung around and walked swiftly away.

She'd heard him go, literally running up the steps. He'd definitely been in a hurry to be gone.

He'd shut the door, not with a bang but firmly.

A short silence had followed, then had come the horrible, loud grating noise, followed by several—she thought three—solid *thumps*.

Thumps so heavy, the ground beneath her had juddered.

*Those thumps were not a good sign.*

If Ecton had put her in some cellar, what did those thumps mean?

Reluctantly, she accepted that she had no real idea where she was. Even if she freed herself of the hood and her bindings, she didn't know whether she could get out.

And if Gregory was injured...

Beneath the hood, her eyes narrowed.

*Ten to one, Ecton's story was a ruse. He's captured you to force Gregory to sell the Hall to him.*

The important part in that was that there was no reason to suppose Gregory was incapacitated. And if he wasn't, he would come for her.

Once he realized she was missing.

Daniel and several others knew she'd gone to see Mrs. Poole. When she didn't return for afternoon tea, they would search and...

There'd been no witnesses to Ecton's attack. How would Gregory know Ecton had taken her?

Doubt seeped into her mind. Cold dread followed. How long would she have to wait in this cold darkness? Would they even find her?

Obviously, at some point, Ecton would taunt Gregory with her where-abouts, but how long would he drag the matter out? If Ecton was wise, he would wait until Gregory grew frantic before hinting that he might know where she was.

How long before Ecton spoke? Before he renewed his twice-rejected offer for Bellamy Hall?

For several long moments, she dwelled on those questions before thrusting them to the back of her mind.

Instead, she thought of Gregory—of his hazel eyes and smiling lips. Of the warmth of his arms and the passion in his kiss.

Resolutely, she fixed his image in her mind and reminded herself of the shared future he and she were determined to build at Bellamy Hall.

A future rich with promise and with love and affection of so many different stripes.

She clung to the gilded vision and a no-matter-how-irrational certainty that Gregory would come for her.

She held both in the forefront of her mind to keep the darkness at bay.

# CHAPTER 15

*W*ith Caitlin's cousins and her uncle at his back, Gregory rode up the curving drive of Ecton Hall.

As a group, they rounded the last bend, and the house rose before them.

As one, they slowed.

They halted their horses at the edge of the weed-strewn forecourt and stared at the dilapidated building.

Bellamy Hall might be a gothic monstrosity, yet despite its size, it was lovingly tended, well-maintained, and in excellent condition.

Ecton Hall hadn't been loved for years. It had once been a neat, Georgian-style gentleman's residence of three stories, built of local stone, with windows spaced symmetrically to either side of the central door and the long, vertical window above it and what once, no doubt, had been manicured lawns in front and to either side—exactly what one might imagine as the seat of a minor lord.

Now, the house was run-down to just short of falling down. There were visibly damaged tiles on the roof, and several wooden shutters hung askew. Paint, what was left of it, peeled and flaked from the window frames, and the glass in the windows looked like it hadn't been cleaned for a decade.

Weeds sprouted between the cracked stones forming the steps and the front porch, but the front door, protected by the porch, looked as if it was still in use.

Rory shifted in the saddle on the heavy hunter halted alongside Gregory's mount. "You sure he'll have brought her here?"

"No. But this is the first place we need to check." Gregory glanced around. "We might do better to leave our horses here." Tied to the skeletal trees that bordered the drive.

Rory grunted in agreement, and the five of them dismounted and secured their horses.

As Gregory turned back to Ecton Hall, he saw movement in the distance, some way to the rear of the derelict house.

A small mob were striding purposely toward them.

Hamish had followed Gregory's gaze. He squinted. "Is that the folk from the Hall?"

Gregory nodded. "It really isn't that far across the fields. I think that's the boundary fence they're climbing over. They'll be here soon."

Frowning, Patrick glared at the house. "What I don't understand is why this Ecton thought kidnapping Caitlin was a good idea."

Gregory scanned the house, searching for any sign of occupation. "Just before you arrived, I received a letter from my younger brother. He's in London and, with others, has been investigating Ecton, trying to discover why Ecton wants Bellamy Hall. On the face of it, that seemed absurd." He waved at the house. "As we can see and from all we've heard, Ecton doesn't like living in the country. From what I've learned, we can safely assume that Ecton wants money, and my brother's information suggests that Ecton's offer to buy Bellamy Hall is contingent on him selling the combined estates to a mining company."

"Mining?" Hamish frowned. "I wouldn't have thought this area, so close to the river, would be of much use to any miner."

"Whatever Ecton's pitch to the mining companies is, there's a good chance it's fraudulent. But he needs Bellamy Hall to add to Ecton Hall to make a parcel of land large enough for any mining company to even consider." With his gaze on the mob fast approaching, thankfully quietly, Gregory went on, "While it's possible Ecton somehow learned that Caitlin is wealthy—in which case, he's either intending to marry her and claim her inheritance or he's holding her for ransom—I suspect his intention is more along the lines of forcing me to part with Bellamy Hall."

Patrick continued to frown.

Before his putative uncle-in-law could return to his question of why Ecton would think Caitlin an effective pawn to force Gregory to sell—an issue he would prefer not to address at that precise moment—he went on.

"Either motive is possible for the same reason—Ecton wants money, and his need might well be desperate."

"And," Rory rumbled, still staring at the house, "desperate men are prone to doing desperate things."

Gregory glanced at Caitlin's relatives. "Whatever happens, I suggest we avoid mentioning Caitlin's wealth. If Ecton doesn't know—and there's really no reason he would—there's no sense in giving him that information."

Stony-faced, Patrick nodded. "Especially if, as you say, he's after money."

Rory looked to Gregory. "How do you want to handle this?"

Gregory was grateful that Rory was asking and not simply charging ahead.

"The place looks deserted," Daniel observed. "But it's big enough that doesn't mean there's no one inside."

"Indeed." Gregory turned to the denizens of the Hall as they arrived en masse. He looked over his troops, all angrily determined, and nodded to Joshua, Jenkins, and Henry. "Can you three take your workers, skirt around, and check the rear?"

Henry tipped him a salute. "Consider it done."

The three and their helpers divided into two parties and, keeping to the lawns, set off in opposite directions to swiftly circle the house.

Gregory surveyed the rest of Caitlin's would-be rescuers. As well as Vernon and his apprentice, Julia and Millie were there and, in common with everyone who had come across the fields, were armed with whatever implements they'd had to hand. In Julia's case, it was a wicked-looking digging tool, while Millie held a small hand scythe. The group were studying the house and, possibly in reaction to its unsettling appearance, had spread out, facing the place. No one had their backs to it.

"I want to wait to see what the others find," Gregory said, "but I take it Ecton Hall didn't always look like this."

Her gaze fixed on the house, Julia answered, "No. This is ghastly. When the current Lord Ecton's parents were alive, it was a lovely, welcoming place." She huffed. "They would be turning in their graves if they could see it now."

Parker appeared around the side of the house, jogging around the line of the circling trees.

He slowed as he reached them and nodded to Gregory. "No sign of anyone at all, but we found a flashy curricle and a couple of nags in a broken-down stable out back. The horses have definitely been out recently." Parker's expression darkened. "But there's no one about to even give them a rubdown, and their tack's just been tossed any old how over a rail." Condemnation rang in his tone.

Gregory nodded. "Thank you." He glanced at those around him. "So it appears Ecton drove here after kidnapping Caitlin. If he realized Hattie saw him seizing Caitlin, he'll be expecting me." He glanced at the house. "So I'm going to go in via the front door."

"I'll go with you," Patrick Fergusson declared in a tone that brooked no argument.

The man was Caitlin's guardian. Gregory inclined his head. "That might be wise."

"Meanwhile"—Rory straightened—"Hamish, Daniel, and I will circle around and see if there's some other way into the house."

Hamish snorted. "With such a ramshackle place, there's sure to be somewhere around by the kitchens where we can get in."

Without waiting for further discussion, Rory led the other two off, following the path Parker had used to reach them.

Parker watched the trio go, then looked at Gregory. "I'll go and let the others know what's happening, sir."

Gregory nodded, and Parker saluted and trotted after the brothers.

Watching Caitlin's cousins tread lightly as they went, their eyes searching the house's façade for possible entry points, Gregory recalled comments she'd made regarding their stalking skills—Rory's and Hamish's especially—and decided he didn't need to worry about them.

"Right, then." He looked at the others gathered to either side; they appeared ready to storm any bastion. "At this point, I'd like you all to remain here, while Mr. Fergusson and I and Caitlin's cousins see what we can learn. If we need assistance, we'll call." He studied the house. "If we leave the front door open, you'll be able to hear us easily enough."

There were rumblings, but he didn't wait for any argument. He glanced at Patrick Fergusson. "Ready, sir?"

Patrick waved at the front door. "You know the man. Lead on."

Gregory did, striding swiftly to the front steps and climbing to the front porch. The bell chain hanging beside the door was broken, and the knocker looked to have been wrenched off; all that remained was a darker spot on the door.

He raised a fist and thumped on the door.

He and Patrick waited, but no response was forthcoming.

Patrick's eyes narrowed. "Perhaps we've caught him napping."

"Whether literally or figuratively..." Gregory shrugged and reached for the doorknob.

That, at least, still worked. The door swung inward on a long, loud *creak.*

Gregory stepped into a front hall that bore no resemblance whatsoever to any he'd previously seen. Cobwebs wreathed the old chandelier and draped outward to festoon the paneled walls. Dim light slanted down the stairwell, illuminating the dust that lay thick on the floor and coated the few pieces of furniture remaining—like the battered suit of rusty armor standing by an open door. The rug that covered the center of the floor had probably once held a pattern, but it was indistinguishable now.

Gregory walked forward, and Patrick followed, leaving the front door open.

Looking around, Gregory noticed that, except for the door beside the suit of armor, all other doors leading off the hall appeared well and truly closed. Judging by the cobwebs and dust, they hadn't been opened for quite some time.

He met Patrick's eyes, then raised his voice. "Ecton!"

"In here," came the immediate response, predictably issuing from beyond the open door.

Frowning, Gregory stalked in that direction.

"He likes to play games," Patrick muttered as he followed.

One behind the other, they strode into the room. A desk faced them, but the chair behind it was unoccupied.

They halted, but before they could look around, Gregory heard a *click* from their left and swung in that direction.

Ecton was seated in a wing chair beside a hearth in which a miserable fire spat and smoldered. Smiling smugly, he held a pistol trained on Gregory's chest.

Ecton's eyes widened as he took in Patrick. "Ah, you brought a friend. I hadn't anticipated that but..." Lightly, Ecton shrugged and returned his gaze to Gregory's face. "No matter. The situation between us remains the same."

Gregory arched a supercilious brow. "And what situation is that?"

With his legs elegantly crossed at the knees, Ecton smiled and swung one booted foot. "Why, dear boy, the one in which, in return for me telling you where you can find your missing chatelaine, you sign the agreement waiting for you over there"—Ecton nodded toward the desk —"on the dotted line." His smile deepened. "That's really all you have to do."

Clenching his jaw against the all-but-overwhelming urge to fling himself on Ecton and throttle him before beating him senseless with his own pistol, Gregory forced himself to turn and walk nonchalantly to the desk.

After the slightest hesitation, Patrick followed.

They halted before the desk and, side by side, looked down at the documents spread on the dusty surface. An inkwell, open and half full, and a pen were arranged on the desk above the documents.

After casting his eyes over the pages, Patrick murmured, "I'm accustomed to the Scottish system. Is this what I think it is?"

Gregory murmured back, "It's a legal document registering the sale of the Bellamy Hall estate. Effectively, if I sign this, it will transfer ownership of Bellamy Hall to Ecton, without any recourse whatsoever." Without shifting his gaze, he raised his voice and asked, "Where is Miss Fergusson, Ecton?"

Ecton's chair creaked. Gregory glanced his way and saw that he'd uncrossed his legs, but the pistol still remained trained on Gregory.

Ecton met his eyes and smiled, still smug. "At this point, it would, no doubt, be wise for me to state—categorically—that she's not here. I've left her hidden in a place that you will never find, not without me telling you of it. I should add that she's tied up, with no access to food or water —or indeed, heat." Studying Gregory's impassive face, Ecton evenly continued, "I seriously doubt she'll survive for long—a few days at most, and they won't be pleasant. But if you wish to cut short her ordeal"—with his head, he indicated the page Gregory's hand rested upon—"I suggest you sign that agreement."

With the dirty windows and anemic fire, the light in the room was poor, and the shadows in the corner of the room behind Ecton's chair were impenetrable. Nevertheless, in staring at Ecton, at the edges of his vision, Gregory saw the shadows ripple and shift.

Smoothly, he returned his attention to the pages on the desk. "Strange. I don't recall making any agreement with you."

Ecton sighed mightily. "Surely you're not going to try to negotiate at this hour?"

Gregory glanced once more at Ecton, careful to keep his gaze on the man and resist the temptation to peer into the shadows behind him. Gregory also couldn't risk glancing at Patrick to see if he, too, had noticed that they and Ecton were no longer the only ones in the room. Instead, to keep Ecton's attention focused on him, Gregory said, "Satisfy my curiosity. Why do you—who everyone knows hates living in the country—want to buy Bellamy Hall?"

Ecton's grin was self-confidence incarnate. "You are, of course, correct. I abhor the countryside. Sadly, however, to live in London in the manner to which I've grown accustomed, I need funds." He leaned back in the chair and regarded Gregory. "With your background, you'll be aware of how expensive every last thing is in the capital. Unfortunately, my attempts to sell this dismal place—" He waved a hand to indicate their surroundings, and Gregory seized the opportunity to look past Ecton's chair, confirming that Rory, Hamish, and Daniel had come through a connecting door and all three were—amazingly silently for such large men—creeping up on Ecton.

Gregory returned his gaze to Ecton's face as, entirely oblivious, Ecton continued "—were met with a complete lack of interest. But then the craze about ironstone mining in Northamptonshire struck and attained such a pitch that it reached even my ears, and I hit upon the notion of using that—of there being ironstone under my lands—as a means of pushing through a sale."

He beamed at Gregory. "And I was right. The mining companies are clamoring for ironstone deposits and will pay quite ridiculous sums for potential sites. The only fly in the ointment was that this estate is too small to interest any company, but if I were to add the Bellamy Hall acres to mine, then the sale is all but guaranteed."

Ecton looked utterly confident, convinced of his own brilliance.

Beside Gregory, Patrick shifted.

Gregory glanced his way; by now, Patrick had to have seen his sons creeping closer.

Sensibly, Patrick's frowning gaze was fixed—severely and censoriously—on Ecton. "I've long had an interest in mining, from when I worked as an engineer." He glanced at Gregory. "Before my brother died, that was."

From the corner of his eye, Gregory saw the idea that their father might possibly learn something useful strike Rory, Hamish, and Daniel, and the three froze. In the lead, Rory was only a long step from the back of Ecton's chair.

Patrick returned his gaze to Ecton. "I still read a lot and keep up with developments, so I've heard about the ironstone deposits south of Kettering."

Ecton smiled. "Excellent. So you'll know that, with interest in this area reaching such heights, now is the perfect time to approach a company with the prospect of mining ironstone on my acres." He inclined his head Gregory's way. "Once Cynster's acres are combined with mine, that is. Given you understand my point, perhaps you can convince Cynster here that I am entirely in earnest. I'll make a very tidy profit when I sell the land." He looked at Gregory, and his features hardened. Pugnaciously, he stated, "I want that land."

Giving no sign he was aware of his sons, Patrick rocked on his toes. "Son, I don't know who's been pulling your leg or if you know that what you've just said is balderdash, because the land down here, barely above a river, isn't likely to contain minable ironstone. No mining company will buy land like this and certainly not for ironstone sands, which are found at considerable depths."

Ecton stared at Patrick, and for a moment, Gregory wasn't sure whether Patrick had just shattered Ecton's dreams or whether...

Then Ecton's oiliest smile bloomed. "Very good, sir." Beyond smug, he arched his brows. "But you might be surprised by what a little salting of ironstone sand here and there plus greasing the right palms can achieve. I've already got several companies interested."

Given what Gregory now understood of Ecton, that rang true.

Patrick was now glowering. "Let me see if I understand this correctly. You've kidnapped my niece to force Cynster to sign over the neighboring estate so you have enough land to swindle some mining company and their investors?"

Ecton opened his eyes wide as if innocently surprised. "She's your niece?" Then his far-too-smug smile returned, and he nodded. "But otherwise, you are entirely right."

"You *worm*." Disgust laced Patrick's voice. He raised his gaze to his sons.

Hamish took that as his cue. He reached around the side of the wing chair and snatched the gun from Ecton's relaxed grasp.

In the same instant, Rory reached over the back of the chair, locked a beefy arm around Ecton's throat, and pulled tight. Muscles bulged in Rory's arm.

Ecton gasped and rose in the chair, desperate to ease the pressure on his neck and failing.

Rory leaned forward and, from close quarters, grinned at Ecton, who was vainly tugging at Rory's sleeve. Ecton's eyes bulged as they met Rory's.

Rory showed his teeth. "How about you tell us where you've put our cousin, and in return, I won't break your neck?"

Ecton paled, but then his lips thinned. "You wouldn't dare!"

Rory tightened his hold. "I'm not English. How do you know what I will or won't do?"

Ecton's gaze flicked to Gregory. He struggled for breath, then defiantly spat, "I won't tell you a damn thing. Miss Fergusson's whereabouts is my ace in this game. If you kill me, you'll never find her." His lips twisted mockingly. "At least not alive."

Gregory froze, along with all four Fergussons. Searching Ecton's eyes, Gregory saw no sign that the man was bluffing. He wasn't going to tell them where Caitlin was; he'd spoken the truth—her location was his only leverage, and he wasn't about to give it up.

His features like stone, Gregory looked at Rory and Hamish. "Tie him up and lock him away—in the cellar here, if it's strong enough. If not, we'll take him back to the Hall." He cast a scathing look at Ecton. "After we search this wreck of a place."

From the flare of satisfaction he glimpsed in Ecton's eyes, he was almost willing to wager they'd find nothing in Ecton Hall. But they—and Caitlin—couldn't take the risk that he was reading Ecton wrongly. Or being deliberately misled, something else he wouldn't put past the bastard.

Battling back a surge of fury combined with fear, Gregory swung round and stalked out, leaving Ecton to Rory's and Hamish's tender mercies.

Daniel hung back to help his brothers, but Patrick was on Gregory's heels. "What do you plan to do?" Patrick asked. "We have to find her!"

"Indeed," Gregory growled. "That's exactly what we're going to do—find her and take her home." To Bellamy Hall, where she belonged.

With him and all the others now waiting in the front hall.

He walked to the center of the hall, and everyone gathered around him.

"We heard," Henry rumbled.

Parker nodded. "The cowardly little prick is going to make us hunt for her."

Gregory was glad he didn't have to recount the recent exchange and what Ecton had claimed regarding Caitlin's danger. He looked around the cobweb-draped hall. "We can't trust anything he says, so the first thing we need to do is thoroughly search this mausoleum."

"You said you wanted him put in the cellar," Henry said. "Blackie and I know where it is."

Blackie nodded. "Good solid foundations, this place has. The cellar should still be sound."

Gregory tipped his head toward the drawing room as the sound of a pained "oof!" emanated from it. "In that case, perhaps you and Blackie should help the lads take his lordship there."

Henry smiled, and Blackie's grin turned positively evil. "Be happy to," Henry replied, and with unabashed eagerness, he and Blackie made for the open doorway.

Consigning thoughts of Ecton's continued health to the farthest recesses of his mind, Gregory surveyed the small army remaining. More people had arrived while he'd been talking to Ecton. "Right, then." He looked around the sea of willing faces. "This is what we'll do."

He divided the company into groups of three and sent them off to scour the house. As Ecton Hall was a more conventional structure than Bellamy Hall, a comprehensive search was much easier to organize.

As Gregory and Patrick climbed the stairs in the wake of the mob, Gregory murmured, "As much as I doubt she'll be here, we need to eliminate the possibility before we direct our attention farther afield."

Patrick grunted. "We'd look right idiots if he's been silly enough—or clever enough, depending on how you look at it—to put her in one of the bedrooms here." He joined Gregory in searching one of the larger suites, then they moved on to the next room along the corridor.

Given their number, it didn't take long to cover both the ground and first floors, after which most of the crew climbed the stairs to comb through the rooms in the attics.

Waiting with Patrick at the top of the main stairs for those searching above to report back, Gregory seized the moment to ask the older man, "In your opinion, could Ecton have convinced some mining company to buy the combined parcel of land?"

Patrick gazed at the floor—at the threadbare carpet—for a full minute, then vouchsafed, "Depending on how he went about it, then aye, he might have pulled it off." Patrick raised his head and, his expression hard, met Gregory's eyes. "Mind you, he'd need to have an assayer in his pocket, but given his cockiness and the amounts of money we're talking about, it seems likely he's already got that in hand." Patrick let out a gusty breath. "And the final point that has me leaning toward him pulling it off is that, in the current climate, while mining companies are falling over themselves to do deals for ironstone sands, and make no mistake, once their people actually got here, they would immediately know they'd been sold a dud, yet at that point, the very last thing they would want is for the management's gullibility to become known."

"So they would hide the crime?"

"Oh aye—you can bet your last farthing on that. So it's likely clever boy downstairs would have got away with the money and not even a slap on the wrist."

Gregory's jaw set. "A crime where the victims refuse to admit they've been wronged."

"Exactly."

He hesitated, but from the sound of footsteps on the floor above, the others were still searching. "No one has mentioned any mining at Benbeoch."

"Nah, not there." Patrick glanced at the ceiling. "I was part of a company operating out of Glasgow. Still have an interest in it, which is why I keep up with things, but I had to give up the engineering itself when m'brother died. Benbeoch needed a steady hand, someone to take care of the place and the clan, and there was no one else." He shrugged his heavy shoulders. "So I left mining and went home."

From beneath his lashes, Gregory studied Patrick's weathered face. For all that the Scotsman was a man of bluff bluster, he cared—deeply—for his family, for his clan. Perhaps he tried too hard to manage everyone—that certainly seemed to be the case—but having been thrust into the position in the way he had... Somewhat unexpectedly, Gregory felt a certain kinship with the older man. The weight of responsibility for others' livelihoods was something with which he was now well-acquainted.

Patrick looked toward the attic stairs as the thunder of footsteps heralded the return of the searchers. There'd been no cries of success and relief, confirming Gregory's assessment that Ecton hadn't hidden Caitlin in the house.

As, grim-faced, the others gathered, he declared, "Just to be certain, we'll need to search the cellars."

Everyone followed as he and Patrick led the way into the kitchen, where they found lamps and candles and passed them around, then continued through an ancient doorway and down a set of stone stairs to the dank, cold cellar.

Once there, the company spread out. The search didn't take long, and as expected, they discovered no sign of Caitlin.

Meanwhile, from behind the locked door of an old storeroom guarded by Rory and Hamish, Ecton laughed at their efforts.

The mood of the crowd that, finally, gathered at the base of the cellar stairs was, unsurprisingly, dark.

Gregory glanced at the faces, then simply said, "Wait here."

To that point, he'd been driven mostly by fear and panic and the resulting burning need to act—to do something and find Caitlin—but the minutes spent in the fruitless search had allowed his brain to start analyzing and thinking, and gradually, rational thought had come to the fore.

He tweaked Patrick's sleeve, turned, and with the older man falling in at his back, strode for the storeroom. The assembled company had earned the right to hear what was said.

Rory saw Gregory coming, took in his expression, and unbarred the door and hauled it open. Hamish held up a lantern to light the space inside.

Gregory halted on the threshold. The lantern beam fell full on their prisoner. The men had literally hog-tied Ecton and dumped him on his side in a pile of old straw. Other than a discarded crate and a disintegrating barrel that might once have held apples, there was little else left in the long-abandoned storeroom.

Despite his inelegant position, Ecton squinted up at Gregory and grinned. "Have you found her yet?"

Gregory folded his arms and leaned his shoulder against the door frame. "No. Are you sure you don't want to tell us where she is?"

Ecton chuckled. "She's my trump card, so no. I'll wait until you realize that I have you stymied."

His tone made it clear that it hadn't occurred to him to think of Caitlin or, indeed, anyone beyond himself.

"I see." Gregory turned his head and, over his shoulder, called, "Joshua?"

Seconds later, Joshua materialized at his elbow. "Yes?"

His gaze on Ecton, Gregory said, "Take one of his lordship's horses and ride to Loxton Park. Tell Lord Loxton that Ecton has kidnapped Miss Fergusson and hidden her away, and he refuses to reveal where she is. He's attempting to use her as a hostage to force me to give him Bellamy Hall."

Ecton's eyes widened.

Calmly, Gregory went on, "Use my name and ask his lordship if he would join us here at his earliest convenience."

Joshua grinned. "My pleasure." With a jaunty salute, he strode off.

Ecton was frowning and testing his bonds. "I say, Cynster! That's not the way we play this game!"

"Ecton," Gregory said, his tone one of utter contempt, "this is no game. And even if there was a game, none of us are willing to play any game of any sort with the likes of you."

With that, he pushed away from the door frame, unfolded his arms, turned on his heel, and left.

Hamish pulled back, and Rory swung the door closed and dropped the bar back into place.

Gregory took in the gathering at the bottom of the cellar stairs. Everyone was looking to him to lead. He nodded up the stairs. "Let's talk in the kitchen." He glanced back at the storeroom, indicating that he didn't want Ecton to overhear what was said.

They trooped up and congregated in the empty space in which a central bench should have stood.

Rory was the last one up the stairs. He shut the cellar door, then said to Gregory, "Henry and I checked. That storeroom door's sound, and there's no other way out. He won't escape."

Gregory nodded and turned to address the group. "It's already well into the afternoon. I'll have to wait for Lord Loxton and explain matters to him and, I hope, hand Ecton into his keeping. However, we need to search the immediate surroundings. We know Caitlin isn't in the house, but Ecton was already here, in the drawing room, waiting for us when we arrived. He didn't have time to go far to hide her. She has to be somewhere close."

A murmur of agreement rose from the group.

"So," Gregory concluded, "we need to search all the outbuildings and anywhere else the blackguard could have hidden her."

Henry and Jenkins exchanged a look, then both stepped forward. "We know the place as well as anyone here," Henry said.

Jenkins nodded. "We'll organize a search and see it done."

Gregory exhaled. "Thank you. I'll leave it to all of you. I'll be in the drawing room." He turned toward the front hall and arched a brow at Patrick.

The older man grumped, "I'll wait with you. I want to hear what this Lord Loxton says."

Gregory inclined his head and led the way back to the drawing room.

He and Patrick settled in the dusty chairs by the fireplace. A few minutes later, Rory, Hamish, and Daniel joined them.

Hamish waved toward the kitchen. "They don't need us. Apparently, this is a pretty small holding."

Gregory nodded, and after hunting about the room, the three found chairs they could trust and brought them over.

Once they'd sat, Patrick—who was plainly chafing with worry for his niece—glowered at them. "This would never have happened—our Caitlin would never have been in any danger at all—if you lot hadn't let her scarper off." Patrick's eyes narrowed on his sons. "Or should I say *helped* her scarper off?"

Rory, Hamish, and Daniel stared at their father, then exchanged a long, three-way glance.

Finally, Rory looked back at Patrick. "As you've realized, we actively helped her leave, and if you'd spent any time down here with her—as we three have—you'd have seen how she's blossomed and bloomed. Much as it might pain you to admit it, she needed the space, aye, and the role and the encouragement to fill it, that she found here. She's...becoming all she could be here." He shook his head with certainty. "She would never have managed that at Benbeoch, and not just because you're there, always ready to do everything that needs doing. You and those who, like you, still view her as a child were set on keeping her wrapped in wool padding, safely tucked away from life."

"And then"—with his arms folded across his chest, Hamish took up the baton—"you tried to ram marriage to one of us down her throat. After that, of course we helped her leave. And for much the same reason, we followed her. And that, all of that, was *your* doing, Da. You and no one else. So don't blame us for what happened after and for where things stand right now."

Gregory expected an explosion from Patrick, but instead, the elder

Fergusson grumbled incoherently and continued to glower...but he didn't contradict what his sons had said.

*Interesting.*

The resulting heavy, brooding silence lengthened and intensified.

Eventually, Gregory observed, "If there's one thing I've learned through the recent months of dealing with the menagerie that is Bellamy Hall, it's that there never is any value in apportioning blame for past mistakes. What is useful is to focus on rectifying any problems or issues regardless of how they arose and steadily moving forward on a path that benefits everyone involved." He doubted he'd ever spoken truer words. He straightened in the chair. "At present, that means finding Caitlin. At this time, that is our paramount and, indeed, singular goal."

Daniel stirred. "I've been thinking about what you said earlier." He met Gregory's eyes. "You pointed out that Ecton hadn't had much time to hide Caitlin away. I've been trying to estimate how much time he actually had. He was in that curricle of his, and once he'd driven off with Caitlin, we know Hattie found William straightaway, and William came running as fast as he could—and he is a fast runner. If you think of how long it took us to realize it was Ecton, get on the horses, and ride over here...it really wasn't all that long."

Frowning, Gregory suggested, "Twenty minutes?"

Rory huffed. "Certainly not more than half an hour."

"And don't forget," Hamish put in, "after he got back here, he'd had time to unharness his horses."

Gregory pointed at Hamish. "That's an excellent point."

"And he had his pistol and paper ready when we walked in." Patrick nodded at the desk, where the agreement lay unsigned.

"Indeed." Swiftly canvassing the implications, Gregory stated, "This was no spur-of-the-moment kidnapping. Ecton had this entire sequence of events planned. He had the pistol ready and primed, the agreement laid out on the table, with pen and ink no less, and then...he must have been following Caitlin, waiting for a moment when she was alone and out of sight—or at least out of reach—of anyone else."

Rory leaned forward, forearms on his knees. "He'll have had his hiding place prepared, too. He must have, to have managed to hide her away in such a short time."

Inspired, Gregory said, "We need to—" He broke off as the front door creaked open, and the tap of a cane and the stump of heavy footsteps reached them.

"Good Lord!" came from the front hall. "That wretched boy has let this place go completely to rack and ruin!"

A murmur followed, and the tapping and stumping resumed, drawing nearer.

Gregory and the Fergussons got to their feet as Gerald, Lord Loxton, entered the room.

His lordship halted, momentarily oblivious to their presence as he gazed around him in disbelief. "I remember this place when his parents were alive. Quite lovely, it was. Now..." He gestured. "It's a wreck." He sniffed disparagingly. "Typical of that blighter. He was a bad 'un from the cradle."

Lord Loxton sighed, lowered his gaze, and looked inquiringly at the company. His gaze came to rest on Gregory. "Cynster!" His lordship exchanged nods, then stumped forward. "What's this I hear about Miss Fergusson being kidnapped, heh?"

"Indeed, sir. She has been." Gregory waved at the others. "These are Miss Fergusson's relatives." In the interests of brevity, he added, "Visiting from Scotland."

Loxton exchanged another round of nods, then Gregory waved him to the armchair he'd vacated.

After settling himself, his lordship clasped his hands over the head of his cane and, his gaze shrewd, looked at Gregory. "So what's the blighter been up to now?"

Gregory told him. Mercifully, the Fergussons kept their mouths shut while, in concise fashion, Gregory outlined Ecton's perfidy.

At the end of his recitation, Lord Loxton smiled chillingly. "I'm sorry Miss Fergusson's been embroiled in this, but given our dastardly villain, sadly, I'm not surprised. I'll be happy to take Ecton off your hands and deal with him through the courts. However"—his gaze swept the group —"finding Miss Fergusson and making sure she's unharmed must be our highest priority."

"Indeed, sir." Gregory had managed to rein in his impatience until then, but with what they'd recently discussed circling in his brain, he wanted to get out and find her. *Now.* "As you're willing to assume responsibility for Ecton, we'll—"

He broke off as a clatter of boots heralded Henry Kirk, closely followed by everyone else from Bellamy Hall. The group clustered behind Henry as he dipped his head to Lord Loxton, but it was to Gregory whom Henry reported, "It's not that big an estate, and we've searched every inch. Caitlin's definitely not hidden anywhere here. We found no sign of her at all."

Grimly, Gregory nodded. "All right. We've eliminated all the obvious places. We need to think, and Daniel and the rest of us have been estimating how much time Ecton had to hide Caitlin away. Even if he'd planned it, he had only minutes—five or ten. Something of that order. So"—he peered at the faces he could see behind Henry, and obligingly, Henry stepped to the side, revealing the company crowding behind him —"we need to put ourselves in Ecton's shoes. We know he drove off with Caitlin from just north of the Osiery. He had to have taken the arm of the lane that runs along the riverbank. If he hadn't, he would have driven to the Hall, which he didn't. So he drove along the riverbank, along a short section of lane, and into the Ecton Hall drive. As far as we can tell, Caitlin wasn't with him when he reached Ecton Hall lands, which means he hid her somewhere along the riverbank."

He regarded the assembled people of Bellamy Hall. "You know that area better than I or"—he gestured to Lord Loxton and the Fergussons —"the others here. So think—where along that stretch did Ecton hide her?"

Joshua frowned. "That stretch is mostly Bellamy Hall land—just like the smarmy bastard to hide her on our lands rather than his."

"Oh."

The simple exclamation had everyone looking at Blackie—at the expression of enlightenment that bloomed across his old, worn features.

Blackie looked at Gregory and, in a tone of revelation, said, "The ruins."

When Gregory looked puzzled, Blackie explained, "There's a track— just a rough trail, really, but if he didn't care about his horses, he could have taken them most of the way along. It's on the other side of the abbey from the Hall and leads from the riverbank up to the ruins. If you go up it, you can reach the ruins without risking anyone from the Hall seeing you." Blackie hauled in a breath and added, "And I'm thinking, were it me and I had to hide a person, I'd use the old crypt, down under the altar. Far as I know, it's still open, and sure as heck, the smarmy bastard will have stashed Miss C down there."

Everyone stared at Blackie. No one disagreed with his assessment.

Before Gregory could order everyone on their way to the ruins, Lord Loxton harrumphed and, when everyone looked his way, imperiously waved them off. "Go, go! I've brought two men with me. Send them in, tell them where that blackguard Ecton is, and you may leave it to us to take care of him." He locked his gaze with Gregory's. "Just send word when you find her."

Gregory nodded and started for the door, and the people of Bellamy Hall streamed forth ahead of him.

# CHAPTER 16

*W*ith the people of Bellamy Hall behind him, Gregory strode up the last section of the sloping track leading from the riverbank to the ruins of Coldchurch Abbey. He hadn't been into the abbey church for years, but the otherworldly atmosphere that perennially hovered like a ghostly shroud over the remnants of walls, arches, and shattered stones at the top of the rise hadn't changed.

The afternoon was waning, the sun sinking toward the horizon and sending shadows stretching across the rubble-strewn ground.

He crested the rise and stepped onto the plateau on which the ruins lay, scattered in clumps over the ground between him and the house. He paused, and a cry rose behind him. With everyone else, he swiveled and looked back.

Lower on the track, people clustered together, then from the center of the group, Millie pushed through and came hurrying on to Gregory and the Fergussons, who had halted around him.

Others gave way, smiling as they saw what Millie held in one hand. Nearing Gregory, she waved a piece of white cloth.

Beaming, she halted before him. "It's hers—Miss C's!" Between her fingers, she spread the material. "See? Here." She pointed at a corner. "CF."

"Let me see, lass." Rory bent and peered at the handkerchief, then straightened and nodded at Gregory. "It's hers, right enough. She always was good with her needle."

Looking down the slope toward the river, Gregory scanned the area across which the rough track had led them. "There's no reason she would ever have come this way, not of her own accord, so she must have dropped the handkerchief when Ecton brought her here." His heart lifted, and he turned to face the ruins. "Blackie was right. She's here somewhere."

The pronouncement was greeted with exclamations of relief, and everyone still on the track came hurrying up. On reaching the cusp where Gregory and the Fergussons were standing, scanning the ruins and getting their bearings, the rest of the party spread out along the lip of the rise.

Blackie pointed at the single half-ruined arch that was all that remained of the church's glory. "Sure as eggs are eggs, she'll be in the crypt. The entrance is behind the altar."

Gregory remembered and, with hope rising, started picking his way over the rubble. Approached from this direction, the way to the church was much less clear than when coming from the house.

The others spread out, flanking him as everyone scrambled over the jumble of toppled stones.

They had to go around the remnants of an old wall—part of the monk's dorter—before they could see the area in which the entrance to the crypt lay.

Gregory reached the wall first. Eagerly, he rounded its end and came to an abrupt halt.

Rory, following at Gregory's heels, bumped into him, making Gregory stumble forward.

Then Rory stopped, too, and stared. "What the devil?"

Grimly, Gregory felt his face set. "The devil, indeed."

Others scrambled up and around the wall, fanning out about Gregory and the Fergussons as curses filled the air.

Julia was as incensed as anyone. "The bastard's tried to bury her!"

Gregory stared at what Ecton had wrought.

"It wasn't like that before," Henry growled.

"No," Joshua agreed. "Our painters would have noticed and said something."

"No way those stones fell by themselves." Hamish pushed past and went to take a closer look.

"Them blocks used to be balanced up there." Blackie pointed to the top of the wall at the rear of the altar. "They was leaning a bit. He must've tipped them off."

Patrick, too, walked forward, frowning at the three massive rectangular blocks, each as long as a man was tall and half as wide and deep, that had fallen from the wall. Then he swung to face Gregory. "Where's the crypt door?"

Silently, Gregory nodded at the three massive blocks. "Directly behind those."

"It was Ecton," Hamish called, grim certainty in his voice. "There are ropes half buried here."

Others went to look, and curses rained freely on Ecton's head.

Frowning, Rory muttered, "But why?"

Feeling very much as if every emotion inside him had shut down—that his entire inner self was a calculating void—Gregory replied, "Because he assumed Caitlin would be the only witness to her kidnapping." His mind pieced together the information and supplied him with Ecton's likely plan. "Ecton didn't expect to be seen by anyone other than Caitlin, but although he was, he didn't care. Hattie was the only other person who saw him, and he could rely on his rank to dismiss or discredit any testimony she made."

Patrick was nodding. "If you'd signed those papers—as he was sure you would—he might have told you she was here or somewhere else, but regardless, by the time you discovered this, he would have been far away. Off to London, most like." Patrick turned bleak eyes Gregory's way. "This was his way of ensuring you didn't go straight after him, and by the time anyone caught up with him, he'd deny all knowledge. He would have said you were making it up, that you'd lost to him at cards or some such thing and had to sell to him to cover your debts." Patrick looked at the tumbled stones. "Something like that."

"His reasons don't matter." Gregory was certain of that. "Lord Loxton has Ecton in custody. All *we* need to do is get Caitlin out of there."

Everyone stared at him.

Hamish waved a hand at the blocks. "How? Each of these weighs a ton."

Gregory met Hamish's eyes and smiled. "That's the one thing Ecton didn't allow for—we're in the country." He looked at Jenkins. "We have Clydesdales, do we not?"

"Ah." Jenkins's face cleared. "Of course." He whirled, searched the faces, then pointed at his stable lads. "You, you, and you. Go and fetch the draft horses. All four. Fast as you can."

"And don't forget their yokes and harnesses," Gregory called after the already running lads.

Patrick was shaking his head. "Ecton truly is a fool through and through. You don't even need to send to neighbors for the beasts."

Gregory's smile widened, and his confidence grew. "That's one of the benefits of a place like Bellamy Hall."

～

The light was failing by the time they got the horses there and harnessed with the right gear to haul away the stones.

With his knowledge of stone, Hamish had been a big help, and Patrick, with his engineering expertise, had been crucial in working out how to best construct the net they'd fashioned to loop about the stones and in which direction to pull each away.

Several of those who had stormed Ecton's dilapidated house had returned to the Hall to carry the news to those who'd remained behind. As a result, a large contingent, including Cromwell and the painters, had come hurrying to the ruins with lanterns and blankets and shawls. And to hold the chill at bay, jugs of ale and cider—the painters' contribution, which was welcomed by all.

As the sun slipped beneath the horizon, the cold intensified.

Each block required all four horses to drag it away. They got the first hauled off sufficiently far to the right easily enough, but the second had tipped as it fell and wedged into place and, consequently, proved a lot more difficult to dislodge. Eventually, Hamish set to with a huge chisel and hammer he'd had fetched. The sound of metal striking metal rang out eerily over the landscape of dark, shattered, jutting rocks.

Gregory couldn't drag his gaze or his awareness from the lantern-lit scene about the blocked doorway. Caitlin was in there; he told himself she was, yet still he feared. Until he set eyes on her again—or better yet had her in his arms—he couldn't relax, couldn't stand down.

She was everything to him.

He made a silent vow that, when he next had a moment alone with her, he would tell her exactly what she meant to him.

Better yet, he would show her.

Even better, he would do both.

Then Hamish stepped back, examined his handiwork, and signaled to Henry and Jenkins, who were waiting at the horses' heads, and the huge beasts leaned into their yokes once more, and this time, with a hideous screeching scrape, the second stone started moving.

Everyone cheered.

As soon as the second block was out of the way, willing hands fell to, unhooking and dismantling the net of ropes and leathers they'd cobbled together to haul the blocks, and finally, they approached the last massive stone.

Inside the crypt, Caitlin blinked and blinked, then cursed at her continued inability to see. Or to reach up and dab the tears from her eyes.

They were coming—truly coming to get her out. That horrible screeching, grating sound—followed by cheers—set the matter beyond doubt.

The relief that had already flooded her rose even higher and caught in her throat.

She'd been lying there, feeling increasingly anxious and helpless with it, but then she'd heard voices—distant and indistinct—yet they'd continued and hadn't faded away.

They—her rescuers, she assumed, and thanked God for them—had remained outside for quite some time, but in the dark, she really had no idea how long it had been. She'd puzzled over why they hadn't come to fetch her and had reasoned that the fiend had somehow blocked the door.

With all sounds deadened by the earth and stone surrounding her and muffled even more by the black hood, she'd been reduced to guessing what was going on, but those loud and happy cheers surely indicated that, whoever had found her, they were making progress toward getting her out.

*Gregory.*

He would be there; she was sure of it.

Behind the black material, she smiled and tried to take a deep, calming, reassuring breath, then remembered and cut off her inhale.

*Breathe slowly and shallowly.*

Soon she would be free and wouldn't have to be so miserly over air.

She just had to wait.

Gregory would be with her as soon as he could.

Until she'd found herself in the dark, left to face her thoughts, fears, hopes, and dreams, she hadn't realized just how dear he'd become to her

—how much he'd become the center of her existence—but she now knew that as truth. Her truth.

She knew others saw her as the central figure in the Bellamy Hall universe, but everyone needed someone else—some special person—to anchor them and give their life meaning.

For her, Gregory was that person.

He'd come to Bellamy Hall and surprised them all by staying, yet he hadn't tried to take over, as she'd feared he would.

Instead, he'd worked with her, alongside her, and she'd discovered she truly liked and valued the companionship that had engendered. That sense that they were both working to the same end, toward the same goal.

That keeping Bellamy Hall and its eccentric residents and esoteric businesses afloat was a shared endeavor.

She hadn't realized how much that meant to her until she'd been left in utter darkness with nothing else to think about other than what she stood to lose.

But she understood now—so much—and as soon as she saw Gregory, she would tell him of all she'd learned of herself while lying alone in the dark.

~

The instant the third massive stone block was hauled away, revealing the crypt door, cheers erupted on all sides.

Too tense to smile, Gregory seized the lantern Blackie had been holding and leapt down to the level of the door. The latch lifted easily. With Rory at his back, Gregory shouldered the door wide, stepped inside, and held the lantern high.

The beam illuminated a set of stone steps leading down to a cavernous chamber full of tombs and shadows. Some graves were carved into the walls, while sepulchers stood in haphazard ranks, taking up most of the floor.

Memories from when he'd last been there with his siblings, exploring and playing among the tombs, rushed back to him.

"*Mm!*" The distant muffled sound reached him, followed by a dull *thump*, as if boots were striking the dusty floor.

Hope—nay, joy—surged through him. "Caitlin!"

The sound came again, and lowering the lantern to light the stairs, he hurried down. He hit the paved floor and strode on, down one of the two narrow aisles.

Rory, with Hamish on his heels, both also carrying lanterns, followed.

Gregory raised his lantern and played the light around, searching for some sign of Caitlin. Hamish and Rory did the same.

From the earlier sounds, Gregory thought she was somewhere deeper in the crypt. "Where are you?"

The thumping came again, clearer this time, and with a muttered curse, he forged ahead.

He went past her before a muffled murmur and a *thud* drew him back to a narrow passage between two tombs. He directed the lantern beam along the passage, then into the space at its end, and finally saw a blue coat and woolen skirts and a pair of half-boots bound with rope.

"Caitlin!" To the others, he called, "She's here!"

A second later, he knelt beside her and set down the lantern. "Hold on —let's get you free."

Hamish called up the steps, "We've found her!"

Gregory helped her into a sitting position as a mumble that might have been "Thank God!" came from beneath the black hood.

Rory, followed by Hamish, squeezed into the narrow passage and hovered.

Gregory tugged at the rope binding Caitlin's wrists, but she shook her head vigorously and incoherently expostulated, and he switched to prying at the knot in the scarf wound about the hood and her lower face.

Rory crouched and started working on the rope around her ankles.

Finally, Gregory got the knot undone and tugged the scarf away.

The instant the hood loosened, Caitlin dragged in a massive breath. She let it out with, "Thank heavens! I haven't been able to breathe properly ever since the fiend tied that on."

Although Gregory was hugely relieved to hear her voice, strong and sure and steady, as he reached for the hood, he exchanged a look with Rory, one that suggested it was just as well Ecton was nowhere within easy reach. Smoothly, Gregory drew the black material off Caitlin's head, and she sighed with relief and blinked in the lantern light. Then she focused on him and beamed.

Something in his chest clenched tight, and uncaring of the others watching, he hauled her to him and planted a swift, hard kiss on her lips —lips that met his with equal fervor. Indeed, she raised her bound hands, seized his lapels, and pressed her own heated kiss on him.

Reluctantly, they ended the exchange, and he released her and turned his attention to the rope about her wrists. "Thank God you're all right." Her kiss had answered that unvoiced question.

Rory drew the rope from about her feet and patted her calf awkwardly. "Did he hurt you at all, lass?"

"No. He just dumped me here like a sack of potatoes and rushed off."

"Good," Rory said, then winced. "Well, obviously not good, but…you know what I mean."

Caitlin smiled reassuringly at him.

And seeing her face, her usual relaxed, confident, self-assured expression, Gregory realized that, like her, he hadn't been breathing freely, not since he'd learned she'd been taken.

He drew a deep, steadying breath and felt something large and powerful settle, soothed, inside him.

She turned her radiant smile back on him. "You came for me—I knew you would."

He hid his pleasure at seeing that truth blazoned in her eyes and huffed. "Everyone came for you." He waved toward the distant steps. "Come and see."

Some others were coming down the steps, sending lantern beams striking through the dimness in all directions.

Hamish and Rory retreated to the main aisle, and Gregory helped Caitlin to her feet.

She wobbled, and he seized her anew and steadied her. "Let me go first. Hold on to the tombs and to me."

With an arm looped supportively about her waist, he sidled along the passage, keeping her upright as, concentrating on placing her feet, she followed.

Waving Hamish and Rory back toward the steps and the oncoming others, Gregory stepped free of the passage and into the wider aisle. The instant Caitlin edged out of the passage, he stooped and swept her into his arms.

"Oh!" She looped her arms around his neck and whispered, "I can walk, you know."

He set his jaw. "Not well enough to get out of the ruins."

She looked around. "We're in the abbey ruins?"

"In the crypt."

"I wondered where he'd left me." Then she sobered. "What happened?"

He looked ahead at those approaching. "It's a long story—we'll tell you later. But Ecton is presently languishing in Lord Loxton's hands. I doubt you'll see him again."

Caitlin shuddered. "I have no ambition to set eyes on that man ever again."

Then Rory and Hamish, who'd been ambling ahead of them, squeezed to either side, and she saw the man who was walking toward them. Her jaw dropped. "Uncle Patrick?"

He beetled his brows at her. "Aye, it's me." His jaw clenched, but then he nodded at her and included Gregory in the approving—for him, almost benevolent—gesture. "Glad to see you're safe, miss."

The aisle between the tombs wasn't that wide. Her uncle, Rory, and Hamish—and Cromwell and Henry, who had come down as well—had to turn and retreat ahead of her and Gregory, but all went with smiles on their faces and relief in their eyes.

Gregory slowed as the others reached the steps and went up, carrying the news that she was unharmed, and cheers rose from a large number of throats.

Startled, she looked at Gregory. "How many are there outside?"

"Most of the Hall's residents. And others, like Julia, were here, but have gone back to wait in the house." He smiled at her. "Virtually everyone turned out to find you—you are much loved here. Never doubt it."

Even in the diffuse light of the lantern he held hooked over the fingers of one hand, the expression in his eyes sent her heart soaring.

He reached the bottom of the steps and paused. He glanced briefly up, and she did, too. The others had vanished into the twilight above.

She tightened her arms about his neck, and as she looked his way again, he bent his head, and she stretched up and drew his lips to hers.

The kiss was full of emotion—some of it tentative, but all of it real—as recognition, understanding, and acceptance flowed between them.

As they reluctantly drew back, she murmured, "I would have panicked, but I knew you would come for me."

He rested his forehead against hers. "Just the thought of losing you...I couldn't bear it. Couldn't even stomach thinking of it." He raised his head and looked into her eyes. "You have to marry me and put me out of my misery."

She smiled mistily and knew her heart shone in her eyes. "You haven't asked me yet."

"I plan to—you know that. But for you…I want to do it properly, with the right fanfare and atmosphere and everything else you deserve."

She wouldn't care but sensed that for him, "doing it properly" meant something, so she inclined her head and, still smiling, replied, "And when you do, just so you know, I plan to say yes."

He smiled, then lightly laughed and bent and kissed her again, and she welcomed the caress and returned it and rejoiced.

"A-hem!"

The noisy clearing of a large throat had them breaking apart and glancing up at the top of the steps.

Rory stood silhouetted against the darkening sky, haloed by the lanterns of those still waiting on them. "If you two lovebirds are quite finished, there's a small army waiting to see with their own eyes that Caitlin's all right."

She laughed, and Gregory smiled and obediently carried her up the steps and into the evening's gloom that was held at bay by the lanterns carried by a cheering throng.

As people gathered around, patting her shoulders, arms, or legs or catching her free hand and squeezing it, Gregory's words, "you are much loved here," echoed in her mind.

These were the people she'd spent the past years helping, and they'd turned out en masse to help her.

Her heart swelled as every last one crowded close to reassure themselves she was unharmed, unhurt, and in good spirits.

Millie handed back Caitlin's handkerchief, and others praised her for her quick thinking in dropping it.

"Gave us heart, it did," Jenkins informed her.

Old Blackie grinned at her. "Finding it told us we were on the right track."

But Millie had started frowning. "But what about your legs? Why is Mr. Cynster carrying you?"

That was an excellent question. Caitlin arched a brow at the gentleman in question. "I'm perfectly all right, and I'm sure I can walk."

His lips compressed, and she felt his grip on her side and legs tighten. "You were wobbling in the crypt, and the ground out here is the definition of uneven." He raised his head and, to the others, confidingly said, "Best, I think, that I carry our chatelaine-cum-steward safely to the house."

Unsurprisingly, there were murmurs of agreement, some tinged with concern at the suggestion, however vague, of any lingering weakness.

Caitlin suppressed the urge to insist she was perfectly capable of walking the hundred or so yards to the house. If she was going to accept Gregory's offer of marriage, presumably she would have to grow accustomed to such displays of protectiveness.

Especially as her cousins and uncle were only too likely to step up in Gregory's stead.

"Right, then." Plainly taking her silence as acquiescence to his cosseting, Gregory hefted her slightly and stepped forward. "Let's get you back to the Hall."

He started walking, carefully stepping over the rocks and shattered stones littering the ground, and the others fanned out to either side and followed, an escort of happy, relieved friends bearing them forward on a wave of affection.

Caitlin relaxed in Gregory's arms and watched the outline of Bellamy Hall, in all its gothic extravagance, rise up against the sky before them.

Lamps burned in many windows, casting golden light in welcome and greeting, and the solidity of the structure, as always, was both comforting and reassuring.

*Home.*

She'd never felt so strongly settled, so anchored by place at Benbeoch Manor. She'd been born there, but it had never felt like hers—her place to nurture.

Bellamy Hall did. In the welcome she'd found there, she'd grown and set down roots. This was where she should and would remain.

All that was very clear to her now, and the notion of remaining in Gregory's arms was the icing on her cake.

Smiling to herself, she leaned her head against his chest.

She felt him look down at her and murmured, low so only he would hear, "You're carrying me away from an altar, you know."

She sensed him smiling down at her. "I don't think the abbey any longer qualifies as consecrated ground, so I'll have to search for another to haul you before."

She opened her eyes wide and trained them on him. "Haul? Doesn't the general concept of matrimony rather assume any hauling done is the other way around?"

His smile deepened. "But this is us. Neither you nor I—nor, indeed, any of those at Bellamy Hall—necessarily follow anyone else's rules."

She conceded that with a tip of her head. "True."

Still smiling, he looked ahead, and she followed his gaze to where Alice and Julia stood holding open the south door.

"Actually," he murmured, "as matters are shaping up, I suspect I'll be carrying you all the way to your room."

Her squawked "I'm sure I've recovered my balance by now" was dismissed as irrelevant by everyone.

~

With Alice and Julia fussing on either side, Gregory carried Caitlin through the corridors, up the main stairs, and all the way to her bedchamber, allowing those who had waited in the house to reassure themselves that she was, in fact, all right.

"*Perfectly* all right," as she kept insisting.

Yet despite the pointed looks she threw him, no one made the slightest attempt to suggest that he allow her to walk on her own two feet, and for that, he was grateful. He honestly didn't know whether he could force himself to let her go.

But once they reached her room, Alice, backed by Julia, demanded he deposit Caitlin on the pretty blue counterpane on her bed and leave her to their ministrations.

When Caitlin was moved to protest that she didn't need to lie on her bed, she was firmly overruled, although Alice promised that, once she had checked her for any and all injuries, she would be free to go downstairs.

Forced to accept that, Gregory laid Caitlin down and retreated. He went first to his room to change his scuffed and dusty clothes, then descended the stairs and joined Patrick, the other Fergussons, and the regular contingent of Hall residents in the drawing room.

Everyone, including Patrick Fergusson, had spruced themselves up, as it was nearly time for dinner.

Sherry was passed around, and minor toasts were drunk while everyone waited for the lady of the moment to arrive.

When, escorted by Alice and Julia, Caitlin finally appeared, the room erupted in cheers.

Gregory rose from his armchair as she glided across the room, a smile just for him on her lips. He reached for her hand and, when she surrendered it, grasped her fingers, smoothly raised her hand to his lips, and brushed a kiss to her knuckles, to the open delight of most of those watching and the narrowing-eyed interest of her uncle.

Blushing prettily, Caitlin turned and, standing beside Gregory with her hand still in his, thanked everyone for their concern and for coming to her aid and, smiling at Alice, confirmed she'd been given a clean bill of health.

"Which," Caitlin confided, her smiling gaze raking the attentive faces, "is just as well, for I was determined to join you for dinner. You must tell me all that occurred when you confronted that fiend, Lord Ecton."

Numerous voices assured her the tale was one worth telling, but before any could commence it, a beaming Cromwell appeared to announce that dinner was served.

Gregory offered Caitlin his arm, and she laid her hand on his sleeve, and in happy anticipation, they led the company, bubbling with good spirits, into the dining room.

He sat Caitlin at the foot of the table, then returned to his place at the table's head. Patrick had been shown by a deferential Cromwell to the chair on Gregory's right.

As Gregory settled in his seat, he caught Patrick's eye and nodded down the table, at the unruly, happy, laughing company, which now included three of his sons. "This," Gregory said, "is the reality of Bellamy Hall."

Patrick's lips pursed, but his expression plainly stated that he appreciated the togetherness that was so much on show and that despite the misgivings he must have entertained on his journey down from Scotland, he was quietly reassured.

Gregory caught Rory's eye, and Hamish's as well, and saw that Patrick's elder sons were reading their father's reaction to the Hall's residents much as Gregory was. Their relief and the nascent hope it birthed was clear, at least to Gregory.

He waited while the footmen charged their wine glasses and Cromwell dispensed the first course—a hearty partridge and pigeon soup —then as Cromwell drew back, Gregory raised his glass. "Today, the residents of Bellamy Hall—those here tonight and also those who live elsewhere on the estate—saw off a major threat to our collective welfare. We did that by sticking together, by being prepared to stand shoulder to shoulder and confront our enemy. As the owner of Bellamy Hall, I applaud our collective effort and thank you all for your help and support."

Glasses were raised, and "Hear, hear!" and "To Bellamy Hall!" rang out around the table.

Then with excellent appetites, they settled to consume what Nessie clearly intended to be a celebratory meal complete with roast venison, roasted kid, and stuffed piglet. The vegetables were succulent and plentiful, and Patrick, with an appetite as hearty as that of any of his sons, was patently impressed.

Dabbing his lips with his napkin, he reached for his wine glass and, with his other hand, gestured to the sumptuous spread. "You..." He paused, then amended, "All of you here live very well."

Gregory smiled. "We try, and business by business, improvement by improvement, I believe we're succeeding"

Patrick humphed and took a long swallow of the wine.

From the other end of the table, Caitlin viewed her uncle's expression with well-concealed surprise. His attitude to all that was Bellamy Hall seemed far more interested and even accepting than she'd imagined would ever be possible.

Somehow—in just a few short hours, no less—Gregory had performed an eye-opening miracle, meaning he'd succeeded in opening her uncle's usually heavily blinkered eyes to the notion that other ways of doing things, ways that weren't his, might actually work and, more, be advantageous.

Watching with wary hope, she prayed that would auger well for the revelations and confrontation that, now Patrick was there, had to come.

To distract herself from that looming reality, she glanced at Rory, seated beside her. "No one has yet told me what happened after Ecton kidnapped me." She looked questioningly around the table. "I now know Ecton put me in the crypt and pulled the stones down to block the door, but how did you find me so quickly?"

She listened as, while they steadily consumed their feast, Rory, Hamish, Joshua, and Julia between them explained how, from a distance, Hattie had witnessed the abduction and told William what she'd seen and sent him racing to the Hall, and how, after Hattie and Gregory between them identified Ecton as the villain of the piece, the residents of the estate —all those who could hoist arms at a moment's notice—had gone en masse to Ecton Hall. There, they'd waited while Gregory, assisted by her uncle and her cousins, had dealt with Ecton, who had refused to divulge where he'd put her. They'd eventually locked him in a cellar storeroom and scoured the old house and grounds for any sign of her, to no avail.

"Then," Joshua said, "Cynster realized how tight the time was, which meant that Ecton had to have hidden you somewhere along the riverbank."

"Blackie remembered the old track leading from the river to the ruins and suggested that, had he been in Ecton's shoes, he would have put you in the crypt," Julia explained. "So we hurried over there, and then Millie"—she smiled at the younger woman—"found your handkerchief, so we knew we were on the right track."

"I'd forgotten about dropping my handkerchief," Caitlin said. "Thanks to that wretched hood, I was completely disoriented and had no idea where he was taking me. The handkerchief was all I could think of that might mark the place."

"It gave us heart." Millie beamed at her. "And after finding it and then the stones tumbled over the crypt door, we knew we were right, and you had to be inside."

Caitlin listened as the group explained what had been done to free her, and in turn, she described how little she'd been able to hear from inside the crypt. "Gregory mentioned that Ecton is now in Lord Loxton's hands."

"Yes, indeed." Joshua looked up the table. "And I haven't yet reported what his lordship said to me when I rode to Loxton Park to tell him about us finding you and how Ecton had sealed the crypt, possibly in an attempt to permanently silence you."

At the other end of the table, Gregory arched a dark brow. "What did Lord Loxton say?"

Joshua grinned. "That he was very glad to hear Miss Fergusson had been retrieved unharmed and that he intended to keep Ecton in the local cells and bind him over for trial at the next assizes on charges of attempted fraud and attempted blackmail and was now of a mind to add attempted murder to the list of the blackguard's crimes. He said to tell you he'd taken the prepared contract as evidence and will call tomorrow to take statements from all who were in the drawing room and heard Ecton explain his scheme."

Smiling delightedly, Joshua looked around the table. "His lordship is confident that at the very least, Ecton will be transported."

While Caitlin wasn't surprised by the relief she felt, she saw the feeling mirrored in many eyes. Ecton had threatened not just her but everyone there—everyone who had become a part of Bellamy Hall.

Joshua's tale had reminded many there, including Caitlin, that she didn't actually know what Ecton's plan had been. When she posed the question, Gregory explained Ecton's demand that Gregory sign over ownership of Bellamy Hall in order to learn Caitlin's whereabouts, then added the information that he'd received that day from his brother in London. He then turned to Patrick and invited her uncle to explain what he'd deduced through questioning Ecton.

Patrick readily complied, to the general fascination of all those about the table. "He was a fraud through and through," her uncle concluded. "Not only was he no real gentleman, but he wasn't and never would be the owner of land with genuine deposits of ironstone sands. First to last, his scheme was a fabrication with the sole purpose of cheating some mining company and their investors out of a very large sum."

"Well, I, for one," Vernon declared, "am exceedingly grateful that, through this incident, we've rid not just ourselves but this district of the fiend."

"Hear, hear," Percy said. "And might I suggest that, now we've successfully removed Ecton from our orbit, we should celebrate that achievement with suitable gusto?"

"And thankfulness," Julia declared and held up her glass in a toast. "To Bellamy Hall!"

The words were echoed up and down the table, and as one with the company, Caitlin raised her glass and drank.

Later, after they'd done justice to the three delicious desserts Nessie had concocted and retreated to the drawing room to talk and exclaim and realign themselves with the less-dramatic demands of their normal lives, Caitlin found herself standing beside Gregory and listening as the others described Ecton Hall as they'd found it—an absolute wreck was the general consensus—and discussed what might now happen to the place.

Whether Gregory had ambled up to her or she had found her way to him, she couldn't have said, but it seemed that he and she now felt most comfortable, most at ease, by each other's side.

Together, they stood before the fireplace and chatted and laughed with the others as speculation as to who might take over Ecton Hall and what they might make of the old house grew ever more fanciful and wild.

Smiling, she surveyed the faces around her and detected a certain degree of smug happiness over being denizens of Bellamy Hall rather than of anywhere else, with secure and satisfying lives anchored by the place itself. Or more accurately, by what the estate had evolved into.

All those there—excluding only her uncle—plainly felt embraced, nurtured, and supported by the community that had grown within the estate's boundaries.

It wasn't anything to do with bricks and mortar or even land and lines on a map. Community was all about people, and they'd created a wonderful one there.

Her earlier thought of the Hall being her home echoed and resonated inside her. She knew that, within hours, she would have to make a decision and a declaration, but what that decision would be had never been clearer.

She glanced sidelong at Gregory and allowed her gaze to drink in his features—relaxed and plainly happy, indeed, content—and was struck by the simple epiphany that the biggest, heaviest, most powerful anchor holding her at Bellamy Hall was him.

Him and what he'd fostered there.

She was in no doubt that, had some other man come to fill the shoes of the owner of Bellamy Hall, this group and their collective contentment would not exist, not as it did now. The group as it was when he'd arrived would not have evolved as they had, into such a tightly knit crew, not without his input. Lady Bellamy had planted the seed, and Timms had steadily watered it, but it was Gregory who had given the entity the older ladies had created the opportunity and space to grow.

In that instant, she saw him clearly.

Just as she, fleeing from an untenable situation under her uncle's regime at Benbeoch Manor, in taking refuge at Bellamy Hall on that long-ago winter's night, had stumbled into her own true place—the role in which she fitted best and could do most good with her life—so, too, he had surely come to Bellamy Hall searching for his true place, and like her, he'd found it.

He'd recognized the possibility, seen the opportunity, and had carved out the role that now was his.

Smiling, she wondered if what they shared in emotional evolution was part of the attraction that simmered and thrummed beneath her skin.

Beneath his, too, as she was well aware.

He'd noticed her smile, and as his eyes trapped hers, he raised a questioning brow.

She let her smile deepen, boldly linked her arm with his, and eased a touch closer.

Under cover of the conversations rolling on around them, he dipped his head and murmured, "I suspect your uncle would like to have a word with you, and I would certainly appreciate exchanging several words with him regarding you."

She glanced up, eyes widening.

*Does he mean...?*

He met her gaze and, with his own steady as a rock, murmured, "Are you up for that?"

Beaming, she let her answer shine in her eyes. "Indeed, I am." Her uncle was chatting with Percy and Vernon while closely observing his sons. She waved in his direction. "Lead on."

# CHAPTER 17

*W*ith Gregory, Caitlin collected her uncle and cousins and led the group to the privacy of the library.

There, they settled in the armchairs about the nicely blazing fire, and Gregory handed out tumblers of whisky to her cousins and her uncle. The latter took one grudging sip, then, shocked, raised the glass and stared at the rich amber liquid.

Amused, Rory huffed. "It's Glencrae." He tipped his head toward Gregory. "He's related to the earl."

Patrick's eyes narrowed on Gregory as he took a larger sip.

Smiling, Gregory smoothly said, "As I've already mentioned, I'm also related to the current Lady of the Vale of Casphairn and her twin, Marcus Cynster, who owns the old Hennessy estate and also helps his wife, Niniver, manage the even older Carrick estate, Niniver being the head of that clan. That"—he waved a long-fingered hand—"is by way of demonstrating that I have a connection with the area in which Benbeoch Manor lies and some understanding and affinity for Scottish ways as a prelude, Mr. Fergusson, to formally requesting your permission to pay my addresses to your niece and ward, Caitlin."

Only a small flare of surprise gleamed in her uncle's eyes; he'd suspected that request was coming. After a second's hesitation, he snorted. "Do you think what I saw today will sway me to give you the nod?"

Wishing she'd asked more questions about what had occurred that day, especially between her uncle and her putative fiancé, she looked at Gregory.

Somewhat to her surprise, he held Patrick's gaze unflinchingly. "Yes."

For a second, her uncle stared back, then she realized he was fighting to straighten his lips.

He raised his glass and, from behind it, said, "Well, you don't lack for confidence. I'll give you that."

Gregory inclined his head. "Be that as it may, after the events of today, I feel that stating my case point by point would be superfluous. What you saw today is what I would offer your niece—a place by my side, the same one she already fills to remarkable effect, and a future here, as the lady of Bellamy Hall. A future in which her many talents are appreciated and valued and where respect and, most importantly, deep affection will always be hers."

He paused, then continued, "Over the past months, I've realized that what's here at Bellamy Hall"—his gesture encompassed all that surrounded them—"is unique and precious." His gaze rested steadily on her uncle's face. "And as I told you today, entirely truthfully, I would lay it all in the scales if that was the price for keeping Caitlin safe."

The simple unadorned statement of what she meant to him and the sincerity in his voice resonated inside Caitlin, and emotion rose to clog her throat.

She drew in a tight breath and looked at her uncle. She got the impression he wished he could argue, but after several fraught seconds, his gaze flicked to her.

"What say you, niece?"

She studied him, then looked at Gregory and, matching his honesty, simply said, "My heart lies here."

The warmth in his gaze would have melted stone.

She looked back at her uncle. "When he offers for my hand, I will accept."

His brows beetling, Patrick stared at her.

Calmly, she looked back and said nothing more.

She trusted Gregory's judgment; if he said Patrick had seen enough to judge his qualities, then there was no need to further elaborate. From what she'd learned of Gregory's actions in commanding the denizens of the Hall and orchestrating her rescue, his leadership abilities, understated though those often were, had shone, and Patrick, of all men, would have seen and appreciated that and approved. He also knew her well enough to understand that her own straightforward words hid feelings that were as deep as they were powerful.

Eventually, still studying her, he said, "I suppose I always knew this day would come—feared it, too—but at least you've chosen wisely." He looked at Gregory and inclined his head. "You have my permission."

Caitlin locked her eyes with Gregory's and smiled as widely as he did. They'd just cleared the biggest hurdle between them and their desired future, and how ironic that the ease with which they'd managed that was due, in large part, to that fiend, Ecton.

However, they weren't over the rough ground yet.

She drew in a breath and refocused on her uncle. "We'll live here, of course. At least for the most part." For clarity's sake, she rephrased, "Bellamy Hall will be our primary residence."

Patrick frowned, then, somewhat to her surprise, reluctantly nodded. "Aye." His blue eyes met hers. "I've seen and heard enough of how the people here regard you—how they look to you, and you, in turn, manage them." Approval tinged his gaze as he went on, "You've built something here—crafted a position for yourself—that would have been difficult if not impossible for you to accomplish at Benbeoch. And I can see it suits you—that it gives you something you need."

When she allowed her surprise to show, Patrick humphed. "You positively glow with happiness, girl." More sadly, he said, "You've never looked like that at home."

As she stared at her uncle, taking in the emotion that lay beneath those words, her perspective shifted a critical degree, and with sudden clarity, she saw—and appreciated—what he'd actually tried to do for her.

He hadn't understood that she'd had other ideas, so his "what was best for her" hadn't been what she'd wanted or needed. But his intentions had always stemmed from the right source. Like his sons, like her fiancé-to-be, in his own way, he'd been trying his best to protect her and give her the best in life.

As understanding poured through her, she smiled, then glanced at Gregory. "I expect we'll visit Benbeoch Manor for several weeks each year."

He nodded. "Undoubtedly."

Patrick huffed. "Just as well. Eventually, you'll need to take on the management of the estate from me."

Gregory inclined his head. "That will be an honor."

Caitlin's heart warmed, and judging by her uncle's expression, his heart softened further.

But then his gaze shifted to his three older sons, and his features hardened. Perhaps it was the insight she'd just gained into what drove her sometimes—ofttimes—irritatingly dictatorial uncle, but behind the harshness in his face, she saw a mix of worry and concern.

Deciding that leaving them—four men—to negotiate the minefield between them would lead to disaster, she elected to confront the issue directly. Looking at her cousins, she asked, "Now you've spent some time here, what do you three want to do?" *With your lives* was implied.

Rory looked at his father and met his blue gaze. "I've found a good place here. I've made friends and met people I like working with, and I'm well on the way to establishing a business of my own. And then there's Millie, if she'll have me, but we've a way to go before we get to that point." With rocklike certainty, he told his father, "You don't need me at the manor. It never was our home—for us lads, that was in Glasgow and is long behind all of us now. But I've found my place here, and it suits me." He glanced at Caitlin and Gregory. "If these two will have me, I'll stay."

Immediately, Gregory responded, "Everyone here is hoping you will. Martin Cruickshank sings your praises, and I've seen the interest in your instruments build—and the profit you can turn on them." Gregory flashed Rory a grin. "And then, as you say, there's Millie, and none of us want to disappoint her."

Rory sent Gregory a grateful look and shifted his gaze to his father. "So that's what I'll do."

"As for me," Hamish leapt in, "like Rory, I've found my talents as well as my knowledge can be put to good use here. I can't keep up with the demand for stonemasonry, and it's not just for building walls, and helping out at Home Farm keeps my hand in with the sheep." He met Patrick's eyes. "This place has given me the sort of chance that anyone with a brain knows comes only once in a lifetime."

He looked at Caitlin and smiled surprisingly sweetly. "When I followed you and Rory south, I had no idea that I would stumble onto such a chance, such a place. So if you'll have me, I'll be staying on, too."

Caitlin arched her brows. "And Madge?"

Hamish looked at her warily. "Madge and I…share a lot of likes and dislikes. What might come of that…?" He shrugged his big shoulders.

"The answer can only come with time, but I admit I'd like to find out what it is."

Smiling, Caitlin inclined her head and slanted a glance at Gregory. "If you truly wish to stay, we'll be happy to have you."

"Indeed," Gregory affirmed.

"Hmm." Patrick eyed his eldest sons. "Well, you're men grown, and if you're sure...?"

"We are," Rory and Hamish said in unison.

"Benbeoch won't be able to support you," Patrick warned.

Grinning, Rory replied, "That's all right. Bellamy Hall doesn't pay us, either—our businesses already do."

Surprise showed in Patrick's expression, but after a second of reading his sons' expressions as well as Caitlin's and Gregory's, he accepted that as fact. A difficult fact to swallow, but a fact, nevertheless.

Patrick shifted his gaze to his third son, and his expression grew stony. "I hope you're not going to try to tell me that your daubs are turning a profit?"

Entirely unperturbed, Daniel smiled—and in her quieter cousin, Caitlin saw a flash of inner confidence that reminded her forcibly of Gregory. "It's too early to claim that," Daniel said, "so instead, I'm going to ask Gregory to explain how the Bellamy Hall system works and how it is that the estate boasts not one not two but three other painters, all of whom are making good livings from their works. What's more, those three think my daubs, as you call them, fit nicely alongside theirs, and they've invited me to join them in responding to an invitation from a London art dealer, one who runs an exclusive Mayfair gallery, to show our pieces."

Head tipping, Daniel paused, then admitted, "One can't, of course, say for certain—not about anything to do with art—but those who know about such things think my style will appeal to many within the ton."

Patrick looked thoroughly disconcerted; it was clear he'd expected Daniel, at least, to meekly go home with him. He looked at Gregory, his expression equal parts uncertainty and disbelief.

Smiling faintly, Gregory said, "The three gentlemen involved in the Hall's painting business feel there's a definite place for Daniel and his paintings within that enterprise. I've seen for myself that his style with watercolors, educated by his years of painting misty Scottish scenes, is peculiarly suited to the current craze of ghostly scenes of gothic ruins and atmospheric landscapes. While I'm no art expert, given my uncle is Sir

Gerrard Debbington, I'm reasonably confident in knowing what will sell to the ton."

Patrick grunted.

Gregory's lips curved. "Now, as to how the Hall's business collective operates..."

Caitlin watched her uncle's expression as Gregory outlined the structure that lay beneath the Hall's businesses, tying them together in a mutually supportive way. Listening to his exposition, she realized that, under his direction, that structure had grown significantly stronger, more able to withstand the vicissitudes of shifting market demands for this business or that.

Apparently comprehending the disbelief that lingered in her uncle's eyes, with an understanding smile, Gregory concluded by admitting, "When I inherited the estate and arrived at the Hall, it took me quite some time before I believed such a system could possibly work. But after I'd gone through the accounts"—he tipped his head Caitlin's way—"which your niece so conscientiously keeps, I was completely won over. In terms of keeping an estate of this size, with the type of land and agriculture it can support, permanently on a solid financial footing, having the other businesses—in general, built upon the original and necessary agricultural framework—to balance the collective books makes the estate as a whole well-nigh impervious to any ill winds that might blow."

Her uncle's disbelief had faded, but he remained unconvinced.

"For instance," Gregory went on and nodded at Rory, "Rory's business of crafting musical instruments is an addition to the carpentry workshop, which itself grew out of the handymen's workshop and also the carriage works, and the carriage works, in turn, grew out of the stable. If you consider the forge, which was originally an adjunct to the stable, as well as the standard blacksmith's business run by Henry Kirk, the forge also supports his daughter Madge's ironwork sculptures—which have grown very popular in the district—as well as giving rise to the glassblowing workshop, which utilizes the same furnace as the forge. And the glassblowing business is currently poised to expand significantly into London and the ton.

"Each business that runs on the estate enables the business owners to build wealth from their profits, while the collective fund ensures they will always have a roof over their heads and food on the table, regardless of the vicissitudes of fortune." Gregory met Patrick's eyes. "As one responsible for an agricultural estate in these uncertain times, you'll appreciate that such certainty is a huge advantage."

Patrick made a gruff sound of agreement. "You'll get no argument from me on that score."

"In addition," Gregory said, "as Rory and Hamish have mentioned, they are also active in two of the other businesses, namely with Nene Farm, our cattle stud, and Home Farm, which runs our sheep flock, respectively. They each earn a stipend from those businesses. As for Daniel"—Gregory looked at Caitlin's younger cousin and smiled—"I've been waiting for him to declare his decision regarding whether he will remain here or not to suggest that, given what I understand was his experience at Benbeoch Manor, he should work alongside both Caitlin and myself, initially as my assistant, but with the goal of becoming the estate's steward, a position that we really need to fill."

Gregory met Patrick's eyes and calmly stated, "That will give him a second string to his bow as well as benefit the Hall business community as a whole."

Daniel's face had lit at the suggestion; no one needed to ask if he thought it a good idea.

Patrick humphed and, frowning, stroked his chin, but Caitlin sensed most of his resistance to his sons' defections had been overcome. After a moment, he looked at Rory and Hamish, then at Daniel. "Regardless, you'll essentially remain landless, and in the future..."

A father's very understandable anxiety resonated beneath the words.

"As to that," Gregory smoothly said, "I've a suggestion to make." He turned to Caitlin and held out a hand, and when she surrendered hers, he closed his fingers gently over hers and met her eyes. "Tell me what you think of this—Benbeoch is yours, after all."

She shook her head and swiveled to face him. "It will soon be yours as much as mine." She arched her brows. "Indeed, some would no doubt say more yours than mine." She suppressed the urge to glance at Patrick.

His expression growing serious, Gregory held her gaze. "You know that's not the way I think."

She nodded. "So tell us your idea."

Gregory looked at Patrick. "Obviously, this is predicated on Caitlin and I marrying, but assuming we do, then given the way the Hall operates, we'll need to spend the bulk of the year here. At the most, we might manage a month or two in Scotland, at the height of summer when there's less happening here." He glanced at Caitlin. "Do you agree?"

She thought, then nodded. "Realistically, we'll both be needed here through much of the year." Here, where both of them had found their true place.

Gregory looked back at Patrick. "What I propose is that, as part of the marriage settlements, your sons, including Morgan, will each receive a fifteen percent share of the Benbeoch estate, with the residual forty percent remaining with Caitlin, myself, and our descendants." He glanced at Rory, Hamish, and Daniel, who all looked stunned. "If you three remain here, building your businesses and lives at Bellamy Hall, then I would imagine that we—the three of you and Caitlin and myself—would make an arrangement with your brother Morgan under which he would continue to manage the combined estate."

Rory was clearly envisioning the situation in his mind. He blew out a breath, then glanced at Hamish. "Hamish and I could liaise with Morgan about improving the sheep and the cattle at Benbeoch. I've already got some ideas just from what I've seen thus far down here."

Hamish was nodding. "And we could visit more often—several times a year."

Daniel had stars in his eyes. "I'd be happy to help Morgan with the paperwork I've been taking care of to date. I can do much of that from here just as easily as there, and the other painters and I would want to visit a few times a year to paint as well."

Gregory was watching Patrick, as was Caitlin. Her uncle was blinking and blinking again as he absorbed what Gregory's idea would mean.

Smoothly, Gregory summarized, "Such a proposal should, I believe, set your mind at rest, sir. While giving Rory, Hamish, and Daniel the freedom to pursue their passions, it will also ensure that, if for whatever reason they fail, they have land and an income to fall back on. To go home to. In addition, the arrangement will allow Morgan to become established as an estate manager, which occupation I gather he enjoys, with his own parcel of land and income, and will also leave the reins of the Benbeoch Manor estate in the hands of the one most capable of managing them."

Caitlin allowed her approval—and her admiration—to color her expression. "That's a *brilliant* notion. It resolves everything."

Almost accusingly, Patrick looked Gregory in the eye. "You've been thinking of this for some time."

Gregory inclined his head. "For a few days. I could see the potential issues and felt sure we could find some way to address everyone's reservations."

Patrick continued to frown, then glanced at his sons.

All three looked eager, indeed, keen to have him agree.

When he only frowned harder, Gregory prompted, "Well, sir? Will such a proposal, executed via the marriage settlements, be agreeable to you?"

Patrick regarded him for several seconds, then humphed. "Given you're apparently to be my nephew-by-marriage, I suppose it behooves me to agree."

Caitlin uttered a sound of suppressed delight that bordered on a squeal. She leapt up and swooped on her uncle, bussing him on the cheek. "You won't regret it, Uncle Patrick. That, I can safely swear."

Patrick blushed and all but scowled at her. "No need for histrionics, my girl." He paused, considering her, then said, "Just as long as you're happy…"

She beamed and looked at Gregory. "I am happy—truly, truly happy!"

Not only for herself but for them all.

~

Gregory and Caitlin were the last to climb the stairs. They were both still smiling; he didn't think he'd stopped since Patrick had agreed to his proposal for the marriage settlements.

Their proposal.

He glanced at Caitlin. Her hand lay snugly in his as they ascended the stairs. The others had gone ahead and were already striding to their rooms. Before they reached the landing, they heard the doors, one after another, close.

"Four." Gregory glanced at his love and smiled. "We're alone."

She sighed happily, her lips still delectably curved. "Indeed." She leaned her head against his shoulder. "This is one of the times in our day that I treasure."

They stepped off the stairs and into the gallery. They'd developed the habit of ending their evenings there, alone, in the comfortable shadows.

As one, they turned toward the arm of the gallery that led to Gregory's room, away from the entrances to the corridors to the other wings.

An alcove a little way along had become their evening haunt, a place in which they could share whispers, hopes, and dreams, and kisses and caresses as well.

Over the past weeks, those wordless exchanges had grown more heated, more poignant, more meaningful, but also increasingly laced with a building urgency.

Now, at last, he felt free to move ahead—to take the next step, one he and she had been waiting to broach.

He stepped into the alcove, drawing her with him, and as they usually did, they looked out on the moonlit ruins. Mist lay heavy on the stone-strewn ground and cloaked the ancient soaring arch in drifting, translucent scarves.

Tonight, there was little they needed to share in words; after the long discussion in the library, their thoughts were assuredly aligned.

He breathed in and, using the hand he held, drew her to face him.

She turned readily and looked up, into his eyes. Her lips glimmered, sheened by the moonlight, temptation incarnate, but tonight, first...

Despite the weightiness of the moment, he felt his lips curve. "I've never done this before."

She understood perfectly, yet with passable innocence, she arched a questioning brow. "This what?"

He raised her hand to his lips and kissed the backs of her fingers, holding her widening eyes all the while. "Proposing marriage to the lady I love."

Teasingly, she widened her eyes. "Have you proposed marriage to someone *other* than the lady you love?"

He laughed softly and met her eyes again.

Caitlin looked into the wicked hazel depths as, still smiling, he murmured, "No, I haven't. This will be the first and, I fervently hope, my one and only attempt to offer for a lady's hand."

Without warning, he stepped back and went down on one knee.

Her heart leapt and lodged in her throat. Her lips formed a soundless O.

He looked up at her, and she stared into his moss-and-gold eyes and felt bathed in a glow of fond affection—bathed in his love.

Through their nighttime excursions into passion, restrained by circumstance though those had been, she'd grown increasingly aware and increasingly certain of that emotional bond solidifying between them.

Growing stronger each day and more intense with every night.

"Caitlin Susanna Madeline Fergusson, will you do me the honor of becoming my wife, to stand by my side through thick and thin as we steer our crazy household and all those on the Bellamy Hall estate into a glorious future?"

It was her turn to smile, then laugh.

When Caitlin met Gregory's eyes again, hers were radiant, the most glorious sight he ever hoped to see.

Then with commendable brevity, she simply said, "Yes, Gregory Cynster. I will be utterly delighted to be your wife."

He was on his feet in the next heartbeat and drawing her into his arms.

He bent his head, and their lips met—in a kiss that was almost reverent.

A kiss that promised and lured, then hunger broke its bonds, and their passions roared.

He swept her into his arms, and she was already there, already stretching up to meet his greedy need with her own. To encourage and incite, with her lips and tongue to meet every demand he made and, in return, impress her own wants and desires on him.

Boldly, she moved into him, pressing her curves to his harder frame.

His breath hitched, and he desperately tried to grab hold of the reins that had slid from his grasp and were fast disappearing…

"We don't have to stop." She murmured the words against his lips, then dove again into the kiss.

His head swam, and he plunged into the heady delights of the heated haven of her mouth.

Without his conscious direction, his hands slid from her back, skating over her trim waist, then one rose to cup her breast, swollen and straining beneath her tight bodice.

It was her turn to lose her breath, then she made an inarticulate sound and wantonly pressed the firm mound and tight peak into his greedy palm.

He closed his hand and let his fingers play as, between them, the flames of desire rose ever higher.

*This* was the moment all those previous interludes and resisted temptations had been leading to.

*This* was the inevitable culmination—an irresistible conflagration of hunger, need, desire, and passion that razed their defenses, seized their senses, and swept them away.

Into a physical longing so deep and profound, neither had any hope of holding back.

Or even of controlling it; the urgency bit too deep.

On a gasp, she broke the kiss and, her violet eyes ablaze, trapped his gaze. "Tonight," she all but panted, as desperately needy as he, "we don't have to stop."

She hauled his lips to hers and kissed him with an ardor so heated it set him alight.

Molten passion incinerated the last vestige of his control. He hauled her against him, and his fingers tangled in her hair as he gripped her head and altered the angle of the kiss, the better to devour.

Heartbeat by heartbeat, their urgency built, higher, more turbulent, more compelling, until it reared and broke like a wave over them.

Passion lashed, and desire burned, and they were helpless to hold against the compulsion. The raging tide propelled them on, eradicating any chance of either stepping back.

Neither could, not from this—from what, together, they'd fed, then unleashed.

He forced himself to draw back enough to growl, "I want you."

Her gasped reply came instantly. "And I want you."

From beneath heavy lids, he looked into her star-filled, violet-blue eyes and understood that, for them both, in that instant, their mutual need was the only thing that mattered. "Your room or mine?"

Caitlin didn't need to think. "Yours." Rory's room was two doors from hers, and Cromwell had put her uncle across the corridor. "Definitely yours."

Besides, she'd fantasized about finding herself in his bed.

Their lips met again, too hungry, it seemed, to part for long.

Unwilling to break from the kiss, unable, it seemed, to drag their hands from each other, they progressed down the wing in a waltzing rush, then the door at the end of the corridor was there, and he opened it, and they whirled through.

Her skin was already on fire. The instant she heard the door shut, she could no longer contain the near-ravenous need to feel his hard hands and his wickedly knowing fingers on her bare skin.

Couldn't wait an instant longer to get her hands on him.

With her lips still locked with his, she reached for buttons and frantically undid them, his first, but hers as well, anything to get rid of all the layers between them.

*This is passion. This is desire.*

Both were a wonder to her. She'd never experienced either, only with him and, even then, not to this degree, to where the compulsion to know and feel—to embrace and, ultimately, to take him inside her—was an unrelentingly compulsive beat.

One that thudded inexorably through her veins and sent heat flaring beneath her skin.

Their clothes fell away, hers and his, discarded wherever they landed.

And suddenly, in the shadowed dark, when he drew her hard against him, hot skin met hot skin, and something within her positively purred.

Need and want collided, and she spread her hands, palms and fingers flat, to his upper chest. The resilience of the muscles beneath the taut skin fascinated her senses.

The immediate tension that infused those muscles she stroked and admired mesmerized her.

Then one of his hands closed about her bare breast, and every sense she possessed lost touch with the world.

His fingers artfully caressed, and she gasped. Their lips parted, and she let her head fall back as, eyes closed, she followed every tantalizing touch.

Never had her nerves sparked like this. Never had her mind felt so utterly overwhelmed by sensation.

Against the softness of her belly, the hard ridge of his erection, iron encased in hot velvet, was another sensual distraction. Another unvoiced demand.

And with every expert touch, every knowing caress, he introduced her to new delights, to fresh fields of tactile stimulation. And with every gasp he drew from her, every moan that marked the expanding of her senses, her wits fell back just a little further, until her entire conscious mind was totally given over to feeling.

Feeling and emotion and the compulsion to come together with him.

His caresses grew more daring, more explicit, and with her hands, lips, and tongue, she urged him on.

Then his long fingers dipped into the hollow between her thighs, and her lungs seized as her mind and her senses reveled in the resultant glory.

She forgot to breathe as he gently probed, then pressed. Abruptly, her knees weakened, but he caught her, then he stooped and swept her into his arms and carried her to the bed.

He threw back the covers and laid her on the ivory sheets, then followed her down.

Her wits had surfaced enough for her to admire the long, lean length of him, the sleek line of the muscles in his thighs and the breadth of his powerful shoulders.

*Mine, all mine.*

The thought set her lips curving, and she reached for him.

Gregory looked down at her, at the desire that wreathed her features. His breathing was already ragged. He knew she was an innocent in this sphere, that this would be her first time lying with a man, yet the rake within him found himself stunned with admiration at the openhearted ardor with which she embraced the pleasure to be had in this, their first journey to paradise.

She took his breath away. She was all sultry siren as she lay gloriously naked on his sheets and, with one small hand, gripped his bicep and determinedly tugged, encouraging him to cover her.

They were both heated, with passion burning steadily through them and desire a damp sheen on their skins.

There was no reason not to comply with her wordless direction, with her eager, urgent entreaty.

He dipped his head and took her mouth again—a succulent delight she immediately surrendered—and lifted over her. Spreading her thighs with his, he lowered his body to hers.

That first flash of sensation as he settled upon her raced through him as well as her. Her skin was indescribably silky and soft, welcoming and alluring; he could only imagine what his hair-dusted limbs felt like to her, but other ladies in the past had informed him the sensation was evocative.

He sank into her mouth and plundered, deliberately reclaiming her attention. He could feel the slick, scalding evidence of her readiness bathing the head of his erection. He waited until he was sure her awareness had returned to the evocative thrust of his tongue against hers, then he flexed his hips and thrust into her welcoming warmth.

Her strangled cry was trapped between their lips, and beneath him, she froze, but a heartbeat later, she softened, bit by aching bit, then he felt her relax. A second later, her fingers, gripping his upper arms, tightened, and she tilted her hips experimentally, and he released the breath he'd been holding and drove even deeper.

He halted, fully sheathed in the incredible softness of her body— taking just that moment to glory in the sensation—then he withdrew and, as gently as he could, thrust in again.

Two more thrusts, and Caitlin had had enough of "gently." She tipped back her head, breaking the kiss, and commanded, "Harder. Faster."

He gave a dark chuckle and complied. "As my lady orders."

The words reached her on a gravelly growl, but as he immediately did as she'd asked and moved more powerfully, thrusting and retreating to a steady beat, joining and linking them in this dance that, despite her lack of experience, her body seemed to recognize and effortlessly follow, she merely smiled and gave herself up to the moment.

To the pleasure and delight.

But it seemed they'd stoked their fires too well. The flames built rapidly, and soon, they were both gasping, both striving, reaching as one for some elusive prize.

Harder, faster, more deeply he plunged, and she rode with him, writhing and seeking and urging him ever on.

Tension built deep inside her, winding tighter with every second, ratcheting more and more until a frantic desperation seized her.

And then, quite suddenly, he thrust one last time, and the unforgiving tension snapped, and a starburst of sensation exploded in her mind, and all she was unraveled as glory streaked down her nerves, pleasure flooded her veins, and bliss swamped her mind.

He stiffened in her arms, and with a hoarse, guttural cry half smothered in the curve of her throat, he spilled into her, then slumped in her arms, apparently as boneless as she.

A wave of sated pleasure rolled over her, of a sort she'd never felt before.

The ultimate in intimate comfort, that pleasure reassured and soothed.

As, unresisting, she let the tide take her, she felt him do the same, and she smiled and, safe with him, let go and sank beneath the waves.

Sometime later—she couldn't have said how long—he stirred, raised his head, and looked down at her.

She felt his loving gaze lingeringly trace her features, but she couldn't summon the strength to lift her lids and meet it.

Then she heard him chuckle softly—an elemental sound of male pride —and he dropped a kiss on her swollen lips, disengaged, and lifted from her.

As he immediately dropped to the bed beside her, flicked the covers over them, then gathered her into his arms, turning her so her head was pillowed on his chest, she didn't feel any need to protest.

Instead, she snuggled to get comfortable, glorying in the warmth of his hard, hot limbs over and around which hers were now draped. She felt him press a soft kiss to her temple, and she relaxed again, expecting oblivion to reclaim her.

Instead, she found her mind cataloging the subtle signs as he—his body—relaxed as well, and he surrendered to sleep. She listened to his heartbeat, strong and steady now beneath her ear, noted how his breathing slowed.

Her eyes remained closed, but she felt her lips curve.

They'd started almost as foes, wary, watchful, with each suspicious of the other, but working together for the good of the people of Bellamy Hall, through what they'd shared in that common cause, they'd grown to be friends.

Now, they'd become lovers and soon would be husband and wife.

An evolution nearly completed for him. For her, a journey embarked on with the end finally in sight.

Contentment lay heavy upon her. Still smiling, with her head pillowed on his chest, she settled beneath the reassuring weight of his arm and waited for slumber to claim her.

She was drifting in that hazy world between wakefulness and sleep, with visions of their wedding circling, when an errant thought floated across her mind.

She hadn't yet asked him how he felt about bagpipes.

# EPILOGUE

## MAY 1, 1852. BELLAMY HALL,
## NORTHAMPTONSHIRE

The entire household, wedding guests and all, had been woken at dawn by the haunting strains of bagpipes floating out from the ruins.

Needless to say, Tristan, Melrose, and Hugo had been beyond ecstatic and had been there to record the sight of Rory, Hamish, Daniel, and Morgan, in full Fergusson clan regalia, pacing back and forth under the abbey's ancient arch as they played.

The wedding itself, held at All Saints Church in Earls Barton and proudly officiated over by Reverend Millicombe, had been an exceptionally well-attended affair. Every resident of the Hall estate, plus all the members of the wider congregation as well as assorted other local figures, had packed the small church and crowded around the open doorway. Inside, the church had been crammed with Caitlin's Scottish kin and the even larger contingent of Gregory's relatives and numerous Cynster connections.

Caitlin had been thrilled to have all her family around her. Her uncle had given her away and had been brimming with pride as he did.

He and Morgan had arrived at Bellamy Hall several days prior, and she'd been both surprised and relieved to note how much Morgan—who was the same age as she—had matured as well as grown. He'd been ready and willing to take on the responsibility of Benbeoch Manor and had wholeheartedly welcomed the settlements Gregory had arranged.

Consequently, Rory, Hamish, and Daniel were now free to pursue their passions, and as Caitlin had walked down the aisle to take the final step in securing her own passionately desired future, she'd sent up a prayer of thanks that in following her path all the way to the end, she'd created the setting for her cousins—all four—to find their own true places.

That had set a special seal to what was proving to be a magical day.

The ceremony had passed off without a hitch. As Gregory had whispered, while under the watchful eyes of Julia, Alice, and Gregory's sister, Therese, nothing would dare go wrong.

Accompanied by her handsome husband and their children, Therese had arrived days early to help oversee the preparations. She'd visited several times since Caitlin and Gregory had announced their betrothal, and she and Caitlin had quickly settled into an easy friendship. Indeed, Therese had been instrumental in smoothing Caitlin's path into the large and boisterous Cynster family.

Included in that number, and also among those who had arrived early, were Gregory's relatives from north of the border. The Carricks—Lucilla, Thomas, and their children—and Marcus and Niniver Cynster had bolstered the Scottish influence, and all had been patently delighted at the news that, in marrying Caitlin, Gregory would be strengthening Cynster ties to the area in which both couples lived.

Caitlin had found talking with Lucilla and Niniver, both of whom had been born and had grown up mere miles south of Benbeoch Manor, hugely reassuring and distinctly heartening.

And to remind Caitlin of Scotland, Marcus and Niniver had brought two Scottish wolfhound puppies as a wedding gift. Both hounds had instantly attached themselves to Caitlin and taken to following her everywhere—which after the incident with Ecton, Gregory found reassuring—but at night, when she retreated to Gregory's room and shut the door on the dogs, the pair had quickly and utterly shamelessly found their way to the kitchens and made a place for themselves by Nessie's hearth.

Now, with the wedding breakfast in full swing, the pups had been banished to the stable. Niniver had declared that the presence of far too many enticing dishes, all within hound reach, would be unfair temptation to the young dogs, so after cavorting about the lawns while the staff and all those on the estate had lined the forecourt and nearer reaches of the drive to welcome Gregory and Caitlin, now man and wife, to their future home, the pups had been dispatched to the stable in the arms of two grinning stablemen.

The wedding feast had followed, the dishes an unexpected blend of English and Scottish fare. Julia, Joshua, and Nessie had done their homework—and had consulted Therese and, through her, Lucilla and Niniver —and the result had been spectacular.

Once the platters were emptied and the desserts were served only to vanish, the speeches began. Caitlin had never laughed so hard in her life —nor been so irresistibly moved to tears by her uncle's poignant address, which had touched on her parents' hopes for her and her bravery, in his eyes, in finding her own way.

After the last speech—Gregory's thanks on behalf of them both to all who had come and contributed to their wonderful day—the musicians started playing, with English and Scottish blending seamlessly in waltzes, polkas, jigs, and country reels.

Everyone—literally everyone, even Gregory's grandmama—was captured by the evocative beat, and if feet weren't flying in the dance, they were tapping on the floor.

Unable to stop smiling, Caitlin danced the wedding waltz with Gregory, then she was swept into a jig by Rory. From his arms, she was drawn into a country dance by Gregory's older brother, Christopher, then Hamish reclaimed her for the Scottish side. And so it went on—one partner English, the next Scottish. Laughing, she gave herself up to the moment and the music and her enthusiastic partners.

Gregory watched his wife—his at last and forever to be so—go down a reel with Morgan.

Gregory, too, couldn't stop smiling. The day—their special day— truly had been perfect.

"Well!" Martin appeared by his side and nodded to the throng of whirling dancers. "This has been quite a show."

Gregory arched a brow. "Have you enjoyed yourself?"

Martin looked faintly surprised. "I have, as it happens."

Gregory shifted to face him. "Before I forget, I owe you our thanks for learning what you did about Ecton. No one else had managed to unearth even a hint, and without the insight you provided, I might not have instantly leapt to the conclusion that Caitlin's kidnapper was him, and of course, time was of the essence in rescuing her."

Martin flashed him a grin. "Pleased to have been able to help." He glanced at the dancers, locating Caitlin. "She's a lovely lady. You've chosen well."

"So I think."

"Well!" A hand landed on Gregory's shoulder, and Christopher halted beside him. "It's done now—you're a staid married man."

"Indeed." Devlin, Therese's husband, came up on Christopher's other side. He nodded to Martin and gestured to the dancers. "This has been remarkably uplifting. There's something about such uninhibited exhibitions of energy that sets the blood flowing. Judging by comments made by our better halves, this wedding breakfast has set a high bar for the future."

"Hmm." Christopher looked over the heads. "Speaking of the future, I wonder who among the Cynsters will be next?"

Gregory glanced at Martin; his younger brother, too, was scanning the dancers, apparently certain the answer would be one of them.

Devlin, however, was looking at Martin, and after making a show of surveying the crowd, Christopher, too, brought his gaze back to rest on Martin.

Eventually feeling the weight of their combined gazes, Martin glanced their way, then laughed and shook his head. "No point looking at me. That, I can promise. I'm far too busy building my empire to spare time to look about me for a wife."

Devlin grinned. "Just so you know, that's not how it works."

"No, indeed." Christopher nodded. "Fate has a habit of working to her own agenda."

Martin made a scoffing sound. "Whoever's next, I can promise it won't be me. At least at present, I'm firmly in charge of my own destiny, and I can assure you that while I have nothing against the institution of marriage, for the foreseeable future, there is no space in my life for a wife." He shifted. "And now, if you'll excuse me, I need a word with Jason—I'm driving him back to London tonight."

With a salute to the three of them, Martin walked off.

Gregory, Christopher, and Devlin watched him go.

"To my ears," Christopher said, "that sounded awfully like a challenge."

Devlin shook his head. "Tossing down gauntlets at Fate's feet is never a wise idea."

"No, indeed." His gaze on Martin's back, Gregory smiled. "But he'll learn. That said, he's right—whichever Cynster falls next, it won't be him. He, Jason, Toby, and that crew have years to go yet before they reach the restless stage where men like us start to think of marriage."

Reluctantly, Christopher nodded. "True. Most likely, it'll be one of your peers. Who do you think it'll be? Justin, Evan, Nicholas, Aiden, or even Julius? Me, I'd wager on Justin. He's the more serious one."

"Evan, for my money," Devlin said, getting into the spirit of the thing. "He's playing the field with a vengeance these days. I suspect that will come back to bite him."

Gregory found one dark head amid the throng of people on the dance floor. "Nicholas," he said. "He's the one who—like Martin—isn't expecting it. And Fate—as we three can attest—likes nothing better than turning the tables on unsuspecting males."

Both Christopher and Devlin conceded that truth, then Therese and Ellen returned to claim their husbands, and Caitlin rushed up to claim Gregory's hand and drag him into a jig.

～

The music and dancing stretched on into the night.

Later, after the traditional throwing of the bride's bouquet, Gregory and Caitlin stole away, not to their now-very-much-shared apartment but to the abbey ruins.

The moon was out and full, lighting their way with a silvery wash that, as Caitlin remarked, their four painters would have gone into paroxysms over had they been in any state to appreciate the sight. All four were still dancing in the ballroom, swept away by the music and the excellent company.

Holding firmly to Caitlin's hand, Gregory helped her over the strewn rocks. They climbed to where the edge of the rise gave them the best view of the Hall and its lands.

There, they sat side by side on one of the larger stones and looked down on what was now their shared responsibility.

Caitlin lifted her face to the light breeze, then looked at the roofs and turrets of the Hall. "When I first arrived here, it seemed like an almost magical place—a different realm, where matters were handled in unexpected ways."

Clasping her hand between both of his, Gregory nodded. "A magical realm is a good way of describing it. When we visited as children, it always had that aura. A place where unexpected things could happen." He paused, then went on, "From what I now understand, Sir Humphrey laid the groundwork for what we now have, tilled the soil and planted the seed, if you will, and Minnie nurtured that seed until it germinated and grew."

"And when Minnie passed on," Caitlin took up the tale, "Timms watched over that first nascent shoot and encouraged it to grow into a sapling."

"And we've now taken on the task of protecting and growing that sapling into a fully-fledged tree." When Caitlin glanced at him, Gregory met her gaze. "That's the legacy those three left to you and me."

She smiled, turned her hand in his, and squeezed. "Just as well we're both up for the challenge."

The smile they shared was confident and assured.

They knew where they were headed, and for both of them, dedicating themselves to furthering the enterprise that was Bellamy Hall promised a lifetime of challenges to meet and people to help, with the prospect of unlimited shared satisfaction.

Looking back at the house, Gregory raised Caitlin's hand and pressed a kiss to her knuckles. "We came here—both of us—each in our own way searching for our place. The right place in which to put down roots and grow. We've been blessed to find that place here, together, giving life to the dream Sir Humphrey, Minnie, and Timms made a reality."

Her gaze on the Hall, slumbering in the moonlight, Caitlin nodded. "And now we'll be steering that dream—our reality—into the future."

Gregory gazed at the Hall—now their home—and smiled. "I feel certain that, at this very moment, Minnie and Timms will be looking down on us in benediction."

Caitlin laughed and glanced upward. "Yes, indeed—and they'll be smiling in smug delight."

∼

∼

Dear Reader,

Through the past several volumes dealing with his siblings' romances,

Gregory's dissatisfaction with his life and, indeed, his prospects has grown increasingly clear. Finally came the time when he unexpectedly inherited Bellamy Hall and from that point, Fate—assisted by Minnie and Timms—took a firm grip on his reins.

Returning to Bellamy Hall—the scene of Gregory's parents, Vane and Patience's romance, as told in *A Rake's Vow* all those many years ago—has been a real delight. In following Gregory's journey to find his true place in life, I had a great deal of fun learning about all the arts and crafts that flourished in the English countryside at that time. I hope you enjoyed our exploration of the "small businesses" of that period.

I hope you enjoyed reading of Gregory and Caitlin's evolving understanding of what love and family mean to them.

As usual, buried in the Epilogue is a hint of which Cynster is next in line for his story, and in this instance, there were two hints—Gregory's younger brother, Martin, and also his cousin, Nicholas. So in order to complete Vane and Patience's branch of the family tree, I'm leaping ahead 11 years to bring you the tale of Martin's Cynster's inevitable tumble into love. Given his declaration here that he has no time for a wife, his story is fittingly titled *The Time For Love*, and will be released in August, 2022.

With my best wishes for unfettered happy reading!


*Stephanie.*

For alerts as new books are released, plus information on upcoming books, exclusive sweepstakes and sneak peeks into upcoming novels, sign up for Stephanie's Private Email Newsletter http://www.stephanielaurens. com/newsletter-signup/

Or if you don't have time to chat and want a quick email alert, sign up and follow me at BookBub https://www.bookbub.com/authors/stephanie-laurens

The ultimate source for detailed information on all Stephanie's published books, including covers, descriptions, and excerpts, is Stephanie's Website www.stephanielaurens.com

You can also follow Stephanie via her Amazon Author Page at http:// tinyurl.com/zc3e9mp

Goodreads members can follow Stephanie via her author page https:// www.goodreads.com/author/show/9241.Stephanie_Laurens

You can email Stephanie at stephanie@stephanielaurens.com

Or find her on Facebook
https://www.facebook.com/AuthorStephanieLaurens/

**COMING NEXT:**

**THE TIME FOR LOVE**
**Cynster Next Generation Novel #11**
**To be released in August, 2022.**

*Martin Cynster arrives at the Carmichael Steelworks in Sheffield intent on buying the business, but on meeting the majority owner, Miss Sophia Carmichael, and unexpectedly rescuing them both from a deadly accident, he embraces the necessity of completely rescripting his no-longer-just-business proposal.*

Available for pre-order from May, 2022.

**RECENTLY RELEASED:**

**THE MEANING OF LOVE**
**A spin-off from Lady Osbaldestone's Christmas Chronicles**

*#1* New York Times *bestselling author Stephanie Laurens explores the strength of a fated love, one that was left in abeyance when the protagonists were too young, but that roars back to life when, as adults, they meet again.*

*A lady ready and waiting to be deemed on the shelf has her transition into spinsterhood disrupted when the nobleman she'd once thought she loved*

*returns to London and fate and circumstance conspire to force them to
discover what love truly is and what it means to them.*

What happens when a love left behind doesn't die?

Melissa North had assumed that after eight years of not setting eyes
on each other, her youthful attraction to—or was it infatuation with?—
Julian Delamere, once Viscount Dagenham and now Earl of Carsely,
would have faded to nothing and gasped its last. Unfortunately, during the
intervening years, she's failed to find any suitable suitor who measures up
to her mark and is resigned to ending her days an old maid.

Then she sees Julian across a crowded ballroom, and he sees her, and
the intensity of their connection shocks her. She seizes the first chance
that offers to flee, only to discover she's jumped from the frying pan into
the fire.

Within twenty-four hours, she and Julian are the newly engaged toast
of the ton.

Julian has never forgotten Melissa. Now, having inherited the earl-
dom, he must marry and is determined to choose his own bride. He'd
assumed that by now, Melissa would be married to someone else, but
apparently not. Consequently, he's not averse to the path Fate seems to be
steering them down.

And, indeed, as they discover, enforced separation has made their
hearts grow fonder, and the attraction between them flares even more
intensely.

However, it's soon apparent that someone is intent on ensuring their
married life is cut short in deadly fashion. Through a whirlwind courtship,
a massive ton wedding, and finally, blissful country peace, they fend off
increasingly dangerous, potentially lethal threats, until, together, they
unravel the conspiracy that's dogged their heels and expose the villain
behind it all.

*A classic historical romance laced with murderous intrigue. A novel
arising from the Lady Osbaldestone's Christmas Chronicles. A full-length
historical romance of 127,000 words.*

**THE SECRETS OF LORD GRAYSON CHILD**

## Cynster Next Generation-Connected Novel
(following on from The Games Lovers Play)

*#1* New York Times *bestselling author Stephanie Laurens returns to the world of the Cynsters' next generation with the tale of an unconventional nobleman and an equally unconventional noblewoman learning to love and trust again.*

*A jilted noblewoman forced into a dual existence half in and half out of the ton is unexpectedly confronted by the nobleman who left her behind ten years ago, but before either can catch their breaths, they trip over a murder and into a race to capture a killer.*

Lord Grayson Child is horrified to discover that *The London Crier*, a popular gossip rag, is proposing to expose his extraordinary wealth to the ton's matchmakers, not to mention London's shysters and Captain Sharps. He hies to London and corners *The Crier's* proprietor—only to discover the paper's owner is the last person he'd expected to see.

Izzy—Lady Isadora Descartes—is flabbergasted when Gray appears in her printing works' office. He's the very last person she wants to meet while in her role as owner of *The Crier*, but there he is, as large as life, and she has to deal with him without giving herself away! She manages—just—and seizes on the late hour to put him off so she can work out what to do.

But before leaving the printing works, she and he stumble across a murder, and all hell breaks loose.

Izzy can only be grateful for Gray's support as, to free them both of suspicion, they embark on a joint campaign to find the killer.

Yet working side by side opens their eyes to who they each are now—both quite different to the youthful would-be lovers of ten years before. Mutual respect, affection, and appreciation grow, and amid the chaos of hunting a ruthless killer, they find themselves facing the question of whether what they'd deemed wrecked ten years before can be resurrected.

Then the killer's motive proves to be a treasonous plot, and with others, Gray and Izzy race to prevent a catastrophe, a task that ultimately falls to them alone in a situation in which the only way out is through selfless togetherness—only by relying on each other will they survive.

*A classic historical romance laced with crime and intrigue. A Cynster*

*Next Generation-connected novel—a full-length historical romance of 115,000 words.*

## THE GAMES LOVERS PLAY
### Cynster Next Generation Novel #9

*#1* New York Times *bestselling author Stephanie Laurens returns to the Cynsters' next generation with an evocative tale of two people striving to overcome unusual hurdles in order to claim true love.*

*A nobleman wedded to the lady he loves strives to overwrite five years of masterful pretence and open his wife's eyes to the fact that he loves her as much as she loves him.*

Lord Devlin Cader, Earl of Alverton, married Therese Cynster five years ago. What he didn't tell her then and has assiduously hidden ever since—for what seemed excellent reasons at the time—is that he loves her every bit as much as she loves him.

For her own misguided reasons, Therese had decided that the adage that Cynsters always marry for love did not necessarily mean said Cynsters were loved in return. She accepted that was usually so, but being universally viewed by gentlemen as too managing, bossy, and opinionated, she believed she would never be loved for herself. Consequently, after falling irrevocably in love with Devlin, when he made it plain he didn't love her yet wanted her to wife, she accepted the half love-match he offered, and once they were wed, set about organizing to make their marriage the very best it could be.

Now, five years later, they are an established couple within the haut ton, have three young children, and Devlin is making a name for himself in business and political circles. There's only one problem. Having attended numerous Cynster weddings and family gatherings and spent time with Therese's increasingly married cousins, who with their spouses all embrace the Cynster ideal of marriage based on mutually acknowledged love, Devlin is no longer content with the half love-match he himself engineered. No fool, he sees and comprehends what the craven act of denying his love is costing both him and Therese and feels compelled to rectify his fault. He wants for them what all Therese's married cousins enjoy—the rich and myriad benefits of marriages based on acknowledged mutual love.

Love, he's discovered, is too powerful a force to deny, leaving him wrestling with the conundrum of finding a way to convincingly reveal to Therese that he loves her without wrecking everything—especially the mutual trust—they've built over the past five years.

*A classic historical romance set amid the glittering world of the London haut ton. A Cynster Next Generation novel—a full-length historical romance of 110,000 words.*

## The fourth instalment in Lady Osbaldestone's Christmas Chronicles
## LADY OSBALDESTONE'S CHRISTMAS INTRIGUE

*#1* New York Times *bestselling author Stephanie Laurens immerses you in the simple joys of a long-ago country-village Christmas, featuring a grandmother, her grandchildren, her unwed son, a determined not-so-young lady, foreign diplomats, undercover guards, and agents of Napoleon!*

At Hartington Manor in the village of Little Moseley, Therese, Lady Osbaldestone, and her household are once again enjoying the company of her intrepid grandchildren, Jamie, George, and Lottie, when they are unexpectedly joined by her ladyship's youngest and still-unwed son, also the children's favorite uncle, Christopher.

As the Foreign Office's master intelligencer, Christopher has been ordered into hiding until the department can appropriately deal with the French agent spotted following him in London. Christopher chose to seek refuge in Little Moseley because it's such a tiny village that anyone without a reason to be there stands out. Neither he nor his office-appointed bodyguard expect to encounter any dramas.

Then Christopher spots a lady from London he believes has been hunting him with matrimonial intent. He can't understand how she tracked him to the village, but determined to avoid her, he enlists the children's help. The children discover their information-gathering skills are in high demand, and while engaging with the villagers as they usually do and taking part in the village's traditional events, they do their best to learn what Miss Marion Sewell is up to.

But upon reflection, Christopher realizes it's unlikely the Marion he was so attracted to years before has changed all that much, and he starts to wonder if what she wants to tell him is actually something he might want to hear. Unfortunately, he has set wheels in motion that are not easy to redirect. Although Marion tries to approach him several times, he and she fail to make contact.

Then just when it seems they will finally connect, a dangerous stranger lures Marion away. Fearing the worst, Christopher gives chase—trailed by his bodyguard, the children, and a small troop of helpful younger gentlemen.

What they discover at nearby Parteger Hall is not at all what anyone expected, and as the action unfolds, the assembled company band together to protect a secret vital to the resolution of the war against Napoleon.

*Fourth in series. A novel of 81,000 words. A Christmas tale of intrigue, personal evolution, and love.*

## PREVIOUS CYNSTER NEXT GENERATION RELEASES:

## THE INEVITABLE FALL OF CHRISTOPHER CYNSTER
### Cynster Next Generation Novel #8

*#1* New York Times *bestselling author Stephanie Laurens returns to the Cynsters' next generation with a rollicking tale of smugglers, counterfeit banknotes, and two people falling in love.*

*A gentleman hoping to avoid falling in love and a lady who believes love has passed her by are flung together in a race to unravel a plot that threatens to undermine the realm.*

Christopher Cynster has finally accepted that to have the life he wants, he needs a wife, but before he can even think of searching for the right lady, he's drawn into an investigation into the distribution of counterfeit banknotes.

London born and bred, Ellen Martingale is battling to preserve the fiction that her much-loved uncle, Christopher's neighbor, still has his wits about him, but Christopher's questions regarding nearby Goffard Hall trigger her suspicions. As her younger brother attends card parties at the Hall, she feels compelled to investigate.

While Ellen appears to be the sort of frippery female Christopher abhors, he quickly learns that, in her case, appearances are deceiving. And through the twists and turns in an investigation that grows ever more serious and urgent, he discovers how easy it is to fall in love, while Ellen learns that love hasn't, after all, passed her by.

But then the villain steps from the shadows, and love's strengths and vulnerabilities are put to the test—just as Christopher has always feared. Will he pass muster? Can they triumph? Or will they lose all they've so recently found?

*A historical romance with a dash of intrigue, set in rural Kent. A Cynster Next Generation novel—a full-length historical romance of 124,000 words.*

## A CONQUEST IMPOSSIBLE TO RESIST
### Cynster Next Generation Novel #7

*#1* New York Times *bestselling author Stephanie Laurens returns to the Cynsters' next generation to bring you a thrilling tale of love, intrigue, and fabulous horses.*

*A notorious rakehell with a stable of rare Thoroughbreds and a lady on a quest to locate such horses must negotiate personal minefields to forge a greatly desired alliance—one someone is prepared to murder to prevent.*

Prudence Cynster has turned her back on husband hunting in favor of horse hunting. As the head of the breeding program underpinning the success of the Cynster racing stables, she's on a quest to acquire the necessary horses to refresh the stable's breeding stock.

On his estranged father's death, Deaglan Fitzgerald, now Earl of Glengarah, left London and the hedonistic life of a wealthy, wellborn rake and returned to Glengarah Castle determined to rectify the harm caused by his father's neglect. Driven by guilt that he hadn't been there to protect his people during the Great Famine, Deaglan holds firm against the lure of his father's extensive collection of horses and, leaving the stable to the care of his brother, Felix, devotes himself to returning the estate to prosperity.

Deaglan had fallen out with his father and been exiled from Glengarah over his drive to have the horses pay their way. Knowing Deaglan's wishes and that restoration of the estate is almost complete, Felix writes to the premier Thoroughbred breeding program in the British Isles to test their interest in the Glengarah horses.

On receiving a letter describing exactly the type of horses she's seeking, Pru overrides her family's reluctance and sets out for Ireland's west coast to visit the now-reclusive wicked Earl of Glengarah. Yet her only interest is in his horses, which she cannot wait to see.

When Felix tells Deaglan that a P. H. Cynster is about to arrive to assess the horses with a view to a breeding arrangement, Deaglan can only be grateful. But then P. H. Cynster turns out to be a lady, one utterly unlike any other he's ever met.

Yet they are who they are, and both understand their world. They battle their instincts and attempt to keep their interactions businesslike, but the sparks are incandescent and inevitably ignite a sexual blaze that consumes them both—and opens their eyes.

But before they can find their way to their now-desired goal, first one accident, then another distracts them. Someone, it seems, doesn't want them to strike a deal. Who? Why?

They need to find out before whoever it is resorts to the ultimate sanction.

*A historical romance with neo-Gothic overtones, set in the west of Ireland. A Cynster Next Generation novel—a full-length historical romance of 125,000 words.*

**The first volume of the Devil's Brood Trilogy
THE LADY BY HIS SIDE
Cynster Next Generation Novel #4**

*A marquess in need of the right bride. An earl's daughter in search of a purpose. A betrayal that ends in murder and balloons into a threat to the realm.*

Sebastian Cynster knows time is running out. If he doesn't choose a wife soon, his female relatives will line up to assist him. Yet the current debutantes do not appeal. Where is he to find the right lady to be his marchioness? Then Drake Varisey, eldest son of the Duke of Wolverstone, asks for Sebastian's aid.

Having assumed his father's mantle in protecting queen and country, Drake must go to Ireland in pursuit of a dangerous plot. But he's received an urgent missive from Lord Ennis, an Irish peer—Ennis has heard something Drake needs to know. Ennis insists Drake attends an upcoming house party at Ennis's Kent estate so Ennis can reveal his information face-to-face.

Sebastian has assisted Drake before and, long ago, had a liaison with Lady Ennis. Drake insists Sebastian is just the man to be Drake's surrogate at the house party—the guests will imagine all manner of possibilities and be blind to Sebastian's true purpose.

Unsurprisingly, Sebastian is reluctant, but Drake's need is real. With only more debutantes on his horizon, Sebastian allows himself to be persuaded.

His first task is to inveigle Antonia Rawlings, a lady he has known all her life, to include him as her escort to the house party. Although he's seen little of Antonia in recent years, Sebastian is confident of gaining her support.

Eldest daughter of the Earl of Chillingworth, Antonia has abandoned the search for a husband and plans to use the week of the house party to decide what to do with her life. There has to be some purpose, some role, she can claim for her own.

Consequently, on hearing Sebastian's request and an explanation of what lies behind it, she seizes on the call to action. Suppressing her senses' idiotic reaction to Sebastian's nearness, she agrees to be his partner-in-intrigue.

But while joining the house party proves easy, the gathering is thrown into chaos when Lord Ennis is murdered—just before he was to speak with Sebastian. Worse, Ennis's last words, gasped to Sebastian, are: *Gunpowder. Here.*

Gunpowder? And here, where?

With a killer continuing to stalk the halls, side by side, Sebastian and Antonia search for answers and, all the while, the childhood connection that had always existed between them strengthens and blooms...into something so much more.

*First volume in a trilogy. A Cynster Next Generation Novel – a classic historical romance with gothic overtones layered over a continuing intrigue. A full-length novel of 99,000 words.*

**The second volume of the Devil's Brood Trilogy**
**AN IRRESISTIBLE ALLIANCE**

### Cynster Next Generation Novel #5

*A duke's second son with no responsibilities and a lady starved of the excitement her soul craves join forces to unravel a deadly, potentially catastrophic threat to the realm - that only continues to grow.*

With his older brother's betrothal announced, Lord Michael Cynster is freed from the pressure of familial expectations. However, the allure of his previous hedonistic pursuits has paled. Then he learns of the mission his brother, Sebastian, and Lady Antonia Rawlings have been assisting with and volunteers to assist by hunting down the hoard of gunpowder now secreted somewhere in London.

Michael sets out to trace the carters who transported the gunpowder from Kent to London. His quest leads him to the Hendon Shipping Company, where he discovers his sole source of information is the only daughter of Jack and Kit Hendon, Miss Cleome Hendon, who although a fetchingly attractive lady, firmly holds the reins of the office in her small hands.

Cleo has fought to achieve her position in the company. Initially, managing the office was a challenge, but she now conquers all in just a few hours a week. With her three brothers all adventuring in America, she's been driven to the realization that she craves adventure, too.

When Michael Cynster walks in and asks about carters, Cleo's instincts leap. She wrings from him the full tale of his mission—and offers him a bargain. She will lead him to the carters he seeks if he agrees to include her as an equal partner in the mission.

Horrified, Michael attempts to resist, but ultimately finds himself agreeing—a sequence of events he quickly learns is common around Cleo. Then she delivers on her part of the bargain, and he finds there are benefits to allowing her to continue to investigate beside him—not least being that if she's there, then he knows she's safe.

But the further they go in tracing the gunpowder, the more deaths they uncover. And when they finally locate the barrels, they find themselves tangled in a fight to the death—one that forces them to face what has grown between them, to seize and defend what they both see as their path to the greatest adventure of all. A shared life. A shared future. A shared love.

*Second volume in a trilogy. A Cynster Next Generation Novel – a classic historical romance with gothic overtones layered over a continuing intrigue. A full-length novel of 101,000 words.*

**The third and final volume in the Devil's Brood Trilogy
THE GREATEST CHALLENGE OF THEM ALL
Cynster Next Generation Novel #6**

*A nobleman devoted to defending queen and country and a noblewoman wild enough to match his every step race to disrupt the plans of a malignant intelligence intent on shaking England to its very foundations.*

Lord Drake Varisey, Marquess of Winchelsea, eldest son and heir of the Duke of Wolverstone, must foil a plot that threatens to shake the foundations of the realm, but the very last lady—nay, noblewoman—he needs assisting him is Lady Louisa Cynster, known throughout the ton as Lady Wild.

For the past nine years, Louisa has suspected that Drake might well be the ideal husband for her, even though he's assiduous in avoiding her. But she's now twenty-seven and enough is enough. She believes propinquity will elucidate exactly what it is that lies between them, and what better opportunity to work closely with Drake than his latest mission, with which he patently needs her help?

Unable to deny Louisa's abilities or the value of her assistance and powerless to curb her willfulness, Drake is forced to grit his teeth and acquiesce to her sticking by his side, if only to ensure her safety. But all too soon, his true feelings for her show enough for her, perspicacious as she is, to see through his denials, which she then interprets as a challenge.

Even while they gather information, tease out clues, increasingly desperately search for the missing gunpowder, and doggedly pursue the killer responsible for an ever-escalating tally of dead men, thrown together through the hours, he and she learn to trust and appreciate each other. And fed by constant exposure—and blatantly encouraged by her—their desires and hungers swell and grow...

As the barriers between them crumble, the attraction he has for so long restrained burgeons and balloons, until goaded by her near-death, it erupts, and he seizes her—only to be seized in return.

Linked irrevocably and with their wills melded and merged by passion's fire, with time running out and the evil mastermind's deadline looming, together, they focus their considerable talents and make one last push to learn the critical truths—to find the gunpowder and unmask the villain behind this far-reaching plot.

Only to discover that they have significantly less time than they'd thought, that the villain's target is even more crucially fundamental to the realm than they'd imagined, and it's going to take all that Drake is—as well as all that Louisa as Lady Wild can bring to bear—to defuse the threat, capture the villain, and make all safe and right again.

As they race to the ultimate confrontation, the future of all England rests on their shoulders.

*Third volume in a trilogy. A Cynster Next Generation Novel – a classic historical romance with gothic overtones layered over an intrigue. A full-length novel of 129,000 words.*

If you haven't yet caught up with the first books in the Cynster Next Generation Novels, then BY WINTER'S LIGHT is a Christmas story that highlights the Cynster children as they stand poised on the cusp of adulthood – essentially an introductory novel to the upcoming generation. That novel is followed by the first pair of Cynster Next Generation romances, those of Lucilla and Marcus Cynster, twins and the eldest children of Lord Richard aka Scandal Cynster and Catriona, Lady of the Vale. Both the twins' stories are set in Scotland. See below for further details.

## BY WINTER'S LIGHT
### Cynster Next Generation Novel #1

*#1 New York Times bestselling author Stephanie Laurens returns to romantic Scotland to usher in a new generation of Cynsters in an enchanting tale of mistletoe, magic, and love.*

It's December 1837 and the young adults of the Cynster clan have succeeded in having the family Christmas celebration held at snow-bound Casphairn Manor, Richard and Catriona Cynster's home. Led by Sebastian, Marquess of Earith, and by Lucilla, future Lady of the Vale, and her twin brother, Marcus, the upcoming generation has their own plans for the holiday season.

Yet where Cynsters gather, love is never far behind—the festive occasion brings together Daniel Crosbie, tutor to Lucifer Cynster's sons, and

Claire Meadows, widow and governess to Gabriel Cynster's daughter. Daniel and Claire have met before and the embers of an unexpected passion smolder between them, but once bitten, twice shy, Claire believes a second marriage is not in her stars. Daniel, however, is determined to press his suit. He's seen the love the Cynsters share, and Claire is the lady with whom he dreams of sharing *his* life. Assisted by a bevy of Cynsters —innate matchmakers every one—Daniel strives to persuade Claire that trusting him with her hand and her heart is her right path to happiness.

Meanwhile, out riding on Christmas Eve, the young adults of the Cynster clan respond to a plea for help. Summoned to a humble dwelling in ruggedly forested mountains, Lucilla is called on to help with the difficult birth of a child, while the others rise to the challenge of helping her. With a violent storm closing in and severely limited options, the next generation of Cynsters face their first collective test—can they save this mother and child? And themselves, too?

Back at the manor, Claire is increasingly drawn to Daniel and despite her misgivings, against the backdrop of the ongoing festivities their relationship deepens. Yet she remains torn—until catastrophe strikes, and by winter's light, she learns that love—true love—is worth any risk, any price.

*A tale brimming with all the magical delights of a Scottish festive season. A Cynster Next Generation novel – a classic historical romance of 71,000 words.*

## THE TEMPTING OF THOMAS CARRICK
### Cynster Next Generation Novel #2

*Do you believe in fate? Do you believe in passion? What happens when fate and passion collide?*
*Do you believe in love? What happens when fate, passion, and love combine?*
*This. This…*

*#1* New York Times *bestselling author Stephanie Laurens returns to Scotland with a tale of two lovers irrevocably linked by destiny and passion.*

Thomas Carrick is a gentleman driven to control all aspects of his life.

As the wealthy owner of Carrick Enterprises, located in bustling Glasgow, he is one of that city's most eligible bachelors and fully intends to select an appropriate wife from the many young ladies paraded before him. He wants to take that necessary next step along his self-determined path, yet no young lady captures his eye, much less his attention...not in the way Lucilla Cynster had, and still did, even though she lives miles away.

For over two years, Thomas has avoided his clan's estate because it borders Lucilla's home, but disturbing reports from his clansmen force him to return to the countryside—only to discover that his uncle, the laird, is ailing, a clan family is desperately ill, and the clan-healer is unconscious and dying. Duty to the clan leaves Thomas no choice but to seek help from the last woman he wants to face.

Strong-willed and passionate, Lucilla has been waiting—increasingly impatiently—for Thomas to return and claim his rightful place by her side. She knows he is hers—her fated lover, husband, protector, and mate. He is the only man for her, just as she is his one true love. And, at last, he's back. Even though his returning wasn't on her account, Lucilla is willing to seize whatever chance Fate hands her.

Thomas can never forget Lucilla, much less the connection that seethes between them, but to marry her would mean embracing a life he's adamant he does not want.

Lucilla sees that Thomas has yet to accept the inevitability of their union and, despite all, he can refuse her and walk away. But how *can* he ignore a bond such as theirs—one so much stronger than reason? Despite several unnerving attacks mounted against them, despite the uncertainty racking his clan, Lucilla remains as determined as only a Cynster can be to fight for the future she knows can be theirs—and while she cannot command him, she has powerful enticements she's willing to wield in the cause of tempting Thomas Carrick.

*A neo-Gothic tale of passionate romance laced with mystery, set in the uplands of southwestern Scotland. A Cynster Next Generation Novel – a classic historical romance of 122,000 words.*

## A MATCH FOR MARCUS CYNSTER
### Cynster Next Generation Novel #3

*Duty compels her to turn her back on marriage. Fate drives him to protect her come what may. Then love takes a hand in this battle of yearning hearts, stubborn wills, and a match too powerful to deny.*

*#1* New York Times *bestselling author Stephanie Laurens returns to rugged Scotland with a dramatic tale of passionate desire and unwavering devotion.*

Restless and impatient, Marcus Cynster waits for Fate to come calling. He knows his destiny lies in the lands surrounding his family home, but what will his future be? Equally importantly, with whom will he share it?

Of one fact he feels certain: his fated bride will not be Niniver Carrick. His elusive neighbor attracts him mightily, yet he feels compelled to protect her—even from himself. Fickle Fate, he's sure, would never be so kind as to decree that Niniver should be his. The best he can do for them both is to avoid her.

Niniver has vowed to return her clan to prosperity. The epitome of fragile femininity, her delicate and ethereal exterior cloaks a stubborn will and an unflinching devotion to the people in her care. She accepts that in order to achieve her goal, she cannot risk marrying and losing her grip on the clan's reins to an inevitably controlling husband. Unfortunately, many local men see her as their opportunity.

Soon, she's forced to seek help to get rid of her unwelcome suitors. Powerful and dangerous, Marcus Cynster is perfect for the task. Suppressing her wariness over tangling with a gentleman who so excites her passions, she appeals to him for assistance with her peculiar problem.

Although at first he resists, Marcus discovers that, contrary to his expectations, his fated role *is* to stand by Niniver's side and, ultimately, to claim her hand. Yet in order to convince her to be his bride, they must plunge headlong into a journey full of challenges, unforeseen dangers, passion, and yearning, until Niniver grasps the essential truth—that she is indeed a match for Marcus Cynster.

*A neo-Gothic tale of passionate romance set in the uplands of southwestern Scotland. A Cynster Next Generation Novel – a classic historical romance of 114,000 words.*

And if you want to discover where the Cynsters began, return to the iconic

## DEVIL'S BRIDE

the book that introduced millions of historical romance readers around the globe to the powerful men of the unforgettable Cynster family – aristocrats to the bone, conquerors at heart – and the willful feisty ladies strong enough to be their brides.

# ABOUT THE AUTHOR

#1 *New York Times* bestselling author Stephanie Laurens began writing romances as an escape from the dry world of professional science. Her hobby quickly became a career when her first novel was accepted for publication, and with entirely becoming alacrity, she gave up writing about facts in favor of writing fiction.

All Laurens's works to date are historical romances, ranging from medieval times to the mid-1800s, and her settings range from Scotland to India. The majority of her works are set in the period of the British Regency. Laurens has published over 75 works of historical romance, including 40 *New York Times* bestsellers. Laurens has sold more than 20 million print, audio, and e-books globally. All her works are continuously available in print and e-book formats in English worldwide, and have been translated into many other languages. An international bestseller, among other accolades, Laurens has received the Romance Writers of America® prestigious RITA® Award for Best Romance Novella 2008 for *The Fall of Rogue Gerrard.*

Laurens's continuing novels featuring the Cynster family are widely regarded as classics of the historical romance genre. Other series include the *Bastion Club Novels*, the *Black Cobra Quartet*, the *Adventurers Quartet,* and the *Casebook of Barnaby Adair Novels.*

For information on all published novels and on upcoming releases and updates on novels yet to come, visit Stephanie's website: www.stephanielaurens.com

To sign up for Stephanie's Email Newsletter (a private list) for heads-up alerts as new books are released, exclusive sneak peeks into upcoming books, and exclusive sweepstakes contests, follow the prompts at http://www.stephanielaurens.com/newsletter-signup/

To follow Stephanie on BookBub, head to her BookBub Author Page: https://www.bookbub.com/authors/stephanie-laurens

Stephanie lives with her husband and a goofy black labradoodle in the hills outside Melbourne, Australia. When she isn't writing, she's reading, and if she isn't reading, she'll be tending her garden.

www.stephanielaurens.com
stephanie@stephanielaurens.com

CPSIA information can be obtained
at www.ICGtesting.com
Printed in the USA
LVHW012120030722
722686LV00002B/211